apoleon's retreat through the streets of Leipsic after his defeat by the allied armies of Austria, Russia and Prussia

Painting by L. Braun

THE GREAT EVENTS

BY

FAMOUS HISTORIANS

A COMPREHENSIVE AND READABLE ACCOUNT OF THE WORLD'S
HISTORY, EMPHASIZING THE MORE IMPORTANT EVENTS, AND PRE-
SENTING THESE AS COMPLETE NARRATIVES IN THE MASTER-WORDS
OF THE MOST EMINENT HISTORIANS

NON-SECTARIAN   NON-PARTISAN   NON-SECTIONAL

ON THE PLAN EVOLVED FROM A CONSENSUS OF OPINIONS GATH-
ERED FROM THE MOST DISTINGUISHED SCHOLARS OF AMERICA
AND EUROPE, INCLUDING BRIEF INTRODUCTIONS BY SPECIALISTS
TO CONNECT AND EXPLAIN THE CELEBRATED NARRATIVES, AR-
RANGED CHRONOLOGICALLY, WITH THOROUGH INDICES, BIBLIOG-
RAPHIES, CHRONOLOGIES, AND COURSES OF READING

EDITOR-IN-CHIEF

ROSSITER JOHNSON, LL.D.

ASSOCIATE EDITORS

CHARLES F. HORNE, Ph.D.
JOHN RUDD, LL.D.

With a staff of specialists

VOLUME XV

The National Alumni

CONTENTS

VOLUME XV

	PAGE
An Outline Narrative of the Great Events, . .	xiii
CHARLES F. HORNE	

Union of Ireland with Great Britain
The Great Irish Rebellion (A.D. 1800), . . .   I
WILLIAM O'CONNOR MORRIS

Rise of the Democratic Party in the United States
(A.D. 1801)
Jefferson's Inaugural, ... :   18
HERMANN VON HOLST
THOMAS JEFFERSON

The Louisiana Purchase (A.D. 1803), . . .   39
HENRY S. RANDALL

The Tripolitan War (A.D. 1804), ...   58
J. FENIMORE COOPER

The Coronation of Napoleon (A.D. 1804), . .   76
WILLIAM HAZLITT

The Lewis and Clark Expedition (A.D. 1804), .   84
JAMES DAVIE BUTLER
ROBERT SOUTHEY

The Battle of Trafalgar (A.D. 1805)
England becomes Mistress of the Seas, . . .   105
ROBERT SOUTHEY

The Battle of Austerlitz (A.D. 1805), . . .   115
PIERRE LANFREY

PAGE

The British Acquisition of Cape Colony (A.D. *1806*), 127
HENRY A. BRYDEN

Prussia Crushed by Napoleon (A.D. *1806*), . . 140
SIR WALTER SCOTT

The First Practical Steamboat (A.D. *1807*), . . 159
JAMES RENWICK

Wellington's Peninsular Campaign (A.D. *1808–1813*), 170
JOHN RICHARD GREEN

Brazil becomes Independent (A.D. *1808–1822*), . 181
DANIEL P. KIDDER

The Revolution in Mexico (A.D. *1810*), . . . 189
JOEL R. POINSETT

The Uprising in South America (A.D. *1810*)
The Career of Bolivar, the Liberator, . . . 205
ALFRED DÉBÉRLE

The Massacre of the Mamelukes (A.D. *1811*), . . 223
ANDREW A. PATON

Napoleon's Russian Campaign (A.D. *1812*), . . 231
CHARLES A. FYFFE
FRANÇOIS P. G. GUIZOT

War on the Canadian Border (A.D. *1812–1814*), . 241
AGNES M. MACHAR
JAMES GRAHAME

Perry's Victory on Lake Erie (A.D. *1813*), . . 268
THEODORE ROOSEVELT

The Uprising of Germany (A.D. *1813*)
The Battle of the Nations at Leipsic, . . . 281
WOLFGANG MENZEL

The Burning of Washington (A.D. *1814*), . . 295
RICHARD HILDRETH
GEORGE R. GLEIG

CONTENTS

PAGE

*The Congress of Vienna (*A.D. *1814),*   .   .   .   310
HENRY M. STEPHENS

*The Hartford Convention (*A.D. *1814)*
Protests against the War of 1812, ...   326
SIMEON E. BALDWIN
JOHN S. BARRY

*The Battle of New Orleans (*A.D. *1815)*
The End of the War of 1812, ...   343
JAMES PARTON

*The Battle of Waterloo (*A.D. *1815),*   .   .   .   363
WOLFGANG MENZEL
WILLIAM SIBORNE
VICTOR HUGO

*Universal Chronology (*A.D. *1800–1815),*   .   .   393
JOHN RUDD

LIST OF ILLUSTRATIONS

VOLUME XV

PAGE

Napoleon's retreat through the streets of Leipsic after his defeat by the allied armies of Austria, Russia, and Prussia (page 294),   .   Frontispiece

Painting by L. Braun.

Admiral Nelson on board the frigate Victory in the Battle of Trafalgar, ...   110

Painting by W. H. Overend.

AN OUTLINE NARRATIVE

TRACING BRIEFLY THE CAUSES, CON-
NECTIONS, AND CONSEQUENCES OF

THE GREAT EVENTS

(THE NAPOLEONIC ERA)

CHARLES F. HORNE

O conqueror since the days of Charlemagne has so altered the political boundaries of Europe as did Napoleon, and none has so changed the minds of men. Intentionally or not, he became one of the greatest bene-factors of the human race. In France he suppressed the Republic; but abroad he was its apostle, and spread its basic principle of equality over the en-tire face of civilization. Future ages may date an epoch from him as having been the last great military conqueror; for the ideas established by him and by his generation seem to have made further conquests like his own impossible.

If we try to imagine the French Revolution without Napo-leon, we must picture it driven back within French borders by the armies of united Europe, with its principles perhaps per-mitted to continue in feeble existence among Parisian philoso-phers, but inoperative and even unknown among the mass of men. It is true that the United States was at the same moment displaying to the world a noble example of the success of repub-lican government; but the United States was feeble, distant, and little understood. France was the centre of civilization, the heart of the world, leader of Europe in intellect and culture; and the French Republic in 1799 seemed staggering to its fall, beaten down by the armies of kings, tangled in the meshes of an im-practicable constitution, given over to the rule of incompetence and corruption.

Then stepped forward General Bonaparte. In 1795 he had

rescued his country from the rule of King Mob; in 1799 he saved it from its feeble government of paper, defended it against the cannon of Europe. He assumed a military dictatorship, swept away the inefficient constitution, and substituted one of his own which left all power with himself. In name, however, the country continued a republic, and the common folk of Europe were little likely to appreciate the meaning of Bonaparte's changes. Indeed, Frenchmen themselves remained a bit confused, and years afterward, even when their chief had assumed the rank of Emperor, their coins were inscribed "Napoleon, Emperor of the French Republic." So it was still as the champion of liberty that Napoleon appealed to Europe.

As soon as he assumed power the whole aspect of affairs changed. In 1800 he crossed the Alps with an army, and for the second time drove the Austrians out of Italy. His chief lieutenant, Moreau, gained a decisive victory over Austrians and Germans at Hohenlinden. A peace was established which left Bonaparte the chief potentate of Europe.

The many minute details arranged by this treaty dragged its final settlement on until 1803. Then emerged from it a new and wholly reconstructed Central Europe, with France made more than ever its chief State. A row of little republics, dependent on French support, extended over Italy, Switzerland, Holland, and most of Germany. The tiny German States, previously near four hundred in number, were reduced to forty; and most of these were included in a "Confederation of the Rhine," from which both Prussia and Austria were shut out.

The next year General Bonaparte definitely assumed the title of Emperor Napoleon I, was crowned by the Pope, and began changing his set of dependent republics into kingdoms, to be ruled by his lieutenants and members of his family. His ambition to become the successor of Charlemagne, to unite Germans and French in one huge empire, was clearly announced; and the cry of "Liberty," by which France had everywhere summoned the common people to her aid, began to fail her. Even Napoleon could scarce continue to assert himself the high priest of that republicanism which he was suppressing on every hand.[1]

[1] See *Coronation of Napoleon*, page 76.

STRIFE OF FRANCE AND ENGLAND

So strong was the power the dictator had established, that there might have been none to dispute it but for England. England, finding her commercial supremacy threatened by the astonishing strides of France, had become Napoleon's most persistent enemy, and he returned her antagonism in kind. His ill-fated expedition to Egypt had been partly an attack upon her trade. But the destruction of his fleet by Nelson in the Battle of the Nile, had made England as powerful on the seas as France on land. Neither State could match the other on its chosen element.

England, however, has always one vulnerable point, Ireland. The last great Irish rebellion had arisen in 1798; and in 1800 the country was finally united with England under a single government. Irish members entered Parliament, to continue there the weary struggle for liberty which they had so long maintained at home.[1] Napoleon was constantly seeking to arouse rebellion anew in the dependent island; and at length in 1804 he gathered an enormous army on the shores of the English Channel with the avowed intention of invading England and crushing forever her opposition to him and to freedom.

In face of this tremendous danger the British Government bestirred itself vigorously. Austria, Russia, Sweden, and Naples were persuaded to join it in what is known as the "Third Great Coalition" against Napoleon; and from Britain's wealth large sums were distributed to the allies to enable them to put their armies in motion. At the same time an English fleet defeated a portion of the French and, occupying the Channel, made the threatened invasion temporarily impossible.

Napoleon promptly turned his army against his other foes. By a campaign considered his military masterpiece he compelled a huge Austrian army to surrender at Ulm in Germany. Then pressing on into Austria he seized Vienna and met the combined Russian and Austrian forces under command of their sovereigns themselves at Austerlitz.[2] This, the "Battle of the Three Emperors," was Napoleon's most important success. The Rus-

---

[1] See *Union of Ireland with Great Britain: The Great Irish Rebellion*, page 1.

[2] See *Battle of Austerlitz*, page 115.

sians fell back defeated, into their own land.   Austria, helpless at the conqueror's feet, submitted to whatever terms he chose to dictate.   The following year the Austrian ruler even abandoned his title of Emperor of Germany.   The ancient empire which had maintained a precarious existence for more than a thousand years (800–1806) disappeared at last, and gave place to the new French empire, which extended over much of Germany.

To offset this greatest of Napoleon's triumphs, came the Battle of Trafalgar, in which, but two days after the surrender at Ulm, Nelson, greatest of England's naval heroes, crushed the combined fleets of France and her unwilling ally, Spain.[1]

Remembering the victories of Frederick the Great, and believing themselves to be invincible in arms, the Prussians had watched not unwillingly the overthrow of their ancient rival, Austria, and had protested little against the annihilation of a German Empire in which they could hold only a secondary place. But by degrees the exactions of Napoleon, the insolence of his demands, became such as no State could submit to, except as an acknowledged dependent.   Prussia, which for a dozen years had refused all the overtures of the other powers to join the alliance against France, suddenly declared war single-handed.[2]

Her ill-commanded, antiquated troops were defeated with ridiculous ease at Jena and Auerstadt by the veterans of Napoleon (1806); and the conqueror entered a new capital, Berlin, as he had entered Rome and Vienna.   Russia, safe in its distance from the arch-enemy, had taken up Prussia's cause, so Napoleon, pressing farther east than his standards had yet been seen, encountered the Russians on their own borderland in two bloody battles at Eylau and Friedland (1807).   The first of these was indecisive, the second a severe defeat for Russia, and following it came the famous interview of the young czar, Alexander, with his rival, on a raft in the Niemen, Russia's boundary river.

Which of the two Emperors had the better of the meeting has been much discussed.   Certain it is that they clasped hands and came to a friendly agreement to divide Europe between them. Napoleon was to do what he liked in the west.   Alexander seized

[1] See *The Battle of Trafalgar*, page 105.
[2] See *Prussia Crushed by Napoleon*, page 140.

from Sweden the east coast of the Baltic Sea, thus extending Russia's northwest limits where they stand to-day; and he also appropriated liberal slices of Turkey and Prussian Poland.

In return the Czar pledged himself to support Napoleon in the vast commercial warfare which the latter was planning against England. The wealth of the island empire consisted in her commerce; she supplied the wants of Europe. Now, every European port was to be closed against her. This policy of course bore quite as hard upon the lands which sold and the lands which purchased goods, as it did on England which transported them; and to the installation of this mistaken system, to the attempt to enforce it, is commonly traced the downfall of Napoleon. The common folk of Europe who had at first admired the "man of destiny," grew resentful and rebellious under their privations.

DOWNFALL OF NAPOLEON

No one man can be stronger than all men. Those who seem to us most powerful in dominance over the age in which they live, have in reality only recognized the current of the times and swept along upon its surface, guiding it perhaps, but never thwarting it. Napoleon in his earlier career had been in harmony with his age, with its revolt against old formulas, its defiance of absolutism, its insistence on individual worth, recognition of the man and not the title. More and more, however, did he in his overweening self-confidence set himself in opposition to the new influences by which he had risen. He became but another oppressor, replacing those he had overthrown.

Especially was this manifest in Spain. There the ancient royal family had proved so worthless, so subservient to his will, that at length he deposed them entirely and declared his own feeble brother, king. The deposed Bourbons resisted as little as the conqueror expected; but there was in the Spaniards themselves a changelessness, a loyal conservatism, that made them intensely patriotic. They could not stand against the trained armies of France, which easily established Joseph Bonaparte in Madrid, but all over the country arose a guerilla warfare which not even the greatest of the Bonapartes was able to subdue. Portugal also insisted on keeping her ports open to

English commerce. So Napoleon attacked her, too. England eagerly accepted this chance of renewing the war against her enemy, and sent troops to the aid of both Portgual and Spain. Wellington began in that desolate Peninsula the strife which was to lead him to Waterloo.[1]

Next Austria revolted against French tyranny and rose in her turn, not now at the command of her sovereign, but at the insistence of her people. Napoleon left Spain and came in person to suppress the rebellion. He succeeded, but not until the Austrians had inflicted on him at Aspern the first defeat of his career. The Prussians also were grown savage against him. The very men who had cheered him on his entry to Berlin in 1806, saluted him with such grim reluctance in 1812, that he marvelled at the change. At last Alexander of Russia declared he would no longer ruin his country by excluding British ships from her ports. Napoleon in answer planned his great Russian campaign of 1812.[2]

Its issue is too well known to need repetition. The once invulnerable conqueror was defeated not more by the severity of the Russian winter, than by the unity of the Russian people in resistance against him. As he fled back to Paris, nation after nation rose behind him in rebellion, not in obedience to their kings, but answering to the cry for "freedom," which France herself had first sent out.

There is something awe-inspiring in that uprising of Europe. The Prussians led the way; then the other German peoples, then Austria, joined with the advancing Russians. The Spaniards led by Wellington swarmed over the Pyrenees. The Britons crossed from their island refuge. The Swedes came down from the North.

And there was much that was heroic in Napoleon's defiance. He raised a new army from exhausted France, an army of old men and boys. Never did he conduct a more masterly campaign. But the men he was facing now were not mere military machines. When the Prussians found their powder worthless, they charged French cannon with their clubbed muskets and beat their way to victory through sheer brute desperation. At

[1] See *Wellington's Peninsular Campaign*, page 170.
[2] See *Napoleon's Russian Campaign*, page 231.

the Katzbach they annihilated an entire army. Napoleon himself was defeated in the great "Battle of the Nations" at Leipsic, different indeed from the "Battle of the Emperors" at Austerlitz. The vanquished victor fled back to France with the remnant of his army.[1] Still did he fight battle after battle, still with impotent genius resist the irresistible. At last the allies forced their way to Paris, and his own Senate declared the Emperor deposed. He yielded and was exiled to the island of Elba, over which he was permitted to rule.

The delighted monarchs of Europe gathered in the celebrated "Congress of Vienna" to rearrange their household, readjust the boundary lines which France had so tumultuously disarranged. Each king was warm in congratulations and gratitude to his people who had rescued him. Each promised them the liberty they desired. As a matter of fact, however, the monarchs proved less interested in arranging constitutions for their subjects than in grasping territory for themselves. So loud grew the wrangling at Vienna that it seemed the result must be another war, one of the ancient kind where kings fought for provinces and the people had no part except in the slaughter.[2]

Napoleon, seeing his opportunity in this disunion, left his little kingdom of Elba and reappeared suddenly in France. His old soldiers flocked to his standard; the allies for a moment hesitated; and soon the Emperor was firm upon his throne as ever. He led his armies hurriedly to the frontier to attack those which Prussia and England, his two most obstinate enemies, were gathering against him. For a moment the old days of his victories seemed come again; but English steadiness and Prussian vengefulness overthrew him at Waterloo.[3] He was exiled to St. Helena, where he died a prisoner. The monarchs returned to their bargaining at Vienna; and the people resumed their waiting for the constitutions they had earned.

THE OTHER CONTINENTS

The wild confusion which Napoleon had caused in Europe, found naturally its echo in other parts of the world. In 1806

---

[1] See *Uprising of Germany*, page 281.
[2] See *The Congress of Vienna*, page 310.
[3] See *Waterloo*, page 363.

England, taking advantage of the league into which all Europe had been forced against her, wrenched South Africa from the Dutch.[1] After Napoleon had been driven from Egypt, British forces were landed there to take advantage of the civil strife to which the inhabitants had been abandoned. The expedition was unsuccessful, but it opened the way for a daring adventurer, Mehemet Ali, to establish himself as Pacha of Eygpt. Ali threw off all but a nominal allegiance to Turkey; he massacred the "Mamelukes," and thus made himself practically absolute monarch of a new and independent State.[2]

When in 1807 the royal family of Portugal were driven to flee from the troops of France, they took refuge in their colony of Brazil, and seeing its vastness proclaimed it an American empire.[3] When the Spanish colonies in America found that they were receiving orders from three different governments at home, that of Jerome Bonaparte, of the Bourbons, and of a revolutionary tribunal; when, moreover, they found each government threatening them with death if they obeyed the others; and when they realized that no one of the governments was able to enforce its threats or uphold its officials—naturally in this dilemma they began governing themselves. The Mexican Revolution began in 1810, but independence was not won till 1822.[4]

The colonies were stimulated by the cry of "liberty" which was everywhere upon the air. Over all South America one rebellion flamed up after another. The yoke of helpless Spain was everywhere thrown off. The freedom of America from Europe which the United States had proclaimed in the North, the Spanish States now echoed through the South. The gospel of equality which America had taught to France, and France to Europe, now returned from Europe to America.[5]

ADVANCE OF DEMOCRACY IN AMERICA

Meantime, what had been the experiences of the United States? While in Europe democracy was being trampled down, first by Napoleon whom it had placed upon his throne,

[1] See *The British Acquisition of Cape Colony*, page 127.
[2] See *Massacre of the Mamelukes*, page 223.
[3] See *Brazil Becomes Independent*, page 181.
[4] See *Revolution in Mexico*, page 189.
[5] See *Uprising in South America : Career of Bolivar*, page 205.

then by the monarchs whom it had rescued from his grip, in America it was being ever more widely extended. Scarce was Washington dead ere his cautious conservatism was brushed aside, and a new party, vigorously proclaiming its trust in the "common people," rose to power under Thomas Jefferson. The older statesmen lamented his election to the Presidency as an evil almost equal to revolution. They felt that the "madness of the mob" was upon them, and feared to see repeated in their own country the excesses of the French Reign of Terror.[1]

Nothing of the sort happened. Democracy, frenzied in Europe, proved admirably calm and self-controlled in America; and out of the bitter political controversies of its earliest years, the United States passed into a period of calm, wherein the great majority of its leaders were closely agreed as to measures and policies. The "era of good feeling" began.

Most important of the great measures for which Jefferson was responsible, was the purchase of Louisiana. This was another of the consequences of the great European strife. Napoleon had taken Louisiana from Spain. He had visions of building there a vast colonial empire; but England's complete mastery of the sea soon rendered any such hope chimerical. When in 1803 the conqueror began planning his huge English campaign, it was obvious that at the first note of war the British navy could seize Louisiana, unopposed. To prevent this he sold—or gave would be the better word—gave Louisiana to the United States. An almost worthless gift men thought it then, this vast unpeopled wilderness. Many Americans protested against the President's paying even three million dollars for it. They saw in the treaty only a shrewd Napoleonic move to embroil their nation with Great Britain, a Democratic scheme to bind them closer to democracy in France.[2]

But war did not immediately follow; and the internal development of the country during this period of peace was so enormous as soon to give a new importance to the purchased territory. In 1804 Lewis and Clark were despatched on their famous exploring expedition to the Northwest, upon the results of which

[1] See *Rise of the Democratic Party in the United States*, page 18.
[2] See *Purchase of Louisiana*, page 39.

the United States based its claim to the Oregon region.[1]   In the
East, roads were everywhere built; and in 1807 Fulton's invention of a practical steamboat revolutionized commerce, made of
every one of the vast rivers of the continent a highway, inexpen-
sive, swift, and safe.   The wilderness ceased to be remote.[2]

Intercourse with foreign nations during this time consisted
chiefly of trying to keep out of trouble.   All Europe was at war.
If the United States could keep at peace with the needy nations, vast commercial profits were to be gained.   The trade of
all the world might be gathered in her hands.   American ships
were seen in every ocean of the globe.   Britain, hampered by
Napoleon's decrees, could scarce compete with this new and
daring rival.   Naturally there was constant friction.

Since Europe was too busy, or too little interested, the United
States in 1801 and 1803 undertook the chastisement of the Barbary powers, whose plundering hampered her merchant-ships.[3]
Twenty years before, Paul Jones, appearing suddenly upon
European coasts, had been called a pirate; but here was a full-
armed, full-manned fleet-of-war sailing into European waters from
another continent.   Such an event had not occurred since the
days of the Saracens.   Except from invaders dwelling around the
Mediterranean it had never occurred.   It was an epoch in history, the first sign of the fading of European supremacy.

Both England and France began taking measures against
the American trading invasion.   Decree after decree was issued
against our ships.   The situation grew ever more strained.
There would have been war, only the United States knew not
which of its huge hectoring antagonists to attack, and could
hardly fight both.   Finally Napoleon made an offer of amity,
and instantly the United States attacked England (1812).

Canada saw in this war only an attempt of the overgrown
and grasping Republic to conquer her; and indeed it must be
admitted that for a time the contest had somewhat of that aspect.[4]   England, involved in her huge European struggle, could
do little to aid Canada; and though the New England States in

---

[1] See *The Lewis and Clark Expedition*, page 84.
[2] See *The First Practical Steamboat*, page 159.
[3] See *The Tripolitan War*, page 58.
[4] See *War on the Canadian Border*, page 241.

particular felt small enthusiasm for the war, yet American troops gradually increased in numbers along the border, and bade fair to overwhelm the brave resistance of the Canadians. The central victory of the frontier contest was that of Perry on Lake Erie. He built a fleet to match that of the Canadians, completely overwhelmed his opponents, and thus gained control of the lake. With it came American supremacy over all the vague Northwest.[1]

At sea, meanwhile, the tiny American navy was covering itself with glory, its individual ships meeting those of England with unexpected success. The privateers of each nation did great havoc to the other's trading-vessels, while France looked on with delight at the mutual destruction. Of course, in the end England's huge fleets drove the American men-of-war from the seas; and the shrewd traders of New England saw ruin staring them in the face. In 1814 a convention met in Connecticut, at Hartford, to protest against the war. There was nothing really treasonable in this, but through the excited country the cry of treason was raised and believed, and gave the final blow to the ever-fading Federalist party of New England.[2]

Napoleon's defeat and first abdication early in 1814 caused a complete change in the American war. England found herself dictator of a triumphant European peace; and all her fleets and veteran armies were free for use in America. She turned them immediately to that purpose. The presumptuous State which had dared to dispute her commercial supremacy, was to be crushed completely. Three powerful expeditions were sent out, one to strike southward from Canada, one to ravage the coast midway, and one to penetrate northward from New Orleans.

The central expedition reflected little credit on either of the contestants. A force of hardly four thousand British broke through a large number of bewildered militia, and burned Washington, committing such irreparable and profitless destruction as civilization has grown to regard as mere vandalism. They treated the city as even infuriated Europe in the same year had not dreamt of treating captured Paris. The marauders then assailed Baltimore but were repelled.[3]

[1] See *Perry's Victory on Lake Erie*, page 268.
[2] See *The Hartford Convention*, page 326.
[3] See *The Burning of Washington*, page 295.

To north and south there was a different tale to tell. The powerful Canadian expedition, attempting to penetrate by Lake Champlain, was met by a few militia and an American squadron feebler than its own. The Britons were completely defeated, their fleet destroyed, and their army driven back to Canada. The New Orleans invasion was met by General Jackson and his straight-shooting frontiersmen. The determined resolution of the defenders of their homes, the deadly aim of the men, and the military instinct of their leader proved irresistible. The entire force of British veterans, long trained to European victory in Wellington's wars, suffered that most disastrous defeat which Louisiana still celebrates as a yearly holiday.[1]

Both Britain and the United States grew wise. Nay, perhaps the whole world had learned its lesson, that invasion of the homes of a resolute people is a far different and far more difficult matter than ordinary even-sided battle. France at the outset of her revolution had hurled back all the armies of Europe. Yet the insulted Prussians in their hour of vengeance had annihilated the invading troops of France. Even the irregular guerillas of Spain in defence of home had proved able to maintain themselves against all the genius of Napoleon. The United States had twice failed to conquer Canada. Britain had failed even more signally to conquer the United States. Neither party has ever renewed the futile attempt.

The War of 1812 has been called America's "Second War of Independence." In Europe the era of 1815 left democracy bewildered and helplessly entangled, but in the United States it was free, triumphant, and advancing. What wonder that the one continent should progress more rapidly than the other, that its example, its attraction, should prove irresistible in allurement to the down-trodden common folk of Europe.

[1] See *The Battle of New Orleans ; End of the War of 1812*, page 343.

[FOR THE NEXT SECTION OF THIS GENERAL SURVEY SEE VOLUME XVI]

UNION OF IRELAND WITH GREAT BRITAIN

THE GREAT IRISH REBELLION

A.D. 1800

WILLIAM O'CONNOR MORRIS

For more than three centuries the condition and claims of Ireland have engaged the attention of the world. That country is often spoken of as having been during this long period in a state of "chronic rebellion" against English rule. Of the actual organized rebellions which mark its history from 1565 to 1870, no fewer than nine distinct outbreaks or serious demonstrations are recorded. Among these the "Great Rebellion" of 1798 was the most formidable. Although unsuccessful, it taught the insurgents how better to estimate the forces at their command for advancing the country's interests, and gradually led to more intelligent and systematic endeavors in the fields of discussion and statesmanship. From time to time, during the nineteenth century, clear gains for the cause of Irish liberty were won by her champions in Parliament, on the hustings, and in the ranks of literature.

The "Great Rebellion" was preceded by the organization of many Irish societies in hostility to the British Government. Chief among them was the Society of United Irishmen, founded at Belfast, in 1791, mainly by Theobald Wolfe Tone, a young barrister of English descent, and, like most of the members of the society, a Protestant.

At first the United Irishmen formed an open organization, whose chief avowed aims were parliamentary reform, repeal of the penal laws, and Catholic emancipation. Later it became a secret society with revolutionary objects. The story of its acts, of the rebellion which it was instrumental in causing, and of the union with Great Britain which soon followed, is well told by Morris, long a member of the Irish judiciary, and one of the most competent historians of these events.

UNITED Irish leaders, seeing there was no hope of accomplishing their ends by constitutional means, began, as Tone had done from the first, to think that revolution was their only chance. Their organization was made military; their societies were prepared for a call to the field; supplies of arms were eagerly sought; the districts in which they possessed influence were placed under the command of officers; and attempts were made secretly to enroll and drill levies capable of an armed rising. The emissaries sent to France became more numerous; the principal of these was Lord Edward Fitzgerald, a scion of the great Geraldine name; and the heads of the French Republic were invited to strike England through Ireland, and to set the Irish people free. At the same time, true to their policy from the first, the United Irishmen made renewed efforts to drag Catholic Ireland into their wake; the confiscation of the land was held out as a bribe to the peasantry; Irishmen were to have their own when they were released from the bonds of landlords and the collectors of tithe. A movement, now distinctly rebellious, was thus linked with a movement springing from the land; thousands of Catholics fell into the United Irish ranks; agrarian outbreaks, in many places, assumed the aspect of a predial war; and the tendency of Irish agrarian trouble to resist the power of the State, and to become revolutionary, grew very manifest. As yet, however, the United Irishmen, except in Ulster, were hardly organized; and the Catholic peasantry were still a chaotic mass, tossed hither and thither, without real leaders.

A movement, meanwhile, of a very different kind, directly opposed to that of the United Irishmen, but indirectly giving it powerful aid, had been acquiring considerable strength in Ulster, and even extending beyond its limits. In the Northern Province, the Celtic Irish, all Catholic, and the Protestant descendants of the old settlers, were, in many districts, closely intermixed; perennial feuds had existed between them. This state of disorder had greatly increased, as lawlessness had spread through parts of Ulster; and from 1791 to 1795 the Protestant "Peep o' Day Boys," as they were called, and the Catholic "Defenders" came into repeated conflict. The first-named body, largely composed of members of the Established Church, disliked the Presbyterian and United Irish movement, which Catholic Ireland was invited to join, and formed the "Orange" Society. The ranks of the Orangemen rapidly increased; their organization became powerful, and spread even to the Southern provinces; undoubtedly it obtained the support of a considerable number of the Ulster gentry, and possibly even of the Irish Government.

It is certain, however, that the Irish Catholics were not prepared to attempt to rise against the State in force. Wolfe Tone landed at Havre, France, in the first months of 1796—one of other emissaries but their born leader—and his capacity and earnestness made a real impression on the Directory, then in the seat of power in Paris. He advocated a formidable descent on Ireland, with the arguments of an enthusiast; it is to his credit that he made scarcely a stipulation for himself, and that he tried to obtain pledges that, in the event of success, his country was not to be made a dependency of France. A large fleet carrying fifteen thousand troops, under the command of the illustrious Hoche, set sail from Brest, in December, upon the enterprise. It is remarkable that it did not make for Dublin, or a port of Ulster, as Tone had advised; it sought to effect a landing on the extreme verge of Munster, perhaps because an attempt of the kind had proved successful more than a century before. The French navy, however, was in a wretched state; Hoche, in a frigate, never reached the Irish coast, and the principal part of the invading fleet, after making Bantry Bay in safety, was driven out to sea by a furious tempest. It has been thought, however, that Grouchy, the second in command, might have landed with a not inconsiderable force; if so Munster might have been overrun, and become, for a time, a French province; on this occasion, as on the day of Waterloo, Grouchy perhaps did England really good service. The failure of the expedition has been ascribed to chance. History more justly points out that it is not easy to invade an island, cut off from the Continent by a dangerous and most stormy sea, especially with an inferior naval force.

The failure at Bantry did not change the purpose of the United Irish leaders; but it made them cautious, and they resolved, if possible, not to attempt a rising before the French had made a successful landing. Ulster, nevertheless, and other parts of Ireland, were in a state of hardly suppressed rebellion, sustained by a savage war of classes, throughout nearly the whole of 1797. A United Irish Directory had been formed in Belfast, enforcing its mandates far and wide; an insurrectionary army was held in the leash, drilled, and to a certain extent, disciplined; it may have numbered, on paper, one hundred thousand men. Another United Irish Directory had its seat in Dublin; some of its leaders were able men; but their chief trust was placed in

Lord Edward Fitzgerald who was to command the armed levies of the South, and whose great name seemed a tower of strength. These levies, it was said, numbered two hundred thousand men —an estimate, beyond doubt, excessive; but tens of thousands of the Catholic peasantry had by this time become United Irishmen, and many of them had been rudely armed and disciplined. The plan of the conspirators was to seize the Castle of Dublin, as in 1641, to occupy the capital, and to make the men in power prisoners; and then to rise generally throughout the country, when the invasion of the French had been made certain. In the interval of time remaining, fresh efforts were made to exasperate and extend the agrarian war; maps of the old confiscated lands were prepared; old prophecies that the Saxon was to be expelled from Ireland were noised abroad, and the peasantry were told that their alien masters were doomed. In this way the rebellious and the agrarian movements became thoroughly united in some districts; plantations were cut down and smithies blazed for the manufacture of a formidable weapon, the pike; and the organization of the "Whiteboy" system with its central and local secret societies, was set on foot to promote the United Irish cause. This combination, however, does not appear to have been complete in more than a few counties; and it did not exist, it has been said, in Connaught.

This state of things in Ireland was perilous in the extreme; affairs in Europe, and even in England, increased the peril. Notwithstanding the failure of 1796, a great French fleet had assembled at Brest, and a Dutch fleet was at anchor near the Texel, in order to renew a descent on Ireland—Tone had indefatigably pressed on the enterprise; France had already nearly mastered the Continent; the very naval power of Great Britain had been shaken, especially by symptoms of disaffection in the fleet. The Irish Government was perfectly justified in resolving to crush out rebellion in time; Clare, its master spirit, deserves credit for a resolution and daring worthy of Strafford. But it was more unfortunate that it had not the support of a regular and well-organized military force. The army in Ireland was only a few thousand men; the militia had become deeply tainted; the men at the "Castle" had largely to rely on the yeomanry, a numerous volunteer levy, raised to a great extent by the local gentry, and mostly Protestants. Ulster was selected as the first point of attack; the leaders of the conspiracy were arrested; the incendiary press was scattered to the winds; a general process of seizing and collecting arms was enforced in the Province without scruple or mercy. Houses were burned down wholesale to compel the surrender of weapons; bands of yeomen harried the Catholic districts; confessions were extorted by atrocious methods; wherever an attempt at resistance was made, it was repressed by wild and relentless cruelties. In a word, a kind of savage guerilla warfare not unlike that of the Desmond conflict, and aggravated by a furious strife of race and creed, raged for a time in many parts of Ulster; and hundreds of captives were hurried off, and put on board the fleet—an event ominously connected with the Mutiny at the Nore. The head of the rebellion was broken; it should be added that, ruthless as the means were, they had been sanctioned by the Irish Parliament. The Government, after a pause of a few weeks, turned against the conspiracy in the capital. It must be borne in mind that though a French invasion had been stopped by the great fight of Camperdown, the warrior of Italy was at this very moment on the French coasts, planning a descent on England. Spies and informers had kept Camden, Clare, and the Council apprised of all that was going on; the members of the Directory were made prisoners; and the arrest and subsequent death of Lord Edward Fitzgerald deprived the leaders of the intended rising of a head in whom they placed extraordinary trust, though there was little to recommend him except a name, still a spell of power among the peasantry of the South.

If excesses had already occurred, the Irish Government, up to this point of time, recollecting the situation, can be hardly blamed. The brain of the conspiracy had, so to speak, been smitten; but the paralyzed members still stirred with life; all prospects of a rising had not disappeared. Fitzgibbon knew that the plan of the leaders was not to move until the French had landed; he seems, like Claverhouse, to have deliberately resolved to force insurrection into premature being and to stifle it before it could obtain aid from abroad. By his counsels more than by those of any other personage, the system which had succeeded in the North was carried out in parts of the Southern provinces. This policy, which, be it observed, was denounced by Abercromby, the commander-in-chief of the regular army, and a true soldier, had the result expected from it. It became impossible to await the coming of the French; the people in several counties were driven into revolt; and the sanguinary rebellion of 1798 broke out on May 23d in that year.

The rising was confined to a part of Leinster; it was generally feeble and ill-combined, it became formidable in a nook of the province only. An attempt to attack Dublin from without, connected with an insurrection within, was easily quelled by the armed force on the spot, and though deeds of blood were done, Kildare, Carlow, and Meath were quickly subdued. The rising, however, was universal and fierce in the two beautiful counties of Wicklow and Wexford, the fairest part of the southeastern tract of Ireland. In this prosperous region, the strife between the Orangemen and Defenders had raged for some months, and the efforts of the Government to bring rebellion to a head had been marked with peculiar cruelties. The conflict from the first was a savage war of religion; it was also to some extent a struggle of race; but, in this instance, the double lines of distinction in Ireland did not coincide, the rebels were for the most part of Anglo-Norman or English descent; it was a war of armed Protestants, backed by a military force, waged with a Catholic peasantry, half maddened by wrong. For nearly a month the issue of the contest was very doubtful; it assumed a terrible and hideous aspect; it is impossible to adjust the balance of evil deeds done on either side. The horrors of the scene are relieved by the proofs of devoted courage that were shown; the Protestants fought with the reckless pride characteristic of a dominant race; the Catholics exhibited heroic daring, at Vinegar Hill, Oulart, and New Ross; the fowling-piece and the long pike had great effect in brave and resolute hands; and one of the rebel leaders displayed a capacity worthy of a born general. After many efforts the rising was at last quenched, in ashes and blood; but the Catholics had occupied the town of Wexford for a time, and, had the march of the Catholics on Arklow proved successful, the capital would have been probably taken.

The uprising scarcely made a sign in Connaught; it appeared in Munster in only a few weak gatherings. Ulster, where the conspiracy had been most deeply laid, did not stir during the war in the southeast. The causes of this deserve passing notice. The preparations for a rising had been already prevented; the Presbyterians waited the advent of the French; they resented, too, a quarrel between France and the United States. But the most effective cause of their inaction was this: the struggle in Wicklow and Wexford was one of religions; and the United Irishmen of Ulster stood aloof from a purely Protestant and Catholic conflict which ran counter to their hopes and sympathies. The rebellion of 1798 was almost wholly fought out by Irishmen; it had nearly ceased when troops poured in from England; but it had called out high Irish qualities. By this time Camden had been replaced by Cornwallis, a capable and humane soldier; but a kind of guerilla struggle lingered for a few months among the valleys and hills of Wicklow, the fastness of the Celtic mountaineers of old.

Nevertheless the state of Ireland was lamentable after the close of 1798; it left a legacy of blighted hopes and most evil memories. It was not only that fair parts of the country had been ravaged by a barbarous strife; the material was as nothing to the moral ruin. The influences that had, for many years, seemed to lessen the differences of blood and faith, and even to have healed many wounds of the past, had disappeared in an inhuman struggle; the old distinctions had come out, deeply marked as ever; the conflict, if not wholly, had been in the main a war of race, and above all, of religion. The hopeful visions of the United Irishmen had gradually disappeared; the ideal of Grattan had proved impossible; the aspirations of a new era had been as idle as the French dreams of 1789. The ruling orders of Ireland had been made revengeful; the classes beneath them had beheld the prospect of enlarged liberties suddenly withdrawn; the lines of demarcation between the owners and occupiers of the soil, and between Catholic and Protestant, had been greatly widened. This change for the worse, which put the whole country back, was very marked in the Irish Parliament; it had become a mere court to register what the Castle and Clare ordered; the independent party in it had dwindled almost to nothing; and Grattan and his followers, indignant at recent events, unable to check the course of the Government, and saddened at the failure of the hopes of 1782, had seceded from it in anger and despair. Long before this time they had made a last fruitless effort in the cause of Catholic emancipation and Parliamentary reform.

Before the end of the struggle, a French squadron, and a few hundred men, had landed near Killala, on the coast of Mayo. Napoleon had taken the main fleet of France to the East, where it perished in the great battle of the Nile; he had no taste for rebellion, Irish or other; the French Directory sent only an insignificant force to the shores of Ireland. Its leader, Humbert, however, was a brilliant soldier; he routed a body of militia, threefold in numbers, in a combat known as the "Race of Castlebar"; he gave Cornwallis much to do before he was compelled to surrender. Another petty French descent was remarkable only for the capture of Wolfe Tone after a sharp engagement. The unfortunate chief of the United Irish movement— he had served in the expedition to Bantry and had witnessed the disaster of Camperdown—was doomed to the ignominious death of a felon, though he held the commission of a French general, and only averted his fate by suicide. Tone was unquestionably the first of the Irish leaders; he had capacity, resource, true faith in his cause, and patriotism; his figure will live in Irish history. After a few severe examples had been made, the conspirators, who had fallen into the hands of the Irish Government, were amnestied, under not unfair conditions; their lives were spared, but they had to leave the country. They were, none of them, men of marked powers; but some won honor in foreign lands; two or three gallantly followed Napoleon's eagles; more than one made a name for himself in America. Much in their conduct is to be sternly condemned; yet, at this distance of time, it deserves a kind of sympathy. They had at first only constitutional reforms in view; they were drawn into rebellion in part by the revolutionary ideas of France, but in part by the mistakes of the Irish Government.

The rebellion of 1798 had only just ended, when Pitt began to lay grounds for the Union. The contest had been tardily put down; reënforcements from England had come in late; but we may summarily reject the wicked myths—evil phantoms rising from a field of carnage—that Pitt fomented a rising in arms, and

let Irish factions tear each other to pieces in order to promote a
measure he had at heart. The Union of Great Britain and Ireland had not only been projected by many able thinkers; it had
been in the minds of several English statesmen, ever since the
Revolution of 1782. Apart, however, from this, Pitt, it is evident from his letters and speeches, did not thoroughly comprehend the whole reasons that made a union a necessity of state at
this time, or perceive the consequences that might flow from it.
He saw, as the "Regency Question" had made manifest, that the
two legislatures might dangerously clash; he saw, too, the danger of this at a period of war, though, in England's struggle with
Revolutionary France, the Irish Parliament had given him most
cordial support. He saw also that probably the best means to
secure the Established Church in Ireland, to keep the land in
Protestant hands, in a word to maintain what he called "the
Protestant Settlement," was to make Ireland one with Great
Britain; nor was he blind to the possible evils of the existing
state of Catholic Ireland. But, though he was not insensible to
them, he did not completely grasp the truths that, after the horrors of 1798, the only hope for Ireland, torn as she had been by
a barbarous strife of race and faith, was to bring her under the
control of an imperial parliament; and that the only wise policy
for a British minister was, with the aid of a strong and just government, to place Catholic and Protestant, Saxon and Celt, on
an equal level of civil and religious rights. This justification of
the Union he did not fully realize, at least he did not act boldly
as if he did; and we may smile at his notions that the introduction of Irish members into the United Parliament might largely
increase the power of the Crown, and that a union would cause
Irish faction quickly to cease. Pitt, in fact, as we have before
remarked, was ignorant of the true state of Ireland, and in the
case of Ireland as in that of France in 1792–1793, he had not the
genius to perceive what was beyond his immediate ken.

It was the wish of Pitt to combine the Union with the emancipation of the Irish Catholics, and with measures to provide
funds for the support of the Catholic Irish priesthood, and for
the commutation of the tithes of the Established Church; he had
seen, we have said, the bad effects of this impost. This policy
was in the right direction; but it was not original, as has been

alleged; the Irish Parliament would have conceded the Catholic claims in 1795; the payment of the priests was an old idea, and had been advocated by Irish writers and statesmen; the commutation of the tithe was a favorite plan of Grattan. Pitt, however, did not persist in the project, which he had hoped to make an essential part of the Union; he yielded to the counsels of Clare, greatly trusted by him in Irish affairs, and consented to deprive his measure of these features; he knew, too, at this time, that George III was obstinately opposed to the demands of the Catholics. This was the first of his grave mistakes on the subject; it is the more to be blamed because Cornwallis, able to gauge Irish opinion on the spot, always insisted that the Union could not succeed, if Catholic emancipation was not made, so to speak, its gift.

Means were taken, toward the close of 1798, to ascertain the judgment of Irishmen on the question of Union and Catholic emancipation. A few of the great peers agreed to support the scheme, should it serve their interests; a number of members of the Irish Houses were ready to obey the minister on the usual terms; some of the independent landed gentry, alarmed at the events of 1798, beheld in the Union safety for themselves; the leading men of Catholic Ireland, much as they had resented Fitzwilliam's recall, were not unwilling so consider the subject. But an immense majority of the Irish Protestants, the trading classes of Dublin almost to a man, and nine-tenths, at least, of the Irish bar, were indignant at the very thought of a union, and expressed their sentiments in emphatic language: this is the more remarkable because the country was held down by a British armed force, and the views of the British Ministry were perfectly well known. In these circumstances, Robert Stewart, Lord Castlereagh, the chief secretary of Cornwallis, announced, somewhat vaguely, the policy of Pitt, in the Irish House of Commons in a speech on the address made in January, 1799; but an amendment was rejected by one vote only; and, as this was plainly equivalent to a defeat, the measure was permitted to drop for a time.

Though the Government had been baffled in the Irish Lower House, it obtained a large majority in the Irish House of Lords, where the influence of Clare was easily supreme. The British

Parliament had, about the same time, passed resolutions in favor of the Union by an overwhelming majority of votes; and Pitt insisted that the measure could be carried out in Ireland. But it was far from easy to give his purpose effect; and means were adopted, the exact nature of which has been matter of controversy ever since, but of which the general character is not doubtful. The Irish Parliament had long been swayed by corrupt influence; this had probably increased since 1782; it had been openly exercised on the "Regency Question." Direct bribery was not employed; but promises of peerages were lavishly scattered; places were created and places unscrupulously filled, in order to obtain support for the scheme; officials were threatened with dismissal if they did not vote for the Government; appeals were persistently made to the hopes and the fears of the members in both parts of the Irish Parliament. Simultaneously, pledges were given that immense sums were to be paid to the patrons and the proprietors of the numerous boroughs to be disfranchised; and one of the reforms effected in 1793, by which placemen in the House of Commons were compelled to vacate their seats, was twisted into a method to secure a majority. By these expedients, regarded by Cornwallis with disgust, but employed by his chief secretary with unflinching boldness, the Irish Parliament was packed to vote for a union; but it is only just to add that, from the first, many of its members—and the number certainly tended to increase—conscientiously approved of Pitt's policy.

Recourse, too, was had to other means to influence Irish opinion outside the Parliament in behalf of the contemplated measure. Able pamphlets were published, and the press subsidized; Cornwallis went through different counties, to canvass, so to speak, for the Union; and many favorable addresses were obtained, though these were of a questionable kind, and the adverse petitions were much more numerous. The Irish Government, however, chiefly directed its efforts to enlist Catholic Ireland on its side; and incidents occurred, even yet obscure, that form an unhappy passage in Irish history. Pitt had informed Cornwallis that the Union was to be a "Protestant Union," in the phrase of the time; he told the Lord-Lieutenant, very plainly, that Catholic emancipation was to be no part of the measure.

But his own speeches in the British House of Commons implied that he approved of the Catholic claims, and that they might be conceded when the Union had become law; he certainly encouraged Cornwallis, and gave him power to bid openly for Catholic support; he perhaps authorized Cornwallis to assure the Irish Catholic leaders that their cause was his own. That upright but not very astute nobleman, always the earnest champion of the Irish Catholics, placed his own interpretation on Pitt's hints and words: he had many conferences with the heads of Catholic Ireland, and entreated them to use their influence to promote the Union; he unquestionably held out hopes, if he did not make promises; he left them under the impression that their emancipation was certain and at hand. It should be added that, before this time, Cornwallis had been negotiating with the Irish Catholic bishops, with reference to a provision for the priesthood; Pitt seems to have been not aware of this; but the fact is, not the less, of extreme significance. The broad result was that the Catholic leaders generally threw in their lot with the Union, and drew the Catholic masses with them; Catholic Ireland, in the main, declared for the measure; and this, Pitt and Cornwallis agreed, was of supreme importance. A small minority, however, of the Irish Catholics, with more insight, and perhaps with more ambitious views, protested vehemently against the proposed scheme: among these was Daniel O'Connell, a young lawyer, just beginning his career.

The devices employed to bring about the Union made their effects apparent in the Irish Parliament, when it assembled again in January, 1800. An amendment to the "Address," by which it was sought to stop the progress of the measure, was rejected; the "Question" was introduced, a few days afterward, by a message from the Viceroy sending to both Houses the resolutions voted by the British Parliament, and recommending the policy sanctioned by it. The debates on the subject, arising in different ways, were impassioned, and took up much time; but they are marked by ability of a very high order. Castlereagh advocated the scheme, with calm power and thoroughness; Clare, in a speech of real insight and force, insisted that in a union lay the only hope of property, of law, and of the Established Church in Ireland. A fine array of eloquence was mar-

shalled on the other side; the bar engaged its most brilliant ornaments, Saurin, Plunket, Bushe, and other eminent worthies;
the Speaker, Foster, rose to the height of a great argument, in
a most weighty and thoughtful harangue.   But Grattan towered
above all his fellows—he had lately returned to the House of
Commons.   In language of singular beauty and pathos, accompanied by solemn and prophetic warnings, he advised the Parliament not to destroy itself, and to preserve its existence for
the Irish "nation."   All opposition, however, proved vain; the
Government retained the majority it had procured; resolutions,
passed by the Irish Parliament, in favor of a union, were translated into articles and bills, and the measure of Pitt received the
sanction of both the Irish and the British Parliaments.   It deserves notice that a proposal to refer the decision of the question
to the Irish electorate was angrily resented by Pitt and Castlereagh; the voice even of Protestant Ireland, though that of a
minority of the Irish people, and of a minority in the main
loyal, was not allowed to pronounce on this matter.   It is certain, however, that, in its later stages at least, the measure did
not provoke widespread discontent; there was no passionate
outburst of opinion against it.   Dublin and the Irish bar, indeed, remained bitterly hostile; but there was little murmuring
in the country districts; the mass of Catholic Ireland did not
stir; its leaders looked forward with anxious hope; the trading
classes were induced to expect that the Union would bring them
large benefits; Presbyterian Ireland seems to have thought that
its favorite linen manufacture would make great progress.   The
attitude of the majority of the people was one of apathy; it
was felt that a measure, backed by the British Parliament and
the British army, could not be withstood; but unquestionably a
minority, growing in strength, inclined very decidedly toward a
union.

The Union was accomplished by questionable means; nor
was it a well-conceived measure, even within the narrow limits
traced out by Pitt.   The Irish and British Legislatures were
merely combined, and emerged in a single imperial Parliament;
Ireland retained the viceroy, a separate Government, a separate
Administration, separate courts of justice, even separate exchequers for a considerable time, and the shadow of an inde-

pendent state was suffered to exist. The remaining portions of
the scheme were of less importance and do not deserve particular attention.

The maintenance of the Established Church was made a solemn and fundamental law; with what results time was to show
in its fulness; the settlement of the land was left of course, as it
was; but undoubtedly the hope of preserving this had weight
with numbers of the landed gentry alarmed at the threats uttered
in 1798 to undo the confiscations of the past. The fiscal arrangements were harsh to Ireland; she was to contribute two-
seventeenths to the imperial expenditure, a proportion certainly
in excess; her trade was somewhat further enlarged, and ultimately was to be completely free; but the commercial benefits
which Castlereagh declared would follow the Union were not
realized. The Irish peers lost their seats in the Irish House of
Lords; a small body of the order have ever since been chosen to
represent them in the imperial Parliament; the three hundred
members of the Irish House of Commons were reduced to one
hundred in the imperial House, a number that ought to have
been adequate to make the will of Ireland sufficiently felt. For
the rest, while much that the Union should have contained was
unhappily not comprised in it, much that was discreditable in
its incidents was faithfully carried out; the borough-mongering
nobles and commoners were gorged with the spoil that had
been promised; and the pledges of corruption were duly fulfilled.

Pitt was a large-minded and enlightened statesman; he certainly desired, when the Union was secure, to carry out the measures of relief for the Irish Catholics which, from the outset, he
had had in view. He probably reckoned on his prodigious influence; but he had unhappily kept the King in the dark, though
fully aware of the King's sentiments; a ministerial cabal was
formed against him; and George III, on a preposterous plea,
pressed with the obstinacy of a distempered mind, peremptorily
refused to listen to the Catholic claims. The subsequent conduct of Pitt in this matter has indisputably thrown a shadow on
his name. He resigned his office, when he had persuaded himself that he could not carry out his Irish Catholic policy; he is
entitled to every credit attaching to the act. But in a very short

time he let his master know that he would not urge the question again; he supported a violent Anti-Catholic Ministry; he returned to office, but took no steps to vindicate the demands of Catholic Ireland.

All this has exposed his memory to grave suspicion; and history can hardly withhold its censure. It is idle to say that he told Cornwallis that the Union was to be a Protestant one only: he held out hopes himself to the Irish Catholics; he invited Cornwallis to do the same; he carried the Union, to some extent at least, by obtaining Irish Catholic support, secured only by what were deemed promises that Catholic relief would certainly follow. In these circumstances, it was not enough to have simply abandoned the helm; he ought to have insisted on the King's adopting his measures; and had he done so, he must have attained his object; and his subsequent attitude has a look of insincerity, if not worse. We fear it must be said that, in his wish to accomplish the Union, he did not scruple to allow the Irish Catholics to entertain hopes which, he well knew, might not be fulfilled; that he all but pledged himself to them, through the Lord Lieutenant, though he felt he might not be able to redeem the pledge; and that he thought his conscience absolved by a resignation—which he took care should not last long—without even trying to give effect to a policy to which he stood committed as a man and a minister. The best excuses, perhaps, to be made for him are that, in his ignorance of Ireland and her real state, he did not understand all that was involved in the course he took, and that, in the death struggle of the rebellion, he believed it was his duty to become the head of the state, without regard to consistency or too fine a sense of honor.

Under the Constitution of 1782 Ireland unquestionably made social and material progress; the ancient divisions of blood and creed, which for centuries have kept her races apart, and her feuds of class, had to some extent disappeared. In these circumstances it was not impossible, though in our judgment it was not probable, that Grattan's ideal might have, with a free Parliament and a powerful landed gentry, the respect of a contented peasantry. But the French Revolution scattered these hopes to the winds; its destructive influence was as fatal, perhaps, in Ireland, as in any part of Europe; it blighted the fair promise of the close of the eighteenth century. We must add, too, that having regard to the relations it created between Great Britain and Ireland, the Constitution of 1782 was not likely to endure; it was hardly compatible with the security of the British empire; it was distrusted by British statesmen. Be this as it may, the French Revolution, searching Irish institutions to the very core, proved how errors of policy and faults of the British and Irish Governments prevented reforms which might, conceivably, have averted the disastrous events that followed. Rebellion, however, began to lift its head; a revolutionary movement to combine Irishmen in a league against England, the common enemy, and to stir up anarchical strife, was crossed and baffled by another movement, characteristic of the ill-feeling of the past; and the end was a horrible war of race and religion. For much that was done in 1798, Clare and the men at the Castle are to be severely blamed; but their position, we must recollect, was difficult in the extreme; and if they forced civil war to come to a head, they certainly prevented a worse catastrophe. As affairs stood when the rebellion had ended, a union had become a necessity of state, in the interest of Ireland and of Great Britain alike; but Pitt managed the settlement badly; and the Union was an ill-designed measure, carried by sinister means through the Irish Parliament, and accompanied by an act of wrong to Catholic Ireland, of which the results were long felt. Still Pitt must not be too harshly judged; in the existing state of the world he was bound to accomplish a union at almost any risk or cost.

Ireland entered into a union with England under unhappy conditions, and at an inauspicious time. The Catholic question was one of pressing importance, and, if unsettled, certain to cause trouble; the country required other reforms, the necessity of which had begun to be seen by some of the best men in the Irish Parliament. Ireland was in want of a strong but progressive government; but she had been united with Great Britain at the very time when the conflict with France was soon to become one of life and death; when all hopes of changes in the state seemed gone; when reactionary ideas had immense force; when unbending Toryism was supreme, nay absolute. And the reforms she needed were, in some instances, in direct conflict with

British ideas; in others, were little understood by British states-men; and Ireland was to be ruled by a Parliament that knew her not, and by politicians well meaning, indeed, but often ill-informed and without sympathy; it being doubtful, too, if in the peculiar state of her representation, she would possess sufficient influence of her own. The prosperity of Ireland had been largely destroyed; the land had been devastated by civil war; the dregs of rebellion lingered; animosities of race and faith had been fearfully revived; and the island was behind England in culti-vation and wealth. These circumstances alone made it no easy task to govern Ireland well in an imperial Parliament, and by ministers dependent on it. If the Union was a necessity of the time; if, on the whole, it was to effect good, it was to be seen that it was not an unmixed blessing, and that it was to be accom-panied, at least, with some real evils.

RISE OF THE DEMOCRATIC PARTY IN THE UNITED STATES

JEFFERSON'S INAUGURAL

A.D. 1801

HERMANN von HOLST   THOMAS JEFFERSON

Among the political parties which have appeared in the United States since the founding of the Republic many arose through temporary influences and, with or without accomplishing noteworthy aims, came to an end. Of those which, whatever changes at one time or another they may have undergone, have long remained as persistent factors in American politics, that which almost from its origin has been known as the Democratic party is the oldest and at many periods has been the dominant party of the country. It has controlled the national or the executive Government under nine Presidents—Jefferson, Madison, Monroe, Jackson, Van Buren, Polk, Pierce, Buchanan, and Cleveland.

Under Washington and John Adams the national executive was controlled by the Federalists, a party formed in 1787 to support the Federal Constitution. Its importance ceased soon after the War of 1812. It was opposed by the Anti-Federal party, which stood against strengthening the National Government at the expense of the States. The name Anti-Federal went out of use about 1794, and the opponents of the Federal party took the name of Republicans. Their party was afterward called the Democratic-Republican, and still later (1828) the Democratic party, a name chosen as being "novel, distinct, and popular." Of this party — as the Democratic-Republican — Jefferson is regarded as the founder, and the Democratic party to the present day is often called the "party of Jefferson," while the term " Jeffersonian Democracy " is as frequently applied to its principles.

In the survey of Von Holst, an eminent authority on the political foundation and development of the United States, the origin and principles of the Democratic party are clearly set forth, and in Jefferson's first inaugural, which follows, the political faith of the party, as given by himself, is definitely stated.

HERMANN VON HOLST[1]

WASHINGTON'S presence made Adams's inauguration a moving spectacle. Adams remarked that it was difficult to say why tears flowed so abundantly. An ill-defined feeling filled

[1] From Von Holst's *Constitutional and Political History of the United States* (New York : Callaghan and Company), by permission.

all minds that severer storms would have to be met now that the one man was no longer at the head of the state, who, spite of all oppositions, was known to hold a place in the hearts of the entire people. The Federalists of the Hamilton faction gave very decided expressions to these fears, and Adams himself was fully conscious that his lot had fallen on evil days. It was natural that the complications with France should for the moment inspire the greatest concern. The suspicion that France was the quarter from which the new administration was threatened with greatest danger was soon verified by events.

The inaugural address touched on the relations between France and the United States only lightly. Adams had contented himself with speaking of his high esteem for the French people, and with wishing that the friendship of the two nations might continue. The message of May 16, 1797, on the other hand, addressed to an extraordinary session of Congress, treated this question exclusively. The President informed Congress that the Directory had not only refused to receive Pinckney, but had even ordered him to leave France, and that diplomatic relations between the two powers had entirely ceased. In strong but temperate language he counselled them to unanimity, and recommended that "effectual measures of defence" should be adopted without delay. It is necessary "to convince France and the world that we are not a degraded people, humiliated under a colonial spirit of fear and sense of inferiority, fitted to be miserable instruments of foreign influence, and regardless of national honor, character, and interest." At the same time, however, he promised to make another effort at negotiation.

Pinckney, Marshall, and Gerry were chosen to make an effort to bring about the resumption of diplomatic relations and the friendly settlement of the pending difficulties. Their efforts were completely fruitless. The Directory did not indeed treat them with open discourtesy, but met them in such a manner that only new and greater insults were added to the older. Gerry, for whom Adams entertained a feeling of personal friendship, was most acceptable to the Directory, because he was an Anti-Federalist. Talleyrand endeavored to persuade him to act alone. There can be no doubt whatever that Gerry had no authority to do so. Partly from vanity, and partly from fear of the consequences of a complete breach, he went just far enough into the adroitly laid snares of Talleyrand to greatly compromise himself, his fellow-ambassadors, and the Administration. The want of tact was so much the greater, as Talleyrand, by three different mediators, gave the ambassador to understand that the payment of a large sum of money was a condition precedent of a settlement.

In the early part of April, 1798, the President laid before the House of Representatives all the documents bearing on this procedure. If, even before his administration had begun, the general feeling of the country had been constantly turning against France, now a real tornado of ill-will broke forth.

The Anti-Federalists would willingly have given currency to the view that the ambassadors had been deceived by common cheats. But their ranks grew so thin that they were obliged to proceed with great caution.

While Jefferson had called the President's message of March 19th mad, he now declared: "It is still our duty to endeavor to avoid war; but if it shall actually take place, no matter by whom brought on, we must defend ourselves. If our house be on fire, without inquiring if it was fired from within or from without, we must try to extinguish it. In that, I have no doubt, we shall act as one man." That such would have been the case will be scarcely questioned now. But although the Anti-Federalists did not think of playing the part of traitors, and although they gave expression to their sympathy for France only in a suppressed tone, Jefferson was right when he said that "party passions were indeed high." The visionaries became sober, and those who had been sober intoxicated. Hence the discord grew worse than ever.

A small number of the Federalists were anxious for war, and the rest of them considered it at least as probable as the preservation of peace. Warlike preparations were therefore pushed forward with energy. But it was not considered sufficient to get ready to receive the foreign enemy; it was necessary to fetter the enemy at home. The angry aliens were to be gotten rid of while it was not yet too late, and the extreme Anti-Federalists were to be deterred from throwing too great obstacles, at this serious time, in the way of the Administration. In the desire to effect both of these things, the so-called Alien and Sedition laws, which sealed the fate of the Federal party and gave rise to the doctrine of nullification, had their origin.

The plan of this work does not permit us to dwell on the contents of these laws. Suffice it to say that for a long time they have been considered in the United States as unquestionably unconstitutional. At the time, however, there was no doubt among all the most prominent Federalists of their constitutionality. Hamilton even questioned it as little as he did their expediency. But he did not conceal it from himself that their adoption was the establishment of a dangerous precedent. Lloyd of Maryland had on June 26th introduced a bill more accurately to define the crime of treason and to punish the crime of sedition, which bill was intended for the suppression of all exhibitions of friendship for France, and for the better protection of the Government. Hamilton wrote to Wolcott in relation to this bill that it endangered the internal peace of the country, and would "give to faction body and solidity."

Lloyd's bill did not come up to be voted upon in its original form; but the Alien and Sedition laws were of themselves sufficient to realize Hamilton's fears. The supremacy of Massachusetts and Connecticut had become so unbearable to the South that the idea of separation arose again in May. The influential John Taylor of Virginia thought "that it was not unwise now to estimate the separate mass of Virginia and North Carolina with a view to their separate existence." Jefferson wrote him in relation to this advice, on June 1, 1798, "that it would not be wise to proceed immediately to a disruption of the Union when party passion was at such a height. If we now reduce our Union to Virginia and North Carolina, immediately the conflict will be established between those two States, and they will end by breaking into their simple units."

As it was necessary that there should be some party to oppose, it was best to keep the New England States for this purpose. He had nothing to say against the rightfulness of the step. He contented himself with dissuading from it on grounds of expediency. He counselled patience until fortune should change, and the "lost principles" might be regained, "for this is a game in which principles are the stake."

Considering these views, it is not be to wondered at that, in consequence of the Alien and Sedition laws, Jefferson began to see the question in a different light.   We shall have something to say later on the question whether, and to what extent, he considered it timely to discuss the secession of Virginia from the Union.   But he was soon satisfied that his opponents had bent the bow too nearly to the point of breaking, to permit him to look upon further patient waiting for better fortune as the right policy.   It was no longer time to stop at the exchange of private opinion and the declarations of individuals.   The moment had now come when the "principles" should be distinctly formulated and officially proclaimed and recognized.   Not to do this would be to run the risk of being carried away by the current of facts to such a distance that it would be difficult and perhaps impossible to get hold of the principles again.   But if, on the other hand, this were done, everything further might be calmly waited for, and the policy of expediency again brought into the foreground.   The protest was officially recorded; and so long as it was not, either willingly or under completion, as officially recalled, or at least withdrawn, it was to be considered as part of the record which might be taken advantage of at any stage of the case.   Herein lies the immense significance of the Virginia and Kentucky resolutions.

Their importance is enhanced by the fact that Madison, who had merited well of the country, on account of his share in the drawing up and adoption of the Constitution, and whose exposition of it is therefore of the greatest weight, was the author of the Virginia resolution of December 24, 1798, and by the further fact that Jefferson, the oracle of the Anti-Federalists, had written the original draft of the Kentucky resolutions of November 10, 1798.

Although not in accord with chronological order, it is advisable to consider the Virginia resolutions first, for the reason that they do not go as far as the Kentucky resolutions.   According to the testimony of their authors, the resolutions of both Legislatures had the same source, and there were special reasons why it was necessary to make the Virginia resolutions of a milder character.   Although a violation of chronological order, it seems, therefore, proper to consider these as the basis of the Kentucky resolutions, or rather as a lower round of the same ladder.

The paragraph of the Virginia resolutions of most importance for the history of the Constitution is the following:

"Resolved, That this Assembly doth emphatically and peremptorily declare that it views the powers of the Federal Government as resulting from the compact to which the States are parties as limited by the plain sense and intention of the instrument constituting that compact, as no further valid than they are authorized by the grants enumerated in that compact; and that in case of a deliberate, palpable, and dangerous exercise of other powers, not granted by the said compact, the States who are parties thereto have the right, and are in duty bound, to interpose for arresting the progress of the evil and for maintaining within their respective limits the authorities, rights, and liberties appertaining to them."

The Legislature of Kentucky disdained to use a mode of expression so vague and feeble or to employ language from which much or little might be gathered as occasion demanded.   In the first paragraph of the resolutions of November 10, 1798, we read:

"Resolved, That whenever the General Government assumes undelegated powers, its acts are unauthoritative, void, and of no force; that to this compact each State acceded as a State, and is an integral party; that this Government, created by this compact, was not made the exclusive or final judge of the extent of the powers delegated to itself, since that would have made its discretion, and not the Constitution, the measure of its powers; but that, as in all other cases of compact among parties having no common judge, each party has an equal right to judge for itself as well of infractions as of the mode and measure of redress."

Thus were the "principles" established.   But in order that they might not remain a thing floating in the air it was necessary to provide another furmula, by which the States might be empowered to enforce the rights claimed, or at least to find a word which would presumably embody that formula, and which was sufficient so long as they limited themselves to the theoretical discussion of the question. The Legislature of Kentucky, in its resotions of November 14, 1799, gave the advocates of State rights the term demanded, in the sentence:

"Resolved, That the several States who formed that instrument being sovereign and independent, have the unquestionable right to judge of the infraction; and that a nullification by these sovereignties, of all unauthorized acts done under color of that instrument, is the rightful remedy."

In later times the admirers of Madison and Jefferson who were true to the Union have endeavored to confine the meaning of these resolutions within so narrow limits that every rational interpretation of their contents has been represented by them as arbitrary and slanderous. When about the end of the third and the beginning of the fourth decade of this century, the opposition to the Federal Government in Georgia, and especially in South Carolina, began to assume an alarming form, the aged Madison expressly protested that Virginia did not wish to ascribe to a single State the Constitutional right to hinder by force the execution of a law of the United States. "The resolution," he wrote, March 27, 1831, "was expressly declaratory, and, proceeding from the Legislature only, which was not even a party to the Constitution, could be declaratory of opinion only." In one sense, this cannot be questioned. In the report of the committee of the Virginia Legislature on the answers of the other States to the resolutions of 1798 we read as follows: "The declarations are expressions of opinion unaccompanied by any other effort than what they may produce on opinion, by exciting reflection." But to concede that this was the sole intention of the resolutions of December 24th, is to deprive the words, according to which the States had the right and were in duty bound to "interpose" in case the General Government had in their opinion permitted itself to assume ungranted power, of all meaning.

But it has never yet been denied that these few words express the pith of all the resolutions. More was claimed than the right to express opinions—a right which had never been questioned. If expression was not clearly and distinctly given to what was claimed, it was to leave all possible ways open to the other States to come to an agreement in all essential matters.

Jefferson was in this instance less cautious than Madison, and his vision was more acute. He thought that the crisis of the Constitution had come, and therefore assumed a standpoint from which he could not be forced back to the worthless position adopted by Madison in his celebrated report of 1800. Jefferson allowed it to depend on the further course of events whether force should be used, or whether only the right to employ force should be expressly and formally claimed. At first he was anxious that a middle position should be assumed, but a middle position which afforded a secure foothold. The Legislature of Kentucky had done this, inasmuch as it had adopted that passage in his draft in which it was claimed that the General Government and the States were equal parties, and in which it was recognized that the latter had "an equal right to judge" when there was a violation of the Constitution, as well as to determine the ways and means of redress.

Madison, and, later, Benton, as well as all the other admirers of the "Sage of Monticello," who were opposed to the later school of secessionists, have laid great weight on the fact that the word nullification, or anything of a like import, is to be found only in the Kentucky resolutions of 1799, which did not originate with Jefferson. This technical plea in Jefferson's behalf has been answered by the publication of his works. Among his papers two copies of the original draft of the Kenucky resolutions of 1798 have been discovered in his own handwriting. In them we find the following: "Resolved, That when the General Government assumes powers which have not been delegated, a nullification of the act is the rightful remedy: that every State has a natural right, in cases not within the compact (*casus non fœderis*), to nullify of their own authority all assumptions of power by others within their limits."

That Jefferson was not only an advocate, but the father, of the doctrine of nullification is thus well established. It may be that Nicholas secured his assent to the striking out of these sentences, but no fact has as yet been discovered in support of this assumption. Still less is there any positive ground for the allegation that Jefferson had begun to doubt the position he had assumed. Various passages in his later letters point decidedly to the very opposite conclusion.

The Virginia and Kentucky resolutions produced no further immediate consequences. The recognized leaders of the Anti-Federalists or Republicans had given their interpretation of the Constitution, and of the Union created by it. Their declarations remained a long time unused, but also unrecalled and unforgotten. The internal contests continued and their character remained the same. The revolution in the situation of parties now necessitated a change of front on both sides, and for a time also the battles between them were waged over other points and in part in another way.

The next collision was an actual struggle for supremacy. An inadequate provision of the Constitution alone made this battle a possibility to the Federalists; but the struggle over the question of the Constitution was after all considered only as a mere accidental collateral circumstance.

The Republicans (Democrats) had won the Presidential election by a majority of eight of nine electoral votes. Their two candidates, Jefferson and Aaron Burr, had each received seventy-three votes. They intended that Jefferson should be President and Burr Vice-President. Spite of this, however, they gave both the same number of votes, either not to endanger Burr's election or because he became a candidate only on that condition. This was, considering Burr's reputation and the boldness of his character, a dangerous experiment. Judge Woodworth charged that Burr had won over one of the electors of New York to withhold his vote from Jefferson, and that this was prevented only by the fact that the other electors of the State had discovered it in time. If this charge be well founded, it was by mere accident that the country escaped electing a man President whose name had never yet been connected with the Presidency by any party.

If an equal number of electoral votes should be cast for two or more candidates, the House of Representatives would have to elect one of them to the Presidency. In this case, the votes would be cast by States, and it would be necessary that a majority of all the States should vote for one of the candidates in order to have a valid election. The Federalists had a majority in the House of Representatives, but voting by States they could control only one-half the votes. This was just sufficient to prevent an election.

No one denied that the majority of the people, as well as the Republican electors, desired to make Jefferson President. But party passion had reached such a feverish height that the Federalists resolved, spite of this, to plant themselves on the letter of the Constitution, and to hinder Jefferson's election. The possibility of electing their own candidates[1] was completely excluded by the Constitution. They could therefore do nothing except to obtain for Burr a majority of the votes of the States, or prevent an election. In case no President was elected by the States, they thought of casting the election on the Senate. The Senate was to elect a provisional President—from among the Senators or not—who then might be declared President of the United States. Such a proceeding could not be justified by any provision of the Constitution; the case had not been provided for at all. It is impossible to say whether this is the reason why the plan was soon dropped; certain it is, however, that Gibbs's statement, that such a plan never existed, is incorrect.

After some hesitation they resolved to try to elect Burr. Only six States, it is true, voted for him, but it was necessary to win over only four votes in order to guarantee him the legal majority of nine States. The prospect of the success of both plans was at least great enough to inspire the Republicans with serious fear. Jefferson had written on December 15th to Burr that "decency" compelled him to remain "completely passive" during the campaign. But now he considered the situation so serious that he thought himself no longer bound by "decency." He personally requested Adams to interfere by his veto, if the Federalists should attempt to turn over the Government, during an interregnum, to a President *pro tem*. Although he declared that such a measure would probably excite forcible resistance, Adams refused to be guided by his advice.

Madison proposed another means of escape. He thought that an interregnum until the meeting of Congress in December, 1801, would be too dangerous; Jefferson and Burr should therefore call Congress together by a common proclamation or recommendation. This step could no more be justified by any provision of the Constitution than an interregnum under a provisional President. Madison himself conceded that it would not be "strictly regular." But the literal interpretation was presumably the alpha and omega of the political creed of the Republicans. Spite of this the notion met with Jefferson's approbation.

Between the two parties, or rather above them, stood the founder of the Federalist party himself. Even Hamilton advised

[1] Adams and Pinckney.—ED.

that a concession should be made to the interests of political expediency.   The possibilities which the equal electoral vote placed
in the hands of the Federalists in the House of Representatives
were to be used wherever possible, to force certain promises from
Jefferson.   But Hamilton did not wish to go any further.   He
declared the project of the interregnum to be "dangerous and un-
becoming," and thought that it could not possibly succeed.   Jefferson or Burr was the only question.   When his party associates also
seemed to have adopted this view, he used his whole influence to
dissuade them from smuggling Burr into the White House.   He
had written to Wolcott on December 16th, that he expected that
at least New England would not so far lose her senses as to fall
into this snare.   When he was mistaken in these expectations he
wrote letter after letter to the most prominent Federalists who
might exert an influence directly or indirectly on the election.
"If there be a man in the world," he wrote to Morris, "I ought
to hate, it is Jefferson."   Spite of this, however, he pleaded for
Jefferson's election harder than any Republican: "for in a case
like this," he added, "it would be base to listen to personal considerations."   Besides, he always dwelt with emphasis on the
folly, the baseness, the corruption and impolicy of the Burr intrigue.   In all these letters, some of which are very lengthy, he
shows himself the far-seeing statesman, and examines everything
with calmness and incision; but at times he rises to a solemn
pathos.   With the greatest firmness, but at the same time with a
certain amount of regret, he writes to Bayard: "If the party shall,
by supporting Mr. Burr as President, adopt him for their official
chief, I shall be obliged to consider myself as an isolated man.
It will be impossible for me to reconcile with my motives of honor
or policy the continuing to be of a party which, according to my
apprehension, will have degraded itself and the country."

Hamilton's intellectual superiority was still recognized by the
Federalists, but spite of this he stood almost isolated from every
one.   The repulsive virulence with which the party war had been
waged during all these years, and the consciousness that their
defeat was in a great measure due to the bitter and exasperating
contentions among themselves, had dulled the political judgment
and political morals of most of the other leaders.   Hamilton's
admonitions were not without effect, but he was not able to bring

about a complete surrender of the plan which was as impolitic as
it was corrupt.   The electoral contest in the House of Representatives continued from February 11th to the 17th.   Not until the
thirty-sixth ballot did so many of the Federalists use blank ballots
that Jefferson received the votes of ten States and was declared
the legally elected President.   According to the testimony of the
Federalist Representatives themselves, the field would not even
yet have been cleared were it not that Burr had surrendered his
ambiguous position.   He could not completely and formally renounce his Republican friends, and hence the Federalists received
from him only vague and meaningless assurances.   All the dangers to the party and the country which would have been the consequence of the success of their intrigues, they would have know-
ingly entailed in order to place at the head of the Government one
whom they believed would turn his back on them the moment
they had helped him into power.   They would have been throwing dice to determine the future of the Union simply for the satisfaction of venting their hatred on Jefferson.

Everyone was fully conscious of the magnitude of the crisis.
Bayard wrote to Hamilton on March 8th concerning the last
caucus of the Federalists: "All acknowledged that nothing but
desperate measures remained, which several were disposed to
adopt and but few were willing openly to disapprove.   We broke
up each time in confusion and discord, and the manner of the last
ballot was arranged but a few minutes before the ballot was
given."   Some years later he repeated the assertion under oath,
that there were some who thought it better to abide by their vote,
and to remain without a President, rather than choose Jefferson.
But reason and patriotism at length obtained the mastery.   Bayard seems to have been the instrument of this decision.

How much Hamilton contributed to the defeat of the advocates of the *va banque!* it is not easy to estimate.   Randolph, at the
time a member of the House of Representatives, often expressed
his conviction that the safety of the Republic was due to Hamilton.   There was no difference of opinion in the two parties on
this, that the victory of the stubborn Federalists would have
seriously endangered the Republic.

One month before the balloting began we find the conviction
prevalent among the Federalists that the Republicans would, un-

der no circumstances, be satisfied with an interregnum or with the election of Burr. James Gunn, a Federal Senator from Georgia, wrote to Hamilton on January 9th: "On the subject of choosing a President some revolutionary opinions are gaining ground, and the Jacobins are determined to resist the election of Burr at every hazard. I am persuaded that the Democrats have taken their ground with the fixed resolution to destroy the Government rather than yield their point."

The Republicans did not oppose this conviction, but declared it to be well founded with all the emphasis with which such declarations have always been made in America. Jefferson wrote to Monroe on February 15th, two days before the election: "If they (the Federalists) had been permitted to pass a law for putting the Government into the hands of an officer, they would certainly have prevented an election. But we thought it best to declare openly and firmly, one and all, that the day such an act was passed, the Middle States would arm, and that no such usurpation, even for a single day, should be submitted to. This first shook them, and they were completely alarmed at the resource for which we declared; to wit, a convention to reorganize the Government and to amend it." Armed resistance, followed by a peaceful revolution; such was the last word of the Republicans. The Federalists rightly considered this ultimatum to be no vain threat. In a letter written the day after the election to Madison, Jefferson speaks of the "certainty" that legislative usurpation would have met with armed resistance. And Jefferson's testimony is by no means the only evidence. Even the press began to treat the subject of "*bella, horrida bella!*" More than this; in Virginia, where the excitement was greatest, establishments had already been erected to supply the necessary arms, and even troops. John Randolph, in the speech already mentioned, had completely lifted the curtain that hung over this subject. Reliance was to be placed on Dark's brigade, which had promised to take possession of the arms in the United States armory at Harper's Ferry.

The idea of waging war on the Union with its own weapons is very old; the secessionists did nothing more than carry out the plan which the "fathers" of the Republic had considered as embodying the proper course under certain contingencies.

The victory of the Republicans did not by any means produce the revolution in internal politics which was to be expected. When the electoral vote had been made known, Jefferson, in the first transports of his joy over the victory, blew with all his might the trumpets of the opposition. He tendered Chancellor Livingston a place in his Cabinet, that he might be of some service in the "new establishment of Republicanism; I say for its new establishment, for hitherto we have only seen its travesty." The stubborn resistance of the Federalists, which wounded his vanity not a little, increased his angry feeling against them. On February 18th he furnished Madison with an account of the election. He lays particular stress on the fact that the Federalists did not finally vote for him, but that there was an election only because a part of them abstained from voting, or only used blank ballots. "We consider this, therefore," he says, "a declaration of war on the part of this band."

These utterances are thoroughly in keeping with Jefferson's preceding course, and with his words and actions toward the Federalists and their policy. Spite of this, however, his own future policy is not to be inferred from them. Hamilton did not fall into this error, because he was well acquainted with the main traits of Jefferson's character, and estimated their relative value correctly, although his judgment on the whole may have been somewhat too severe. He therefore saw and foretold the character of Jefferson's policy better than Jefferson himself could have done while under the influence of the excitement of the political campaign. Hamilton writes to Bayard, January 16, 1801: "Nor is it true that Jefferson is zealot enough to do anything in pursuance of his principles which will contravene his popularity or his interest. He is as likely as any man I know to temporize, to calculate what will be likely to promote his own reputation and advantage; and the probable result of such a temper is the preservation of systems, though originally opposed, which being once established could not be overturned without danger to the person who did it. To my mind, a true estimate of Mr. Jefferson's character warrants the expectation of a temporizing rather than of a violent system."

This judgment of Hamilton found its confirmation in the inaugural address of the new President. In it Jefferson counsels that the rights of the minority should be held sacred, that a union in heart and soul should be brought about, and that an effort should be made to do away with despotic political intolerance as religious intolerance had already been done away with. "We have called by different names brothers of the same principle. We are all Republicans—we are all Federalists."

Jefferson could not only use such language without danger, but it was unquestionably the best key in which he could have spoken, although the extreme Republicans would have much preferred to listen to a *væ victis!* He had asserted as early as the spring of 1796, that "the whole landed interest," and therefore a large majority of the people, belonged to the Republican party. There is now little difference of opinion on the point that Jefferson would immediately have followed Washington in the Presidential chair, if the electors had been nothing but the men of straw into which they afterward degenerated. But even if this could be rightly questioned, it would not yet follow that the majority of the people were then really inclined to the Federal party. The Republicans were far inferior to the Federalists in the numbers and the ability of their leaders; and, moreover, the great moneyed interests of the Northern States were the cornerstone of the Federal party. These were two elements which might very well keep them in power awhile longer, even if the majority of the people were in reality more attached to the principles of their antagonists. But they were not a support on which they could establish lasting rule. In a democratic republic, the political influence of the moneyed interests, when they have not attained the immense proportions they have in the America of to-day, is, as a rule, very limited, and that of talent is very frequently still smaller.

Hamilton's lead was followed as long as the pressure of necessity was felt. But as soon as the most difficult labor of organization was done, his superiority became one of the greatest obstacles which stood in the way of his public activity. Not only did the Federalists put him aside by degrees, but their faultfinding with his actions and omissions began here and there to partake of the tone of the most odious attacks made by the Republicans on his policy. This was a sign of the times which deserved the most earnest consideration. When in a political party, in a popular state, a breach occurs between its founders and the masses that compose it, its days are, as a rule, numbered.   If the breach takes place after the essential idea on which the party was founded has been realized, it will not, and cannot, be long survived.

This one essential idea, which constituted the real spark of vitality in the Federalist party, had been realized before the end of Washington's second term as President, and the existence of the work as well secured as was possible under the circumstances. The force which moved the pendulum in its forward motion was exhausted.   And if it did not begin its backward course immediately, but seemed to stand for a moment in suspense, it was because an accidental force acted upon it from without.   The prolongation of the supremacy of the Federal party was due mainly to the unhealthy attitude assumed by the Anti-Federalists toward France.   When the fruits of this began to be reaped in the transactions under the government of the Directory, the power of the Federalists, which was then declining, at once mounted to its zenith.   The Congressional elections of 1797 were very favorable to them.   The value of this success, however, must not be overestimated, as it was owing to a question of external politics.   Only in case foreign politics, by the outbreak of war, should be kept most prominently in the foreground, could they hope that their success would obtain a more lasting character.   But the quarrel between France and the United States had reached its height with the "X. Y. Z."[1] affair and with Gerry's return. When Adams, contrary to a former solemn assurance, resolved to send a new embassy to France, the Republicans soon regained the ground they had lost; for the attitude of the people toward questions of home politics remained essentially unaltered.

The position of the Federalists in the Presidential election of 1801 had been a desperate one.   The hopelessness of their situation drove them to the rash and despicable game in the House of Representatives.   They would have been deterred from it if they could have ascribed their defeat to accidental and transitory

[1] The X. Y. Z. Mission, an American embassy to France in 1797, consisting of C. C. Pinckney, John Marshall, and Elbridge Gerry.   An attempt was made by three French agents (disguised as X., Y., and Z.) to bribe them.—ED.

causes. The correspondence of their leaders, however, shows plainly that their faint hope of better success after four years was only a hope against their better judgment. The reaction had fairly set in. The Republicans did not dare to touch the essential things which had been accomplished during the twelve years' victory of the Federalists over them, and did not even desire to do so; for the same matter is seen very differently from the point of view of the Administration and of the opposition. It might not be expected of them that they would intentionally increase the heritage left them, but if they would not immediately squander it, the capital would bear interest and increase. More was not to be expected. The defeat of the Federalists was a decisive one, for even the citadel of their strength was undermined. While in the Southern States a more temperate feeling prevailed, the Republicans in the New England States began to celebrate triumphs. The decisive point, however, was that they obtained a firm footing in the rural districts, whereas, hitherto, they had found adherents only among the more mercurial population of the large towns. The choice troops of the Federalists began to waver on every side, and the intrigues of the leaders in the House of Representatives gave the impulse to the complete dissolution of their ranks. Yet neither the sense of honor, nor the healthy judgment which drew from Hamilton the declaration that he must renounce a party which had thus soiled its name, was wanting among the masses. It was seen at the moment how great was the mistake made. Even during the balloting in the House of Representatives, the Federalists went over in swarms to the enemy; every vote for Burr was another nail in the coffin of the party. This sudden and violent fall of the Federal party explains the security which the continuance of the Union enjoyed during the two following decades. The party which represented particularistic tendencies was in possession of power, and had an overwhelming majority. In the next Presidential election Jefferson and Clinton received each one hundred sixty-two electoral votes, while Charles C. Pinckney and Rufus King received only fourteen each, and in 1805 there were only seven Federalists in the Senate. But even if the probability of a disruption was therefore very small the character of the internal struggle remained the same. This character was even placed in a clearer light by the fact that the parts played by each were changed, so far as the question of right was concerned, and that the opposition, spite of its weakness, was not satisfied with wishes and threats of separation, but began in earnest to devise plans of dissolution.

THOMAS JEFFERSON

Called upon to undertake the duties of the first executive office of our country, I avail myself of the presence of that portion of my fellow-citizens which is here assembled, to express my grateful thanks for the favor with which they have been pleased to look toward me, to declare a sincere consciousness that the task is above my talents, and that I approach it with those anxious and awful presentiments which the greatness of the charge, and the weakness of my powers, so justly inspire. A rising nation, spread over a wide and fruitful land, traversing all the seas with the rich productions of their industry, engaged in commerce with nations who feel power and forget right, advancing rapidly to destinies beyond the reach of mortal eye; when I contemplate these transcendent objects, and see the honor, the happiness, and the hopes of this beloved country committed to the issue and the auspices of this day, I shrink from the contemplation and humble myself before the magnitude of the undertaking. Utterly indeed should I despair, did not the presence of many, whom I here see, remind me, that, in the other high authorities provided by our Constitution, I shall find resources of wisdom, of virtue, and of zeal, on which to rely under all difficulties. To you, then, gentlemen, who are charged with the sovereign functions of legislation, and to those associated with you, I look with encouragement for that guidance and support which may enable us to steer with safety the vessel in which we are all embarked, amid the conflicting elements of a troubled world.

During the contest of opinion through which we have passed, the animation of discussions and of exertions has sometimes worn an aspect which might impose on strangers unused to think freely and to speak and to write what they think; but this being now decided by the voice of the nation, announced according to the rules of the Constitution, all will of course arrange themselves under the will of the law, and unite in common efforts for the common good. All too will bear in mind this sacred principle, that though the will of the majority is in all cases to prevail, that will, to be rightful, must be reasonable; that the minority possess their equal rights, which equal law must protect, and to violate would be oppression.

Let us then, fellow-citizens, unite with one heart and one mind, let us restore to social intercourse that harmony and affection without which liberty, and even life itself, are but dreary things. And let us reflect that having banished from our land that religious intolerance under which mankind so long bled and suffered, we have yet gained little, if we countenance a political intolerance, as despotic, as wicked, and capable of as bitter and bloody persecutions. During the throes and convulsions of the ancient world, during the agonizing spasms of infuriated man, seeking through blood and slaughter his long lost liberty, it was not wonderful that the agitation of the billows should reach even this distant and peaceful shore; that this should be more felt and feared by some and less by others; and should divide opinions as to measures of safety; but every difference of opinion is not a difference of principle. We have called by different names brethren of the same principle. We are all Republicans: we are all Federalists.

If there be any among us who would wish to dissolve this Union, or to change its republican form, let them stand undisturbed as monuments of the safety with which error of opinion may be tolerated, where reason is left free to combat it. I know indeed that some honest men fear that a republican government cannot be strong; that this Government is not strong enough. But would the honest patriot, in the full tide of successful experiment, abandon a government, which has so far kept us free and firm, on the theoretic and visionary fear that this Government, the world's best hope, may, by possibility, want energy to preserve itself? I trust not. I believe this, on the contrary, the strongest government on earth. I believe it the only one, where every man, at the call of the law, would fly to the standard of the law, and would meet invasions of the public order as his own personal concern. Sometimes it is said that man cannot be trusted with the government of himself. Can he then be trusted with the government of others? Or have we found angels, in the form of kings. to govern him? Let history answer this question.

Let us then, with courage and confidence, pursue our own federal and republican principles; our attachment to union and representative government.   Kindly separated by nature and a wide ocean from the exterminating havoc of one-quarter of the globe; too high-minded to endure the degradations of the others, possessing a chosen country, with room enough for our descendants to the thousandth and thousandth generation, entertaining a due sense of our equal right to the use of our own faculties, to the acquisitions of our own industry, to honor and confidence from our fellow-citizens, resulting not from birth, but from our actions and their sense of them, enlightened by a benign religion, professed indeed and practised in various forms, yet all of them inculcating honesty, truth, temperance, gratitude and the love of man, acknowledging and adoring an overruling Providence, which by all its dispensations proves that it delights in the happiness of man here, and his greater happiness hereafter; with all these blessings, what more is necessary to make us a happy and a prosperous people?   Still one thing more, fellow-citizens, a wise and frugal government, which shall restrain men from injuring one another, shall leave them otherwise free to regulate their own pursuits of industry and improvement, and shall not take from the mouth of labor the bread it has earned.   This is the sum of good government; and this is necessary to close the circle of our felicities.

About to enter, fellow-citizens, on the exercise of duties which comprehend everything dear and valuable to you, it is proper you should understand what I deem the essential principles of our Government, and consequently those which ought to shape its administration.   I will compress them within the narrowest compass they will bear, stating the general principle, but not all its limitations.   Equal and exact justice to all men, of whatever state or persuasion, religious or political: peace, commerce, and honest friendship with all nations, entangling alliances with none: the support of the State governments in all their rights, as the most competent administrations for our domestic concerns, and the surest bulwarks against antirepublican tendencies: the preservation of the General Government in its whole constitutional vigor, as the sheet anchor of our peace at home and safety abroad; a jealous care of the right of election by the people, a mild and safe corrective of abuses which are lopped by the sword of evolution, where peaceable remedies are unprovided: absolute acquiescence in the decisions of the majority, the vital principle of republics, from which is no appeal but to force, the vital principle and immediate parent of despotism: a well-disciplined militia, our best reliance in peace, and for the first moments of war, till regulars may relieve them: the supremacy of the civil over the military authority: economy in the public expense, that labor may be lightly burdened: the honest payment of our debts and sacred preservation of the public faith: encouragement of agriculture, and of commerce as its handmaid: the diffusion of information, and arraignment of all abuses at the bar of the public reason: freedom of religion; freedom of the press; and freedom of person, under the protection of the *habeas corpus;* and trial by juries impartially selected.

These principles form the bright constellation, which has gone before us, and guided our steps through an age of revolution and reformation.   The wisdom of our sages, and blood of our heroes, have been devoted to their attainment:—they should be the creed of our political faith; the text of civic instruction, the touchstone by which to try the services of those we trust; and should we wander from them in moments of error or of alarm, let us hasten to retrace our steps, and to regain the road which alone leads to peace, liberty, and safety.

I repair, then, fellow-citizens, to the post you have assigned me.   With experience enough in subordinate offices to have seen the difficulties of this the greatest of all, I have learned to expect that it will rarely fall to the lot of imperfect man to retire from this station with the reputation, and the favor, which bring him into it.   Without pretensions to that high confidence you reposed in our first and greatest Revolutionary character, whose preëminent services had entitled him to the first place in his country's love, and destined for him the fairest page in the volume of faithful history, I ask so much confidence only as may give firmness and effect to the legal administration of your affairs.

PURCHASE OF LOUISIANA

A.D. 1803

HENRY S. RANDALL

After the framing and adoption of the Federal Constitution, the most important civil event in the history of the United States is the great land acquisition known as the Louisiana Purchase. Already, even before the Declaration of Independence, a movement of population from the eastern shores to the region beyond the Alleghanies had begun, and this advance toward the country's interior had much to do with making conditions favorable to the new expansion when the opportunity for it came.

The Ohio and Mississippi rivers were at once seen to be available as great water routes of commerce, and these natural advantages rapidly led to a continued westward migration. To meet the new conditions in the Mississippi Valley, many modifications of eastern modes and institutions were made, and the increasing complexity of society, together with foreign control of the Mississippi country, rendered the problem of further national expansion in that direction difficult to deal with. It was finally solved without the help of precedents and without serious complications.

Toward the end of the eighteenth century, forces long at work determined events in the direction of American control of the Mississippi Valley, to which the French, old enemies of the British colonists, laid claim. Spain, the earlier claimant, had refused free navigation of the Mississippi to American settlers, but finally in 1794 this was granted. Then, in 1800, the country which became known as the Louisiana Purchase, including New Orleans and all the land from the Mississippi to the Rocky Mountains, and between the Gulf of Mexico and British America, was ceded by Spain to France, in which country Napoleon had lately made himself first consul. Here Randall's account takes up the history, in which the next and most important of all changes in the possession of the trans-Mississippi lands gave them into the permanent keeping of the United States.

INTELLIGENCE of the cession of Louisiana and the Floridas by Spain to France reached the United States. The important changes this event caused in our own foreign relations, and the new and decisive line of policy it at once suggested to President Jefferson, should be given in his own words. He wrote to Mr. Livingston, the American minister in France, April 18, 1802:

"The cession of Louisiana and the Floridas by Spain to France works most sorely on the United States. On this subject the Secretary of State has written to you fully, yet I cannot forbear recurring to it personally, so deep is the impression it makes on my mind. It completely reverses all the political relations of the United States, and will form a new epoch in our political course. Of all nations, of any consideration, France is the one which, hitherto, has offered the fewest points on which we could have any conflict of right, and the most points of a communion of interests. From these causes, we have ever looked to her as our natural friend, as one with which we never could have an occasion of difference. Her growth, therefore, we viewed as our own: her misfortune ours. There is on the globe one single spot, the possessor of which is our natural enemy. It is New Orleans, through which the produce of three-eighths of our territory must pass to market, and from its fertility it will ere long yield more than half of our whole produce and contain more than half of our inhabitants.

"France, placing herself in that door, assumes to us the attitude of defiance. Spain might have retained it quietly for years. Her pacific dispositions, her feeble state, would induce her to increase our facilities there, so that her possession of the place would be hardly felt by us, and it would not, perhaps, be very long before some circumstance might arise which might make the cession of it to us the price of something of more worth to her. Not so can it ever be in the hands of France: the impetuosity of her temper, the energy and restlessness of her character, placed in a point of eternal friction with us, and our character, which, though quiet and loving peace and the pursuit of wealth, is high-minded, despising wealth in competition with insult or injury, enterprising and energetic as any nation on earth; these circumstances render it impossible that France and the United States can continue long friends when they meet in so irritable a position.

"They, as well as we, must be blind if they do not see this; and we must be very improvident if we do not begin to make arrangements on that hypothesis. The day that France takes possession of New Orleans fixes the sentence which is to restrain her forever within her low-water mark. It seals the union of two nations, who, in conjunction, can maintain exclusive possession of the ocean. From that moment we must marry ourselves to the British fleet and nation. We must turn all our attention to a maritime force, for which our resources place us on very high ground: and having formed and connected together a power which may render reënforcement of her settlements here impossible to France, makes the first cannon which shall be fired in Europe the signal for tearing up any settlement she may have made, and for holding the two continents of America in sequestration for the common purposes of the united British and American nations. This is not a state of things we seek or desire. It is one which this measure, if adopted by France, forces on us, as necessarily as any other cause by the laws of nature brings on its necessary effect.

"It is not from a fear of France that we deprecate this measure proposed by her. For however greater her force is than ours, compared in the abstract, it is nothing in comparison to ours when to be exerted on our soil. But it is from a sincere love of peace, and a firm persuasion that, bound to France by the interests and the strong sympathies still existing in the minds of our citizens, and holding relative positions which insure their continuance, we are secure of a long course of peace. Whereas, the change of friends, which will be rendered necessary if France changes that position, embarks us necessarily as a belligerent power in the first war of Europe. In that case, France will have held possession of New Orleans during the interval of a peace, long or short, at the end of which it will be wrested from her. Will this short-lived possession have been an equivalent to her for the transfer of such a weight into the scale of her enemy? Will not the amalgamation of a young, thriving nation continue to that enemy the health and force which are at present so evidently on the decline? And will a few years' possession of New Orleans add equally to the strength of France? She may say she needs Louisiana for the supply of her West Indies. She does not need it in time of peace, and in war she could not depend on them [supplies], because they would be so easily intercepted. I should suppose that all these considerations might, in some proper form, be brought into view of the Government of France. Though stated by us it ought not to give offence; because we do not bring them forward as a menace, but as consequences not controllable by us, and inevitable from the course of things. We mention them, not as things which we desire by any means, but as things we deprecate; and we beseech a friend to look forward and to prevent them for our common interests.

"If France considers Louisiana, however, as indispensable for her views, she might perhaps be willing to look about for arrangements which might reconcile it to our interests. If anything could do this it would be the ceding to us the island of New Orleans and the Floridas. This would certainly, in a great degree, remove the causes of jarring and irritation between us, and perhaps for such a length of time as might produce other means of making the measure permanently conciliatory to our interests and friendships. It would, at any rate, relieve us from the necessity of taking immediate measures for countervailing such an operation by arrangements in another quarter. But still we should consider New Orleans and the Floridas as no equivalent for the risk of a quarrel with France, produced by her vicinage.

"I have no doubt you have urged these considerations on every proper occasion, with the Government where you are. They are such as must have effect, if you can find means of producing thorough reflection on them by that Government. The idea here is that the troops sent to Santo Domingo were to proceed to Louisiana after finishing their work in that island. If this were the arrangement, it will give you time to return again and again to the charge. For the conquest of Santo Domingo will not be a short work. It will take considerable time and wear down a great number of soldiers. Every eye in the United States is now fixed on the affairs of Louisiana. Perhaps nothing since the Revolutionary War has produced more uneasy sensations through the body of the nation. Notwithstanding temporary bickerings have taken place with France, she has still a strong hold on the affections of our citizens generally. I have thought it not amiss, by way of supplement to the letters of the Secretary of State, to write you this private one, to impress you with the importance we affix to this transaction."

This letter was to be sent to M. de Nemours, who was about to proceed from the United States to France. As he did not call for it, the President forwarded it to him open; requesting him to possess himself thoroughly of its contents, and then seal it. His object was thus explained:

"I wish you to be possessed of the subject, because you may be able to impress on the Government of France the inevitable consequences of their taking possession of Louisiana; and though, as I here mention, the cession of New Orleans and the Floridas to us would be a palliation, yet I believe it would be no more, and that this measure will cost France, and perhaps not very long hence, a war which will annihilate her on the ocean, and place that element under the despotism of two nations, which I am not reconciled to the more because my own would be one of them. Add to this the exclusive appropriation of both continents of America as a consequence. I wish the present order of things to continue, and with a view to this I value highly a state of friendship between France and us. You know too well how sincere I have ever been in these dispositions, to doubt them. You know, too, how much I value peace, and how unwillingly I should see any event take place which would render war a necessary resource, and that all our movements should change their character and object. I am thus open with you, because I trust that you will have it in your power to impress on that Government considerations in the scale against which the possession of Louisiana is nothing. In Europe nothing but Europe is seen, or supposed to have any right in the affairs of nations; but this little event, of France's possessing herself of Louisiana, which is thrown in as nothing, as a mere make-weight in the general settlement of accounts—this speck which now appears as an almost invisible point in the horizon, is the embryo of a tornado which will burst on the countries on both sides of the Atlantic, and involve in its effects their highest destinies. That it may yet be avoided is my sincere prayer; and if you can be the means of informing the wisdom of Bonaparte of all its consequences, you have deserved well of both countries. Peace and abstinence from European interferences are our objects, and so will continue while the present order of things in America remains uninterrupted."

This was a bold experiment on the ruler of France—the first general and one of the least timid statesmen and diplomatists of modern times. The morality of the President's attitude rests on the basis of necessity—the right to do that which is indispensable to self-preservation. The practical consequences involved were the same in a single point—so far as Louisiana was concerned—as those contemplated in Hamilton's Miranda scheme. But the latter made conquest its primary object, and it proposed to fall upon another power because it was weak and defenceless, not because it was dangerously strong. It indeed made some late show of acting for the purpose of guarding against precisely what now had taken place; but if we should assume this to be a sincere ground of action, it would only have put our country in the posture of plundering a weak neighbor to prevent a more dangerous neighbor from plundering it—doing a moral wrong in anticipation, for fear some other power might do that moral wrong. This would be a plea on which nations or individuals could always found a right to rob the weaker.

But when France actually obtained a title to these contiguous provinces and proposed to make herself our neighbor, she voluntarily, and by no fault of ours, practically commenced a step which all Americans agreed in considering fraught with the extremest danger to our country. Even then we did not attempt secretly to form confederacies to wrest her property from her. We went to her frankly and told her our views. We went boldly to the then strongest nation on earth, and informed her if she persisted in colonizing at a point which gave her the key of our western possessions, she must prepare for war with us and such friends as we could secure to our alliance. And neither was this made the alternative of her yielding up anything that belonged to her without a rightful equivalent. It was the purpose of our Cabinet, the moment it was found France would negotiate on the basis of parting from her newly acquired possession, to offer her far more for them than they had cost her. Our Cabinet might or might not judge correctly of our danger. But there was nothing dishonorable or immoral in its conduct. There was nothing which required a covering of false pretences to deceive our people or to draw them into a war on fictitious grounds, when, had they known them, they would have abhorred the true ones. There was nothing in the transaction, or in any of its connections, which would require them to be forgotten or disavowed by chief actors within that brief period in which ordinary memories preserve transactions of very secondary importance.

We are not prepared to deny, however, that the President's letter to Livingston showed high diplomatic skill—that it made the most of the circumstances—that it was a shrewd and singularly daring effort to beat the French Consul at a game he was himself very fond of playing toward other nations. The further chances of the game—the skill of the players—the end which tests the wisdom of the beginning—are to be hereafter recorded.

The French Government, however, studiously avoided giving our minister any information of its purchase of Louisiana or its non-purchase of Florida. The reason will presently appear in a despatch of Livingston. The latter, according to his instructions, attempted as a primary object to prevent the French continental acquisitions, and next, if they took place, to attempt to obtain that portion of them east of the Mississippi, and particularly West Florida, in order to secure the outlets to the Gulf of Mexico furnished by its rivers, especially the Mobile. In this Livingston met with no encouragement. On his hinting at a purchase the minister told him "none but spendthrifts satisfied their debts by selling their lands." De Marbois—a steady friend of the United States—informed him that the French Government considered the acquired possessions an excellent "outlet for their turbulent spirits." He soon learned that their colonization was a favorite scheme of the First Consul. Some passages in a despatch of Livingston, of January 13, 1802, deserve particular attention:

"By the secrecy and duplicity practised relative to this object, it is clear to me that they apprehend some opposition on the part of America to their plans. I have, however, on all occasions declared that as long as France conforms to the existing treaty between us and Spain, the Government of the United States does not consider herself as having any interest in opposing the exchange. The evil our country has suffered by their rupture with France is not to be calculated. We have become an object of jealousy both to the Government and people.

"The reluctance we have shown to a renewal of the treaty of 1778 has created many suspicions. Among other absurd ones, they believed seriously that we have an eye to the conquest of their islands. The business of Louisiana also originated in that; and they say expressly that they could have no pretence, so far as related to the Floridas, to make this exchange, had the treaty been renewed, since by the sixth article they were expressly prohibited from touching the Floridas. I own I have always considered this article, and the guaranty of our Independence, as more important to us than the guaranty of the islands was to France: and the sacrifices we have made of an immense claim to get rid of it, as a dead loss."

By comparing this with Jefferson's letter of April 18, 1802, it will be seen how completely the President's views differed from Mr. Livingston's in regard to the consequences of a French colonization of Louisiana, and in regard to the proper policy to be adopted by the United States if it was attempted. And the further despatches show that no change took place in the minister's views until he received the letter of the President. The policy which secured the purchase of Louisiana was purely original with the latter. Not a distant hint, not even an analogous idea, was received from any other quarter.

The minister again wrote home, March 24th, that the colonization of New Orleans was "a darling object of the First Consul"—that he "saw in it a mean to gratify his friends and dispose of his enemies"—that it was thought "that New Orleans must command the trade of our whole western country" —that the French had been persuaded "that the Indians were attached to France and hated the Americans"—that "the country was a paradise," etc. The minister then proposed that the United States establish a port at Natchez, or elsewhere, and give it such advantages "as would bring our vessels to it without touching at New Orleans."

He wrote, April 24th, that the French minister "would give no answer to any inquiries he made" on the subject of Louisiana; that the Government was "at that moment fitting out an armament" to take possession, consisting of "between five and seven thousand men, under the command of General Bernadotte," who would shortly sail for New Orleans, "unless the state of affairs in Santo Domingo should change their destination." He declared his information certain, and again pressed his Government "immediately to take measures to enable Natchez to rival New Orleans."

Some other letters passed which are not necessary to be mentioned. On July 30th Livingston wrote the Secretary of State that he had received his despatches of May 1st and 11th, the President's letter through Dupont de Nemours, of the preceding April 18th (1802), and that he was preparing a memoir to the French Government.

The formal instructions of May 1st and 11th fell far short of the scope or decision of the President's private letter which he had sent to Dupont de Nemours open, expressly and avowedly to have its contents made known to the French Government. The former, however, directed the minister to urge upon France "an abandonment of her present purpose." Those of the 1st directed him to endeavor to ascertain at what *price* she would relinquish the Floridas—those of the 11th, to employ "every effort and address" to procure the cession of all territory east of the Mississippi, including New Orleans—and he was authorized, should it become absolutely necessary in order to secure this, to guarantee the French possessions west of the river.

The discrepancy between the instructions and private letter admits of a ready explanation. The one exhibited the official attitude which it was considered prudent to take—the other gave warning of the inner and entire feelings and purposes, in a form which would have its full effect, but which could not be officially recognized and therefore construed into a menace, or made the subject of official discussion and disclosure. The unofficial letter, in effect, converted the propositions of the official ones into ultimata. If France would cede to the United States New Orleans and all the territory east of the Mississippi, for an equivalent in money, then the "marrying" with England would not take place, and France could have the benefit of another American guaranty. But what was a guaranty worth which would fall with the first collision of the parties between whom the predicted "friction" would not be in the least reduced by the proposed arrangement? What would the remaining territory be worth to France—never worth a thousandth part as much to her as to the United States—in the then situation of the world, without any navigable approach to the greater portion of it, except through a river of which the United States would hold the absolute control?

To accept the President's offer would be to give up the most valuable part of the possession and the key to all the remainder, for the purpose of having the remainder secured from England. Yet, if the reasoning in the President's letter was sound—which enforced the first cession—the rest would inevitably soon follow that cession. In fact, the first cession would render the second more inevitable, and a thousand times less capable of being forcibly prevented. The President's idea, then, amounted practically to this: that if France would sell us all we then needed of her territory, for either commercial, military, or any other purposes, we would help her—or rather allow her to help us—keep the other part from a more dangerous occupant, until we also had need for that other part. Precisely in this light the French Government viewed this offer. Talleyrand emphatically declared that if the French Government gave up what we then asked, what was left was worthless to France.

We neither accuse nor suspect Mr. Jefferson of insincerity. There is no doubt he would have respected his guaranty; and that he would have remained adverse to taking any unjust advantage. But he foresaw, and clearly and warningly pointed to, the train of causes which must inevitably end, sooner or later, in the overthrow of any French power on the Mississippi. Having done this, he took middle ground—ground that would neither disgust France nor mankind by its rapacity—and awaited the result. We have no doubt that having such intellects as Bonaparte's and Talleyrand's to deal with, he very strongly anticipated the result which finally took place. It was to be ready for this, or some other equivalent or similar proposition, that he sent Monroe to France, with verbal instructions extending to any contingency.

The President's views produced no immediate visible change in Bonaparte's plans. Livingston informed his Government, November 11th, that the military expedition to New Orleans was about embarking, and he feared "no prudence would prevent hostilities ere long." Some of his later despatches were rather more hopeful in their tenor; but no marked change occurred in the open aspect of things until the news reached France of the war flame that was burning in Congress, on account of the proceedings of Morales at New Orleans. The Federalists, who were so vehemently laboring to overthrow the Administration on that question, were unconsciously playing into its hands, and as effectually serving one of its great objects—the greatest object of its foreign policy—as if they had been employed expressly for that purpose.

When intelligence of war resolutions, vehement speeches in Congress, and of every other apparent indication of a popular ferment and of a national explosion in the United States was wafted across the Atlantic, the French Consul—used to the fiery energy of democratic legislatures—unable to discern distinctly at such a distance between parties—finding one set openly talking war and the other only asking for privacy in the deliberations on the question—observing that all were in favor of firm declarations and provisional warlike preparations—fancied he saw the American scenes of 1798 about to be reënacted. He saw the United States again preparing with the prodigal bravery which distinguishes an aroused democracy, to tauntingly defy France to the combat; and he doubtless believed this was the first act of the drama which the President's letter had foreshadowed.

It would be something worse than ridiculous to suppose that Bonaparte was intimidated, or that the Directory were intimidated in 1798. But the question was, in commercial phrase, would the contest "pay"? Was it worth while to wage a war with so distant a power while the marine of France was so inferior to that of England, the sure ally of the enemies of France? Was it worth while to attempt to garrison a wilderness, destitute even of provisions, against five millions of contiguous people, who could reach it by a large number of navigable rivers? Was it worth while to expose the French West India possessions to the attacks of such a neighbor? Was it worth while to tempt a partition of all the colonial possessions of France between the United States and England? Was it worth while to "marry" these powers in the bonds of a common interest, and induce their allied maritime flags to "maintain exclusive possession of the ocean," and fix "the sentence which was to restrain France forever within her low-water mark"? The shattered ships of France bore good testimony whether the menaces of the Presi-

dent in the last particular would prove bagatelles, if the policy
he threatened was entered upon.

The victor of Lodi, Abukir, and Marengo — the dictator
of Southern Europe—could have laughed at the President's
threats if nothing but the Rhine or the Pyrenees had separated
the domains over which they ruled. But circumstances sometimes more than counterbalance strength. A mountaineer in a
pass is more formidable than a battalion on a plain. The United
States held the unapproached maritime supremacy of the western hemisphere. She held more. Maritime skill and maritime
victory were hers by birthright. Never man for man and gun for
gun had her flag been struck to Christian or corsair; and now the
Levantine seas were witnessing her avenging chastisement of
those to whom Europe paid tribute. United with England, and
only given time to build—in the mechanical sense of the term—
fleets, and no ocean or sea could float a sail which was not under
the protection of their associated flags.

But independently of such future results, and looking only
to existing facts, Bonaparte was not weak enough in military capacity to suppose for a moment he could hold a level and comparatively unfortified mud-bank, inhabited by a few thousand
creoles, and a vast wilderness occupied only by savages, with
the Atlantic between it and France, against the fighting men of
five millions of people, and with England joyfully and eagerly
ready to intercept every succor he could send, so that not a regiment would reach America without in part owing it to favoring
accidents.

The moment, therefore, he believed the President's avowals
had been made in earnest, and that the American people were
ready to uphold them: ready to fight for the territory—and
what could he expect if the American Republicans, the only
party that could ever tolerate France, should lead in the war
feeling?—his strong sagacity at once foresaw that his colonization projects were at an end; that these new domains were
worthless to France, and must soon pass entirely from its grasp.
Measuring as he always did the sentiment of America toward
France by the Federal standard, he probably considered any
guaranty the latter could receive from the former as a far weaker
and more ephemeral engagement than it would actually have

proved. Necessity would have broken it. But he believed the merest pretext would suffice. It was both for his advantage and credit, then, to get rid of it for the best equivalent he could obtain, before another war should break out between France and England.

On April 30th—just eleven days before Lord Whitmouth received his passports and left France—a treaty and two conventions were entered into between the American and French ministers, by which France ceded the entire province of Louisiana to the United States, for the sum of sixty millions of francs, to be paid to France: twenty millions to be paid to citizens of the United States due from France, for supplies, embargoes, and prizes made at sea; and in further consideration of certain stipulations in favor of the inhabitants of the ceded territory, and certain commercial privileges secured to France.

It was provided that the inhabitants of Louisiana should "be incorporated into the Union of the United States, and admitted as soon as possible, according to the principles of the Federal Constitution, to the enjoyment of all the rights, advantages, and immunities of citizens of the United States; and, in the mean time, they should be maintained and protected in the free enjoyment of their liberty, property, and the religion which they professed."

It was provided that French or Spanish ships coming directly from their own country, or any of their colonies, and loaded only with the produce or manufactures thereof, should for the space of twelve years be admitted to any port within the ceded territory, in the same manner and on the same terms with American vessels coming from those places. And for that period no other nation was to have a right to the same privileges in the ports of the ceded territory. But this was not to affect the regulations the United States might make concerning the exportation of their own produce and merchandise, or any right they might have to make such regulations. After the expiration of the twelve years, and forever, the ships of France were to be treated upon the footing of the most favored nations in the ports of the ceded territory.

The financial arrangements were included in the "Conventions," as France exhibited a sensitive disinclination to have this territorial transfer formally assume its real character of a sale for money. But a careful inspection of the treaties will show that she had much less reason to blush for her conduct on this occasion than nations commonly have which either cede or acquire territory. Her stipulations in behalf of the existing and future population of Louisiana were most humane and noble, and those which affected her American creditors were conceived in the highest spirit of magnanimity and honor. It is curious to speculate what a different air this international compact might have been made to wear had the superseded Talleyrand been the negotiator instead of the austerely virtuous Marbois. And let us not withhold from the Consul of France the credit which is due him for approaching and approving the proceedings of such a minister.

We think it was Napoleon who said he had noticed that Providence generally favored the heaviest and best disciplined battalions. Fortune wafts on those who seize her at the ebb. The "good-luck" to which it gave the opposition so much consolation to attribute the President's success in the purchase of Louisiana continued. The house of Baring, in London, offered for a moderate commission at once to take the American stocks which were created for the purchase money of Louisiana, at their current value in England, and to meet our engagements to France by stipulated monthly instalments. It is not at all probable that this offer to furnish so large a sum to an enemy could have been made without an understanding with the British Government. Nay, the latter had projected an expedition to capture New Orleans as soon as her war with France should break out, but, on being apprised by Mr. King of the measures of the United States toward a purchase, evinced apparent satisfaction with such an arrangement. And on learning the terms of the cession, even George III, if the well-turned diplomatic language of Lord Hawkesbury may be credited, grew gracious, and expressed high approbation of their tenor.

England had every right to feel gratified. No alliance against her power, no special guaranties against her arms, no injurious discriminations against her navigation had been inserted in the treaties. France was stripped of her American continental possessions, and crippled from ever becoming the rival of England in colonial establishments. The ceded territory had gone into the hands of the only power which could hold it safely from all European rivals, and against which it would have been in vain for England herself to contend for its possession. The sum paid into the coffers of France would not approach that which England would save in sending fleets against and in maintaining possession of Louisiana against both France and the United States, without any hope that possession would be permanent. And finally, England could now concentrate all her force without reference to transatlantic efforts or interruptions, in her death-struggle with that modern Alexander against whom it might soon be necessary to defend even her own shores from invasion.

Livingston and Monroe communicated the result of their negotiations to the American Government, May 13th. It is to be presumed the paper was drawn up by Livingston, and was acquiesced in by Monroe, to escape an eclaircissement which would add to existing irritations. It is said that they (the ministers) "well knew" that "an acquisition of so great extent was not contemplated by their appointment," but "they were persuaded that the circumstances and considerations which induced them to make it would justify them in the measure to their Government and country."

So far as official written instructions were concerned, this was true; but both Livingston's official and Jefferson's inofficial letters show that it was an erroneous view; show that procuring Louisiana had been "contemplated" and made the subject of diplomatic correspondence; show that Jefferson had meditated and resolved on obtaining, if practicable, every foot of the American continental possessions of France, the moment he learned that France had obtained them; show that he had communicated these views to Livingston, while that minister was expressing to the French Government, and no doubt honestly entertaining, a wholly different class of ideas. And there is not a particle of doubt that it was precisely to seize upon a favorable crisis, should it occur, to do exactly what was done, that Monroe was sent charged with his "verbal" instructions.

Mr. Madison's reply—as Secretary of State—to the communication of May 13th, was worded with peculiar care, its object being, without giving offence to Mr. Livingston, to dissent from the statement that the ministers had acted contrary to any previous views or wishes of their Government, or had taken a step which had not been "contemplated" by their Government, or one which they had not been expected to promptly and eagerly adopt if available. After expressing the unequivocal approbation of the Government for the proceedings of the ministers, he said:

"This approbation is in no respect precluded by the silence of your commission and instructions. When these were made out, the object of the most sanguine was limited to the establishment of the Mississippi as our boundary. It was not presumed that more could be sought by the United States, either with a chance of success, or perhaps without being suspected of a greedy ambition, than the island of New Orleans and the two Floridas; it being little doubted that the latter was, or would be, comprehended in the cession from Spain to France. To the acquisition of New Orleans and the Floridas, the provision was, therefore, accommodated. Nor was it to be supposed that in case the French Government should be willing to part with more than the territory on one side of the Mississippi, an arrangement with Spain for restoring to her the territory on the other side, would not be preferred to a sale of it to the United States. It might be added that the ample views of the subject carried with him by Mr. Monroe, and the confidence felt that your judicious management would make the most [of?] favorable occurrences, lessened the necessity of multiplying provisions for every turn which your negotiations might possibly take."

He then very quietly mentioned that it was the tenor of Mr. Livingston's own despatches which had "left no expectation of any arrangement with France, by which an extensive acquisition was to be made, unless in a favorable crisis of which advantage should be taken."

Is it asked if we entertain any doubt that Monroe, with his verbal instructions, would have concurred readily in a treaty based on the President's formal and official offer, that is, on the separate acquisition of the Floridas and New Orleans? No such doubt is entertained. No question is made that the President and the American people would have rested satisfied with that acquisition for a generation to come. But it is not probable that the President expected his official demand would be complied with, and no more. If so, he sent Monroe to France for nothing, and much of his letter to him of January 13, 1803, is wholly unmeaning gibberish. Undoubtedly he hoped for a more favorable arrangement. Undoubtedly he verbally instructed Monroe to acquire as much territory as practicable. Undoubtedly Monroe would never have signed a treaty which did not obtain more than New Orleans—and France did not, as it proved, own the Floridas. After reading the President's letter to Livingston, of April 18, 1802, it would be absurd to declare that he did not "contemplate" the acquisition of Louisiana; that he did not solely originate the idea; that he did not originate and put in motion the train of causes by which it was accomplished.

Monroe, with his customary steady discretion and modesty, kept silent as to his share of the merit of this negotiation. Jefferson's temptation to speak was stronger. The opposition, with its usual variety and diversity of grounds of attack, insisted: First, that the purchase was inexpedient, unconstitutional, and disgraceful in its character; second, that it was the result of "good-luck," and was wholly unforeseen and unthought of; third, that Livingston's energy and tact had broken away from instructions to rescue a feeble and irresolute Administration. The President did once or twice hint to very confidential correspondents that if all the facts were before the public, it would be shown that the ministers had not been compelled to take any unauthorized or unexpected responsibility; and he also hinted that Monroe was entitled to a full share of credit for what had been accomplished. Beyond this he coolly let the newspaper trumpet blare on and reduce him to a secondary attitude to those who, if they had executed well, had acted only as his instruments. He had conceived the design; he had foreseen the occasion; he had even given the signal to strike when the occasion came.

It was no ordinary triumph of which he omitted to claim the glory. When from the *bema* of the Pnyx the flashing eye of Demosthenes glanced from the upturned faces of the people of Athens to the scenes of those heroic achievements which he invoked them to emulate, it looked beyond the Gulf of Salamis and the plain of Marathon. Parnes, in whose rocky gorge stood Phyle, towered before him in the north, and in the south the heights on whose southern bases broke the waves of the Ægean. Almost the whole land of Attica lay under his vision, and near enough to have its great outlines distinguishable. What a world was clustered within that compass!

The land of Attica, whose sword shook and whose civilization conquered the world, had the superficial area and about one-third the agricultural productiveness of a moderate sized county in any of the American States which have been erected in the province of French Louisiana. No conqueror who has trod the earth to fill it with desolation and mourning, ever conquered and permanently amalgamated with his native kingdom a remote approach to the same extent of territory. But one kingdom in Europe equals the extent of one of its present States. Germany supports a population of thirty-seven millions of people. All Germany has a little more than the area of two-thirds of Nebraska, and, acre for acre, less tillable land. Louisiana, as densely populated in proportion to its natural materials of sustentation as parts of Europe, would be capable of supporting somewhere from four to five hundred millions of people. The whole United States became capable, by this acquisition, of sustaining a larger population than ever occupied Europe.

The purchase secured, independently of territory, several prime national objects. It gave us that homogeneousness, unity, and independence which are derived from the absolute control and disposition of our commerce, trade, and industry in every department, without the hinderance or meddling of any intervening nation between us and any natural element of industry, between us and the sea, or between us and the open market of the world. It gave us ocean boundaries on all exposed sides, for it left Canada exposed to us, and not us to Canada. It made us indisputably and forever the controllers of the western hemisphere. It placed our national course, character, civilization, and destiny solely in our own hands. It gave us the certain sources of a not distant numerical strength to which that of the mightiest empires of the past or present is insignificant.

A Gallic Cæsar was leading his armies over shattered kingdoms. His armed foot shook the world. He decimated Europe. Millions on millions of mankind perished, and there was scarcely a human habitation from the Polar Seas to the Mediterranean where the voice of lamentation was not heard over slaughtered kindred, to swell the conqueror's strength and "glory"! And the carnage and rapine of war are trifling evils compared with its demoralizations. The rolling tide of conquest subsided. France shrunk back to her ancient limits. Napoleon died a repining captive on the rock of St. Helena. The stupendous tragedy was played out; and no physical results were left behind but decrease, depopulation, and universal loss.

A republican President, on a distant continent, was also seeking to aggrandize his country. He led no armies. He shed not a solitary drop of human blood. He caused not a tear of human woe. He bent not one toiling back lower by governmental burdens. Strangest of political anomalies; and ludicrous as strange to the representatives of the ideas of the tyrannical and bloody past, he lightened the taxes while he was lightening the debts of a nation. And without interrupting either of these meliorations for an instant; without imposing a single new exaction on his people, he acquired, peaceably and permanently for his country more extensive and fertile domains than ever for a moment owned the sway of Napoleon; more extensive ones than his gory plume ever floated over. Which of these victors deserves to be termed "glorious"?

Yet, with that serene and unselfish equanimity which ever preferred his cause to his vanity, this more than conqueror allowed his real agency in this great achievement to go unexplained to the day of his death, and to be in a good measure attributed to mere accident, taken advantage of quite as much by others as by himself. He wrote no laurelled letter. He asked no triumph.

THE TRIPOLITAN WAR

A.D. 1804

J. FENIMORE COOPER

At the opening of the nineteenth century the United States of America were impelled to resist by force the piratical powers known as the Barbary States, on the northern coast of Africa. These corsairs had long vexed the Mediterranean countries of Europe. Similar annoyances having been suffered by the United States, that country at last inflicted upon one of the offenders—Tripoli—a punishment which proved to be the beginning of the end in the predatory career of all.

During the last years of the eighteenth century the Mediterranean was rendered by these African pirates so unsafe that the merchant-ships of every nation were in danger of being captured by them, unless protected by an armed convoy or by tribute paid to the Barbary powers. With other countries, the United States had made payments of such tribute, but at last, when an increase of such payments was demanded by Tripoli, the Republic refused to comply. In consequence of this refusal Tripoli, June 10, 1801, declared war against the United States. The conflict which ensued is known as the Tripolitan War. It had been anticipated by the United States, which had already sent a squadron to the Mediterranean. No serious collision took place until October, 1803; then, while chasing a corsair into the harbor of Tripoli, the United States frigate Philadelphia, Captain William Bainbridge, struck a sunken rock, and, being unable to use her guns, was captured by the Tripolitans.

On February 16, 1804, Lieutenant Stephen Decatur, under orders of Commodore Edward Preble, performed what Nelson called "the most daring act of the age," which made the young officer one of the most famous among naval heroes. With a captured Tripolitan craft, renamed the Intrepid, and a crew of seventy-five men, he entered the harbor of Tripoli by night, boarded the Philadelphia, "within half gunshot of the pacha's castle, drove the Tripolitan crew overboard, set the ship on fire, remained alongside until the flames were beyond control, and then withdrew without losing a man," though under the fire of one hundred forty-one guns.

The further operations and end of the war are narrated by Cooper, who, although most widely known by his novels, was himself at one time an officer in the United States Navy, of which he is also one of the best historians.

IT was July 21, 1804, when Commodore Preble was able to sail from Malta, with all the force he had collected, to join the vessels cruising off Tripoli. The blockade had been kept up with vigor for some months, and the Commodore felt that the season had now arrived for more active operations. He had with him the Constitution, Enterprise, Nautilus, two bomb-vessels, and six gunboats. The bomb-vessels were of only thirty tons measurement, and carried a thirteen-inch mortar each. In scarcely any respect were they suited for the duty that was expected of them. The gunboats were little better, being shallow, unseaworthy craft, of about twenty-five tons burden, in which long iron twenty-fours had been mounted. Each boat had one gun and thirty-five men; the latter, with the exception of a few Neapolitans, being taken from the different vessels of the squadron. The Tripolitan gunboats were altogether superior, and the duty should have been exactly reversed, in order to suit the qualities of the respective craft; the boats of Tripoli having been built to go on the coast, while those possessed by the Americans were intended solely for harbor defence. In addition to their other bad qualities, these Neapolitan boats were found neither to sail nor to row even tolerably well. It was necessary to tow them by larger vessels the moment they got into rough water, and when it blew heavily there was always danger of dragging them under. In addition to this force, Commodore Preble had obtained six long twenty-six pounders for the upper deck of the Constitution, which were mounted in the waist.

When the American commander assembled his whole force before Tripoli, on July 25, 1804, it consisted of the Constitution 44 guns, Commodore Preble; Siren 16, Lieutenant-Commandant Stewart; Argus 16, Lieutenant-Commandant Hull; Scourge 14, Lieutenant-Commandant Dent; Vixen 12, Lieutenant-Commandant Smith; Nautilus 12, Lieutenant-Commandant Somers; Enterprise 12, Lieutenant-Commandant Decatur; the two bomb-vessels, and six gunboats. In some respects this was a well-appointed force for the duty required, while in others it was lamentably deficient. Another heavy ship, in particular, was wanted, and the means for bombarding had all the defects that may be anticipated. The two heaviest brigs had armaments of twenty-four-pound carronades; the other brig, and two of the schooners, armaments of eighteen-pound carronades; while the Enterprise retained her original equipment of long sixes in consequence of her ports being unsuited to the new guns.

As the Constitution had a gun-deck battery of thirty long twenty-fours, with six long twenty-sixes, and some lighter long guns above, it follows that the Americans could bring twenty-two twenty-fours and six twenty-sixes to bear on the stone walls of the town, in addition to a few light chase-guns in the small vessels, and the twelve-pounders of the frigate's quarter-deck and forecastle. On the whole, there appears to have been in the squadron twenty-eight heavy long guns, with about twenty lighter, that might be brought to play on the batteries simultaneously. Opposed to these means of offence, the pacha had one hundred fifteen guns in battery, most of them quite heavy, and nineteen gunboats that, of themselves, so far as metal was concerned, were nearly equal to the frigate. Moored in the harbor were also two large galleys, two schooners, and a brig, all of which were armed and strongly manned. The American squadron was manned by one thousand sixty persons, all told, while the pacha had assembled a force that has been estimated as high as twenty-five thousand, Arabs and Turks included. The only advantage possessed by the assailants, in the warfare that was so soon to follow, were those which are dependent on spirit, discipline, and system.

The vessels could not anchor until the 28th, when they ran in, with the wind at east-southeast, and came to, by signal, about a league from the town. This was hardly done, however, before the wind came suddenly round to north-northwest, thence north-northeast, and it began to blow strong, with a heavy sea setting directly on shore. At 6 P. M. a signal was made for the vessels to weigh and to gain an offing. Fortunately the wind continued to haul to the eastward, or there would have been great danger of towing the gunboats under while carrying sail to claw off the land. The gale continued to increase until the 31st, when it blew tremendously. The courses of the Constitution were blown away, though reefed, and it would have been impossible to save the bomb-vessels and gunboats had not the wind hauled so far to the southward as to give smooth water. Fortunately, the gale ceased the next day.

On August 3, 1804, the squadron ran in again and got within
a league of the town, with a pleasant breeze at the eastward. The
enemy's gunboats and galleys had come outside of the rocks and
were lying there in two divisions; one near the eastern and the
other near the western entrance, or about half a mile apart. At
the same time it was seen that all the batteries were manned, as
if an attack was not only expected but invited.

At 12:30, noon, the Constitution wore with her head off shore,
and showed a signal for all vessels to come within hail. Each
commander, as he came up, was ordered to prepare to attack the
shipping and batteries. The bomb-vessels and gunboats were
immediately manned, and such was the high state of discipline in
the squadron that in one hour everything was ready for the contemplated service. On this occasion Commodore Preble made
the following distribution of that part of his force which was
manned from the other vessels of his squadron:

One bomb-ketch was commanded by Lieutenant-Commandant Dent, of the Scourge. The other bomb-ketch was commanded by Mr. Robinson, first lieutenant of the Constitution.

First division of gunboats. (1) Lieutenant-Commandant
Somers, of the Nautilus: (2) Lieutenant James Decatur, of the
Nautilus: (3) Lieutenant Blake, of the Argus.

Second division of gunboats. (4) Lieutenant-Commandant
Decatur, of the Enterprise: (5) Lieutenant Bainbridge, of the
Enterprise: (6) Lieutenant Trippe, of the Vixen.

At half-past one the Constitution wore again, and stood toward the town. At two the gunboats were cast off, and formed
in advance, covered by the brigs and schooners, and half an hour
later the signal was shown to engage. The attack was commenced
by the two bombards, which began to throw shells into the town.
It was followed by the batteries, which were instantly in a blaze,
and then the shipping on both sides opened their fire, within
reach of grape.

The eastern, or most weatherly division of the enemy's gunboats, nine in number, as being least supported, was the aim of
the American gunboats. But the bad qualities of the latter craft
were quickly apparent, for as soon as Decatur steered toward the
enemy with an intention to come to close quarters, the division of
Somers, which was a little to leeward, found it difficult to sustain

him. Every effort was made by the latter officer to get far enough to windward to join in the attack; but finding it impracticable he bore up and ran down alone on five of the enemy to leeward and engaged them all within pistol-shot, throwing showers of grape, cannister, and musket-balls among them. In order to do this, as soon as near enough, the sweeps were got out and the boat was backed astern to prevent her from drifting in among the enemy. The gunboat, Number Three, was closing fast, but a signal of recall being shown from the Constitution she hauled out of the line to obey, and losing ground kept more aloof, firing at the boats and shipping in the harbor; while Number Two, Lieutenant James Decatur, was enabled to join the division to windward. Number Five, Lieutenant Bainbridge, lost her lateen-yard, while still in tow of the Siren, but, though unable to close, she continued advancing, keeping up a heavy fire, and finally touched on the rocks.

By these changes, Lieutenant-Commandant Decatur had three boats that dashed forward with him, though one belonged to the division of Lieutenant-Commandant Somers; viz., Number Four, Number Six, and Number Two.

The officers in command of these three boats went steadily on until within the smoke of the enemy. Here they delivered their fire, throwing in a terrible discharge of grape and musket-balls, and the order was given to board. Up to this moment the odds had been as three to one against the assailants; and they were now, if possible, increased. The brigs and schooners could no longer assist. The Turkish boats were not only the heaviest and the best in every sense, but they were much the strongest manned. The combat now assumed a character of chivalrous effort and of desperate personal prowess that belongs rather to the Middle Ages than to struggles of our own time. Its details, indeed, savor more of the tales of romance than of harsh reality, such as we are accustomed to associate with acts of modern warfare.

Lieutenant-Commandant Decatur took the lead. He had no sooner discharged his volley of musket-balls than Number Four was laid alongside of the opposing boat of the enemy. He boarded her, followed by Lieutenant Thorn M'Donough and all the Americans of his crew. The Tripolitan boat was divided nearly in two parts by a long open hatchway, and as the crew of

Number Four came in one side the Turks retreated to the other, making a sort of ditch of the open space. This caused an instant of delay, and perhaps fortunately, for it permitted the assailants to act together. As soon as ready, Decatur charged round each end of the hatchway, and after a short struggle a part of the Turks were piked and bayoneted, while the rest submitted or leaped into the water.

No sooner had Decatur got possession of the boat first assailed than he took her in tow and bore down on the one next to lee-ward. Running the enemy aboard, as before, he boarded him with the most of his officers and men. The captain of the Tripolitan vessel was a large powerful man and Decatur charged him with a pike. The weapon, however, was seized by the Turk, wrested from the hands of the assailant, and turned against its owner. The latter parried a thrust, and made a blow with his sword at the pike, with a view to cut off its head. The sword hit the iron and broke at the hilt and the next instant the Turk made another thrust. The gallant Decatur had nothing to parry the blow but his arm, with which he so far avoided it as to receive the pike only through the flesh of his breast. Tearing the iron from the wound he sprang within the Turk's guard and grappled his antagonist. The pike fell between the two and a short trial of strength succeeded, in which the Turk prevailed. As the combatants fell, however, Decatur so far released himself as to lie side by side with his foe on the deck. The Tripolitan now endeavored to reach his poniard while his hand was firmly held by that of his enemy. At this critical instant, when life or death depended on a moment well employed or a moment lost, Decatur drew a small pistol from the pocket of his vest, passed the arm that was free round the body of the Turk, pointed the muzzle in, and fired. The ball passed entirely through the body of the Mussulman and lodged in the clothes of his foe. At the same instant Decatur felt the grasp that had almost smothered him relax, and he was liberated. He sprang up and the Tripolitan lay dead at his feet.

In such a mêlée it cannot be supposed that the struggle of the two leaders would go unnoticed. An enemy raised his sabre to cleave the skull of Decatur while he was occupied with his enemy, and a young man of the Enterprise's crew interposed an arm to save him. The blow was intercepted, but the limb was severed, leaving it hanging only by a bit of skin. A fresh rush was now made upon the enemy, who was overcome without much further resistance.

An idea of the desperate nature of the fighting that distinguished this remarkable assault may be gained from the amount of the loss. The two boats captured by Lieutenant-Commandant Decatur had about eighty men in them, of whom fifty-two were known to have been killed and wounded, most of the latter very badly. As only eight prisoners were made who were not wounded, and many jumped overboard and swam to the rocks, it is not improbable that the Turks suffered still more severely. Lieutenant-Commandant Decatur himself being wounded, he secured his second prize and hauled off to rejoin the squadron, all the rest of the enemy's division that were not taken having by this time run into the harbor by passing through the openings between the rocks.

When Lieutenant-Commandant Decatur was thus employed to windward, his brother, Lieutenant James Decatur, the first lieutenant of the Nautilus, was nobly emulating his example in Number Two. Reserving his fire, like Number Four, this young officer dashed into the smoke, and was on the point of boarding when he received a musket-ball in his forehead. The boats met and rebounded; and in the confusion of the death of the commanding officer of Number Two, the Turk was enabled to escape, under a heavy fire from the Americans. It was said, at the time, that the enemy had struck before Lieutenant Decatur fell, though the fact must remain in doubt. It is, however, believed that he sustained a very severe loss.

In the mean time, Lieutenant Trippe in Number Six, the last of the three boats that were able to reach the weather division, was not idle. Reserving his fire like the others, he delivered it with deadly effect when closing, and went aboard his enemy in the smoke. In this instance the boats also separated by the shock of the collision, leaving Lieutenant Trippe, with J. D. Henley and nine men only, on board the Tripolitan. Here, too, the commanders singled each other out, and a fierce personal combat occurred while the work of death was going on around them. The Turk was young and of large and athletic build, and soon compelled his slighter but more active foe to fight with caution. Advancing on Lieutenant Trippe he would strike a blow and receive a thrust in return. In this manner he gave the American commander no less than eight sabre wounds in the head and two in the breast; when making a sudden rush he struck a ninth blow on the Lieutenant's head which brought him down upon one knee. Rallying all his force in a desperate effort the latter, who still retained the short pike with which he fought, made a thrust that forced the weapon through the body of his gigantic adversary and tumbled him on his back. As soon as the Tripolitan officer fell the remainder of his crew surrendered.

The boat taken by Lieutenant Trippe was one of the largest belonging to the pacha. The number of her men is not positively known, but, living and dead, thirty-six were found in her, of whom twenty-one were either killed or wounded. When it is remembered that but eleven Americans boarded her the achievement must pass for one of the most gallant on record. All this time the cannonading and bombardment continued without ceasing. Lieutenant-Commandant Somers, in Number One, sustained by the brigs and schooners, had forced the remaining boats to retreat, and this resolute officer pressed them so hard as to be compelled to wear within a short distance of a battery of twelve guns close to the mole. Her destruction seemed inevitable. As the boat came slowly round, a shell fell into the battery and most opportunely blew up the platform, driving the enemy out to the last man. Before the guns could be again used, the boat had got in tow of one of the small vessels.

There was a division of five boats and two galleys of the enemy that had been held in reserve within the rocks, and these rallied their retreating countrymen and made two efforts to come out and intercept the Americans and their prizes; but they were kept in check by the fire of the frigate and small vessels. The Constitution maintained a very heavy fire and silenced several of the batteries, though they reopened as soon as she had passed. The bombards were covered with the spray of shot, but continued to throw shells to the last. At half past four the wind coming round to the northward a signal was made for the gunboats and bomb-ketches to rejoin the small vessels, and another to take them and the prizes in tow. The last order was handsomely executed by the brigs and schooners under cover of a blaze of fire from the frigate. A quarter of an hour later the Constitution herself hauled off and ran out of gunshot.

Thus terminated the first serious attack that was made on the town and batteries of Tripoli. Its effect on the enemy was of the most salutary kind, the manner in which their gunboats had been taken by boarding making a deep and lasting impression. The superiority of the Americans in gunnery was generally admitted before, but here was an instance in which the Turks had been overcome by inferior number, hand to hand, a kind of conflict in which they had been thought particularly to excel. Perhaps no instance of more desperate fighting of the sort, without defensive armor, is to be found in the pages of history. Three gunboats were sunk in the harbor in addition to the three that were taken; and the loss of the Tripolitans by shot must have been very heavy. About fifty shells were thrown into the town, but little damage appears to have been done in this way; very few of the bombs—on account of the imperfect materials that had been furnished—exploding. The batteries were considerably damaged, but the town itself suffered no material injury.

On the American side only fourteen were killed and wounded in the affair; and all of these, with the exception of one man, belonged to the gunboats. The Constitution, though under fire two hours, escaped much better than could have been expected. She received one heavy shot through her mainmast, had a quarterdeck gun injured, and was a good deal cut up aloft. The enemy had calculated his range for a more distant cannonade and generally overshot the ships. By this mistake the Constitution had her main royal yard shot away.

The pacha now became more disposed than ever to treat, the warfare promising much annoyance with no corresponding benefits. The cannonading did his batteries and vessels great injury, though the town probably suffered less than might have been expected, being in a measure protected by its walls. The shells, too, that had been procured at Messina turned out to be very bad, few exploding when they fell. The case was different with the shot, which did effective work on the different batteries. Some idea may be formed of the spirit of the last attack from the report of Commodore Preble, who stated that nine guns, one of which was used but a short time, threw five hundred heavy shot in the course of little more than two hours. Although the delay, caused by the expected arrival of the reënforcement, was used to open a negotiation, it was without effect. The pacha had lowered his demands one-half, but he still insisted on a ransom of five hundred dollars a man for his prisoners, though he waived the usual claim for tribute in future. These propositions were not received, it being expected that, after the arrival of the reënforcement, the treaty might be made on the usual terms of civilized nations.

On August 9th the Argus, Captain Hull, had a narrow escape. That brig having stood in toward the town to reconnoitre, with Commodore Preble on board, one of the heaviest of the shot from the batteries raked her bottom for some distance and cut the planks half through. An inch or two of variation in the direction of this shot would infallibly have sunk the brig, and that probably in a few minutes.

No intelligence arriving from the expected vessels, Commodore Preble, about the 16th, began to make his preparations for another attack, sending the Enterprise, Lieutenant-Commandant Robinson, to Malta with orders for the agent to forward transports with water, the vessels being on a short allowance. On the night of the 17th, Captains Decatur and Chauncey went close in, in boats, and reconnoitred the situation of the enemy. These officers on their return reported that the vessels of the Tripolitan flotilla were moored abreast of each other, from a line extending from the mole to the castle, with their heads to the eastward, making a defence directly across the inner harbor or galley-mole. A gale, however, compelled the American squadron to stand off shore on the morning of the 18th, causing another delay in the contemplated movements. While lying-to in the offing the vessels met the transports from Malta, and the Enterprise returned bringing no intelligence from the expected reënforcement.

On the 24th the squadron stood in toward the town again, with a light breeze from the eastward. At 8 P.M. the Constitution anchored just out of gunshot of the batteries, but it fell calm and the boats of the different vessels were sent to tow the bombards to a position favorable for throwing shells. This was thought to have been effected by 2 A.M., when the two vessels began to throw their bombs, covered by the gunboats. At daylight they all retired without having received a shot in return. Commodore Preble appears to have distrusted the result of this bombardment, the first attempted at night, and there is a reason to think it had but little effect.

The weather proving very fine and the wind favorable, on the 28th Commodore Preble determined to make a more vigorous assault on the town and batteries than any which had preceded it, and his dispositions were taken accordingly. The gunboats and bombards requiring so many men to manage them, the Constitution and the small vessels had been compelled to go into action short of hands in the previous affairs. To obviate this difficulty, the John Adams had been kept before the town, and a portion of her officers and crew, and nearly all her boats, were now put in requisition. Captain Chauncey himself, with about seventy of his people, went on board the flagship, and all the boats of the squadron were hoisted out and manned. The bomb-vessels were crippled and could not be brought into service, a circumstance that probably was of no great consequence on account of the poor ammunition they were compelled to use. These two vessels, with the Scourge, transports, and John Adams, were anchored well off at sea, not being available in the contemplated cannonading.

Everything being prepared, a little after midnight the following gunboats proceeded to the stations, viz., Number One, Captain Somers; Number Two, Lieutenant Gordan; Number Three, Mr. Brooks, master of the Argus; Number Four, Captain Decatur; Number Five, Lieutenant Lawrence; Number Six, Lieutenant Wadsworth; Number Seven, Lieutenant Crane; Number Nine, Lieutenant Thorne. They were divided into two divisions as before, Captain Decatur having become a superior officer, however, by his recent promotion. About 3 A.M. the gunboats advanced close to the rocks at the entrance of the harbor, covered by the Siren, Captain Stewart; Argus, Captain Hull; Vixen, Captain Smith; Nautilus, Lieutenant-Commandant Robinson, and accompanied by all the boats of the squadron. Here they anchored, with springs on their cables, and commenced a cannonade on the enemy's shipping, castle, and town. As soon as the day dawned the Constitution weighed anchor and stood in toward the rocks, under a fire from the batteries, Fort English, and the castle. At this time the enemy's gunboats and galleys, thirteen in number, were closely and warmly engaged with the eight American boats; and the Constitution, ordering the latter to retire by signal, as their ammunition was mostly consumed, delivered a heavy fire of round and grapeshot on the former as she came up. One of the enemy's boats was soon sunk, two were run ashore to prevent them from meeting a similar fate, and the rest retired.

The Constitution now continued to stand on until she had run in within musket-shot of the mole, when she brought up, and opened upon the town, batteries, and castle. Here she lay three-quarters of an hour, pouring in a fierce fire with great effect, until, finding that all the small vessels were out of gunshot, she hauled off. About seven hundred heavy shot were thrown at the enemy in this attack, besides a good many from the chase-guns of the small vessels. The enemy sustained much damage and lost many men. The American brigs and schooners were a good deal injured aloft, as was the Constitution. Although the latter ship was so long within reach of grape, many of which shot struck her, she had not a man hurt. Several of her shrouds, backstays, trusses, springstays, chains, lifts, and a great deal of running rigging were shot away, and yet her hull escaped with very trifling injuries. A boat belonging to the John Adams, under the orders of John Orde Creighton, one of that shipmaster's mates, was sunk by a double-headed shot which killed three men and badly wounded a fourth, but the officer and the rest of the boat's crew were saved.

In this attack a heavy shot from the American gunboats struck the castle, passed through a wall, and rebounding from the opposite side of the room fell within six inches of Captain Bainbridge, who was in bed at the time, and covered him with stones and mortar, from under which he was taken, badly injured, by his officers. More harm was done the town in this attack than in either of the others, the shot appearing to have struck many of the houses. From this time to the close of the month preparations were made to use the bombards again and to renew the cannonading. Another transport arrived from Malta, but without bringing any intelligence of the vessels under the orders of Commodore Barron. On September 3d, everything being ready, at half past two the signal was given for the small vessels to advance. The enemy had improved the time as well as the Americans; they had raised three of their own gunboats that had been sunk in the engagements of August 3d and 28th. These craft were now added to the rest of their flotilla.

The Tripolitans had also changed their mode of fighting. Hitherto, with the exception of the battle of August 3d, their galleys and gunboats had lain either behind the rocks in position to fire over them, or at the openings between them, and they consequently found themselves to leeward of the frigate and small American cruisers, the latter invariably choosing easterly winds to advance with, as such would permit crippled vessels more quickly to retire. On August 3d (the case above excepted), the Turks had been so roughly used when brought to a hand-to-hand struggle—when they evidently expected nothing more than a cannonade—that they were not disposed to venture again outside of the harbor. On September 3d, however, their plan of defence was more judiciously offered. No sooner was it perceived that the American squadron was in motion with the design to attack them than the gunboats and galleys got under way and worked up to windward until they gained a point on the weather side of the harbor, being directly under the fire of Fort English as well as of a new battery that had been erected a little to the westward of the latter.

This disposition of the enemy's force required a corresponding change on the part of the Americans. The bombards were directed to take stations and to commence throwing their shells; while the gunboats in two divisions, commanded as usual by Captains Decatur and Somers and protected by the guns of the brigs and schooners, assailed the enemy's flotilla. This arrangement separated the battle into two distinct parts, leaving the bomb-vessels very much exposed to the fire of the castle, the mole, crown, and other batteries. The Tripolitan gunboats and galleys stood the fire of the American flotilla until the latter had got within musketry-shot, when they retired. The assailants then separated, some of the gunboats following the enemy and pouring in their fire, while the others, with the brigs and schooners, cannonaded Fort English.

In the mean while, perceiving that the bombards were suffering severely from the continuous fire of the guns to which they were exposed, Commodore Preble ran down the Constitution close to the rocks and the bomb-vessels, and brought-to. Here the frigate opened as warm a fire as probably ever came out of a single-decked ship. She was, moreover, in a position where seventy heavy guns could bear upon her. The whole harbor in the vicinity of the town was glittering with the spray of her shot, and each battery, as usual, was silenced as soon as it drew her attention. After throwing more than three hundred round shot, besides grape and cannister, the frigate hauled off, having previously ordered the other vessels to retire from action, by signal. The gunboats in this affair were an hour and fifteen minutes engaged, in which time they threw four hundred round shot besides grape and cannister. Lieutenant Trippe, who had so much distinguished himself and had received so many wounds on August 3d, resumed the command of Number Six, for this occasion. Lieutenant Morris, of the Argus, was in charge of Number Three. As usual, all the small vessels suffered aloft, and the Argus sustained some damage to her hull.

The Constitution was so much exposed in the attack that her escape can only be attributed to the effect of her own heavy fire. It had been found in the previous engagements that so long as she could play upon a battery the Turks could not be kept at its guns; and it was chiefly while she was veering, or tacking, that she suffered. But after making every allowance for the effect of her own cannonading and for the imperfect gunnery of the enemy, it was astonishing that a single frigate could lie exposed to the fire of more than double her own number of available guns, and these, too, mostly of heavier metal and protected by stone walls. On this occasion the frigate was not supported by the gunboats, and was the sole object of the enemy's aim after the bombards had withdrawn.

As might have been expected, the Constitution suffered more in this attack than in any of the previous engagements, though she received nothing larger than grape in her hull. She had three shells through her canvas, one of which rendered the main-topsail temporarily useless. Her sails, standing and running rigging, were also much cut with shot. Captain Chauncey of the John Adams and a party of her officers and crew served in the Constitution again on this day and were of great service. The commander, officers, and crew of the John Adams were always actively employed, although the ship herself could not be brought before the enemy for the want of gun-carriages.

The bombards, being much exposed, suffered accordingly. Number One was so much crippled as to be unable to move without being towed, and was near sinking when she got to the anchorage. Every shroud she had was shot away. Commodore Preble expressed himself satisfied with the good conduct of every man in the squadron. All the vessels appeared to have been well handled and efficient in their several stations.

While Commodore Preble was thus actively employed in carrying on the war against the enemy—this last attack being the fifth made on the town within a month—he had been meditating another manœuvre, and was now ready to put it into execution. The ketch Intrepid, which had been employed by Decatur in burning the Philadelphia, was still in the squadron, having been used of late as a transport between Tripoli and Malta. This vessel had been converted into an "infernal," or, to use more intelligible terms, she had been fitted out as a floating mine, with the intention of sending her into the harbor of Tripoli, to explode among the enemy's cruisers. Such dangerous work could be confided to none but officers and men of known coolness and courage, of perfect self-possession and of tried spirit. Captain Somers, who had commanded one division of the gunboats in the different attacks on the town in a manner to excite the respect of all who witnessed his conduct, volunteered to take charge of this enterprise; and Lieutenant Wadsworth, of the Constitution, an officer of great merit, offered himself as the second in command.

When the Intrepid was last seen by the naked eye she was not a musket-shot from the mole, standing directly for the harbor. One officer on board the nearest vessel, the Nautilus, is said, however, to have never lost sight of her with a night-glass, but even he could distinguish no more than her dim outlines. There was a vague rumor that she touched on the rocks, though it did not appear to rest on sufficient authority to be entitled to much credit. To the last moment she appeared to be advancing. About that time the batteries began to fire. Their shots are said to have been directed toward every point where an enemy might be expected, and it is not improbable that some were aimed at the ketch.

The period between the time when the Intrepid was last seen and that when most of those who watched without the rocks learned her fate, was not long. This was an interval of intense, almost of breathless expectation; and it was interrupted only by the flashes and the roar of the enemy's guns. Various reports exist of what those who gazed into the gloom beheld or fancied they beheld; but one melancholy fact alone would seem to be beyond contradiction. A fierce and sudden light illuminated the scene; a torrent of fire streamed upward, and a concussion followed that made the cruisers in the offing tremble from their trucks to their keels. This sudden blaze of light was followed by a darkness of twofold intensity, and the guns of the battery became mute as if annihilated. Numerous shells were seen in the air, and some of them descended on the rocks where they were heard to fall. The fuses were burning and a few exploded, but much the greater part were extinguished in the water. The mast, too, had risen perpendicularly with its rigging and canvas blazing, but the descent was veiled in the blackness that followed.

So sudden and tremendous was the eruption, and so intense the darkness which succeeded, that it was not possible to ascertain the precise position of the ketch at the moment. In the glaring but fleeting light no person could say that he had noted more than the material circumstance that the Intrepid had not reached the point at which she aimed. The shells had not spread far, and those which fell on the rocks were so many proofs of this important fact. There was nothing else to indicate the precise spot where the ketch exploded. A few cries arose from the town, but the deep silence that followed was more eloquent than any clamor. The whole of Tripoli was like a city of tombs.

If every eye had been watchful previous to the explosion, every eye now became doubly vigilant to discover the retreating boats. Men got over the sides of the vessel, holding lights and placing their ears near the water in the hope of detecting the sounds of even muffled oars; and often it was fancied that the gallant adventurers were near. They never reappeared. Hour after hour went by until hope became exhausted. Occasionally a rocket gleamed in the darkness, or a sullen gun was heard from the frigate as a signal to the boats; but the eyes that should have seen the first were sightless, and the sound of the last fell on the ears of the dead.

The three vessels assigned to that service hovered around the harbor until the sun rose; but few traces of the Intrepid, and nothing of her devoted crew, could be discovered. The wreck of the mast lay on the rocks near the western entrance, and here and there a fragment was visible near it. One of the largest of the enemy's gunboats was missing, and it was observed that two others which appeared to be shattered were being hauled upon the shore. The three that had lain across the entrance had disappeared. It was erroneously thought that the castle had sustained some injury from the concussion, but on the whole, the Americans were left with the melancholy certainty of having met with a serious loss without obtaining any commensurate advantage.

A sad and solemn mystery, after all our conjectures, must forever veil the fate of those fearless officers and their hardy followers. In whatever light we view the affair they were the victims of that self-devotion which causes the seaman and soldier to hold his life in his hand when the honor or interest of his country demands the sacrifice. The name of Somers has passed into a battle-cry in the American marine, while those of Wadsworth and Israel are associated with all that can ennoble intrepidity, coolness, and daring.

The war, in one sense, terminated with this scene of sublime destruction. Commodore Preble had consumed so much of his powder in the previous attacks that it was no longer in his power to cannonade; and the season was fast getting to be dangerous to remain on that exposed coast. The country fully appreciated the services of Commodore Preble. He had united caution and daring in a way to denote the highest military qualities; and his success in general had been in proportion. The attack of the Intrepid, the only material failure in any of his enterprises, was well arranged, and had it succeeded it would probably have brought peace in twenty-four hours. As it was, the pacha was well enough disposed to treat, though he seems to have entered into some calculations in the way of money that induced him to hope that the Americans would yet reduce their policy to the level of his own, and prefer paying ransom to maintaining cruisers so far from home. Commodore Preble, and all the officers and men under his orders, received the thanks of Congress, and a gold medal was bestowed on him. By the same resolution Congress expressed the sympathy of the nation in behalf of the relatives of Captain Richard Somers, Lieutenants Henry Wadsworth, James Decatur, James R. Caldwell, Joseph Israel, and John Sword Dorsey, midshipman, the officers killed off Tripoli.

Negotiations for peace now commenced in earnest, Mr. Lear having arrived off Tripoli for that purpose in the Essex, Captain Barron. After the usual intrigues, delays, and prevarications, a treaty was signed on June 3, 1805. By this treaty, no tribute was to be paid in future, but the sum of sixty thousand dollars was given by America for the ransom of the remaining prisoners after exchanging the Tripolitans in her power man for man.

Thus terminated the war with Tripoli after a duration of four years. It is probable that the United States would have retained in service some officers and would have kept up a small force had not this contest occurred; but its influence on the fortunes and character of the navy was incalculable. It saved the first, in a degree at least, and it may be said to have formed the last.

CORONATION OF NAPOLEON

A.D. 1804

WILLIAM HAZLITT

The Battle of the Nile left Napoleon and his army practically imprisoned in Egypt, held there by British ships. In their absence affairs in Europe went badly for France. A fresh coalition was formed against her in which Russia joined, and Suvaroff, the great Russian General, drove the French from Italy. Napoleon, leaving his army, slipped back secretly to France and was welcomed with intense enthusiasm. He at once undertook a revolution of his own. Appealing to his old comrades of the army, he declared the members of the Government inefficient and turned them out of office. A new Constitution was established and Bonaparte was made " First Consul," an office that practically centred all power in his own hands (1799).

From this time the Republic was practically at an end, Napoleon was dictator, though the empty forms of republicanism continued for another five years. Under the First Consul's direction the French soldiers reëstablished their military supremacy. General Moreau won victory after victory in Germany and finally crushed the Austrians at Hohenlinden. Napoleon himself led an army over the Alps, and surprised and overthrew the Austrians in Italy. He dictated a peace in which all Europe joined (1801). Even England for a time abandoned the strife, though she soon renewed it. Napoleon seized the brief respite to establish extensive internal reforms in France and to consolidate his own power. The consulship had first been given to him for ten years, then it was made a life office; and in 1804 the conqueror abandoned the last pretence of republicanism and had himself elected hereditary Emperor of the French.

Hitherto there had never been more than two emperors, those of Germany whose title had descended through a thousand years and who were in some sort heirs of the Empire of Western Rome, and more recently the emperors of Russia, claiming to carry on the ancient Roman Empire of the East. The empire of Germany had practically ceased to exist, crushed under Napoleon's blows. His assumption of this title was a suggestion to all Europe of his design to ascend its throne and become the successor of Charlemagne as ruler of a reunited Frankish race.

R EPEATED attempts made against the life of the First Consul gave an excuse for following up the design that had been for some time agitated of raising him to the imperial throne and making the dignity hereditary in his family. Not that indeed this

76

would secure him from personal danger, though it is true that
"there's a divinity doth hedge a king"; but it lessened the temptation to the enterprise and allayed a part of the public disquie-
tude by providing a successor.   All or the greater part were satisfied—either from reason, indolence, or the fear of worse—with
what had been gained by the Revolution, and did not wish to
see it launch out again from the port in which it had taken shelter to seek the perils of new storms and quicksands.   If prudence
had some share in this measure, there can be little doubt that
vanity and cowardice had theirs also—or that there was a lurk-
ing desire to conform to the Gothic dialect of civilized Europe in
forms of speech and titles, and to adorn the steel arm of the Republic with embroidered drapery and gold tissue. The imitation,
though probably not without its effect,[1] would look more like a
burlesque to those whom it was intended to please, and could
hardly flatter the just pride of those by whom it was undertaken.

The old Republican party made some stand: the Emigrants
showed great zeal for it, partly real, partly affected. Fouché
canvassed the Senate and the men of the Revolution, and was
soon placed in consequence at the head of the police, which was
restored, as it was thought that fresh intrigues might break out on
the occasion.   The army gave the first impulse, as was but natural; to them the change of style from *Imperator* to "Emperor"
was but slight.   All ranks and classes followed when the example
was once set: the most obscure hamlets joined in the addresses;
the First Consul received wagonloads of them. A register for
the reception of votes for or against the question was opened in
every parish in France—from Antwerp to Perpignan, from Brest
to Mont Cenis.

The *proces-verbal* of all these votes was laid up in the archives
of the Senate, who went in a body from Paris to St. Cloud to present it to the First Consul.   The Second Consul Cambaceres
read a speech, concluding with a summary of the number of
votes; whereupon he in a loud voice proclaimed Napoleon Bonaparte Emperor of the French.   The senators, placed in a line
facing him, vied with each other in repeating " *Vive l'Empereur!* "

---

[1] For instance, would the Emperor of Austria have married his daughter to Bonaparte if he had been only First Consul ?—ED.

and returned with all the outward signs of joy to Paris, where people were already writing epitaphs on the Republic. Happy they whom epitaphs on the dead console for the loss of them! This was the time, if ever, when they ought to have opposed him, and prescribed limits to his power and ambition, and not when he returned weather-beaten and winter-flawed from Russia. But it was more in character for these persons to cringe when spirit was wanted, and to show it when it was fatal to him and to themselves.

Thus then the First Consul became emperor by a majority of two millions some hundred thousand votes, to a few hundreds. The number of votes is complained of by some persons as too small. Probably they may think that if the same number had been against the measure instead of being for it, this would have conferred a right as being in opposition to and in contempt of the choice of the people. What other candidate was there that would have got a hundred? What other competitor could indeed have come forward on the score of merit? *Detur optimo.* Birth there was not; but birth supersedes both choice and merit. The day after the inauguration, Bonaparte received the constituted bodies, the learned corporations, etc. The only strife was who should bow the knee the lowest to the new-risen sun. The troops while taking the oath rent the air with shouts of enthusiasm. The succeeding days witnessed the nomination of the new dignitaries, marshals, and all the usual appendages of a throne, as well with reference to the military appointments as to the high offices of the crown. On July 14th the first distribution of the crosses of the Legion of Honor took place; and Napoleon set out for Boulogne to review the troops stationed in the neighborhood and distribute the decorations of the Legion of Honor among them, which thenceforth were substituted for weapons of honor, which had been previously awarded ever since the first war in Italy.

The Emperor arrogated nothing to himself in consequence of the change in his situation. He had assumed the mock-majesty of kings, and had taken his station among the lords of the earth; but he was still himself, and his throne still stood afar off in the field of battle. He appeared little more conscious of his regal style and title than if he had put on a masquerade dress the evening before, of which if he was not ashamed—as it was a thing of custom—he had no reason to be proud; and he applied himself to his different avocations with the same zeal and activity as if nothing extraordinary had happened. He thought much less, it was evident, of all these new honors than of the prosecution of his operations at Boulogne, on which he labored incessantly. The remoteness or doubtfulness of success did not relax his efforts; having once determined on the attempt, all the intermediate exertions between the will and its accomplishment with him went for nothing, any more than so much holiday recreation. Something more of the *vis inertiæ* would have allayed this inordinate importunity of voluntary power, and led to greater security and repose.

From Boulogne the Emperor went a second time to Belgium, where the Empress joined him; they occupied the palace of Lacken near Brussels, which had formerly belonged to the Archduke Charles. He this time extended his journey to the Rhine; and from Mainz he despatched General Caffarelli to Rome to arrange the visit of the Pope (Pius VII) to Paris. It was from Mainz likewise he sent orders for the departure of the Toulon and Rochefort squadrons as a first step toward carrying into effect the invasion of England; but owing to unforeseen circumstances, it was winter before they sailed.

Bonaparte returned from this tour at the end of October; his attention was engaged during the month of November with the preparations for the coronation, the Pope having set out from Rome for the purpose of performing the ceremony. The court was ordered to Fontainebleau to receive him, the palace there, which had fallen into ruins, having been repaired and newly fitted up by Napoleon. He went to meet the Pope at Nemours; and to avoid formality, the pretext of a hunting party was made use of, the Emperor coming on horseback and in a hunting dress, with his retinue, to the top of the hill, where the meeting took place. The Pope's carriage drawing up, he got out at the left door in his white costume; the ground was dirty, and he did not like to tread upon it with his white silk shoes, but he was at last obliged to do so. Napoleon alighted from his horse to receive him. They embraced. The Emperor's carriage had been driven up and advanced a few paces, as if by accident; but men were posted to hold the two doors open, and at the moment of getting in, the

Emperor took the right door, and an officer of the court handed the Pope to the left, so that they entered the carriage by the two doors at the same moment.   The Emperor naturally seated himself on the right; and this first step decided without negotiation upon the etiquette to be observed during the whole time of the Pope's stay in Paris.

This interview and Bonaparte's behavior was the very highest act and acme of audacity.   It is comparable to nothing but the meeting of Priam and Achilles; or a joining of hands between the youth and the old age of the world.   If Pope Pius VII represented the decay of ancient superstition, Bonaparte represented the high and palmy state of modern opinion; yet not insulting over, but propping the fall of the first.   There were concessions on both sides, from the oldest power on earth to the newest, which in its turn asserted precedence for the strongest.   In point of birth there was no difference, for theocracy stoops to the dregs of earth, as democracy springs from it; but the Pope bowed his head from the ruins of the longest-established authority in Christendom; Bonaparte had himself raised the platform of personal elevation on which he stood to meet him.   To us the condescension may seem all on one side, the presumption on the other; but history is a long and gradual ascent, where great actions and characters in time leave borrowed pomp behind and at an immeasurable distance below them!   After resting at Fontainebleau, the Emperor returned to Paris; the Pope, who set out first and was received with sovereign honors on the road, was escorted to the Tuileries and was treated the whole time of his residence there as if at home.   The novelty of his situation and appearance at Paris excited general interest and curiosity; and his deportment, besides its flowing from the natural mildness of his character, was marked by that fine tact and sense of propriety which the air of the ancient mistress of the world is known to inspire.   Manners have there half maintained the empire which opinion had lost. The Pope was flattered by his reception and the sentiments of respect and good-will his presence seemed everywhere to create, and gave very gracious audiences to the religious corporations which were presented to him and which were at this time but few in number.   To meet this imposing display of pomp and ceremony, Bonaparte was in a manner obliged to oppose a host of ecclesiastics, of old and new nobility, and to draw the lines of form and etiquette closer round him, so as to make the access of old friends and opinions less easy. This effect of the new forms and ceremonies was at least complained of; but if they, thus early, kept out his friends, they did not in the end keep out his enemies.

The day fixed for the coronation arrived. It was December 2, 1804. Notwithstanding the unfavorableness of the weather, the assemblage of the deputations from all the departments, from all the chief towns, and of all the regiments of the army, joined to all the public functionaries of France, to all the generals, and to the whole population of the capital, presented a fine and imposing sight. The interior of the church of Notre Dame had been magnificently embellished; galleries and pews erected for the occasion were thronged with a prodigious concourse of spectators. The imperial throne was placed at one end of the nave, on a very elevated platform; that of the Pope was in the choir, beside the high altar. The Pope set out from the Tuileries, preceded by his chamberlain on an ass—which there was some difficulty in procuring at the moment—who kept his countenance with an admirable gravity through the crowds of observers that lined the streets. The Pope, arriving at the archiepiscopal palace, repaired to the choir of the cathedral by a private entrance.

The Emperor set out with the Empress by the Carrousel. In getting into the carriage, which was open all round and without panels, they at first seated themselves with their backs to the horses, a mistake which, though instantly rectified, was remarked as ominous, and it had all the ominousness which hangs over new power or custom. The procession passed along the Rue St. Honoré to that of the Lombards, then to the Pont au Change, the Palace of Justice, the court of Notre Dame, and the entrance to the archiepiscopal palace. Here rooms were prepared for the whole of the attendants, some of whom appeared dressed in their civil costumes, others in full uniform. On the outside of the church had been erected a long wooden gallery from the archbishop's palace to the entrance of the church. By this gallery came the Emperor's retinue, which presented a truly magnificent sight. They had taunted us with our simplicity and homeliness: Well, then! here was the answer to it.

The procession was led by the already numerous body of courtiers; next came the marshals of the empire, wearing their badges of honor; then the dignitaries and high officers of the crown; and lastly, the Emperor, in a gorgeous state dress. At the moment of his entering the cathedral there was a simultaneous shout, which resembled one vast explosion of " *Vive l'Empereur!* " The immense quantity of figures to be seen on each side of so vast an edifice formed a tapestry of the most striking kind. The procession passed along the middle of the nave, and arrived at the choir facing the high altar. This part of the spectacle was not the least imposing: the galleries round the choir were filled with the handsomest women which France could boast, and most of whom surpassed in the lustre of their beauty that of the rich jewels with which they were adorned.

His holiness then went to meet the Emperor at a desk which had been placed in the middle of the choir; there was another on one side for the Empress. After saying a short prayer there, they returned, and seated themselves on the throne at the end of the church facing the choir: there they heard mass, which was said by the Pope. They went to make the offering, and came back; they then descended from the platform of the throne and walked in procession to receive the holy unction. The Emperor and Empress, on reaching the choir, replaced themselves at their desks, where the Pope performed the ceremony. He presented the crown to the Emperor, who received it, put it himself upon his own head, took it off, placed it on that of the Empress, removed it again, and laid it on the cushion where it was at first.

A smaller crown was immediately put upon the head of the Empress, who, being surrounded by her ladies, everything was done so quickly that nobody was aware of the substitution that had taken place. The procession moved back to the platform. There the Emperor heard *Te Deum:* the Pope himself went thither at the conclusion of the service, as if to say, *Ite, missa est!* The Testament was presented to the Emperor, who took off his glove and pronounced the oath with his hand upon the sacred book. He went back to the episcopal palace the same way that he had come, and entered his carriage. The ceremony was long; the day cold and wet; the Emperor seemed impatient and uneasy a great part of the time, and it was dusk before the cavalcade reached the Tuileries, whither it returned by the Rue St. Martin, the Boulevards, the Place de la Concorde and the Pont-Tournant. The distribution of the eagles took place some days afterward. Though the weather was still unfavorable the throng was prodigious and the enthusiasm at its height; the citizens as well as the soldiers burst into long and repeated acclamations as those warlike bands received from the hands of their renowned leader —not less a soldier for being a king—the pledges of many a well-fought field.

The Cisalpine Republic at the same time underwent a change which was easily managed. The Emperor was surrounded by men, who spared him the trouble of expressing the same wish twice, though many of them afterward pretended that they had sturdily disputed every word and syllable of it, opposing a shadow of resistance to fallen power instead of the substance to the abuse of it, and finding no medium between factious divisions and servile adulation. Lombardy was erected into a kingdom, and the Emperor put the iron crown of Charlemagne upon his head.

THE LEWIS AND CLARK EXPEDITION

A.D. 1804

JAMES DAVIE BUTLER   ROBERT SOUTHEY

More and more, as American history is rewritten, importance is added to this great work of discovery at the opening of the nineteenth century. Next to the purchase of the vast territory called Louisiana, which more than doubled the area of the United States, the most memorable act of President Jefferson was the sending of Meriwether Lewis and William Clark up the Missouri to the great Northwest "where rolls the Oregon" (Columbia).

These explorers were the first to carry the American flag across the continent. In the very year of the Louisiana Purchase (1803) this enterprise, forerunning "the winning of the West," was set on foot. It is difficult to realize the tremendous obstacles and hazards attending its prosecution. For over a year no tidings of the explorers reached the country, and at length they were given up as lost. But their successful work "was the real discovery of the Great West, and indeed of America, to an extent beyond the accomplishment of any similar endeavor before or since."

Lewis and Clark, according to their instructions, kept journals of the expedition, and these proved to be of the greatest value, not only for official purposes, but also for the use of historians. In this work the two commanders were aided by some of their subordinates. The notebooks, as soon as filled, were soldered in water-tight cases, and by such careful preservation were brought back without the loss of a word.

Southey, in England, was an interested student of this expedition and of the explorers' journals, of which he wrote and published an account. He quotes the journals frequently in his appreciative narration, given here in connection with that of James D. Butler, a recent American writer on the subject.

JAMES DAVIE BUTLER

L EWIS and Clark were the first men to cross the continent in our zone, the truly golden zone. A dozen years before them Mackenzie had crossed in British dominions far north, but settlements are even now sparse in that parallel. Still earlier had Mexicans traversed the narrowing continent from the Gulf to

the Pacific, but seemed to find little worth discovery. It was
otherwise in the zone penetrated by Lewis and Clark. There development began at once, and is now nowhere surpassed. Along
their route ten States, with a census, in 1890, of eight and a half
millions, have arisen in the wilderness.

These millions, and more yet unborn, must betake themselves
to Lewis and Clark as the discoverers of their dwelling-places,
as authors of their geographical names, as describers of their
aborigines, as well as of native plants, animals, and peculiarities.
In all these States the writings of Lewis and Clark must be monu-
mental. In disputes about the ownership of Oregon, when it
was urged that the United States could claim only the mouth of
the Columbia because Captain Gray [1] had discovered nothing
more, while a British vessel had been first to sail a hundred
miles up the river, it was answered that the two American captains (Lewis and Clark) had explored it ten times as far. But
they did very much more. They were the first that ever burst
through the Rocky Mountain barrier, and they made known
practicable passes. They first opened the gates of the Pacific
slope, and hence filled the valley of the Columbia with Americans. We thus obtained possession, which is proverbially nine
points, and that while diplomacy was still vacillating.

The credit of our Great Western discovery is due to Jefferson, though he never crossed the Alleghanies. When Columbus
saw the Orinoco rushing into the ocean with irrepressible power
and volume, he knew that he had anchored at the mouth of a continental river. So Jefferson, ascertaining that the Missouri,
though called a branch, at once changed the color and character
of the Mississippi, felt sure that whoever followed it would reach
the innermost recesses of our America. Learning afterward that
Captain Gray had pushed into the mouth of the Columbia only
after nine days' breasting its outward current, he deemed that
river a worthy counterpart of the Missouri, and was convinced
that their headwaters could not be far apart in longitude. In-
augurated in 1801, before his first Presidential term was half
over he had obtained, as a sort of secret-service fund, the small
sum which sufficed to fit out the expedition. He had also se-

[1] Captain Robert Gray, a Boston trader, visited the mouth of the Columbia—which he so named after one of his vessels—in 1792.—ED.

lected his private secretary, Lewis, for its head, and put him in a course of special training. But the actual voyage up the Missouri, purchased April 30, 1803,[1] was not begun till the middle of May, 1804.

Forty-five persons in three boats composed the party. They were good watermen, but navigation was arduous, the river extremely rapid, changeful in channel, and full of eddies and sawyers. The last white settlement was passed within a week, but some meat and corn could be bought of Indians, though delays were necessary for parleys and even councils with them. Others were occasioned by hunting parties, who were kept out in quest of game.

After one hundred seventy-one days the year's advance ended with October, for the river was ready to freeze. The distance upstream they reckoned at sixteen hundred miles, or little more than nine miles a day, a journey now made by railroad in forty-four hours. But it is not likely that any other men could then have laid more miles behind them. In addition to detentions already enumerated, rudders, masts, oars were often broken, and replacing them cost time; boats were swamped or overset, or could be forced onward only with tow-lines.

Winter quarters were thirty miles above the Bismarck of our day. Here they were frozen in about five months. The huts they built, and abundant fuel, kept them warm. Thanks to their hunters and Indian traffic, food was seldom scarce. Officials of the Hudson's Bay Company—who had a post within a week's journey—and many inquisitive natives paid them visits. From all these it was their tireless endeavor to learn everything possible concerning the great unknown of the river beyond. Scarcely one could tell about distant places from personal observation, but some second-hand reports were afterward proved strangely accurate, even as to the Great Falls, which turned out to be one thousand miles away. It was not long, however, before they learned that the wife of Chaboneau, whom they had taken as a local interpreter, was a captive whose birth had been in the Rocky Mountains. She, named the "Bird-Woman," was the only person discoverable after a winter's search who could by any possibility serve them as interpreter and guide among the

[1] Included in the "Louisiana Purchase," of that date.—ED.

unknown tongues and labyrinthine fastnesses which they must encounter.

Early in April, 1805, the explorers, now numbering thirty-two, again began to urge their boats up the river, for their last year's labors had brought them no more than half-way to their first objective, its source. No more Indian purveyors or pilots: their own rifles were the sole reliance for food. Many a wigwam, but no Indian, was espied for four months and four days after they left their winter camp. It was through the great Lone Island that they groped their dark and perilous way. In twenty days after the spring start they arrived at the Yellowstone, and in thirty more they first sighted the Rocky Mountains. Making the portage at the Great Falls had cost them a month of vexatious delay. Rowing on another month brought them on August 12th to a point where one of the men stood with one foot each side of the rivulet, and "thanked God that he had lived to bestride the Missouri, heretofore deemed endless."

They dragged their canoes, however, up the rivulet for five days longer. It was four hundred sixty days since they had left the mouth of the river, and their mileage on its waters had been three thousand ninety-six. A mile farther they stood on the Great Divide, and drank of springs which sent their water to the Pacific. But meantime they had been ready to starve in the mountains. Their hunters were of the best, but they found no game; buffaloes had gone down into the lowlands, the birds of heaven had fled, and edible roots were mostly unknown to them. For more than four months they had looked, and lo! there was no man. It was not till August 13th that, surprising a squaw so encumbered with pappooses that she could not escape, and winning her heart by the gift of a looking-glass and painting her cheeks, they formed friendship with her nation, one of whose chiefs proved to be a brother of their Bird-Woman. Horses were about all they could obtain of these natives, streams were too full of rapids to be navigable, or no timber fit for canoes was within reach. So the party, subsisting on horse-flesh, and afterward on dog-meat, toiled on along one of the worst possible routes. Nor was it till October 7th that they were able to embark, in logs they had burned hollow, upon a branch of the Columbia, which, after manifold portages and perils, bore them to its mouth and the goal of their pilgrimage, late in November. Its distance from the starting-point, according to their estimate, was forty-one hundred thirty-four miles.

A winter of disappointment followed, for no whaler or fur-trader appeared to supply the wayfarers with food or clothing or trinkets for the purchase of necessaries on the homeward journey. Game was so scarce that it is possible they would have starved had not a whale been stranded near them—sent, they said, not as to Jonah, to swallow him, but for them to swallow.

In the spring of 1806, when they turned their despairing faces away from the Pacific, all the beads and gewgaws for presents to savages and procuring supplies during their home-stretch to the Mississippi might have been tied up in two handkerchiefs, if they had had any such articles. Their last tobacco had been consecrated to the celebration of Christmas, and the last whiskey had been drunk on the previous Fourth of July. All roads homeward are down-hill. A forced march of six months brought the discoverers from the ocean to St. Louis, September 23, 1806, though they were obliged to halt a month for mountain snows to melt. From first to last not a man had perished through accident, wild men, or wild beasts, and only one through sickness.

Many an episode in this eventful transcontinental march and countermarch will hereafter glorify with romantic associations islands, rivers, rocks, cañons, and mountains all along its track. Among these none can be more touching than the story of Bird-Woman, her divination of routes, her courage when men quailed, her reunion with a long-lost brother, her spreading as good a table with bones as others could with meat, her morsel of bread for an invalid benefactor, her presence with her infant attesting to savages that the expedition could not be hostile. But when bounties in land and money were granted to others, she was unthought of. Statues of her, however, must yet be reared by grateful dwellers in lands she laid open for their happy homes.

ROBERT SOUTHEY

On April 7, 1805, the adventurers renewed their journey, sending off, at the same time, their barge with despatches to the Government, and the subjects in natural history which they had collected as a present for the President. The party now consisted of thirty-two persons. A French interpreter, by name Chaboneau, had been engaged and it was hoped that his wife would be equally useful, for she was a Snake Indian who had been taken in war by the Minnetarees and sold to her present husband. They went in two large pirogues and six small canoes. The squaw was found serviceable in a way which had not been foreseen. When they stopped for dinner she found out the holes of the mice, opened them with a large stick, and supplied the party with wild artichokes of the Jerusalem (*girasole*) kind, which these creatures hoard in great quantities.

Summer comes close upon the skirts of winter in these climates; five days after they set out several of the men threw off all their clothes, retaining only something round the waist—a fashion which was found more convenient, because the river was so shallow that, in some places, they were obliged to wade. The fashion must have been convenient to the mosquitoes also, who now began to annoy them. On the 14th they reached a part of the river beyond which no white man had ever been. The bluffs along the river bore traces of fire, and, in some places, were actually burning, throwing out much smoke with a strong sulphureous smell; they are composed of a mixture of yellow clay and sand with many horizontal strata of carbonated wood resembling pit-coal, from one to five feet in depth, and scattered through the bluff at different elevations, some as high as eighty feet above the water; great quantities of pumice-stone and lava, or rather earth which seemed to have been boiled and then hardened by exposure, being seen in many parts of the hills where they were broken and washed down into gullies by the rain and melting snow.

Captain Clark says in his note-book that there is reason to believe that the strata of coal in the hills cause the fire. It is the fault of the Government that there was no naturalist in this expedition, and it is to the credit of the officers who conducted it that they should have examined so carefully all they saw, and recorded it as it appeared to them. "We found several stones," they say, "which seemed to have been wood, first carbonated and then petrified by the action of the waters of the Missouri, which has the same effect on many vegetable substances." Patrick Gass saw part of a log quite petrified, and of which good whetstones, or hones, could be made. Salt also is abundantly produced on the surface of the earth; many of the streams which come from the hills were strongly impregnated with it. Up the White-earth River the salts were so abundant as, in some places, to whiten the ground. The party were now tormented with sore eyes occasioned by sand, which was driven from the sandbars in such clouds as often to hide from them the view of the opposite bank. The particles of this sand are so fine and light that it floats for miles in the air like a column of thick smoke and penetrates everything. "We were compelled," says the writer, "to eat, drink, and breathe it very copiously."

On April 26th they reached the Yellowstone River, which they learned from the Indians rises in the Rocky Mountains near the Missouri and the Platte, and is navigable for canoes almost to its head.

The country thus far had presented few striking features. From the mouth of the Missouri to the Platte, about six hundred miles, it is described as very rich land with a sufficient quantity of timber; for fifteen hundred miles, "good second-rate land," rather hilly than level; cottonwood and willows along the course of the streams; the upland almost entirely without trees and spreading into boundless prairies. There are Indian trails along the river, but they do not always follow its windings. There are also paths made by the buffaloes and other animals; the buffalo trail being at least ten feet wide. The appearances of fire had now ceased; the salts were still seen in the ravines and at the base of the small hills.

The general width of the river was now about two hundred yards; it had become very rapid with a very perceptible descent; the shoals were more frequent and the rocky points at the mouth of the gullies more difficult to pass. The tow-line, whenever the banks would permit it, had been found the safest mode of ascending the stream, and the most expeditious, except under a sail with a steady breeze; but this seems not to have been foreseen, or not to have been properly provided for, as their ropes were nearly all made of elk-skin, and much worn and rotted by exposure to the weather. At this time everything depended upon them.

"We are sometimes," says the journal, "obliged to steer the canoes through the points of sharp rocks rising a few inches above the surface of the water, and so near to each other that, if our ropes gave way, the force of the current drives the sides of the canoe against them, and must inevitably upset them or dash them to pieces. Several times they gave way, but fortunately always in places where there was room for the canoe to turn without striking the rock; yet with all our precautions it was with infinite risk and labor that we passed these points."

To add to these difficulties there fell a heavy rain, which made the bank so slippery that the men who drew the towing-lines could scarcely keep their footing, and the mud was so adhesive that they could not wear their moccasins. Part of the time they were obliged to be up to their armpits in the cold water, and frequently to walk over sharp fragments of rock; yet painful as this toil was they bore it not merely with patience, but with cheerfulness. Earth and stones also were falling from the high bluffs, so that it was dangerous to pass under them. The difficulties of this part of the way were soon rewarded by some of the most extraordinary scenery which any travellers have ever described. The description may best be given in the words of the journal:

"We came to a high wall of black rock, rising from the water's edge on the south, above the cliffs of the river; this continued about a quarter of a mile, and was succeeded by a high open plain, till, three miles farther, a second wall, two hundred feet high, rose on the same side. Three miles farther, a wall of the same kind, about two hundred feet high and twelve in thickness, appeared to the north. These hills and river-cliffs exhibit a most extraordinary and romantic appearance. They rise in most places almost perpendicularly from the water to the height of between two hundred and three hundred feet, and are formed of very white sandstone, so soft as to yield readily to the impression of water: in the upper part of which lie imbedded two or three horizontal strata of white free-stone, insensible to the rain, and on the top is a dark rich loam, which forms a gradually ascending plain, from a mile to a mile and a half in extent, when the hills again rise abruptly to the height of about three hundred feet more.

"In trickling down the cliffs, the water has worn the soft sandstone into a thousand grotesque figures, among which, with a little fancy, may be discerned elegant ranges of freestone buildings, with columns variously sculptured and supporting long and elegant galleries, while the parapets are adorned with statuary. On a nearer approach they represent every form of elegant ruins; columns, some with pedestals and capitals entire; others mutilated and prostrate; some rising pyramidally over each other till they terminate in a sharp point. These are varied by niches, alcoves, and the customary appearance of desolated magnificence. The illusion was increased by the number of martins, which had built their globular nests in the niches and hovered over these columns as in our cities they are accustomed to frequent large stone structures.

"As we advance there seems no end of the visionary enchantment which surrounds us. In the midst of this fantastic scenery are vast ranges of walls, which seem the productions of art, so regular is the workmanship: they rise perpendicularly from the river, sometimes to the height of one hundred feet, varying in thickness from one to twelve feet, being equally as broad at the top as below. The stones of which they are formed are black, thick, and durable, and composed of a large portion of earth, intermixed and cemented with a small quantity of sand and a considerable portion of talc or quartz. These stones are almost invariably regular parallelopipeds of unequal size in the wall, but equally deep, and laid regularly in ranges over each other like bricks, each breaking and covering the interstice of the two on which it rests; but though the perpendicular interstice be destroyed, the horizontal one extends entirely through the whole work. The stones too are proportioned to the thickness of the wall in which they are employed, being largest in the thickest walls. The thinner walls are composed of a single depth of the parallelopiped, while the thicker ones consist of two or more depths. These walls pass the river at several places, rising from the water's edge much above the sandstone bluffs, which they seem to penetrate; thence they cross in a straight line on either side of the river to the plains, over which they tower to the height of from ten to seventy feet, until they lose themselves in the second range of hills. Sometimes they run parallel in several ranges near to each other; sometimes intersect each other at right angles, and have the appearance of ancient houses or gardens." Gass also in his brief notes expresses his admiration of this scenery. "The cliffs," he says, "seem as if built by the hand of man, and are so numerous that they appear like the ruins of an ancient city."

On the third day after this remarkable pass they came to a fork in the river which completely perplexed them; for though the Minnetarees had, as they thought, minutely described the course of the Missouri, or the "Ahmateahza" as they called it, they had said nothing of this junction. The north branch was two hundred yards wide, the south three hundred seventy, but the north was the deepest stream; its waters had that muddiness which the Missouri bears into the Mississippi, and its "air and character," in Captain Clark's phrase, so much resembled the Missouri that almost all the men believed that was the course to be pursued. The two leaders thought otherwise; it was known that the Missouri came from the mountains, and they reasoned that this stream would probably be the clearest of the two. There was too much at stake to allow of their proceeding upon any uncertainty.

Captain Lewis, therefore, with six men, went to explore the northern river, while Captain Clark and five others went upon the same errand up the south; the remainder of the party were left to enjoy needful rest; their feet had been much bruised and mangled during the last days, and this respite came seasonably. The former having gone about three-score miles were convinced that the stream came too far from the north for their route to the Pacific. On their return they were exposed to the greatest dangers. The rain had made the bluffs slippery, which as they went gave them risky footing; at a narrow pass some thirty yards in length Captain Lewis slipped, and had he not recovered himself quickly, must have fallen over a precipice of about ninety feet, into the river. One of the men behind him lost his footing about the middle of the pass, and slipped to the verge, where he lay on his face, his right arm and leg over the precipice, while with the other arm and leg he was with difficulty holding on. Captain Lewis, concealing the fear which he felt, told him he was in no danger, and bade him take his knife out of his belt with his right hand, and dig a hole in the side of the bluff for his right foot. With great presence of mind the man did this, and thus raised himself on his knees; he was then directed to take off his moccasins and come forward on hands and knees, holding the knife in one hand and the rifle in the other. In this manner he crawled till he reached a secure spot. The other men who had not attempted this pass were ordered to return and wade the river at the foot of the bluff, where they found it breast-high; and the party finding that any difficulty was preferable to the danger of crossing the slippery heights, continued to proceed along the bottom, sometimes in the mud of the low grounds, sometimes up to their arms in the water, and, when it became too deep to wade, they cut footholds with their knives in the sides of the bank.

Captain Clark meantime having examined the south branch as far as forty-five miles in a straight line, was satisfied that this was the Missouri; the Indians had told him that the falls lay a little to the south of sunset from them, and that the river was nearly transparent at that place. He thought also that if this, which was the wider stream, was not the Missouri, it was scarcely possible that the Indians should not have mentioned it. But all the men were of a contrary opinion; one of them, who was an experienced waterman on this river, gave it as his decided opinion that the north fork was the genuine Missouri; their belief rested upon this, and they said they would willingly follow the Captain wherever he pleased to lead, but they feared that the south fork would soon terminate in the Rocky Mountains, and leave them at a great distance from the Columbia. The captains upon this occasion, with a proper reliance upon their own judgment, and a not less proper respect to the opinions of the men, determined that Captain Lewis should ascend the southern branch by land, till he reached either the falls or mountains, which would decide the question. And here, to lighten the labor as much as possible, they resolved to leave one of the pirogues and all the heavy baggage they could spare, together with some provisions, salt, powder, and tools. The boat was drawn up on the middle of a small island and fastened to the trees. The goods were deposited in a cache, which, like the Moorish *matamore*, is a subterraneous magazine, widening, as it descends, from a very small aperture, the mouth being a circle of about twenty inches in diameter; in this the goods were laid upon a flooring of dry sticks, which were also placed round the sides; they were covered with a dry skin, on which the earth was trodden, and lastly the sod was replaced over the opening so as not to betray the slightest marks of an excavation; the earth as it was dug up having been carefully removed.

On the third day's march the sound of falling waters was heard, and a spray which seemed driven by the high southwest wind rose above the plain like a column of smoke and vanished in an instant. The sound soon became too tremendous to be mistaken for anything but the Great Falls of the Missouri, and having travelled seven miles after first hearing it he reached a scene which had never before been beheld by civilized man. The river forms a succession of rapids, cataracts, and falls for about seventeen miles; at the Great Fall it is three hundred yards wide, for about a third part of which it falls in one smooth even sheet over a precipice of eighty-seven feet; the other part, being broken by projecting rocks, "forms a splendid prospect of perfectly white foam two hundred yards in length," with all that glory of refracted light and everlasting sound and infinity of motion which make a great waterfall the most magnificent of all earthly objects.

There is another fall of fifty feet where the river is at least a quarter of a mile in breadth. In the midst of the river, below a third fall of about twenty-six feet, is a little island well covered with timber, where an eagle had built its nest in a cottonwood tree, amid the eternal mists of the cataract. The Indians had particularly mentioned this striking object. About a mile below the upper fall, and about twenty-five yards from the river, a spring rises which is said to be perhaps the largest in America, but its size is not otherwise described. The water, which is extremely pure and cold, "boils up from among the rocks and with such force near the centre, that the surface seems higher there than the earth on the sides of the fountain, which is surrounded by a handsome turf of green grass." It falls into the river over some steep irregular rocks, with a sudden *ascent* of about six feet in one part of its course: and so great is the quantity of water which it pours forth that "its bluish cast" is distinguishable in the less transparent Missouri for half a mile, notwithstanding the rapidity of the river.

They had seen no Indians from the time they left their encampment; but now, upon renewing their way, they came to a very large lodge, which they supposed to be a great council-house, differing in construction from any which they had seen. It was a circle of two hundred sixteen feet in circumference at the base, composed of sixteen large cottonwood poles, about fifty feet long, the tops of which met and were fastened in the centre. There was no covering; but, in the centre, there were the ashes of a large fire, and round about it the marks of many leathern lodges. Three days afterward, when they were in sight of the Rocky Mountains, they passed about forty little huts framed of willow bushes, as a shelter against the sun, and the track of many horses; they judged them to have been deserted about ten days by the Shoshones, or Snake Indians, of whom they were in search; the same day they came to another lodge, constructed like the former, but only half the dimensions, with the remains of fourscore leathern huts, but which seemed to have been built the preceding autumn.

On July 17th they reached the place where the Missouri leaves its native mountains: the river was deep, rapid, and more than seventy yards across, the low grounds not more than a few yards wide, but allowing room for an Indian road to wind under the hills; the cliffs were about eight hundred feet above the water, of a hard black granite, on which were scattered a few dwarf pine and cedar trees. The navigation was now very difficult. Red, purple, yellow, and black currants were growing there in great abundance, and much exceeding in size those in the Eastern gardens. The sunflower also grew plentifully. The big-horned animals, as they called them, were seen here in great numbers, bounding among precipices, where it seemed impossible that any animal could stand, and where a single false step would have precipitated them at least five hundred feet into the water. The prickly pear, at this time in full bloom, was one of the greatest beauties of the country, but they complained of it, with good reason, as one of the greatest inconveniences also. They were so abundant that it was impossible to avoid them, and the thorns were strong enough to pierce a double sole of dressed doeskin.

A species of flax was observed here, which, it was thought,

would prove a most valuable plant: eight or ten stems sprang from the same root to the height of two and a half or three feet, and the root appeared to be perennial. There were young suckers shooting up, though the seeds were not yet ripe, and they inferred that the stems, which were in the best state for producing flax, might be cut without injuring the root. The heat in these defiles was almost insupportable, and whenever they caught a glimpse of the mountain-tops they were tantalized with a sight of snow. One tremendous pass they named the "Gates of the Rocky Mountains." For nearly six miles, the river, which was there three hundred fifty yards in width, flows between rocks of black granite, which rise perpendicularly from its edges to the height of nearly twelve hundred feet. Nothing, said they, could be imagined more awful than the darkness of these rocks. During the whole distance the water is very deep, even at the edges, and for the first three miles there was not a spot, except one of a few yards, where a man could stand between the water and the wall of rock. Several fine springs burst out from the chasms of the rocks and increase the stream; the current is strong, but they were able to overcome it with their oars, most fortunately, for it would have been impossible to use either the cord or the pole.

A great smoke was perceived the next day, as if the country had been set on fire—the Indians had heard a gun, and, believing that their enemies were approaching, made the signal of alarm and fled into the mountains. Captain Lewis, with Chaboneau, the interpreter, and two other companions, preceded the party now in search of the Shoshones. On August 10th he came to a fork in the Jefferson, beyond which it was not navigable. The next day he perceived, with the greatest delight, a man on horseback, but the man, when they were within a hundred paces of each other, suddenly wheeled round, though every amicable gesture had been made to him, gave his horse the whip and presently disappeared. They followed his track till it was lost, and the next day, proceeding up the stream, they came where it was so narrow that one of the men put his foot across it, and thanked God that he had lived to bestride the Missouri. It was not long before they reached its actual source and drank of the fountain; a situation not altogether unworthy of being compared with that of Bruce at the fountain of the Abyssinian [Blue] Nile. Leaving this memorable spot they got upon the ridge which forms the dividing line between the streams that flow into the Atlantic and Pacific oceans, and there they drank of the waters which run to the Columbia or Oregon, the "Great River of the West."

The fears and suspicions of the Shoshones, and the embarrassments of Captain Lewis after he had met them, and before his companions were arrived, form a very interesting part of his narrative. The two captains went now to the tent of Cameahwait, the chief of this tribe, and sent for Sahcajaweah to be their interpreter.

The accounts which the explorers received of the way before them were most discouraging. To follow the course of the water, Cameahwait said, was impossible, as the river flowed between steep precipices, which allowed of no passage along the banks; and it ran with such rapidity among sharp-pointed rocks that as far as the eye could reach it was one line of foam. The mountains were equally inaccessible; neither man nor beast could pass them, and therefore neither he nor any of his nation had ever attempted it. He had learned from some of the Chopunnish or Pierced Nose [1] Indians, who resided on the river to the westward, that it ran a great way toward the setting sun and there lost itself in a lake of ill-tasting water where the white men lived. Captain Clark, not relying upon this report, went with a guide to reconnoitre the country, and found it equally impracticable to keep the course of the river or cross the mountains in the same direction. The guide, however, said there was a way to some Indian settlements on another river, which was also a branch of the Oregon [Columbia]. The Shoshones all denied this, which was imputed to their desire of keeping among them strangers so able to protect them and so well stocked with valuable commodities; they sold them, however, horses enough for the party, and the adventurers began their journey on August 30th.

They suffered dreadfully from fatigue and hunger; game was so scarce that they were obliged to feed upon their horses; their strength began to fail them; most of the men were now complaining of sickness, and having reached a settlement of the Chopunnish on the Kooskooskee, they determined to build ca-

[1] The Nez Percés, a tribe of the Shahaptian stock.—ED.

noes there. The labor which the men had gone through in the latter part of their way up the Mississippi had made them desirous of travelling on horseback, but they now more gladly returned to their river navigation. September 25th they began to build eight canoes, and having intrusted their remaining horses to the Chopunnish, and buried the saddles in a cache, they embarked on October 7th, accompanied by two chiefs.

On November 2d they perceived the first tide-water; four days afterward they had the pleasure of hearing a few words of English from an Indian, who talked of a Mr. Haley as the principal trader on the coast; and on the 7th a fog clearing off gave them a sight of the ocean. They suffered greatly at the mouth of the river. At one place where they were confined two nights by the wind, the waves broke over them, and large trees which the stream had brought down were drifted upon them, so that with their utmost vigilance they could scarcely save the canoes from being dashed to pieces. Their next haven was still more perilous; the hills rose steep over their heads to the height of five hundred feet; and as the rain fell in torrents, the stones upon their crumbling sides loosened, and came rolling down upon them. The canoes were, in one place, at the mercy of the waves, the baggage in another, and the men scattered upon floating logs or sheltering themselves in the crevices of the rocks and hillside.

In this situation they had nothing but dried fish for food; this weather and these sufferings continued till their clothes and bedding were rotten. At length they reached the open coast, and, having well reconnoitred it, encamped for the winter. This was no very exhilarating prospect. The natives subsisted chiefly on dried fish and roots; the explorers neither liked this diet, nor did there seem enough of it for their supply, nor had they sufficient store of merchandise left to purchase it; they must therefore trust to their hunters for subsistence, and game was not to be found with the same facility here as in the plains of the Missouri. But the sea enabled them to supply themselves with salt, and in about three months trading-vessels were expected, from which, being well provided with letters of credit, they hoped to procure a supply of trinkets for their route homeward. In national expeditions of this nature nothing should be spared which can contribute to the safety and comfort of the persons employed. Captains Lewis and Clark should not have been left to the contingency of obtaining supplies; a ship ought certainly to have been sent to meet them. For want of this they suffered great hardships; game became scarce, and in January nothing but elk was to be seen, which of all others was the most difficult to catch; they could scarcely, they said, have subsisted but for the exertions of one of the party, Drewyer by name, the son of a Canadian Frenchman and an Indian woman, who united in a wonderful degree the dexterous aim of the frontier huntsman with the sagacity of the savage in pursuing the faintest tracks through the forest.

During the winter they sought for all the information in their power concerning the country and the inhabitants, and obtained some account of the number of tribes, languages, and population for about three hundred sixty miles southward along the coast; of those in an opposite direction they learned little more than the names, their encampment being on the south of the Oregon [Columbia].

Captains Lewis and Clark were very desirous of remaining on the coast till the ships arrived, that they might recruit their almost exhausted stores of merchandise; but though they were expected in April, it was found impossible to wait. The elk, on which they chiefly depended, had retreated to the mountains, and if the Indians could have sold food they were too poor to purchase it. About the middle of March, therefore, they began their homeward way; the whole stock of goods on which they were to depend, either for the purchase of horses or of food, during a journey of nearly four thousand miles, being so diminished that it might all be tied in two handkerchiefs. But their muskets were in excellent order, and they had plenty of powder and shot.

The opinion which they had formed of the natives on their way down the river was not improved on their return. It was soon found that nothing but their numbers saved the explorers from being attacked. On one occasion, when Captain Clark could not obtain food, he took a port-fire match from his pocket, threw a small piece of it into the fire, and at the same time taking his pocket compass and a magnet, made the needle turn round

very briskly. As soon as the match began to burn, the Indians
were so terrified that they brought a quantity of wappato¹ and
laid it at his feet, begging him to put out the bad fire. At another
place they were compelled to make the Indians understand that
whoever stole any of the baggage, or insulted any of the men,
would be immediately shot. After some disputes, which ended,
however, without bloodshed, and many difficulties, they came to
the Chopunnish Indians, with whom they had left their horses;
and here they had to wait till the mountains should be pass-
able.

On June 10th they renewed their journey; but on the 17th
they were convinced that it was not yet practicable to cross the
mountains, and therefore were for the first time compelled to
make a retrograde movement. A week afterward they attempted
it again. In the course of that time the snow had melted about
four feet; they had good guides, and it was found better travelling over the snow than over the fallen timber and rocks, which
in summer obstructed the way. Having surmounted the difficulties of this passage, the party separated on the mountain:
Captain Lewis went with nine men by the most direct route to
the Falls of the Missouri, whence he was to ascend Maria River,
and ascertain if any branch of it reached as far south as latitude
50°. Captain Clark, with the rest of the party, made for the
head of the Jefferson; there they divided again. Sergeant Ord-
way and nine men went from there in the canoes down the Missouri; and Captain Clark proceeded to the Yellowstone River,
at its nearest approach to the Three Forks of the Missouri, and
there built canoes to explore that important stream along the
whole of its course. The junction of these two great rivers was
the appointed place of meeting.

Captain Lewis's route was much shorter than that which
they had taken on their outward journey. He got once more
into the land of mosquitoes; the horses suffered so much from
these insects that they were obliged to kindle large fires and
place the poor animals in the midst of the smoke. In such myr-
iads were they that they frequently drew them in with their
breath, and the very dog howled with the torture they gave him.
They came also among their old enemies the bears; but the

¹ A species of arrowhead root.—ED.

abundance of buffaloes after their short commons made amends
for all. These animals seemed to prefer pools, which were so
strongly impregnated with salt as to be unfit for the use of man,
to the water of the river. Captain Lewis proceeded far enough
to ascertain that no branch of the Maria extended as far north
as 50°, and consequently that it would not make the desired
boundary. He fell in with a party of Minnetarees of the north;
the tribe bore a bad character, and these men did not belie it;
for after meeting in apparent friendship and encamping together for the night, they endeavored to rob the Americans of
their horses and guns. In the scuffle that ensued one of the Indians was stabbed through the heart, and Captain Lewis shot
another in the abdomen; the man, however, rose, and fired in
return, and Captain Lewis felt the wind of the ball. He was
destined to a narrower escape a few days afterward, when one of
his own men mistook him for an elk and shot him through the
thigh. When they came to the appointed place of meeting they
saw that Captain Clark had been encamped there, but found no
letter. These words, however, were traced in the sand: "W. C.
a few miles farther down on the right-hand side." Captain
Clark had not intended to trust to a writing in the sand; but
another division of the party arriving before Captain Lewis, and
thinking that he had preceded them, removed his letter.

Captain Clark, on his part, had reached the Yellowstone a
little below the place where it issues from the Rocky Mountains.
It now appeared that the communication between these great
rivers was short and easy. From the Three Forks of the Missouri to this place was forty-eight miles, chiefly over a level
plain; and from the forks of the eastern branch of the Gallatin,
which is there navigable for small canoes, it is only eighteen, with
an excellent road over a high dry country. The Yellowstone here
is a bold, deep, and rapid stream, one hundred twenty yards
wide. As no large timber could be found, Captain Clark made
two small canoes and lashed them together; they were twenty-
eight feet long, about eighteen inches deep, and from sixteen to
twenty-four inches wide. Sergeant Pryor, with two companions,
was then intrusted with the horses to take them to the Mandans,
and the rest of the party began their voyage. The buffaloes
were here in such numbers that a herd of them one day crossing

the river stopped the canoe for an hour; the river, including an island over which they passed, was a mile in width, and the herd stretched as thick as they could swim from one side to another during the whole of that time.

The course of this river, from the point where they reached it till its junction with the Missouri, was computed at more than eight hundred miles, navigable the whole way, without any falls or any moving sandbars (which are very frequent in the Missouri), and only one ledge of rocks, and that not difficult to pass. The point of junction was considered to be one of the best places for an establishment for the Western fur trade. It was impossible to wait here for Captain Lewis because of the mosquitoes; they were in such multitudes that the men could not shoot for them; they could not be kept from the barrel of the rifle long enough for a man to take aim. Pryor and his party soon followed; the horses were stolen from them by some Indians; they then struck for the river, and made skin canoes, or rather coracles, such as they had seen among the Mandans and Ricaras. These vessels were perfect basins, seven feet three in diameter, sixteen inches deep; made of skins stretched over a wooden skeleton; each capable of carrying six or eight men with their loads. They made two that they might divide their guns and ammunition, lest, in case of accident, all should be lost. But in these frail vessels they passed, with perfect security, all the shoals and rapids of the river, without taking in water even during the highest winds. Where a boat is to be committed to the stream, probably no other shape could be so safe.

On August 12th the whole party were once more collected. They found on their return that great changes had taken place in the bed of the Missouri since they ascended it, so shifting are its sands; and they observed that in the course of one thousand miles, though it had received above twenty rivers, some of them of considerable width, besides many smaller streams, its waters were not augmented, so great is the evaporation. When they came to the first village and saw some cows feeding on the bank, the whole party, with an involuntary impulse, raised a shout of joy. Several settlements had been made in this direction during their absence; so fast is the progress of civilization of America, where it is extended by the very eagerness with which men recede from civilized life.   On September 22d they reached the spot from where they had set out, after having travelled nearly nine thousand miles, and performed with equal ability, perseverance, and success one of the most arduous journeys that were ever undertaken.

THE BATTLE OF TRAFALGAR

ENGLAND BECOMES MISTRESS OF THE SEAS

A.D. 1805

ROBERT SOUTHEY

It was impossible for the powers of Europe to submit quietly to the increasing exactions of the new Emperor, Napoleon, until they had once tried their entire united strength against him in an appeal to arms. What is called the "third great coalition" was formed against France in 1805 by Austria, Russia, and England. Sweden, Naples, and other lesser kingdoms were also partners to it. Spain and several of the little German States aided Napoleon.

The vast plans of the French Emperor included an expedition to cross the Channel and crush England, and to accomplish this he gathered all his available French ships and also those of his ally, Spain. These were intended to protect his army in its passage to England, but Nelson met the French and Spanish fleet off the Spanish coast at Cape Trafalgar, and Britain's empire over the seas was established beyond controversy. It has never since been disputed in any considerable naval battle.

NELSON arrived off Cadiz on September 29, 1805—his birthday. Fearing that if the enemy knew his force they might be deterred from venturing to sea, he kept out of sight of land, desired Collingwood to fire no salute and hoist no colors, and wrote to Gibraltar to request that the force of the fleet might not be inserted there in the *Gazette*. His reception in the Mediterranean fleet was as gratifying as the farewell of his countrymen at Portsmouth: the officers, who came on board to welcome him, forgot his rank as commander, in their joy at seeing him again. On the day of his arrival Villeneuve received orders to put to sea the first opportunity. Villeneuve, however, hesitated when he heard that Nelson had resumed the command. He called a council of war, and their determination was that it would not be expedient to leave Cadiz, unless they had reason to believe themselves stronger by one-third than the British force. In the public measures of Great Britain secrecy is seldom practicable and seldom attempted: here, however, by the precautions of Nelson and the wise measures of the Admiralty, the French were for once kept in ignorance; for as the ships appointed to reënforce the Mediterranean fleet were despatched singly, each as soon as it was ready, their collected number was not stated in the newspapers, and their arrival was not known to the enemy.

On October 9th Nelson sent Collingwood what he called in his diary the "Nelson touch." "I send you," said he, "my plan of attack, as far as a man dare venture to guess at the very uncertain position the enemy may be found in; but it is to place you perfectly at ease respecting my intentions, and to give full scope to your judgment for carrying them into effect. We can, my dear Coll, have no little jealousies. We have only one great object in view, that of annihilating our enemies and getting a glorious peace for our country. No man has more confidence in another than I have in you; and no man will render your services more justice than your very old friend, Nelson and Bronte."

The order of sailing was to be the order of battle; the fleet in two lines, with an advance squadron of eight of the fastest sailing two-deckers. The second in command, having the entire direction of his line, was to break through the enemy, about the twelfth ship from their rear; he would lead through the centre, and the advanced squadron was to cut off three or four ahead of the centre. This plan was to be adapted to the strength of the enemy, so that they should always be one-fourth superior to those whom they cut off. Nelson said, "That his admirals and captains, knowing his precise object to be that of a close and decisive action, would supply any deficiency of signals, and act accordingly. In case signals cannot be seen or clearly understood, *no captain can do wrong if he places his ship alongside that of an enemy.*" One of the last orders of this admirable man was that the name and family of every officer, seaman, and marine, who might be killed or wounded in the action, should be, as soon as possible, returned to him in order to be transmitted to the chairman of the patriotic fund, that the case might be taken into consideration for the benefit of the sufferer or his family.

On the 21st, at daybreak, the combined fleets were distinctly seen from the Victory's deck, formed in a close line of battle ahead, on the starboard tack, about twelve miles to leeward, and standing to the south. The English fleet consisted of twenty-seven sail of the line and four frigates; the French, of thirty-three and seven large frigates. The French superiority was more in size and weight of metal than in numbers. They had four thousand troops on board; and the best riflemen who could be procured—many of them Tyrolese—were dispersed through the ships. Little did the Tyrolese, and little did the Spaniards, at that day, imagine what horrors the master whom they served was preparing for their countries.

Soon after daylight Nelson came upon deck. October 21st was a festival in his family, because on that day his uncle, Captain Suckling, in the Dreadnought, with two other line-of-battle ships, had beaten off a French squadron of four sail of the line and three frigates. Nelson, with that sort of superstition from which few persons are entirely exempt, had more than once expressed his persuasion that this was to be the day of his battle also; and he was well pleased at seeing his prediction about to be verified. The wind was now from the west, light breezes with a long heavy swell. Signal was made to bear down upon the enemy in two lines, and the fleet set all sail. Collingwood in the Royal Sovereign, led the leeward line of thirteen ships; the Victory led the weather line of fourteen. Having seen that all was as it should be, Nelson retired to his cabin and wrote the following prayer:

"May the great God, whom I worship, grant to my country, and for the benefit of Europe in general, a great and glorious victory, and may no misconduct in anyone tarnish it; and may humanity after victory be the predominant feature in the British fleet! For myself individually, I commit my life to Him that made me; and may his blessing alight on my endeavors for serving my country faithfully! To him I resign myself, and the just cause which is intrusted to me to defend. Amen, Amen, Amen."

Blackwood went on board the Victory about six. He found him in good spirits but very calm; not in that exhilaration which he had felt upon entering into battle at Abukir and Copenhagen; he knew that his own life would be particularly aimed at, and seems to have looked for death with almost as sure an expectation as for victory. His whole attention was fixed upon the enemy. They tacked to the northward, and formed their line on the larboard tack; thus bringing the shoals of Trafalgar and St. Pedro under the lee of the British, and keeping the port of Cadiz open for themselves. This was judiciously done; and Nelson, aware of all the advantages which it gave them, made signal to prepare to anchor.

Villeneuve was a skilful seaman, worthy of serving a better master and a better cause. His plan of defence was as well conceived and as original as the plan of attack. He formed the fleet in a double line, every alternate ship being about a cable's length to windward of her second ahead and astern. Nelson, certain of a triumphant issue to the day, asked Blackwood what he should consider as a victory? That officer answered that, considering the handsome way in which battle was offered by the enemy, their apparent determination for a fair trial of strength, and the situation of the land, he thought it would be a glorious result if fourteen were captured. He replied, "I shall not be satisfied with less than twenty." Soon afterward he asked him if he did not think there was a signal wanting. Captain Blackwood made answer that he thought the whole fleet seemed very clearly to understand what they were about. These words were scarcely spoken before that signal was made, which will be remembered as long as the language or even the memory of England shall endure: Nelson's last signal—"England expects every man to do his duty!"

It was received throughout the fleet with a shout of answering acclamation, made sublime by the spirit which it breathed and the feeling which it expressed. "Now," said Lord Nelson, "I can do no more. We must trust to the great Disposer of all events, and the justice of our cause. I thank God for this great opportunity of doing my duty."

He wore that day, as usual, his admiral's frock coat, bearing on the left breast four stars, of the different orders with which he was invested. Ornaments which rendered him so conspicuous a mark for the enemy were beheld with ominous apprehension by his officers. It was known that there were riflemen on board the French ships, and it could not be doubted but that his life would be particularly aimed at. They communicated their fears to each other; and the surgeon, Mr. Beatty, spoke to the chaplain, Doctor Scott, and to Mr. Scott, the private secretary, desiring that some person would entreat him to change his dress or cover the stars; but they knew that such a request would highly displease him. "In honor I gained them," he had said, when such a thing had been hinted to him formerly, "and in honor I will die with them."

A long swell was setting into the Bay of Cadiz; our ships crowding all sail moved majestically before it with light winds from the southwest. The sun shone on the sails of the enemy; and their well-formed line, with their numerous three-deckers, made an appearance which any other assailants would have thought formidable; but the British sailors only admired the beauty and the splendor of the spectacle; and in full confidence of winning what they saw, remarked to each other, "What a fine sight yonder ships would make at Spithead!"

The French Admiral, from the Bucentaure, beheld the new manner in which his enemy was advancing—Nelson and Collingwood each leading his line; and pointing them out to his officers, he is said to have exclaimed that such conduct could not fail to be successful. Yet Villeneuve had made his own dispositions with the utmost skill, and the fleets under his command waited for the attack with perfect coolness.

Nelson's column was steered about two points more to the north than Collingwood's, in order to cut off the enemy's escape into Cadiz; the lee line, therefore, was first engaged. "See," cried Nelson, pointing to the Royal Sovereign, as she steered right for the centre of the enemy's line, cut through it astern of the Santa Anna, a three-decker, and engaged her at the muzzle of her guns on the starboard side, "see how that noble fellow, Collingwood, carries his ship into action!" Collingwood, delighted at being first in the heat of the fire, and knowing the feelings of his commander and old friend, turned to his captain and exclaimed, "Rotherham, what would Nelson give to be here!"

The enemy continued to fire a gun at a time at the Victory, till they saw that a shot had passed through her main-topgallant-sail; then they opened their broadsides, aiming chiefly at her rigging in the hope of disabling her before she could close with them. Nelson, as usual, had hoisted several flags, lest one should be shot away. The enemy showed no colors till late in the action, when they began to feel the necessity of having them to strike. For this reason, the Santissima Trinidad, Nelson's old acquaintance, as he used to call her, was distinguishable only by her four decks; and to the bow of this opponent he ordered the Victory to be steered.   Meantime an incessant raking fire was kept up upon the Victory.   The Admiral's secretary was one of the first who fell; he was killed by a cannon-shot while conversing with Hardy. Captain Adair, of the marines, with the help of a sailor, endeavored to remove the body from Nelson's sight, who had a great regard for Mr. Scott; but he anxiously asked, "Is that poor Scott that's gone?" and being informed that it was indeed so, exclaimed, "Poor fellow!"   Presently a double-headed shot struck a party of marines who were drawn up on the poop, and killed eight of them; upon which Nelson immediately desired Captain Adair to disperse his men round the ship, that they might not suffer so much from being together.   A few minutes afterward a shot struck the fore-brace bitts on the quarter-deck, and passed between Nelson and Hardy, a splinter from the bitt tearing off Hardy's buckle and bruising his foot.   Both stopped and looked anxiously at each other, each supposing the other to be wounded. Nelson then smiled and said, "This is too warm work, Hardy, to last long."

The Victory had not yet returned a single gun; fifty of her men had been by this time killed or wounded, and her main-top-mast, with all her studding-sails and their booms, shot away.   Nelson declared that in all his battles he had seen nothing which had surpassed the cool courage of his crew on this occasion.   At four minutes after twelve the Victory opened fire from both sides of her deck.   It was impossible to break the enemy's line without running aboard one of their ships; Hardy informed him of this, and asked him which he would prefer.   Nelson replied, "Take your choice, Hardy; it does not signify much."   The master was ordered to put the helm to port, and the Victory ran aboard the Redoubtable, just as her tiller-ropes were shot away.   The French ship received her with a broadside, then instantly let down her lower-deck ports for fear of being boarded through them, and never afterward fired a great gun during the action. Her tops, like those of all the French ships, were filled with riflemen.   Nelson never placed musketry in his tops; he had a strong dislike to the practice, not merely because it endangers setting fire to the sails, but also because it is a murderous sort of war-

Admiral Nelson on board the Frigate
Victory in the Battle
of Trafalgar
Painting by W. H. Overend.

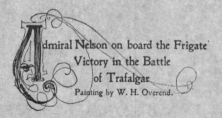

Admiral Nelson on board the Frigate Victory in the Battle of Trafalgar

Painting by W. H. Overend.

out some prospect of life. "Oh, no!" he replied, "it is impossible: my back is shot through; Beatty will tell you so." Captain Hardy then once more shook hands with him, and, with a heart almost bursting, hastened upon deck.

By this time all feeling below the breast was gone; and Nelson, having made the surgeon ascertain this, said to him: "You know I am gone. I know it. I feel something rising in my breast"—putting his hand on his left side—"which tells me so." And on Beatty's inquiring whether his pain was great, he said it was so great that he wished he was dead. "Yet," said he in a lower voice, "one would like to live a little longer, too." And after a few minutes, in the same undertone, he added, "What would become of poor Lady Hamilton if she knew my situation?" Next to his country she occupied his thoughts. Captain Hardy, some fifty minutes after he left the cockpit, returned, and again taking the hand of his dying friend and commander, congratulated him on having gained a complete victory. How many of the enemy were taken he did not know, as it was impossible to perceive them distinctly; but fourteen or fifteen at least. "That's well," cried Nelson, "but I bargained for twenty." And then, in a stronger voice, he said, "Anchor, Hardy, anchor!" Hardy, upon this, hinted that Admiral Collingwood would take upon himself the direction of affairs. "Not while I live, Hardy," said the dying Nelson, ineffectually endeavoring to raise himself from the bed: "Do you anchor!" His previous order for preparing to anchor had shown how clearly he foresaw the necessity of this. Presently, calling Hardy back, he said to him in a low voice, "Don't throw me overboard"; and he desired that he might be buried by his parents, unless it should please the King to order otherwise. Then reverting to private feelings: "Take care of my dear Lady Hamilton, Hardy; take care of poor Lady Hamilton. Kiss me, Hardy," said he. Hardy knelt down and kissed his cheek, and Nelson said: "Now I am satisfied. Thank God, I have done my duty." Hardy stood over him in silence for a moment or two, then knelt again and kissed his forehead. "Who is that?" said Nelson; and being informed, he replied, "God bless you, Hardy." And Hardy then left him—forever.

Nelson now desired to be turned upon his right side, and said, "I wish I had not left the deck; for I shall soon be gone." Death was, indeed, rapidly approaching. He said to the chaplain, "Doctor, I have *not* been a *great* sinner," and after a short pause, "Remember that I leave Lady Hamilton and my daughter Horatia as a legacy to my country." His articulation now became difficult; but he was distinctly heard to say, "Thank God, I have done my duty!" These words he repeatedly pronounced; and they were the last words which he uttered. He expired at thirty minutes after four—three hours and a quarter after he had received his wound.

interest in falling back upon Hungary, to join eighty thousand men of the Archduke Charles. Alexander had committed a first fault in coming, in spite of the remonstrances of his wisest friends, in the midst of his army, where his presence would naturally paralyze brave but servile generals, and, moreover, he was surrounded by young men, full of ardor, courage, and illusions, impatient to distinguish themselves in the eyes of their sovereign, who spoke with the most profound contempt of the dilatory system proposed by Kutuzoff, by the Emperor of Austria, and by the most experienced chiefs of the army. Grave discords that had arisen between the Austrians and the Russians, in consequence of the unfortunate opening of the campaign, also contributed to make both desire a prompt renewal of hostilities, in which each hoped to find his justification.

Napoleon was aware of this state of things and turned it to account with marvellous skill. He had just received, with a great deal of haughtiness, Messieurs de Stadion and Giulay, whom the Emperor of Austria had sent to his camp to make overtures to him. He almost immediately afterward regretted this, on learning that Prussia was on the point of joining his adversaries, and he became as communicative as he had hitherto been haughty and suspicious. On November 25th he despatched Savary to the camp of the allies, with a complimentary letter to the Emperor Alexander, and with a secret mission to observe attentively the army of the enemy, while he felt the ground for a negotiation.

Savary was received with courtesy, but very coldly. He only brought back to his master a curt and evasive letter, which was addressed not to the Emperor, but to the *Chef du Gouvernement Français*. Napoleon, who was so sensitive upon this point, took no offence; he wanted to show that he was superior to the trifles of a vain etiquette, and only became more complaisant. Savary immediately returned to Olmuetz, to propose an interview between Napoleon and the too confiding Alexander. At the same time he was to complete his studies on the Austro-Russian army. Savary, who had the eyes and ears of a future minister of police, observed the size and disposition of the army; he got into conversation with the aides-de-camp, and took note of the rash confidence of the young officers. Alexander refused the interview, but he consented to send to Napoleon his aide-de-camp, the Prince Dolgoruki.

Napoleon took care not to give the Prince the same opportunity for making observations that Savary had had with Alexander. He received him at his advanced posts, and only let him see just enough of his army to deceive him. A few days before, a squadron of his advance guard had been separated and taken prisoner at Wischau. Dolgoruki found the French troops falling back upon all points in order to concentrate themselves in the positions studied long beforehand, toward which Napoleon wished to draw the Austro-Russian army. Crowded in a narrow space, still separated from Bernadotte's corps and Friant's division, which were only to arrive at the last moment, ostensibly occupied in raising intrenchments upon different points as if they feared to be attacked, they could only strike the Prince by the apparent weakness of their force and by their timid and constrained attitude.

After the usual compliments, Dolgoruki went to the object of his mission without any more oratorical precautions. Napoleon has reported the interview with his habitual untruthfulness, seasoning his account with the usual insults toward all men in whom he met with any firmness. He has related in his bulletins that this "puppy" (*freluquet*) went so far as to propose to him the cession of Belgium. It had never been contemplated to demand Belgium from France, and the time would have been badly chosen to put forward such a proposition. Dolgoruki made no proposal of this kind. Alexander had agreed upon a programme when he allied himself to Austria and Prussia, and it was this programme, already discussed a hundred times, that his aide-de-camp submitted to Napoleon. Dolgoruki's report of this interview bears the stamp of truth, and strikingly reminds us of the famous account of Whitworth's interview with Napoleon. As usual, Napoleon speaks as a tempter when he cannot speak as a master. "What do they want of me? Why does the Emperor Alexander make war on me? What does he require? Is he jealous of the aggrandizement of France? Well! let him extend his frontiers at the expense of his neighbors—by way of Turkey; and all quarrels will be terminated!" And as Dolgoruki replied that Russia did not care to increase her territory, but wanted to maintain the independence of Europe, to secure the evacuation of Holland and Switzerland, the indemnity that she had never ceased to claim for the King of Sardinia, Napoleon flew into a violent passion, and exclaimed that he would cede nothing in Italy, "not even if the Russians were encamped upon the heights of Montmartre!" an exclamation that is so much the more probable that we find it textually a few days later in one of his bulletins. These words put an end to a negotiation that had been, on the part of Napoleon, only a ruse of war intended to embolden his enemies, and both sides now thought of nothing but battle.

The positions that Napoleon had occupied to await the collision with the allies were admirably chosen, both for attack and for defence. Backed by the citadel of Bruenn, which would, if it were necessary, insure their retreat into Bohemia; covered on their left by hills thickly wooded, on their front by a deep stream which at certain distances formed large ponds, his troops were intrenched in the right angle made by the two highroads which run from Bruenn, one to Vienna and the other to Olmuetz. They occupied all the villages situated along the stream, from Girszkowitz to Telnitz, where the ponds begin. Opposite to their centre, on the other side of the stream, rose the plateau of Pratzen, a commanding and advanced position, beyond which appeared at some distance the village and château of Austerlitz, which the army of the two emperors already occupied. Napoleon had posted at his left, round a knoll to which the soldiers had given the name of the "Santon," Lannes's *corps d'armée*, on both sides of the Olmuetz road; at his right, from Telnitz to Kobelnitz, he had placed Soult's corps; at his centre, toward Girszkowitz, that of Bernadotte, which had arrived the day before from the Bohemian frontier, and with him Murat's cavalry. He himself formed the reserve with his guard and ten battalions, commanded by Oudinot. Behind his extreme right, at Raygern, in a position far removed from his centre, he detached Davout, with Friant's division and a division of cavalry, in order to bring them down at the decisive moment upon the left of the Russians. The whole of these troops amounted, notwithstanding all that has been said, to a total at least equal to that of the allies; for the three corps d'armée of Soult, Bernadotte, and Lannes, however reduced we may suppose them to have been by their losses and detachments, could not have numbered less than from fifteen to twenty thousand men each; the guard and Murat's cavalry formed at least twenty thousand men, and Davout's detachment counted eight thousand.

This position, almost unassailable in front, was calculated to suggest to the allies the idea of cutting off Napoleon from the route to Vienna, by turning his right, and thus separating him from the rest of his army, which had remained quartered in the neighborhood of the capital. But this operation, hazardous enough if it were undertaken even at a distance by a series of strategical movements with forces only equal to his own, became an act of the most foolish temerity the moment it was attempted under the eyes of so formidable an enemy, within reach of his cannon, and upon the field of battle that he had chosen. Such was, however, the plan which Weyrother ventured to adopt, encouraged no doubt by the apparent and calculated weakness of the detachments of the right near Telnitz, and the approaches of the road to Vienna.

In order to entice him more and more into this perilous path, Napoleon had not only withdrawn the troops from his right, but had not even occupied the plateau of Pratzen, a kind of elevated promontory which advanced toward the centre of the two armies, and from the top of which he would have been able to render the turning movement of the Austro-Russian army very difficult. The allies established themselves upon this plateau, but with insufficient forces, without suspecting the importance of the position and the part that it was to play in the coming battle. On the evening of December 1st, the Russians commenced their flank march, keeping along the Frenchmen's line at two gunshots' distance for about four leagues, in order to turn their right. Napoleon, from his bivouac, saw them rushing to their ruin, with a transport of joy. He allowed them to effect their movement without putting any obstacle in their way, as if he recognized the impossibility of opposing it. Only one small corps of French cavalry showed itself on the plain, and immediately retired as if intimidated by the forces of the enemy.

Napoleon quickly understood, by this commencement, that his efforts to draw the attack upon his right were going to be crowned with success. His conviction in this respect was so firm that the same evening in the proclamation that he addressed to his soldiers he did not hesitate to announce to them the manœuvre that the enemy would make on the morrow at his proper risk and peril. "The positions which we occupy," he said, "are formidable; and while they are marching to turn my right they will present their flank to me. Soldiers, I shall myself direct your battalions. I shall keep out of the fire if with your usual bravery you throw disorder and confusion into the enemy's ranks; but if the victory should be for a moment uncertain, you will see your Emperor the foremost to expose himself to danger!"

This prediction, made with so much assurance, greatly contributed to gain credit for a report, that is still very generally believed in Russia, that Weyrother's plan had been treacherously made known to Napoleon. There is nothing impossible in this fact; for although Weyrother's plan was only communicated to the allied generals very late in the night of December 1st, it was certainly known earlier to a part of the staff. But Napoleon had no need of such a communication to discover a fault, of which he had himself suggested the idea by his own dispositions, and of which he had seen all the preliminary developments with his own eyes. This story is then but of slight importance, and could only be admitted upon formal proofs, which have not hitherto been given.

After having inspected the advanced posts, Napoleon resolved to visit the bivouacs. Being recognized by the soldiers, he was immediately surrounded and cheered. They wished to *fête* the anniversary of his coronation; bundles of straw were hoisted blazing on poles for an impromptu illumination, and an immense train of light along the French line made the allies believe that Napoleon was trying to steal away, by means of a stratagem borrowed from a Hannibal or a Frederick. An old grenadier approached and addressed him in the name of his fellow-soldiers. "I promise thee," he said, "that to-morrow we will bring thee the colors and cannon of the Russian army, to *fête* the anniversary of thy coronation!"—a characteristic harangue which showed that in spite of everything the republican spirit still subsisted in the lower ranks of the army, and that the soldiers regarded Napoleon less as a master than as a former equal, in whom, even in crowning him, they thought they were personifying their own grandeur.

The next morning, December 2, 1805, the rising sun gradually dispelled the fog that covered the country, and showed the two armies ready for the conflict. The Russians had almost entirely evacuated the plateau of Pratzen, and in the valley beneath their columns were distinctly seen advancing in the direction of Telnitz and Sokolnitz. It was there that they hoped to turn the enemy's right, after having forced the Legrand division, which alone held this defile. The execution of this principal manœuvre of Weyrother's plan had been confided to clumsy Buxhoewden, a brave general, but of no ability, who had under his orders a corps of thirty thousand men; and Generals Langeron, Doctoroff, and Przibyszewski. They were to be supported by Kollowrath, who still occupied a part of the plateau. The Russian right, commanded by Bagration, faced Lannes in front of the Santon; in the centre, near Austerlitz, were the two emperors with their guard and the corps d'armée of Prince Lichtenstein. Kutuzoff, discouraged and disheartened by the kind of fetichism that the sacred person of the Czar (Alexander I) inspired in the Russians, followed his master, lamenting beforehand the misfortunes which he foresaw, but without doing anything to ward them off. Bagration himself, on reading in the morning Weyrother's plan, had exclaimed, "The battle is lost!"

The allied army thus formed an immense semicircle, which extended from Holubitz to Telnitz, and closed the angle of which the French occupied the centre. Lying in wait at the bottom of this sort of funnel, concentrated in a narrow space, attentive, motionless, and crouching like a lion preparing to spring upon its prey, the French army was waiting in formidable silence the signal for rushing on the enemy. When the whole of the left of the allies had reached the ponds, and were beginning to attack, at Telnitz, Legrand's division—which was soon to be supported by Davout's corps, recalled from Raygern—Napoleon, who had hitherto kept back his troops, gave the signal, and Soult's divisions rushed to the assault of the heights of Pratzen. There they found Kollowrath's column, marching to rejoin Bux-

hoewden.   In an instant they attacked it in flank and overturned it; immediately after they found the infantry of Miloradovitch, which was drawn up in a second line to support it.
Vandamme's and St. Hilaire's divisions, seconded by Thié-
bault's and Morand's Brigades, threw themselves with the bayonet upon the Russian battalions.   These, stopped short in the
middle of their movement, finding no reserve to support them,
attacked in the rear when they were marching to assail the enemy in front, were driven down the slopes of the plateau under
the eyes of the Emperor Alexander, surprised and dismayed at
the unforeseen catastrophe which had just routed his centre.

While Napoleon was striking with his accustomed rapidity
this decisive blow, which at the beginning of the battle cut the
Russian army in two at its very centre, his own corps d'armée,
boldly deploying by a simultaneous forward march, were performing with almost equal success the task that had been assigned to them.   At the extreme right of the French army, it is
true, Legrand's division, overwhelmed by quadruple forces, had
at first been driven beyond Telnitz and Sokolnitz, but Davout
had soon come to his assistance with Friant's and Bourcier's divisions, so that Legrand's retrograde movement had proved an
advantage rather than otherwise, since it had drawn the Russian
left deeper and deeper into the snare in which it was taken.   From
the centre, Bernadotte had marched upon Blaziowitz; he had
attacked the Russian guard and Prince Lichtenstein's corps,
while Lannes, who formed the right, took Holubitz, in spite of
Bagration's efforts to dispute him this position.   This double
irruption prevented the Russians from reënforcing their troops
at Pratzen.   Lichtenstein's magnificent cavalry, composed of
eighty-two squadrons, called on one side to succor their centre
and charged on the other to support Bagration, could not act
with the harmony that was necessary to the impulse of such an
irresistible mass.   One part of his squadrons engaged with Constantine's ulans in the pursuit of Kellermann's light horse, in the
middle of the French infantry, which crushed it with their fire;
the other charged more successfully Murat's cavalry, but being
unsupported it soon fell back.

At Pratzen, Kamenski's brigade, brought from the Russian
left to the relief of the centre by Prince Wolkonski, had rallied

the remnants of Kollowrath's and Miloradovitch's divisions, and for a moment renewed the combat. Alexander at length understood the importance of the possession of the plateau, but it was impossible for his corps d'armée, engaged so far from this position, which was the first of the whole battle, to send reënforcements in time. Old Kutuzoff, wounded in the head, saw with despair the realization of his fears, and on being asked if his wound was dangerous exclaimed, extending his hand toward Pratzen, "There, there is the mortal wound!" Assailed in front and in flank by all Soult's divisions, Kamenski's brigade heroically resisted their attacks; but soon overwhelmed by numbers, and reduced to half, it was forced down into the bottoms by the side of Birnbaum. It was one o'clock; the centre of the allies was annihilated; their two wings fought still, but without communication and without means of rejoining. In this critical moment the Russian guard, of which the greater part had hitherto remained in reserve, advanced toward the French centre to drive it back, and attempted to retake the heights of Pratzen. One of the French battalions was surprised and overturned by its cuirassiers, but Napoleon's guard rushed up in its turn. The two cavalries charged with fury in a desperate conflict. A hand-to-hand fight began between these choice troops, but terminated in favor of the French. The Russian horse-guards, cut to pieces by the enemy's horsemen, fell back in disorder, and Rapp took Prince Repnine prisoner. At the same time a general movement of the guard and Bernadotte's corps broke the Russian line, which was driven back in the direction of Austerlitz after a frightful slaughter. Napoleon hastened to join a part of these troops to those of Soult in order to make a general attack, under Buxhoewden's corps d'armée.

This general, blindly pursuing his movement round the French right, had not only passed by Telnitz and the defiles that formed the ponds, but had advanced as far as Turas, situated in the enemy's rear, always fighting more or less successfully against Davout's and Legrand's divisions, and without paying any attention to what was taking place in the centre. Recalled by the most peremptory orders, he was now obliged to regain this dangerous route under the fire of all Soult's divisions. Przibyszewski's division, which he had left at Sokolnitz, was surrounded and forced to surrender. He succeeded in bringing back Doctoroff's column as far as Augezd; but at the moment that he was debouching from it Vandamme fell upon him from the heights of Pratzen and cut his column in two, a portion of which only was able to continue the route to rejoin Kutuzoff. The rest of Doctoroff's column and the whole of Langeron's, with Kienmayer's cavalry, were driven over the ponds. Their artillery passed on to a bridge, which broke under it. These troops rushed on to the pond of Telnitz, which had been frozen for two or three days; but Napoleon immediately directed the fire of his batteries upon these unfortunates. The ice was broken by the cannon-balls and by the weight of so great a mass of men: it suddenly gave way, and several thousand soldiers were engulfed in the water. On the morrow their cries and groans were still heard. There remained no other means of escape for Doctoroff and Kienmayer than a narrow road between the two ponds of Melnitz and Telnitz, and it was by this route, under the cross-fire of the French artillery, that these generals executed their retreat with admirable firmness, but sustaining immense losses.

Such were the mournful scenes upon which "the sun of Austerlitz" shone. These scenes had doubtless their grandeur, as have all those in which courage and genius have been displayed, but nothing could henceforth efface the horror of them, for one thing alone has the privilege of purifying and ennobling a field of battle, and that is the triumph of a great idea. Here it was not a principle that was involved, but a man.

The Austro-Russian army had retreated, not to Olmuetz, as Napoleon supposed on the evening of the Battle of Austerlitz, but into Hungary, which in all probability saved it from a still greater disaster. The Russians had lost twenty-one thousand men, dead and wounded; the Austrians nearly six thousand; a hundred thirty-three guns and an immense number of flags had remained in the victor's hands. The French had lost on their side, according to the most probable estimates, about eight thousand five hundred men; for the calculation contained in the Emperor's bulletin, of eight hundred killed and fifteen hundred wounded, can only be regarded as a most puerile falsehood.

Never had Napoleon before carried off such an overwhelming victory: never either had he been so much aided by the faults of his adversaries; but to lead the enemy to commit faults is half the genius of war, and it was in this that he excelled. The victory of Rivoli had been as brilliant by the sureness and precision of the manœuvres, but the results were far from equalling those of Austerlitz. Its immediate consequences were equivalent to the almost complete destruction of the European coalition, which was for a long time reduced to powerlessness. With regard to its future results, they might have been still more satisfactory if a detestable policy had not incessantly called in question the successes obtained by prodigious military genius. But to the end of his career Napoleon proved by his own example that there is an art still rarer and more difficult than the art of using victory—it is the secret of not abusing it.

THE BRITISH ACQUISITION OF CAPE COLONY

A.D. 1806

HENRY A. BRYDEN

When the British established themselves in Cape Colony they took a step which eventually led to an important extension of their vast empire. After the Portuguese discovery of the Cape of Good Hope, near the end of the fifteenth century, no permanent settlement was made there for many years, the Portuguese themselves using the Cape merely as a supply station on the way to India. In 1620 a company of Englishmen landed there and took possession in the name of King James I, but nothing came of this proceeding, and although the Dutch arrived in 1595 they did not stay.

But in 1652 the Dutch made a settlement on the Cape, and in 1658 they had a company of three hundred sixty souls, more than half, however, being negro slaves. The evil effects of this slavery have ever since been felt, although it was long ago extinguished. Throughout the last half of the seventeenth and the whole of the eighteenth century the Dutch settlement made gradual progress. In 1687 there was a French immigration.

The conditions preceding the first British occupation, that event itself, the restoration to the Dutch, and the history of the final acquisition of the Cape by England are shown by Bryden in a clear light. His account is of special value in view of the subsequent course of events in that quarter of the world.

TOWARD the end of the eighteenth century the Dutch settlers had spread far over the Cape country. Their eastern limits were bounded by the Great Fish River; their western boundary, toward the mouth of the Orange, was the Koussie, afterward known as the Buffalo River; and they had settled themselves firmly in the country about the Sneeuwberg Mountains, where the new town and Drosdy of Graaff Reinet had been established. Swellendam had been established as a town and magistracy since 1746. The country northward to the Orange River had been explored; the mouth of the Orange located by Colonel Gordon, a Scottish officer in the service of the Dutch; and so far back as

1761 Hendrik Hop, an enterprising and determined colonist, had crossed the Orange itself and penetrated into Great Namaqualand.

In pushing to the eastward the colonists had come in contact with the Amakosa Kaffirs, a fine, athletic, pastoral, and warlike people, whom they found very different neighbors from the slothful and easily managed Hottentots. In 1779, after various raids, negotiations, and recriminations, the Kaffirs were attacked by the Dutch farmers and their Hottentots, and after some fighting were driven by them beyond the Fish River. It is curious to note that the Hottentots from early times took readily to firearms and horses; they are to this day excellent rifle shots and horsemen, and, whether serving under Dutch or British, have almost invariably proved themselves valuable fighting men. The Kaffirs and Zulus, on the other hand, never showed the same inclination for firearms, preferring rather to trust to their strong arms and sharp assegais.

Even at the present time the bulk of the Kaffirs and Zulus, and the Matabele, are by no means expert gunners or riders. The Bechuanas and Basutos take to horses and rifles more readily, and many good horsemen and fair rifle shots are found among them. In 1789 a second Kaffir war broke out; the Amakosas suddenly invaded the colony west of the Fish River, and, after desultory operations during four years, were still, thanks chiefly to the rapidly decaying Dutch Government, unexpelled from the colonial limits. The gravest dissatisfaction, amounting indeed to disaffection, prevailed among the Swellendam and Graaff Reinet settlers at this period toward their own rulers. Considering that they had lost over sixty thousand head of cattle they had strong reasons for their annoyance. Proclamations from the seat of government were openly scoffed at, and although the settlers had been long forbidden, on pain of corporal or capital punishment and confiscation, to quit their farms and penetrate into the interior, they moved whithersoever it pleased them in search of game, trade, ivory, and fresh pastures. Their warfare with the Bushmen, who dwelt in the mountains, chiefly toward the northern parts of the colony, had been bloody and unceasing for many years past. The Bushmen objected to the white men invading their hunting-grounds, and carried off their cattle and sheep; the

Boers looked upon the Bushmen as nothing better than apes and vermin, and shot them down wherever possible; and the Bushmen in turn defended themselves with poisoned arrows and occasionally descended upon lone farmhouses, when the men were absent, killing women and children and destroying and driving away stock.

It was said of the Sneeuwberg Boers in 1797 that they dared not venture five hundred yards from their own dwellings. As time went on, the reprisals inflicted by either side were distinguished by increasing savagery. The Bushmen, of course, suffered by far the more severely. A Boer thought no more of killing a Bushman than of shooting a Cape partridge, and talked of his feat with as much nonchalance. Commandoes were called out constantly, and the impish Bushmen were hunted down and harried among their fastnesses. The men were invariably killed, and the women and children were made slaves of. In the district of Graaff Reinet alone, between 1786 and 1794, more than two hundred Dutch people and their servants were slain by Bushmen, while of the latter there were shot by the farmers on commando during that period no fewer than two thousand five hundred. The Government at the Cape could, by its very remoteness, exercise no sort of control over these hostilities.

In the year 1781 Great Britain, for the first time in the history of the Dutch settlement, cast an eye upon the Cape Peninsula. England had at this time plenty upon her hands; the revolted American colonists had been joined by the French, and Holland as an ally of France had involved herself in the struggle. England's conquests in India, and her trade with the East, had greatly increased, and the Cape, if it could be captured, offered many attractions as a port of call, a half-way house, a sanatorium, and a place of arms. An English fleet, therefore, under Commodore Johnstone, was despatched with secret orders to seize Cape Town. But, thanks to a smart spy, one De la Motte, the French got wind of the project, and in their turn quietly sent out a fleet, under Admiral de Suffren, to checkmate British designs.

The two fleets by mere accident met at Porto Praya in the Cape Verd Islands, and after a sharp engagement the French, who were beaten off after severely mishandling the English, got clear away, reached Simon's Bay before their rivals, and threw a strong force into Cape Town.   Johnstone, after patching up his crippled vessels, pursued his way to the Cape, where, however, he found the allied French and Dutch forces quite ready for him. Realizing the impossibility of taking the place, he drew off. Looking into the snug Saldanha Bay, a little to the north of the Cape, he found there a rich fleet of the Netherlands Company's Indiamen, homeward bound.   With this capture he enriched himself and went his way.   The once rich and famous Dutch East India Company had about this period been falling upon evil times.   Its ancient prosperity had been slowly departing, and various causes now combined to complete the dry-rot which had set in among the foundations of that great enterprise.

Corruption and misgovernment among its rich islands in the Indies were answerable for some portion of this decay; the war with England, and the many losses incurred during the struggle, may too have contributed to hasten the company's downfall. But, in truth, the Netherlands East India Company had wrought much of its own ruin.   Its absurd and hidebound trade restrictions, with laws and regulations far more fitted for the Middle Ages than for a modern undertaking; these, coupled with ill-chosen servants and rank corruption, contributed to the downfall of this once powerful company.   Even at the perilous time of 1781, when the company was known to be steadily losing twenty-five thousand pounds a year by its Cape possessions, when war had been declared between British and Dutch, and an English fleet was on its way to the Cape, the company's officials could permit themselves to indulge in such insensate folly as the granting of deeds of burghership under such restrictions as the following: The applicant was one Gous, a tailor, formerly a soldier, who was "graciously allowed to practise his craft as a tailor, but shall not be allowed to abandon the same, or adopt any other mode of living, but, when it may be deemed necessary, is to go back into his old capacity and pay, and be transported hence if thought fit."   Under such galling fetters it is small wonder that the Cape colonists of that period were becoming sick of the company's rule.

In spite of approaching ruin and of the fact that repeated demands were being made by deputations of the colonists for a free commerce, the reform of abuses among the officials, and less tyrannous laws, the company managed to keep afloat much in the old way until 1792. By that time it had come to the end of its resources, and disaster was imminent. In 1792 commissioners were appointed by the Stadtholder of the Netherlands to make full inquiry at the Cape, reform abuses, and inaugurate, if possible, a new era of prosperity. The commissioners did what they could. They reduced establishments, rearranged taxation, opened a loan bank, passed new fiscal and trade regulations, and presently departed, leaving the control of affairs to a council of regency, with Commissary-General Sluysken at its head. But troubles came thicker and faster. The back-country colonists of Swellendam and Graaff Reinet refused to pay their taxes, declaring that as the Government could no longer give them aid they would help to maintain it no further.

In 1795 the wild frontier Boers of Bruintjes Hoogte, among them some of the most turbulent and restless spirits in the colony, fine border fighters and forayers, hunters of lions, elephants, and Bushmen, met at Graaff Reinet, expelled the landrost, or magistrate, declared themselves independent, and appointed Adriaan Van Jaarsveld, a noted fighting man against the Kaffirs, as commandant of the new republic. Four months later, in June, 1795, the landrost of Swellendam was expelled in the same manner, and the Boers of that wide district appointed for themselves a "national assembly" and a new magistrate. Looking at the state of general dissatisfaction spreading throughout the colony, it is more than doubtful whether the Dutch authorities at the Cape, even if they had had the opportunity, could ever again have restored order or regained authority among the burghers. As it turned out, deliverance from an almost impossible situation was left to quite other and unexpected hands. Great Britain suddenly appeared upon the scene.

The French Revolution had been creating mighty changes in Europe; its peoples were aflame. In Holland a considerable party were in favor of the French and their new principles, and against their Stadtholder, the Prince of Orange. In 1793 the French declared war upon England, and upon the Government of Holland at that time in alliance with Great Britain. During the hard winter of 1794–1795 the Prince of Orange was compelled to fly to England. It was recognized that the seizure of the Cape by a power hostile to Great Britain would be fatal to her position in India and her trade with the East. The Stadtholder, fully recognizing the weakness of the Cape garrison, was willing that England should hold the place, and gave written orders to the Cape Town authorities to hand over the castle and fortifications to his allies. Armed with this authorization, a fleet and military forces, under Admiral Elphinstone and General Craig, were rapidly fitted out and despatched to the Cape.

In June, 1795, the British fleet sailed into Simon's Bay and dropped anchor, and as speedily as possible the Stadtholder's letter of command was presented to the acting governor of the Cape, Commissary Sluysken. Sluysken was in an extremely awkward position. Personally, it is probable that he and certain members of his council would have preferred to obey the Stadtholder's mandate. But the Prince of Orange was in exile, and Sluysken and his council had already received orders from the "Chamber of Seventeen," representing the Netherlands East India Company, to oppose any landing such as the British proposed to make. Elphinstone and Craig acted with extraordinary forbearance, considering the nature of the times and the chances of a French descent, and actually waited eighteen days before taking action. Finally Sluysken and his council hardened their hearts, declared themselves determined to oppose any invasion, and took measures of defence. They withdrew their forces from Simon's Town and stationed all the troops and burghers they were able to muster at Muizenberg, where a strong and easily defended position, which has been compared with the Pass of Thermopylæ, guarded the road to Cape Town.

Still the British, who expected reënforcements, were very leisurely in their movements. A fortnight after the Dutch had withdrawn from Simons' Town, Craig landed eighteen hundred men and took possession of the quarters abandoned by Sluysken and his military advisers, General de Lille and Colonel Gordon. Sluysken had made a call to arms, and, notwithstanding the disaffection existing throughout much of the colony, had got together sixteen hundred burghers of the Cape and Stellenbosch districts, who, with the Dutch troops stationed at the Cape and a small commando of Hottentots, brought up his available forces to three thousand men. The pass of Muizenberg was strengthened by a battery of artillery, and the formidable heights looking over the serene waters of False Bay were covered with burgher marksmen.

On August 17th General Craig with sixteen hundred men quitted Simon's Town and marched along the seashore for Muizenberg. His force consisted of four hundred fifty men of the Seventy-eighth Regiment, three hundred fifty marines and eight hundred seamen landed from the fleet, under the command of Captains Spranger and Hardy of the Rattlesnake and Echo.

Seldom has a British battle been fought amid more picturesque surroundings. False Bay, with its grand mountains, its sea of glorious blue, and the splendid curve of its shores, stands almost peerless along the African coast. From Muizenberg (the Mountain of Mice), as you look across the bay, the towering sierras of the mainland, arrayed by turns in lovely hues of purple, blue, and brown, terminate in the bold and jutting cape called Hangklip. Southward beyond Simon's Town stretches the rugged mountain backbone of the Cape Peninsula, which terminates, a score of miles away, at its very extremity, in the Cape of Good Hope, fearful to early mariners as the Cape of Storms. As the British general advanced to the attack he was supported by a heavy fire from the British fleet, which had taken up a position commanding the Dutch encampment. The Dutch, notwithstanding the strength of their position, made but a poor stand. It is probable that internal doubts and dissensions had something to do with the matter. De Lille, who was in command of the Cape forces, threw out mounted skirmishers, and opened with his artillery. The skirmishers were quickly driven back, the mountainside commanding the pass was seized by the Naval brigade and part of the Seventy-eighth Regiment, and the Dutch were quickly in flight. The artillery was silenced with no great difficulty, its position was won, and the whole Dutch force, abandoning camps, stores, guns, and ammunition, retreated toward Cape Town. The entire British loss in this action amounted to no more than nineteen killed and wounded. Craig forthwith encamped at Muizenberg and awaited reënforcements.

Early in September an English fleet, bound for India with troops, came into Simon's Bay. Three thousand soldiers were diverted for the completion of South African operations, and on the 14th General Craig, with nearly five thousand men, marched upon Cape Town. The enemy made little further stand. The burgher skirmishers fired at the troops on the march and inflicted some slight loss, but the main Dutch force stationed at Wynberg exhibited but a faint show of resistance. Cape Town lay at Craig's mercy, and within twenty-four hours was formally surrendered. The capitulation was completed at Rondebosch, and the long rule of the Netherlands East India Company had come to an end.

From 1795 to 1803 the Cape was held by the British. During this period the colonists enjoyed an unwonted measure of prosperity. The Dutch restrictions and monopolies were largely removed; trade, so long fettered, at once revived and flourished; at Cape Town a garrison of five thousand men was maintained and British money flowed lavishly. In four years after the occupation property had been raised to double its former value; the paper currency, which had depreciated 40 per cent., was at par; plenty of silver, latterly a rarity indeed, reappeared; two millions of specie were despatched from England and set in circulation. The farmer obtained three rix-dollars for his sheep where a little while before he had obtained but one; exports and imports expanded rapidly. By the year 1801 the revenue had increased threefold, and then amounted to ninety thousand pounds annually. It is worthy of note that in 1795, when the British captured the Cape, the total exports from the colony amounted to no more than fifteen thousand pounds per annum. The total white population at this period was less than twenty-five thousand souls.

In August, 1796, Admiral Elphinstone, who lay with a force of twelve warships in Simon's Bay, received news that a Dutch fleet had left Europe and was then probably near the Cape. The Admiral at once put to sea and came presently upon the Dutch force in Saldanha Bay. Admiral Lucas, the Dutch commander, had under his command nine vessels and about two thousand troops, destined for the recapture of the Cape. As the British stood into Saldanha Bay, the Dutch believed them to be Frenchmen and allies, and cries of pleasure went up. The Hollanders had no chance of escape; General Craig, with a strong force, awaited them on land, Elphinstone covered the mouth of the Bay.

They thought of destroying their ships, but Craig sent word that in that case no quarter would be given. Lucas had nothing for it but to surrender at discretion, which he did on August 18th.

In 1797 Earl Macartney, a veteran public servant, whose name long remained famous for his great embassy to China, became governor at the Cape. In the country districts the Boers were still troublesome and unsettled; Van Jaarsveld, one of their leaders, was arrested for an illegal act, and his neighbors, having risen in insurrection, rescued him from his captors. The insurgents thereupon marched to Graaff Reinet and seized the town. Troops under General Vandeleur were at once despatched to Algoa Bay, and hurried up to Graaff Reinet. The rebellious farmers retired to Bruintjes Hoogte, where they presently yielded. Some twenty of the leaders were condemned to death, others underwent the penalty of kneeling blindfold and having a sword waved over their bare heads; none, as a matter of fact, suffered the extreme penalty, but one was flogged and banished, while two died in prison.

At this time larger numbers of Hottentots in the eastern part of the country had been disarmed of weapons which they had seized from Boer houses during the troubles. They resented this deeply, and, joining themselves with the Amakosa Kaffirs, who were raiding the country toward Sunday River, ravaged a vast district as far as Lange Kloof and the Gamtoos River, plundering, murdering, and burning. The Dutch farmers suffered very severely; some thirty of them and their families were slain, and a whole province lay in ruins. The subsequent settlement, patched up by General Vandeleur, was unsatisfactory, and the Kaffirs and Hottentots escaped practically unpunished.

In 1802 was signed the Peace of Amiens, by which Great Britain agreed to restore the Cape to the Batavian Republic. Early in 1803 General Dundas, the acting governor at Cape Town, handed over the colony to the Dutch commissioner, and the British retired from the scene of their seven and a half years' labors. General Janssens was at once formally installed governor of the colony, which was now divided into six districts instead of four, Tulbagh and Vitenhage being added to the Cape, Stellenbosch, Swellendam, and Graaff Reinet. Janssens was a capable officer and an administrator of excellent intentions. He visited the disturbed eastern districts, pacified the Kaffirs, restored the Hottentots from a debasing slavery to the position of freemen, and in other directions did what he could to further the interests of the colony.   But he could not effect impossibilities. The Batavian Republic itself was in low water, the people of the Cape were starved, and the departure of the moneyed English was severely felt.

Janssens, during his short governorship, seems to have been overcome with despondency at the prospect before him.   In reply to a memorial presented to him he made this doleful speech: "With regard to your inclination to strengthen the Cape with a new settlement, we must to our sorrow, but with all sincerity, declare that we cannot perceive any means whereby more people could find a subsistence here, whether by farming or otherwise. When we contemplate the number of children growing up we frequently ask ourselves, not only how they could find other means of subsistence, but also what it is to end in at last, and what they can lay hands on to procure bread."

Janssens's despairing cry may be said to represent the death-knell of the Batavian power in South Africa.   Far different were his sentiments from those of the British administrators who had already had experience of the Cape.   Whether the Batavian Republic could have supported the colony much longer, or whether, as some statesmen advised, it would have been abandoned, it is now impossible to say.   Other developments were close at hand.   The Peace of Amiens lasted but three short months, and Europe was again in the grip of war.   For two years Janssens was expecting an English descent.   He had been preparing as best he might, strengthening his corps of Hottentots —"Pandours," they were sometimes called—to the number of six hundred, gathering in stores, and arming and drilling the burghers.

The blow fell at last.   On a beautiful evening, January 4, 1806, a great English fleet, numbering, with transports, sixty-three sail, stood in past Robben Island—the "Isle of Seals"— which guards the entrance to Table Bay.   Ship after ship came to anchor opposite the majestic range of Blaauwberg, that rugged chain which, viewed from Cape Town, stands a hazy blue or soft purple in the distance.   Sir Howe Popham commanded the fleet, while the land forces, destined for the assault of the Cape, numbered between six thousand and seven thousand men.   These were under the leadership of Major-General Sir David Baird, a tried and veteran officer, whose merits had already been tested in India, Egypt, and other parts of the world.   Baird had served at the Cape during the British occupation, and had excellent knowledge of the opposition he might expect to meet.

By midday on the 6th the British general's preparations for a landing were complete.   Four warships, the Diadem, Leader, Encounter, and Protector, had moved inshore so as to command the heights above the Blaauwberg Strand, the glittering shore of silvery white sand where the landing was to be made.   The sea was rough and the disembarkation by no means an easy one.   A few Dutch sharpshooters were posted upon the hillside, but the heavy guns of the British warships effactually did their work, and in the whole of the landing no more than four soldiers were wounded, and one killed, by the enemy's fire.   One boat, however, was swamped, and thirty soldiers of the Ninety-third Highlanders were unfortunately drowned.   On this day was landed the Highland brigade, under Brigadier-General Ferguson, consisting of the Seventy-first, Seventy-second, and Ninety-third regiments.   On the 7th a second brigade, comprising the Twenty-fourth, Fifty-ninth, and the Eighty-third regiments, was safely disembarked.   Next morning the two brigades began their march for Cape Town, which lay about eighteen miles distant. Baird had under his command four thousand men, most of them veteran troops, as well as five hundred seamen.   He was but moderately provided with artillery; the Dutch had the advantage of him in this respect, bringing into action sixteen guns as against his eight cannon.   General Janssens, to oppose the British advance, had collected a mixed force, variously estimated at from three thousand to five thousand men.   Of these some were troops of the Batavian Republic, many were mounted burghers—good shots and hardy men of the veldt—some were German mercenaries, others French seamen and marines, the crews of two wrecked vessels, the Atalanta and Napoleon.   Besides these white troops he had an excellent regiment of six hundred Hottentots and a number of trained Malay gunners.

Before dawn on the morning of January 8th the British troops

were in motion. A cloud of Dutch skirmishers and sharpshooters were driven back on their main body, and, at six o'clock in the
morning, rounding the spur of the Blaauwberg, Sir David Baird
saw before him the formidable-looking Dutch array. To prevent the possibility of being outflanked, Baird now extended his
lines and ordered the Highland Brigade, composing his left wing,
to advance. The engagement opened with a hot artillery fire
upon both sides, followed by musketry. The Dutch stood their
ground boldly and answered shot for shot. The Highlanders
were, however, as usual, not to be denied, and getting to close
quarters and charging with the bayonet, the enemy broke and
fled, the Waldeck battalion of Dutch regular troops being the
first to give way. The battle was won, and the victorious British,
looking across to the white houses and citadel of Cape Town, saw
before them the first-fruits of their victory. Baird and his men
had indeed done a good day's work for England. Never since
that January morning of 1806 has the British flag failed to flut-
ter over the Cape Peninsula.

The losses of the Dutch in this engagement—the Battle of
Blaauwberg, as it is called—were heavy. Some writers have put
the number of killed, wounded, and missing as low as three
hundred thirty-seven. Others have placed it as high as seven
hundred. Probably the actual number lies between these two
computations. Upon the British side two hundred twelve were
killed, wounded, and missing. General Janssens had, after his
defeat, retreated to the mountains of Hottentots-Holland, eastward of Cape Town, where he had accumulated magazines and
stores. He had now no real chance of success, however, and he
knew it. On the day following the battle Baird resumed his
march, and occupied a fort on the outskirts of Cape Town. Upon
the following day articles were signed and the town was formally
delivered up by the officer commanding. Janssens himself capitulated eight days later, and under terms of the agreement was,
with his troops and most of the Dutch civil servants, embarked
in British vessels, during the month of March, for Holland. The
last semblance of Batavian authority at the Cape thenceforth disappeared.

In 1813 the Prince of Orange returned from exile and was
reinstated in Holland. At the conclusion of the Napoleonic

struggle, the Prince, now King of the Netherlands, in consideration of the sum of six million pounds sterling, formally ceded the
Cape of Good Hope, together with other trifling settlements, to
the British.   By this time the Cape Dutch were becoming resigned to their new masters, more especially in the vicinity of the
Cape, where the rich and better class of colonists resided.

Here the two races mingled, and even married freely, one with
the other.   In the back country, where the colonists—the real
Boers of South Africa—were of a much ruder and more primitive
type, intercourse with the British was necessarily far more restricted.

PRUSSIA CRUSHED BY NAPOLEON

A.D. 1806

SIR WALTER SCOTT

Austerlitz put an end to the "third great coalition" against France. The Russians retreated to their own country; Austria sued humbly for peace. Prussia had been threatening to join the coalition; now, bewildered by its sudden downfall, her ministers scarce knew where to turn. They signed a hurried treaty with Napoleon, yielding him some German territory and joining him in alliance against England. The English monarch's German duchy of Hanover was thereupon handed over to Prussia.

From this moment Napoleon treated Prussia with insolence, if not contempt. Some historians have believed that he deliberately planned to force Prussia into war at this moment when she would have no allies to join her, when even England was enraged against her because of Hanover. For a dozen years Prussia had kept carefully out of all the French wars. Her King, Frederick William III, was wisely pacific, he had even certain sympathies with the aroused French people; but there had always been a war party at Berlin headed by the heroic Queen Louise. Prussians, remembering the days of Frederick the Great (died 1786), believed themselves invincible in arms. Their King found himself forced at last into a declaration of war.

THE people of Prussia at large were clamorous for war. They, too, were sensible that the late versatile conduct of their cabinet had exposed them to the censure and even the scorn of Europe, and that Bonaparte, seeing the crisis ended, in which the firmness of Prussia might have preserved the balance of Europe, retained no longer any respect for those whom he had made his dupes, but treated with total disregard the remonstrances, which, before the advantages obtained at Ulm and Austerlitz, he must have listened to with respect and deference.

Another circumstance of a very exasperating character took place at this time. One Palm, a bookseller at Nuremberg, had exposed to sale a pamphlet containing remarks on the conduct of Napoleon, in which the Emperor and his policy were treated with considerable severity. The bookseller was seized upon for this offence by the French *gens d'armes*, and transferred to Braunau, where he was brought before a military commission, tried for a libel on the Emperor of France, found guilty, and shot to death in terms of his sentence. The murder of this poor man, for such it literally was, whether immediately flowing from Bonaparte's mandate or the effect of the furious zeal of some of his officers, excited deep and general indignation.

The constitution of many of the states in Germany was despotic; but, nevertheless, the number of independent principalities, and the privileges of the free towns, have always insured to the nation at large the blessings of a free press, which, much addicted as they are to literature, the Germans value as it deserves. The cruel effort now made to fetter this unshackled expression of opinion was, of course, most unfavorable to his authority by whom it had been commanded. The thousand presses of Germany continued on every possible opportunity to dwell on the fate of Palm; and at the distance of six or seven years from his death, it might be reckoned among the leading causes which ultimately determined the popular opinion against Napoleon. It had not less effect at the time when the crime was committed; and the eyes of all Germany were turned upon Prussia as the only member of the late Holy Roman League by which the progress of the public enemy of the liberties of Europe could be arrested in its course.

Amid the general ferment of the public mind, Alexander once more appeared in person at the court of Berlin, and, more successful than on the former occasion, prevailed on the King of Prussia at length to unsheath his sword. The support of the powerful hosts of Russia was promised; and, defeated by the fatal field of Austerlitz in his attempt to preserve the southeast of Germany from French influence, Alexander now stood forth to assist Prussia as the Champion of the North. An attempt had indeed been made through means of D'Oubril, a Russian envoy at Paris, to obtain a general peace for Europe, in concurrence with that which Lord Lauderdale was endeavoring to negotiate on the part of Britain; but the treaty entirely miscarried.

While Prussia thus declared herself the enemy of France, it seemed to follow as a matter of course that she should become once more the friend of Britain; and, indeed, that power lost no time in manifesting an amicable disposition on her part, by recalling the order which blockaded the Prussian ports and annihilated her commerce. But the cabinet of Berlin evinced, in the moment when about to commence hostilities, the same selfish insincerity which had dictated all their previous conduct. While sufficiently desirous of obtaining British money to maintain the approaching war, they showed great reluctance to part with Hanover, an acquisition made in a manner so unworthy; and the Prussian minister, Lucchesini, did not hesitate to tell the British ambassador, Lord Morpeth, that the fate of the electorate would depend upon the event of arms.

Little good could be augured from the interposition of a power that, pretending to arm in behalf of the rights of nations, refused to part with an acquisition which she herself had made contrary to all the rules of justice and good faith. Still less was a favorable event to be hoped for when the management of the war was intrusted to the same incapable or faithless ministers who had allowed every opportunity to escape of asserting the rights of Prussia, when, perhaps, her assuming a firm attitude might have prevented the necessity of war altogether. But the resolution which had been delayed, when so many favorable occasions were suffered to escape unemployed, was at length adopted with an imprudent precipitation, which left Prussia neither time to adopt the wisest warlike measures nor to look out for those statesmen and generals by whom such measures could have been most effectually executed.

About the middle of August Prussia began to arm. Perhaps there are few examples of a war declared with the almost unanimous consent of a great and warlike people which was brought to an earlier and more unhappy termination. On October 1st Knobelsdorff, the Prussian envoy, was called upon by Talleyrand to explain the cause of the martial attitude assumed by his State. In reply a paper was delivered containing three propositions, or rather demands. First: that the French troops which had entered the German territory should instantly recross the Rhine. Second: that France should desist from presenting obstacles to the formation of a league in the northern part of Germany, to comprehend all the states, without exception, which had not been included in the Confederation of the Rhine.

Third: that negotiations should be immediately commenced, for the purpose of detaching the fortress of Wesel from the French Empire, and for the restitution of three abbeys which Murat had chosen to seize upon as a part of his Duchy of Berg.

With this manifesto was delivered a long explanatory letter containing severe remarks on the system of encroachment which France had acted upon. Such a text and commentary, considering their peremptory tone, and the pride and power of him to whom they were addressed in such unqualified terms, must have been understood to amount to a declaration of war. And yet, although Prussia, in common with all Europe, had just reason to complain of the encroachments of France, and her rapid strides to universal empire, it would appear that the two first articles in the King's declaration were subjects rather of negotiation than grounds of an absolute declaration of war, and that the fortress of Wesel, and the three abbeys, were scarce of importance enough to plunge the whole empire into blood for the sake of them.

Prussia, indeed, was less actually aggrieved than she was mortified and offended. She saw she had been outwitted by Bonaparte in the negotiation of Vienna; that he was juggling with her in the matter of Hanover; that she was in danger of beholding Saxony and Hesse withdrawn from her protection, to be placed under that of France: and under a general sense of these injuries, though rather apprehended than really sustained, she hurried to the field. If negotiations could have been protracted till the advance of the Russian armies, it might have given a different face to the war; but in the warlike ardor which possessed the Prussians, they were desirous to secure the advantages which, in military affairs, belong to the assailants, without weighing the circumstances which, in their situation, rendered such precipitation fatal.

Besides, such advantages were not easily to be obtained over Bonaparte, who was not a man to be amused by words when the moment of action arrived. Four days before the delivery of the Prussian note to his minister, Bonaparte had left Paris, and was personally in the field collecting his own immense forces, and urging the contribution of those contingents which the confederate princes of the Rhine were bound to supply. His answer to the hostile note of the King of Prussia was addressed, not to that monarch, but to his own soldiers. "They have dared to demand," he said, "that we should retreat at the first sight of their army. Fools! could they not reflect how impossible they found it to destroy Paris, a task incomparably more easy than to tarnish the honor of the 'Great Nation'? Let the Prussian army expect the same fate which they encountered fourteen years ago, since experience has not taught them that while it is easy to acquire additional dominions and increase of power by the friendship of France, her enmity, on the contrary, which will only be provoked by those who are totally destitute of sense and reason, is more terrible than the tempests of the ocean."

The King of Prussia had again placed at the head of his armies the Duke of Brunswick. In his youth this general had gained renown under his uncle Prince Ferdinand; but it had been lost in the retreat from Champagne in 1792, where he had suffered himself to be outmanœuvred by Dumouriez and his army of conscripts. He was seventy-two years old, and is said to have added the obstinacy of age to other of the infirmities which naturally attend it. He was not communicative nor accessible to any of the other generals, excepting Mollendorf; and this generated a disunion of councils in the Prussian camp, and the personal dislike of the army to him by whom it was commanded.

The plan of the campaign, formed by this ill-fated Prince, seems to have been singularly injudicious, and the more so as it is censurable on exactly the same grounds as that of Austria in the late war. Prussia could not expect to have the advantage of numbers in the contest. It was therefore her obvious policy to procrastinate and lengthen out negotiation until she could have the advantage of the Russian forces. Instead of this, it was determined to rush forward toward Franconia, and oppose the Prussian army alone to the whole force of France, commanded by their renowned Emperor.

The motive, too, was similar to that which had determined Austria to advance as far as the banks of the Iller. Saxony was in the present campaign, as Bavaria in the former, desirous of remaining neuter; and the hasty advance of the Prussian armies was designed to compel the Elector, Augustus, to embrace their cause. It succeeded accordingly; and the sovereign of Saxony united his forces, though reluctantly, with the left wing of the Prussians, under Prince Hohenlohe. The conduct of the Prussians toward the Saxons bore the same ominous resemblance to that of the Austrians to the Bavarians. Their troops behaved in the country of Saxony more as if they were in the land of a tributary than an ally, and while the assistance of the good and peaceable Prince was sternly exacted, no efforts were made to conciliate his good-will or soothe the pride of his subjects. In their behavior to the Saxons in general, the Prussians showed too much of the haughty spirit that goes before a fall.

The united force of the Prussian army, with its auxiliaries, amounted to one hundred fifty thousand men, confident in their own courage, in the rigid discipline which continued to distinguish their service, and in the animating recollections of the victorious career of the Great Frederick. There were many generals and soldiers in their ranks who had served under him; but, among that troop of veterans, Blucher alone was destined to do distinguished honor to the school.

Notwithstanding these practical errors, the address of the Prussian King to his army was in better taste than the vaunting proclamation of Bonaparte, and concluded with a passage which, though its accomplishment was long delayed, nevertheless proved at last prophetic. "We go," said Frederick William, "to encounter an enemy, who has vanquished numerous armies, humiliated monarchs, destroyed constitutions, and deprived more than one state of its independence and even of its very name. He has threatened a similar fate to Prussia, and proposes to reduce us to the dominion of a strange people, who would suppress the very name of Germans. The fate of armies and of nations is in the hands of the Almighty; but constant victory and durable prosperity are never granted save to the cause of justice."

While Bonaparte assembled in Franconia an army considerably superior in number to that of the Prussians, the latter occupied the country in the vicinity of the river Saale, and seemed, in doing so, to renounce all the advantage of making the attack on the enemy ere he had collected his forces. Yet to make such an attack was, and must have been, the principal motive of their

hasty and precipitate advance, especially after they had secured
its primary object, the accession of Saxony to the campaign.
The position which the Duke of Brunswick occupied was indeed very strong as a defensive one, but the means of supporting so large an army were not easily to be obtained in such a
barren country as that about Weimar; and their magazines and
depots of provisions were injudiciously placed, not close in the
rear of the army, but at Naumburg and other places upon their
extreme left, and where they were exposed to the risk of being
separated from them. It might be partly owing to the difficulty
of obtaining forage and subsistence that the Prussian army was
extended upon a line by far too much prolonged to admit of mutual support. Indeed, they may be considered rather as disposed in cantonments than as occupying a military position;
and as they remained strictly on the defensive, an opportunity
was gratuitously offered to Bonaparte to attack their divisions
in detail, of which he did not fail to avail himself with his usual
talent. The headquarters of the Prussians, where were the King
and Duke of Brunswick, were at Weimar; their left, under
Prince Hohenlohe, was at Schleitz; and their right extended
as far as Muehlhausen, leaving thus a space of ninety miles between the extreme flanks of their line.

Bonaparte, in the mean time, commenced the campaign, according to his custom, by a series of partial actions fought on
different points, in which his usual combinations obtained his
usual success; the whole tending to straiten the Prussians in
their position, to interrupt their communications, separate them
from their supplies, and compel them to fight a decisive battle
from necessity, not choice, in which dispirited troops, under baffled and outwitted generals, were to encounter soldiers who had
already obtained a foretaste of victory, and who fought under
the most renowned commanders, the combined efforts of the
whole being directed by the master spirit of the age.

Upon October 8th Bonaparte gave vent to his resentment in
a bulletin in which he complained of having received a letter of
twenty pages, signed by the King of Prussia, being, as he alleged,
a sort of wretched pamphlet, such as England engaged hireling
authors to compose at the rate of five hundred pounds sterling a
year. "I am sorry," he said, "for my brother, who does not un-

derstand the French language, and has certainly never read that rhapsody." The same publication contained much in ridicule of the Queen and Prince Louis. It bears evident marks of Napoleon's own composition, which was as singular, though not so felicitous, as his mode of fighting; but it was of little use to censure either the style or the reasoning of the lord of so many legions. His arms soon made the impression which he desired upon the position of the enemy.

The French advanced, in three divisions, upon the dislocated and extended disposition of the large but ill-arranged Prussian army. It was a primary and irretrievable fault of the Duke of Brunswick that his magazines and reserves of artillery and ammunition were placed at Naumburg, instead of being close in the rear of his army and under the protection of his main body. This ill-timed separation rendered it easy for the French to interpose between the Prussians and their supplies, providing they were able to clear the course of the Saale.

With this view the French right wing, commanded by Soult and Ney, marched upon Hof. The centre was under Bernadotte and Davout, with the guard commanded by Murat. They moved on Saalburg and Schleitz. The left wing was led by Augereau against Kolberg and Saalfeld. It was the object of this grand combined movement to overwhelm the Prussian left wing, which was extended farther than prudence permitted, and, having beaten this part of the army, to turn their whole position, and possess themselves of their magazines. After some previous skirmishes, a serious action took place at Saalfeld, where Prince Louis of Prussia commanded the advanced guard of the Prussian left wing.

In the ardor and inexperience of youth, the brave Prince, instead of being contented with defending the bridge on the Saale, quitted that advantageous position to advance with unequal forces against Lannes, who was marching upon him from Graffenthal. If bravery could have atoned for imprudence, the Battle of Saalfeld would not have been lost. Prince Louis showed the utmost gallantry in leading his men when they advanced, and in rallying them when they fled. He was killed fighting hand to hand with a French subaltern, who required him to surrender, and, receiving a sabre-wound for reply, plunged his sword into the Prince's body. Several of his staff fell around him.

The victory of Saalfeld opened the course of the Saale to the French, who instantly advanced on Naumburg. Bonaparte was at Gera, within half a day's journey from the latter city, whence he sent a letter to the King of Prussia, couched in the language of a victor—for victorious he already felt himself by his numbers and position—and seasoned with the irony of a successful foe. He regretted his good brother had been made to sign the wretched pamphlet which had borne his name, but which he protested he did not impute to him as his composition. Had Prussia asked any practicable favor of him, he said he would have granted it; but she had asked his dishonor, and ought to have known there could be but one answer. In consideration of their former friendship, Napoleon stated himself to be ready to restore peace to Prussia and her monarch; and, advising his good brother to dismiss such counsellors as recommended the present war and that of 1792, he bade him heartily farewell.

Bonaparte neither expected nor received any answer to this missive, which was written under the exulting sensations experienced by the angler when he feels the fish is hooked and about to become his secure prey. Naumburg and its magazines were consigned to the flames, which first announced to the Prussians that the French army had gotten completely into their rear, had destroyed their magazines, and, being now interposed between them and Saxony, left them no alternative save that of battle, which was to be waged at the greatest disadvantage, with an alert enemy, to whom their supineness had already given the choice of time and place for it. There was also this ominous consideration, that, in case of disaster, the Prussians had neither principle nor order nor line of retreat. The enemy were between them and Magdeburg, which ought to have been their rallying-point; and the army of the Great Frederick was, it must be owned, brought to combat with as little reflection or military science as a herd of schoolboys might have displayed in a mutiny.

Too late determined to make some exertion to clear their communications to the rear, the Duke of Brunswick, with the King of Prussia in person, marched with great part of their army to the recovery of Naumburg. Here Davout, who had taken the place, remained at the head of a division of thirty-six thousand men, with whom he was to oppose nearly double the number. The march of the Duke of Brunswick was so slow as to lose the advantage of this superiority. He paused on the evening of the 12th on the heights of Auerstaedt, and gave Davout time to re-enforce the troops with which he occupied the strong defile of Koesen. The next morning, Davout, with strong reënforce-ments, but still unequal in numbers to the Prussians, marched toward the enemy, whose columns were already in motion. The vanguard of both armies met, without previously knowing that they were so closely approaching each other, so thick lay the mist upon the ground.

The village of Hassen-Hausen, near which the opposite armies were first made aware of each other's proximity, became instantly the scene of a severe conflict, and was taken and retaken repeatedly. The Prussian cavalry, being superior in numbers to that of the French, and long famous for its appointments and discipline, attacked repeatedly, and was as often resisted by the French squares of infantry, whom they found it impossible to throw into disorder or break upon any point. The French, having thus repelled the Prussian horse, carried at the point of the bayonet some woods and the village of Spilberg, and remained in undisturbed possession of that of Hassen-Hausen.

The Prussians had by this time maintained the battle from eight in the morning till eleven, and being now engaged on all points, with the exception of two divisions of the reserve, had suffered great loss. The generalissimo, Duke of Brunswick, wounded in the face by a grape-shot, was carried off; so was General Schmettau and other officers of distinction. The want of an experienced chief began to be felt, when, to increase the difficulties of their situation, the King of Prussia received intelli-gence that General Mollendorf, who commanded his right wing, stationed near Jena, was in the act of being defeated by Bona-parte in person. The King took the generous but perhaps des-perate resolution of trying whether in one general charge he could not redeem the fortune of the day, by defeating that part of the French with which he was personally engaged. He ordered the attack to be made along all the line and with all the forces which he had in the field; and his commands were obeyed with gallantry enough to vindicate the honor of the troops, but not to lead to success. They were beaten off, and the French resumed the offensive in their turn.

Still the Prussian monarch, who seems now to have taken the command upon himself, endeavoring to supply the want of professional experience by courage, brought up his last reserves, and encouraged his broken troops rather to make a final stand for victory than to retreat in face of a conquering army. This effort also proved in vain. The Prussian line was attacked everywhere at once; centre and wings were broken through by the French at the bayonet's point; and the retreat, after so many fruitless efforts, in which no division had been left unengaged, was of the most disorderly character. But the confusion was increased tenfold when, as the defeated troops reached Weimar, they fell in with the right wing of their own army, fugitives like themselves, who were attempting to retreat in the same direction. The disorder of two routed armies meeting in opposing currents soon became inextricable. The roads were choked up with artillery and baggage-wagons; the retreat became a hurried flight; and the King himself, who had shown the utmost courage during the Battle of Auerstaedt, was at length, for personal safety, compelled to leave the highroads, and escape across the fields, escorted by a small body of cavalry.

While the left of the Prussian army was in the act of combating Davout at Auerstaedt, their right, as we have hinted, was with equally bad fortune engaged at Jena. This second action, though the least important of the two, has always given the name to the double battle; because it was at Jena that Napoleon was engaged in person.

The French Emperor had arrived at this town, which is situated upon the Saale, on October 13th, and had lost no time in issuing those orders to his marshals which produced the demonstrations of Davout and the victory of Auerstaedt. His attention was not less turned to the position he himself occupied, and in which he had the prospect of fighting Mollendorf and the right of the Prussians on the next morning. With his usual activity he formed or enlarged, in the course of the night, the roads by which he proposed to bring up his artillery on the succeeding day, and, by hewing the solid rock, made a path practicable for guns to the plateau or elevated plain in the front of Jena, where his centre was established. The Prussian army lay before them, extended on a line of six leagues, while that of Napoleon, extremely concentrated, showed a very narrow front, but was well secured both in the flanks and in the rear.

Bonaparte, according to his custom, slept in the bivouac, surrounded by his guards. In the morning he harangued his soldiers, and recommended to them to stand firm against the charges of the Prussian cavalry, which had been represented as very redoubtable. As before Ulm he had promised his soldiers a repetition of the Battle of Marengo, so now he pointed out to his men that the Prussians, separated from their magazines and cut off from their country, were in the situation of Mack at Ulm. He told them that the enemy no longer fought for honor and victory, but for the chance of opening a way to retreat; and he added that the corps which should permit them to escape would lose their honor. The French replied with loud shouts, and demanded instantly to advance to the combat. The Emperor ordered the columns destined for the attack to descend into the plain. His centre consisted of the Imperial Guard and two divisions of Lannes. Augereau commanded the right, which rested on a village and a forest; and Soult's division, with a part of Ney's, was upon the left.

General Mollendorf advanced on his side, and both armies, as at Auerstaedt, were hid from each other by the mist, until suddenly the atmosphere cleared, and showed them to each other within the distance of half cannon-shot. The conflict instantly commenced. It began on the French right, where the Prussians attacked with the purpose of driving Augereau from the village on which he rested his extreme flank. Lannes was sent to support him, by whose succor he was enabled to stand his ground. The battle then became general, and the Prussians showed themselves such masters of discipline that it was long impossible to gain any advantage over men who advanced, retired, or moved to either flank, with the regularity of machines. Soult at length, by the most desperate efforts, dispossessed the Prussians opposed to him of the woods from which they had annoyed the French left; and at the same conjuncture the division of Ney and a large reserve of cavalry appeared upon the field of battle.

Napoleon, thus strengthened, advanced the centre, consisting in a great measure of the Imperial Guard, who, being fresh and in the highest spirits, compelled the Prussian army to give way. Their retreat was at first orderly: but it was a part of Bonaparte's tactics to pour attack after attack upon a worsted enemy, as the billows of a tempestuous ocean follow each other in succession, till the last waves totally disperse the fragments of the bulwark which the first have breached. Murat, at the head of the dragoons and the cavalry of reserve, charged, as one who would merit, as far as bravery could merit, the splendid destinies which seemed now opening to him. The Prussian infantry were unable to support the shock, nor could their cavalry protect them. The rout became general. Great part of the artillery was taken, and the broken troops retreated in disorder upon Weimar, where, as we have already stated, their confusion became inextricable, by their encountering the other tide of fugitives from their own left, which was directed upon Weimar also.

All leading and following seemed now lost in this army, so lately confiding in its numbers and discipline. There was scarcely a general left to issue orders, scarcely a soldier disposed to obey them; and it seems to have been more by a sort of instinct than any resolved purpose, that several broken regiments were directed, or directed themselves, upon Magdeburg, where Prince Hohenlohe endeavored to rally them.

Besides the double battle of Jena and Auerstaedt, Bernadotte had his share in the conflict, as he worsted at Apolda, a village betwixt these two points of general action, a large detachment. The French accounts state that twenty thousand Prussians were killed and taken in the course of this fatal day; that three hundred guns fell into their power, with twenty generals or lieutenant-generals, and standards and colors to the number of sixty.

The mismanagement of the Prussian generals in these calamitous battles and in all the manœuvres which preceded them, amounted to infatuation. The troops also, according to Bonaparte's evidence, scarcely maintained their high character, oppressed probably by a sense of the disadvantages under which they combated. But it is unnecessary to dwell on the various

causes of a defeat, when the vanquished seem neither to have
formed one combined and general plan of attack in the action
nor maintained communication with each other while it endured
nor agreed upon any scheme of retreat when the day was lost.
The Duke of Brunswick, too, and General Schmettau, being
mortally wounded early in the battle, the several divisions of the
Prussian army fought individually, without receiving any general orders, and consequently without regular plan or combined manœuvres. The consequences of the defeat were more
universally calamitous than could have been anticipated, even
when we consider that, no mode of retreat having been fixed on,
or general rallying-place appointed, the broken army resembled
a covey of heath-fowl which the sportsman marks down and
destroys in detail and at his leisure.

Next day after the action a large body of the Prussians, who,
under the command of Mollendorf, had retired to Erfurt, were
compelled to surrender to the victors, and the marshal, with the
Prince of Orange Fulda, became prisoners. Other relics of this
most unhappy defeat met with the same fate. General Kalk-
reuth, at the head of a considerable division of troops, was overtaken and routed in an attempt to cross the Hartz Mountains.
Prince Eugene of Wurtemberg commanded an untouched body
of sixteen thousand men, whom the Prussian general-in-chief
had suffered to remain at Memmingen, without an attempt to
bring them into the field. Instead of retiring when he heard all
was lost, the Prince was rash enough to advance toward Halle,
as if to put the only unbroken division of the Prussian army in
the way of the far superior and victorious hosts of France. He
was accordingly attacked and defeated by Bernadotte.

The chief point of rallying, however, was Magdeburg, under
the walls of which strong city Prince Hohenlohe, though
wounded, contrived to assemble an army amounting to fifty
thousand men, but wanting everything and in the last degree
of confusion. But Magdeburg was no place of rest for them.
The same improvidence which had marked every step of the
campaign had exhausted that city of the immense magazines
which it contained, and taken them for the supply of the Duke of
Brunswick's army. The wrecks of the field of Jena were exposed
to famine as well as the sword. It only remained for Prince Ho-

henlohe to make the best escape he could to the Oder, and, considering the disastrous circumstances in which he was placed, he
seems to have displayed both courage and skill in his proceedings. After various partial actions, however, in all of which he
lost men, he finally found himself, with the advanced guard and
centre of his army, on the heights of Prenzlau, without provisions, forage, or ammunition. Surrender became unavoidable;
and at Prenzlau and Pasewalk, nearly twenty thousand Prussians
laid down their arms.

The rear of Prince Hohenlohe's army did not immediately
share this calamity. They were at Bortzenberg when the surrender took place, and amounted to about ten thousand men,
the relics of the battle in which Prince Eugene of Wurtemberg
had engaged near Weimar, and were under the command of a
general whose name hereafter was destined to sound like a war
trumpet—the celebrated Blucher.

In the extremity of his country's distresses, this distinguished
soldier showed the same indomitable spirit, the same activity in
execution and daringness of resolve, which afterward led to such
glorious results. He was about to leave Bortzenberg on the 29th,
in consequence of his orders from Prince Hohenlohe, when he
learned that general's disaster at Prenzlau. He instantly changed
the direction of his retreat, and, by a rapid march toward Strel-
itz, contrived to unite his forces with about ten thousand men,
gleanings of Jena and Auerstaedt, which, under the Dukes of
Weimar and of Brunswick Oels, had taken their route in that
direction.

Thus reënforced, Blucher adopted the plan of passing the
Elbe at Lauenburg, and reënforcing the Prussian garrisons in
Lower Saxony. With this view he fought several sharp actions
and made many rapid marches. But the odds were too great to
be balanced by courage and activity. The division of Soult,
which had crossed the Elbe, cut him off from Lauenburg, that of
Murat interposed between him and Stralsund, while Bernadotte
pressed upon his rear. Blucher had no resource but to throw
himself and his diminished and dispirited army into Lubeck.
The pursuers came soon up, and found him like a stag at bay.
A battle was fought on November 6th in the streets of Lubeck,
with extreme fury on both sides, in which the Prussians were

overpowered by numbers, and lost many slain, besides four thousand prisoners. Blucher fought his way out of the town, and reached Schwerta. But he had now retreated as far as he had Prussian ground to bear him, and to violate the neutrality of the Danish territory would only have raised up new enemies to his unfortunate master.

On November 7th, therefore, he gave up his good sword, to be resumed under happier auspices, and surrendered with the few thousand men which remained under his command. But the courage which he had manifested, like the lights of St. Elmo amid the gloom of the tempest, showed that there was at least one pupil of the Great Frederick worthy of his master, and afforded hopes, on which Prussia long dwelt in silence, till the moment of action arrived.

The total destruction, for such it might almost be termed, of the Prussian army was scarcely so wonderful as the facility with which the fortresses which defend that country, some of them ranking among the foremost in Europe, were surrendered by their commandants, without shame, and without resistance, to the victorious enemy. Strong towns and fortified places, on which the engineer had exhausted his science, provided too with large garrisons and ample supplies, opened their gates at the sound of a French trumpet or the explosion of a few bombs. Spandau, Stettin, Kuestrin, Hameln, were each qualified to have arrested the march of invaders for months, yet were all surrendered on little more than a summons. In Magdeburg was a garrison of twenty-two thousand men, two thousand of them being artillerymen; and nevertheless this celebrated city capitulated with Marshal Ney at the first flight of shells. Hameln was garrisoned by six thousand troops, amply supplied with provisions and every means of maintaining a siege. The place was surrendered to a force scarcely one-third in proportion to that of the garrison. These incidents were too gross to be imputed to folly and cowardice alone. The French themselves wondered at their conquests, yet had a shrewd guess at the manner in which they were rendered so easy.

When the recreant governor of Magdeburg was insulted by the students of Halle for treachery as well as cowardice, the French garrison of the place sympathized, as soldiers, with the youthful enthusiasm of the scholars, and afforded the sordid old coward but little protection against their indignation. From a similar generous impulse, Schoels, the commandant of Hameln, was nearly destroyed by the troops under his orders. In surrendering the place, he had endeavored to stipulate that, in case the Prussian provinces should pass by the fortune of war to some other power, the officers should retain their pay and rank. The soldiers were so much incensed at this stipulation, which carried desertion in its front, and a proposal to shape a private fortune to himself amid the ruin of his country, that Schoels only saved himself by delivering up the place to the French before the time stipulated in the articles of capitulation.

It is believed that, on several of these occasions, the French constructed a golden key to open these iron fortresses, without being themselves at the expense of the precious metal which composed it. Every large garrison has of course a military chest with treasure for the regular payment of the soldiery; and it is said that more than one commandant was unable to resist the proffer that, in case of an immediate surrender, this deposit should not be inquired into by the captors, but left at the disposal of the governor, whose accommodating disposition had saved them the time and trouble of a siege.

While the French army made this uninterrupted progress, the new King of Holland, Louis Bonaparte, with an army partly composed of Dutch and partly of Frenchmen, possessed himself with equal ease of Westphalia, great part of Hanover, Emden, and East Friesland. To complete the picture of general disorder which Prussia now exhibited, it is only necessary to add that the unfortunate King, whose personal qualities deserved a better fate, had been obliged after the battle to fly into East Prussia, where he finally sought refuge in the city of Koenigsberg. L'Estocq, a faithful and able general, was still able to assemble out of the wreck of the Prussian army a few thousand men for the protection of his sovereign. Bonaparte took possession of Berlin on October 25th, eleven days after the Battle of Jena.

The fall of Prussia was so sudden and so total as to excite the general astonishment of Europe. Its Prince was compared to the rash and inexperienced gambler, who risks his whole fortune on one desperate cast, and rises from the table totally ruined.

That power had for three-quarters of a century ranked among the most important of Europe; but never had she exhibited such a formidable position as almost immediately before her disaster, when, holding in her own hand the balance of Europe, she might, before the day of Austerlitz, have inclined the scale to which side she would. And now she lay at the feet of the antagonist whom she had rashly and in ill time defied, not fallen merely but totally prostrate, without the means of making a single effort to arise. It was remembered that Austria, when her armies were defeated and her capital taken, had still found resources in the courage of her subjects; and that the insurrections of Hungary and Bohemia had assumed, even after Bonaparte's most eminent successes, a character so formidable as to aid in procuring peace for the defeated Emperor on moderate terms. Austria, therefore, was like a fortress repeatedly besieged, and as often breached and damaged, but which continued to be tenable, though diminished in strength and deprived of important outworks.

But Prussia seemed like the same fortress swallowed up by an earthquake, which leaves nothing either to inhabit or defend, and where the fearful agency of the destroyer reduces the strongest bastions and bulwarks to crumbled masses of ruins and rubbish. The cause of this great distinction between two countries which have so often contended against each other for political power, and for influence in Germany, may be easily traced.

The Empire of Austria combines in itself several large kingdoms, the undisturbed and undisputed dominions of a common sovereign, to whose sway they have been long accustomed and toward whom they nourish the same sentiments of loyalty which their fathers entertained to the ancient princes of the same house. Austria's natural authority therefore rested, and now rests, on this broad and solid base, the general and rooted attachment of the people to their prince, and their identification of his interests with their own.

Prussia had also her native provinces, in which her authority was hereditary, and where the affection, loyalty, and patriotism of the inhabitants were natural qualities which fathers transmitted to their sons. But a large part of her dominions consist of late acquisitions obtained at different times by the arms or policy of the Great Frederick; and thus her territories, made up of a number of small and distant states, want geographical breadth, while their disproportioned length stretches, according to Voltaire's well-known simile, like a pair of garters across the map of Europe. It follows as a natural consequence that a long time must intervene between the formation of such a kingdom and the amalgamation of its component parts, differing in laws, manners, and usages, into one compact and solid monarchy, having respect and affection to their king as the common head, and regard to each other as members of the same community. It will require generations to pass away ere a kingdom, so artificially composed, can be cemented into unity and strength; and the tendency to remain disunited is greatly increased by the disadvantages of its geographical situation.

These considerations alone might explain why, after the fatal Battle of Jena, the inhabitants of the various provinces of Prussia contributed no important personal assistance to repel the invader; and why, although almost all trained to arms, and accustomed to serve a certain time in the line, they did not display any readiness to exert themselves against the common enemy. They felt that they belonged to Prussia only by the right of the strongest, and therefore were indifferent when the same right seemed about to transfer their allegiance elsewhere. They saw the approaching ruin of the Prussian power, not as children view the danger of a father, which they are bound to prevent at the hazard of their lives, but as servants view that of a master, which concerns them no otherwise than as leading to a change of their employers.

THE FIRST PRACTICAL STEAMBOAT

A.D. 1807

JAMES RENWICK

That the same year in which Fulton navigated the Hudson River with his improved steamboat also saw the earliest use of fixed steam-engines to drag trains on railways by means of ropes, shows how the great invention improved by Watt was engaging ingenious minds upon the new problems which he and his contemporaries had suggested.

But the fact remains, to the honor of Fulton, that he made steam navigation practicable some years before any workable plan of steam locomotion on land was completed.

The Spaniards claim to have first attempted to propel a vessel by steam in 1543, but the claim rests on doubtful authority. The French physicist Papin, born in 1647, and others in France, England, and the United States, who experimented with more or less result toward the end which Fulton reached, receive at the hands of Renwick the attention due to their efforts, and thus the historical evolution of the steamboat is sufficiently shown in the following account.

Robert Fulton was born at Little Britain, Pennsylvania, in 1765. He went to London and studied painting under Benjamin West, but in 1793 devoted himself wholly to civil and mechanical engineering. In 1794 he removed to Paris, where he conducted many experiments on the lines which finally led to his great achievement. Fulton died in New York in 1815.

UNTIL Watt had completed the structure of the double-acting condensing-engine the application of steam to any but the single object of pumping water had been almost impracticable. It was not enough, in order to render it applicable to general purposes, that the condensation of the water should take place in a separate vessel, and that steam should itself be used, instead of atmospheric pressure, as the moving power; but it was also necessary that the steam should act as well during the ascent as during the descent of the piston. Before the method of paddle-wheels could be successfully introduced it was, in addition, necessary that a ready and convenient mode of changing the motion of the piston into one continuous and rotary should be discovered. All these improvements upon the original form of the steam-engine are due to Watt, and he did not complete their perfect combination before the year 1786.

Evans, who, in America, saw the possibility of constructing a double-acting engine even before Watt, and had made a model of his machine, did not succeed in obtaining funds to make an experiment upon a large scale before 1801. We conceive, therefore, that all those who projected the application of steam to vessels before 1786 may be excluded, without ceremony, from the list of those entitled to compete with Fulton for the honors of invention. No one, indeed, could have seen the powerful action of a pumping-engine without being convinced that the energy, which was applied so successfully to that single purpose, might be made applicable to many others; but those who entertained a belief that the original atmospheric engine, or even the single-acting engine of Watt, could be applied to propel boats by paddle-wheels showed a total ignorance of mechanical principles. This is more particularly the case with all those whose projects bore the strongest resemblance to the plan which Fulton afterward carried successfully into effect. Those who approached most nearly to the attainment of success were they who were farthest removed from the plan of Fulton. His application was founded on the properties of Watt's double-acting engine, and could not have been used at all until that instrument of universal application had received the last finish of its inventor.

In this list of failures, from proposing to do what the instrument they employed was incapable of performing, we do not hesitate to include Savary, Papin, Jonathan Hulls, Perier, the Marquis de Jouffroy, and all the other names of earlier date than 1786, whom the jealousy of the French and English nations has drawn from oblivion for the purpose of contesting the priority of Fulton's claims. The only competitor whom they might have brought forward with some shadow of plausibility is Watt himself. No sooner had that illustrious inventor completed his double-acting engine than he saw at a glance the vast field of its application. Navigation and locomotion were not omitted; but, living in an inland town, and in a country possessing no rivers of importance, his views were limited to canals alone. In this direction he saw an immediate objection to the use of any apparatus of which so powerful an agent as his engine would be the mover; for it was clear that the injury which would be done to the banks of the canal would prevent the possibility of its introduction. Watt, therefore, after having conceived the idea of a steamboat, laid it aside as unlikely to be of any practical value.

The idea of applying steam to navigation was not confined to Europe. Numerous Americans entertained hopes of attaining the same object, but, before 1786, with the same want of any reasonable hopes of success. Their fruitless projects were, however, rebuked by Franklin, who, reasoning upon the capabilities of the engine in its original form, did not hesitate to declare all their schemes impracticable.

Among those who, before the completion of Watt's invention, attempted the structure of steamboats, must be named with praise Fitch and Rumsey. They, unlike those whose names have been cited, were well aware of the real difficulties which they were to overcome; and both were the authors of plans which, if the engine had been incapable of further improvement, might have had a partial and limited success. Fitch's trial was made in 1783, and Rumsey's in 1787. The latter date is subsequent to Watt's double-acting engine; but, as the project consisted merely in pumping in water to be afterward forced out at the stern, the single-acting engine was probably employed. Evans, whose engine might have answered the purpose, was employed in the daily business of a millwright, and, although he might at any time have driven these competitors from the field, took no steps to apply his dormant invention.

Fitch, who had watched the graceful and rapid way of the Indian pirogue, saw in the oscillating motion of the old pumping-engine the means of impelling paddles in a manner similar to that given them by the human arm. This idea is extremely ingenious, and was applied in a simple and beautiful manner; but the engine was yet too feeble and cumbrous to yield an adequate force; and, when it received its great improvement from Watt, a more efficient mode of propulsion became practicable, and must have superseded Fitch's paddles had they even come into general use.

In the latter stages of Fitch's investigations he became aware of the value of Watt's double-acting engine, and refers to it as a

valuable addition to his means of success; but it does not appear
to have occurred to him that, with this improved power, methods
of far greater efficiency than those to which he had been limited
before this invention was completed had now become practicable.

When the properties of Watt's double-acting engine became
known to the public an immediate attempt was made to apply it
to navigation.   This was done by Miller, of Dalswinton, who
employed Symington as his engineer.   Miller seems to have been
its real author; for, as early as 1787, he published his belief that
boats might be propelled by employing a steam-engine to turn the
paddle-wheels.   It was not until 1791 that Symington completed
a model for him, of a size sufficient for a satisfactory experiment.
If we may credit the evidence which has since been adduced, the
experiment was as successful as the first attempts of Fulton; but
it did not give to the inventor that degree of confidence which was
necessary to induce him to embark his fortune in the enterprise.
The experiment of Miller was therefore ranked by the public
among unsuccessful enterprises, and was rather calculated to
deter from imitation than to encourage others to pursue the same
path.

Symington, at a subsequent period, resumed the plans of
Miller, and by the aid of funds furnished by Lord Dundas, put
a boat in motion on the Forth and Clyde canal in 1801.

There can be little doubt that Symington was a mechanic of
great practical skill and considerable ingenuity; but he can have
no claim to be considered as an original inventor; for he was, in
the first instance, no more than the workman who carried into
effect the ideas of Miller, and his second boat was a mere copy of
the first.   It is with pain, too, that we are compelled to notice a
most disingenuous attempt on his part to defraud the memory
of Fulton of its due honor.

In a narrative which he drew up, after Fulton's death, he
states that, while his first boat was in existence, probably in 1802,
he received a visit from Fulton, and, at his request, put the boat
in motion.   Now it appears to be established, beyond all question, that Fulton was not in Great Britain between 1796 and
1804, when he returned to that country on the invitation of Mr.
Pitt, who held out hopes that his torpedoes would be experi-

mented upon by that Government.   At all events, we know that Fulton could not have made the copious notes which Symington says he took, and we have reason to believe that he had never seen the boat of that artisan, for the author of this memoir, long after the successful enterprise of Fulton, actually furnished him, for the purpose of reference, with a work containing a draft of Symington's boat, of which he could have had no need had the assertions of the latter been true.

The experiments of Fitch and Rumsey in the United States, although generally considered as unsuccessful, did not deter others from similar attempts.   The great rivers and arms of the sea, which intersect the Atlantic coast, and still more the innumerable navigable arms of the "Father of Waters," appeared to call upon the ingenious machinist to contrive means for their more convenient navigation.

The improvement of the engine by Watt was now familiarly known, and it was evident that it possessed sufficient powers for the purpose.   The only difficulty which existed was in the mode of applying it.   The first person who entered into the inquiry was John Stevens, of Hoboken, who commenced his researches in 1791.   In these he was steadily engaged for nine years, when he became the associate of Chancellor Livingston and Nicholas Roosevelt.   Among the persons employed by this association was Brunel, who has since become distinguished in Europe as the inventor of the block machinery used in the British navy-yards and as the engineer of the tunnel beneath the Thames.

Even with the aid of such talent the efforts of this association were unsuccessful, as we now know, from no error in principle, but from defects in the boat to which it was applied.   The appointment of Livingston as ambassador to France broke up this joint effort; and, like all previous schemes, it was considered as abortive, and contributed to throw discredit upon all undertakings of the kind.   A grant of exclusive privileges on the waters of the State of New York was made to this association without any difficulty, it being believed that the scheme was little short of madness.

Livingston, on his arrival in France, found Fulton domiciliated with Joel Barlow.   The conformity in their pursuits led to intimacy, and Fulton speedily communicated to Livingston the

scheme which he had laid before Earl Stanhope in 1793. Livingston was so well pleased with it that he at once offered to provide the funds necessary for an experiment, and to enter into a
contract for Fulton's aid in introducing the method into the
United States, provided the experiment were successful.

Fulton had in his early discussion with Lord Stanhope repu-
diated the idea of an apparatus acting on the principle of the foot
of an aquatic bird, and had proposed paddle-wheels in its stead.
On resuming his inquiries after his arrangement with Livingston
it occurred to him to compose wheels with a set of paddles revolving upon an endless chain, extending from the stem to the stern
of the boat.   It is probable that the apparent want of success
which had attended the experiments of Symington led him to
doubt the correctness of his own original views.

That such doubt should be entirely removed he had recourse
to a series of experiments upon a small scale.   These were performed at Plombières, a French watering-place, where he spent
the summer of 1802.   In these experiments, the superiority of the
paddle-wheel over every other method of propulsion that had yet
been proposed was fully established.   His original impressions
being thus confirmed he proceeded, late in the year of 1803, to
construct a working model of his intended boat, which model was
deposited with a commission of French savants.   He at the same
time commenced building a vessel sixty-six feet in length and
eight feet in width.   To this an engine was adapted; and the
experiment made with it was so satisfactory as to leave little
doubt of final success.

Measures were therefore immediately taken preparatory to
constructing a steamboat on a large scale in the United States.
For this purpose, as the workshops of neither France nor America
could at that time furnish an engine of good quality, it became
necessary to resort to England for the purpose.   Fulton had
already experienced the difficulty of being compelled to employ
artisans unacquainted with the subject.   It is indeed more than
probable that, had he not, during his residence in Birmingham,
made himself familiar, not only with the general features, but
with the most minute details, of the engine of Watt, the experiment on the Seine could not have been made.   In this experiment, and in the previous investigations, it became obvious that

the engine of Watt required important modifications in order to adapt it to navigation. These modifications had been planned by Fulton; but it now became important that they should be more fully tested. An engine was therefore ordered from Watt and Bolton, without any specification of the object to which it was to be applied; and its form was directed to be varied from their usual models, in conformity with sketches furnished by Fulton.

The order for an engine intended to propel a vessel of large size was transmitted to Watt and Bolton in 1803. Much about the same time Chancellor Livingston, having full confidence in the success of the enterprise, caused an application to be made to the Legislature of New York for an exclusive privilege of navigating the waters of that State by steam, that granted on a former occasion having expired.

This was granted with little opposition. Indeed, those who might have been inclined to object saw so much of the impracticable and even of the ridiculous in the project that they conceived the application unworthy of serious debate. The condition attached to the grant was that a vessel should be propelled by steam at the rate of four miles an hour, within a prescribed space of time. This reliance upon the reserved rights of the States proved a fruitful source of vexation to Livingston and Fulton, embittered the close of the life of the latter, and reduced his family to penury. It can hardly be doubted that, had an expectation been entertained that the grant of a State was ineffectual, and that the jurisdiction was vested in the General Government, a similar grant might have been obtained from Congress. The influence of Livingston with the Administration was deservedly high, and that Administration was supported by a powerful majority; nor would it have been consistent with the principles of the opposition to vote against any act of liberality to the introducer of a valuable application of science. Livingston, however, confiding in his skill as a lawyer, preferred the application to the State, and was thus, by his own act, restricted to a limited field.

Before the engine ordered from Watt and Bolton was completed, Fulton visited England. Disgusted by the delays and want of consideration exhibited by the French Government, he had listened to an overture from that of England. This was made to him at the instance of Earl Stanhope, who urged upon the Administration the dangers to be apprehended by the navy of Great Britain in case the invention of Fulton fell into the possession of France.   After a long negotiation, protracted by the difficulty of communicating on such a subject between two hostile countries, he at last revisited England.   Here, for a time, he was flattered with hopes of being employed for the purpose of using his invention.   Experiments were made with such success as to induce a serious effort to destroy the flotilla lying in the harbor of Boulogne, by means of torpedoes.   This effort, however, did not produce much effect, and finally, when the British Government demanded a pledge that the invention should be communicated to no other nation, Fulton, whose views had always been directed to the application of these military engines to the service of his native country, refused to comply with the demand.

In these experiments Earl Stanhope took a strong interest, which was shared by his daughter, Lady Hester, whose talents and singularity have since excited so much attention, and who long reigned almost as a queen among the tribes of the Libanus.

Although the visit of Fulton to England was ineffectual, so far as his project of torpedoes was concerned, it gave him the opportunity of visiting Birmingham, and directing in person the construction of the engine ordered from Watt and Bolton.   It could only have been at this time, if ever, that he saw the boat of Symington; but a view of it could have produced no effect upon his own plans, which had been matured in France, and carried, so far as the engine was concerned, to such an extent as to admit of no alteration.

The engine was at last completed, and reached New York in 1806.   Fulton, who returned to his native country about the same period, immediately undertook the construction of a boat in which to place it.   In the ordering of this engine, and in planning the boat, Fulton exhibited plainly how far his scientific researches and practical experiments had placed him before all his competitors.   He had evidently ascertained, what each successive year's experience proves more fully, the great advantages possessed by large steamboats over those of smaller size; and thus, while all previous attempts were made in small vessels, he alone resolved to make his final experiment in one of great dimensions. That a vessel intended to be propelled by steam ought to have very different proportions, and lines of a character wholly distinct, from those of vessels intended to be navigated by sails, was evident to him. No other theory, however, of the resistance of fluids was admitted at the time than that of Bossut, and there were no published experiments except those of the British Society of Arts. Judged in reference to these the model chosen by Fulton was faultless, although it would not stand the test of an examination founded upon a better theory and more accurate experiments.

The vessel was finished and fitted with her machinery in August, 1807. An experimental excursion was forthwith made, at which a number of gentlemen of science and intelligence were present. Many of these were either sceptical or absolute unbelievers. But a few minutes sufficed to convert the whole party and satisfy the most obstinate doubters that the long-desired object was at last accomplished. Only a few weeks before, the cost of constructing and finishing the vessel threatening to exceed the funds with which he had been provided by Livingston, he had attempted to obtain a supply by the sale of one-third of the exclusive right granted by the State of New York. No person was found possessed of the faith requisite to induce him to embark in the project. Those who had rejected this opportunity of investment were now the witnesses of the completion of the scheme, which they had not considered as an adequate security for the desired funds.

Within a few days from the time of the first experiment with the steamboat, a voyage was undertaken in it to Albany. This city, situated at the natural head of the navigation of the Hudson, is distant, by the line of the channel of the river, rather less than one hundred fifty miles from New York. By the old post road the distance is one hundred sixty miles, at which that by water is usually estimated. Although the greater part of the channel of the Hudson is both deep and wide, yet, for about fourteen miles below Albany, this character is not preserved, and the stream, confined within comparatively small limits, is obstructed by bars of sand or spreads itself over shallows. In a few remarkable instances the sloops which then exclusively navigated the Hudson had effected a passage in about sixteen hours, but a whole week was not unfrequently employed in this voyage, and the average time of passage was not less than four entire days. In Fulton's first attempt to navigate this stream the passage to Albany was performed in thirty-two hours, and the return in thirty.

Up to this time, although the exclusive grant had been sought and obtained from the State of New York, it does not appear that either he or his associate had been fully aware of the vast opening which the navigation of the Hudson presented for the use of steam. They looked to the rapid Mississippi and its branches as the place where their triumph was to be achieved; and the original boat, modelled for shallow waters, was announced as intended for the navigation of that river. But even in the very first attempt, numbers called by business or pleasure to the northern or western parts of the State of New York crowded into the yet untried vessel, and when the success of the attempt was beyond question, no little anxiety was manifested that the steamboat should be established as a regular packet between New York and Albany.

With these indications of the public feeling Fulton immediately complied, and regular voyages were made at stated times until the end of the season. These voyages were not, however, unattended with inconvenience. The boat, designated for a mere experiment, was incommodious, and many of the minor arrangements by which facility of working and safety from accident to the machinery were to be insured were yet wanting. Fulton continued a close and attentive observer of the performance of the vessel; every difficulty, as it manifested itself, was met and removed by the most masterly as well as simple contrivances. Some of these were at once adopted, while others remained to be applied while the boat should be laid up for the winter. He thus gradually formed in his mind the idea of a complete and perfect vessel; and in his plan no one part which has since been found to be essential to ease in manœuvring or security was omitted. The eyes of the whole community were now fixed upon the steamboat; and, as all of competent mechanical knowledge were as alive to the defects of the original vessel as Fulton himself, his right to priority of invention of various important accessories has been disputed.

The winter of 1807–1808 was occupied in remodelling and re-building the vessel, to which the name of the Clermont was now given. The guards and the housings for the wheels, which had been but temporary structures, applied as their value was pointed out by experience, became solid and essential parts of the boat. For a rudder of the ordinary form, one of surface much more extended in its horizontal dimensions was substituted; this, instead of being moved by a tiller, was acted upon by ropes applied to its extremity, and these ropes were adapted to a steering-wheel which was raised aloft, toward the bow of the vessel.

It had been shown by the numbers who were transported during the first summer that, at the same price for passage, many were willing to undergo all the inconveniences of the original rude accommodations in preference to encountering the delays and uncertainty to which the passage in sloops was exposed. Fulton did not, however, take advantage of his monopoly, but, with the most liberal spirit, provided such accommodations for passengers as, in convenience and even splendor, had not before been approached in vessels intended for the transportation of travellers. This was on his part an exercise of almost improvident liberality. By his contract with Chancellor Livingston the latter undertook to defray the whole cost of the engine and vessel until the experiment should result in success; but from that hour each was to furnish an equal share of all subsequent investments. Fulton had no patrimonial fortune, and what little he had saved from the product of his ingenuity was now exhausted. But the success of the experiment had inspired the banks and capitalists with confidence, and he now found no difficulty in obtaining, in the way of a loan, all that was needed. Still, however, a debt was thus contracted which the continued demands made upon him for new investments never permitted him to discharge. The Clermont, thus converted into a floating palace, gay with ornamental painting, gilding, and polished woods, commenced her course of passages for the second year in the month of April, 1808.

WELLINGTON'S PENINSULAR CAMPAIGN

A.D. 1808–1813

JOHN RICHARD GREEN

The Treaty of Tilsit saw Napoleon at the height of his power. Russia had become his ally; the rest of Continental Europe was helpless against him. Only England, made safe by that narrow little strip of water between her and France, continued to defy the conqueror. Unable to reach his foe with military arms, Napoleon began against her a tremendous economic war. He forbade Europe to trade with British ships; every port over which his influence extended was closed against them.

Portugal, which was closely connected with England, objected to the Emperor's decrees, and he sent an army which took possession of the hapless little country. This brought French troops into Spain—Spain which had been steadily decaying ever since the days of Philip II, until she had become in these times a mere vassal state to France. Her worthless king, Charles IV, had an equally worthless son, Ferdinand, and a wicked queen. The State was really ruled by the minister, Godoy, who was in Napoleon's pay. Probably the Emperor had long intended to sweep out the whole worthless group and establish one of his own brothers as a monarch in their place. He deemed the present moment, when his troops were establishing themselves in Portugal, as propitious for his purpose.

Unluckily for himself he failed to appreciate the fierce loyalty of the Spaniards. In all his previous conquests he had been able to maintain at least partly the appearance of being a liberator come to rescue the downtrodden common people from their oppressors. The halo of the French Revolutionary movement still clung faintly around him. But in Spain he was openly and undeniably a foreigner trying to force an undesired foreign ruler upon the natives, and he found the opposition very different from any he had before encountered. Though beaten, the Spaniards never remained in subjection, never became his subjects to fight for him against others. "It was the Spanish ulcer," said he himself when he looked back from St. Helena, "that ruined me."

THE effect of the Continental system on Britain was to drive it to a policy of aggression upon neutral states, which seemed to be as successful as it was aggressive. The effect of his system on Napoleon himself was precisely the same. It was to maintain this material union of Europe against Britain that he was driven to aggression after aggression in North Germany, and to demands upon Russia which threatened the league that had been formed at Tilsit. Above all, it was the hope of more effectually crushing the world power of Britain that drove him, at the very moment when Canning was attacking America, to his worst aggression—the aggression upon Spain. Spain was already his subservient ally; but her alliance became every hour less useful. The country was ruined by misgovernment: its treasury was empty; its fleet rotted in its harbors. To seize the whole Spanish Peninsula, to develop its resources by an active administration, to have at his command not only a regenerated Spain and Portugal, but their mighty dominions in Southern and Central America, to renew with these fresh forces the struggle with Britain for her empire of the seas—these were the designs by which Napoleon was driven to the most ruthless of his enterprises.

He acted with his usual subtlety. In October, 1807, France and Spain agreed to divide Portugal between them; and on the advance of their forces the reigning house of Braganza fled helplessly from Lisbon to a refuge in Brazil. But the seizure of Portugal was only a prelude to the seizure of Spain. Charles IV, whom a riot in his capital drove at this moment to abdication, and his son and successor, Ferdinand VII, were alike drawn to Bayonne in May, 1808, and forced to resign their claims to the Spanish crown, while a French army entered Madrid, and proclaimed Joseph Bonaparte as king of Spain.

High-handed as such an act was, it was in harmony with the general system which Napoleon was pursuing elsewhere, and which had as yet stirred no national resistance. Holland had been changed into a monarchy by a simple decree of the French Emperor, and its crown bestowed on his brother Louis. For another brother, Jerome, a kingdom of Westphalia had been built up out of the electorates of Hesse-Cassel and Hanover. Joseph himself had been set as king over Naples before his transfer to Spain. But the spell of submission was now suddenly broken, and the new King had hardly entered Madrid when Spain rose as one man against the stranger. Desperate as the effort of its people seemed, the news of the rising was welcomed throughout England with a burst of enthusiastic joy.

"Hitherto," cried Sheridan, a leader of the Whig opposition, "Bonaparte has contended with princes without dignity, numbers without ardor, or peoples without patriotism. He has yet to learn what it is to combat a people who are animated by one spirit against him." Tory and Whig alike held that "never had so happy an opportunity existed for Britain to strike a bold stroke for the rescue of the world"; and Canning at once resolved to change the system of desultory descents on colonies and sugar islands for a vigorous warfare in the Peninsula. Supplies were sent to the Spanish insurgents with reckless profusion, and two small armies placed under the command of Sir John Moore and Sir Arthur Wellesley for service in the Peninsula.

In July, 1808, the surrender at Baylen of a French force which had invaded Andalusia gave the first shock to the power of Napoleon, and the blow was followed by one almost as severe. Landing at the Mondego with fifteen thousand men, Sir Arthur Wellesley drove the French army of Portugal from the field of Vimiera, and forced it to surrender in the Convention of Cintra on August 30th. But the tide of success was soon roughly turned. Napoleon appeared in Spain with an army of two hundred thousand men; and Moore, who had advanced from Lisbon to Salamanca to support the Spanish armies, found them crushed on the Ebro, and was driven to fall hastily back on the coast. His force saved its honor in a battle before Corunna on January 16, 1809, which enabled it to embark in safety; but elsewhere all seemed lost. The whole of Northern and Central Spain was held by the French armies; and even Saragossa, which had once heroically repulsed them, submitted after a second equally desperate resistance.

The landing of the wreck of Moore's army and the news of the Spanish defeats turned the temper of England from the wildest hope to the deepest despair; but Canning remained unmoved. On the day of the evacuation of Corunna he signed a treaty of alliance with the Junta which governed Spain in the absence of its king; and the English force at Lisbon, which had already prepared to leave Portugal, was reënforced with thirteen thousand fresh troops and placed under the command of Sir Arthur Wellesley. "Portugal," Wellesley wrote coolly, "may be defended against any force which the French can bring against it." At this critical moment the best of the French troops, with the Emperor himself, were drawn from the Peninsula to the Danube; for the Spanish rising had roused Austria as well as England to a renewal of the struggle. When Marshal Soult therefore threatened Lisbon from the north, Wellesley marched boldly against him, drove him from Oporto in a disastrous retreat, and, suddenly changing his line of operations, pushed with twenty thousand men by Abrantes on Madrid. He was joined on the march by a Spanish force of thirty thousand men; and a bloody action with a French army of equal force at Talavera[1] in July, 1809, restored the renown of English arms. The losses on both sides were enormous, and the French fell back at the close of the struggle; but the fruits of the victory were lost by a sudden appearance of Soult on the English line of advance. Wellesley was forced to retreat hastily on Badajoz, and his failure was embittered by heavier disasters elsewhere; for Austria was driven to sue for peace by a decisive victory of Napoleon at Wagram, while a force of forty thousand English soldiers which had been despatched against Antwerp in July returned home baffled after losing half its numbers in the marshes of Walcheren.

The failure at Walcheren brought about the fall of the Portland Ministry. Canning attributed this disaster to the incompetence of Lord Castlereagh, an Irish peer, who after taking the chief part in bringing about the union between England and Ireland, had been raised by the Duke of Portland to the post of Secretary at War; and the quarrel between the two ministers ended in a duel and in their resignation of their offices in September, 1809. The Duke of Portland retired with Canning; and a new ministry was formed out of the more Tory members of the late Administration under the guidance of Spencer Perceval, an industrious mediocrity of the narrowest type; while the Marquis of Wellesley, a brother of the English general in Spain, succeeded Canning as foreign secretary. But if Perceval and his colleagues possessed few of the higher qualities of statesmanship, they had one characteristic which in the actual position of English affairs was beyond all price. They were resolute to continue the war. In the nation at large the fit of enthusiasm had been followed by a fit of despair; and the City of London even

[1] Talavera de la Reina.

petitioned for a withdrawal of the English forces from the Peninsula.

Napoleon seemed irresistible, and now that Austria was crushed and England stood alone in opposition to him, the Emperor determined to put an end to the strife by a vigorous prosecution of the war in Spain. Andalusia, the one province which remained independent, was invaded in the opening of 1810, and, with the exception of Cadiz, reduced to submission, while Marshal Masséna with a fine army of eighty thousand men marched upon Lisbon. Even Perceval abandoned all hope of preserving a hold on the Peninsula in face of these new efforts, and threw on Wellesley, who had been raised to the peerage as Lord Wellington, after Talavera, the responsibility of resolving to remain there.

But the cool judgment and firm temper which distinguished Wellington enabled him to face a responsibility from which weaker men would have shrunk. "I conceive," he answered, "that the honor and interest of our country require that we should hold our ground here as long as possible; and, please God, I will maintain it as long as I can." By the addition of Portuguese troops who had been trained under British officers, his army was now raised to fifty thousand men; and though his inferiority in force compelled him to look on while Masséna reduced the frontier fortresses of Ciudad Rodrigo and Almeida, he inflicted on him a heavy check at the heights of Busaco, and finally fell back in October, 1810, on three lines of defence which he had secretly constructed at Torres Vedras, along a chain of mountain heights crowned with redoubts and bristling with cannon. The position was impregnable: and able and stubborn as Masséna was, he found himself forced after a month's fruitless efforts to fall back in a masterly retreat; but so terrible were the privations of the French army in passing again through the wasted country that it was only with forty thousand men that he reached Ciudad Rodrigo in the spring of 1811.

Reënforced by fresh troops, Masséna turned fiercely to the relief of Almeida, which Wellington had besieged. Two days' bloody and obstinate fighting, however, in May, 1811, failed to drive the English army from its position at Fuentes de Onoro, and the Marshal fell back on Salamanca and relinquished his effort to drive Wellington from Portugal. But great as was the effect of Torres Vedras in restoring the spirit of the English people, and in reviving throughout Europe the hope of resistance to the tyranny of Napoleon, its immediate result was little save the deliverance of Portugal. If Masséna had failed, his colleagues had succeeded in their enterprises; the French were now masters of all Spain save Cadiz and the eastern provinces, and even the east coast was reduced in 1811 by the vigor of General Suchet.

While England thus failed to rescue Spain from the aggression of Napoleon, she was suddenly brought face to face with the result of her own aggression in America. The repeal of the "Non-intercourse Act" in 1810 had in effect been a triumph for Britain: but the triumph forced Napoleon's hand. As yet all he had done by his attack on neutral rights had been to drive the United States practically to join England against him. To revenge himself by war with them would only play England's game yet more; and with characteristic rapidity Napoleon passed from hostility to friendship. He seized on the offer with which America had closed her efforts against the two combatants, and after promising to revoke his Berlin and Milan decrees he called on America to redeem her pledge. In February, 1811, therefore, the United States announced that all intercourse with Great Britain and her dependencies was at an end. The effect of this step was seen in a reduction of English exports during this year by a third of their whole amount. It was in vain that Britain pleaded that the Emperor's promises remained unfulfilled, that neither of the decrees was withdrawn, that Napoleon had failed to return the American merchandise seized under them, and that the enforcement of non-intercourse with England was thus an unjust act and an act of hostility. The pressure of the American policy, as well as news of the warlike temper which had at last grown up in the United States, made submission inevitable; for the industrial state of England was now so critical that to expose it to fresh shocks was to court the very ruin which Napoleon had planned.

During the earlier years of the war, indeed, the increase of wealth had been enormous. England was sole mistress of the seas. The war gave her possession of the colonies of Spain, of

Holland, and of France; and if her trade was checked for a time by the Berlin Decree, the efforts of Napoleon were soon rendered fruitless by the smuggling system which sprang up along the southern coasts and the coast of North Germany. English exports indeed had nearly doubled since the opening of the century. Manufactures were profiting by the discoveries of Watt and Arkwright; and the consumption of raw cotton in the mills of Lancashire rose during the same period from fifty to a hundred millions of pounds. The vast accumulation of capital, as well as the vast increase of the population at this time, told upon the land, and forced agriculture into a feverish and unhealthy prosperity. Wheat rose to famine prices, and the value of land rose in proportion with the price of wheat. Enclosures went on with prodigious rapidity; the income of every landowner was doubled, while the farmers were able to introduce improvements into the processes of agriculture which changed the whole face of the country. But if the increase of wealth was enormous, its distribution was partial.

During the fifteen years which preceded Waterloo, the number of the population rose from ten to thirteen millions, and this rapid increase kept down the rate of wages, which would naturally have advanced in a corresponding degree with the increase in the national wealth. Even manufactures, though destined in the long run to benefit the laboring classes, seemed at first rather to depress them; for one of the earliest results of the introduction of machinery was the ruin of a number of small trades which were carried on at home and the pauperization of families who relied on them for support. In the winter of 1811 the terrible pressure of this transition from handicraft to machinery was seen in the Luddite, or machine-breaking, riots which broke out over the northern and midland counties, and which were only suppressed by military force. While labor was thus thrown out of its older grooves, and the rate of wages kept down at an artificially low figure by the rapid increase of population, the rise in the price of wheat, which brought wealth to the landowner and the farmer, brought famine and death to the poor, for England was cut off by the war from the vast corn-fields of the Continent or of America, which nowadays redress from their abundance the results of a bad harvest. Scarcity was followed by a terrible pauperization of the laboring classes. The amount of the poor-rate rose 50 per cent., and, with the increase of poverty, followed its inevitable result, the increase of crime.

With social and political troubles thus awaking anew to life about them, even Tory statesmen were not willing to face the terrible consequences of a ruin of English industry such as might follow from the junction of America with Napoleon. They were in fact preparing to withdraw the orders in council, when their plans were arrested by the dissolution of the Perceval Ministry. Its position had from the first been a weak one. A return of the King's madness made it necessary in the beginning of 1811 to confer the regency on the Prince of Wales; and the Whig sympathies of the Prince threatened for a while the Cabinet with dismissal. Though this difficulty was surmounted, their hold of power remained insecure, and the insecurity of the Ministry told on the conduct of the war; for the apparent inactivity of Wellington during 1811 was really due to the hesitation and timidity of the Cabinet at home. But in May, 1812, the assassination of Perceval by a madman named Bellingham brought about the dissolution of his Ministry; and fresh efforts were made by the Regent to install the Whigs in office.

Mutual distrust, however, again foiled his attempts; and the old Ministry returned to office under the headship of Lord Liverpool, a man of no great abilities, but temperate, well informed, and endowed with remarkable skill in holding discordant colleagues together. The most important of these colleagues was Lord Castlereagh, who became Secretary for Foreign Affairs. Time has long ago rendered justice to the political ability of Castlereagh, disguised as it was to men of his own day by a curious infelicity of expression; and the instinctive good sense of Englishmen never showed itself more remarkably than in their preference at this crisis of his cool judgment, his high courage, his discernment, and his will, to the more showy brilliancy of Canning. His first work indeed as a minister was to meet the danger in which Canning had involved the country by his orders in council. On June 23d, only twelve days after the Ministry had been formed, these orders were repealed. But quick as was Castlereagh's action, events had moved even more quickly.

At the opening of the year, America, in despair of redress,

had resolved on war; Congress had voted an increase of both army and navy, and laid in April an embargo on all vessels in American harbors. Actual hostilities might still have been averted by the repeal of the orders, on which the English Cabinet was resolved; but in the confusion which followed the murder of Perceval, and the strife of parties for office through the month that followed, the opportunity was lost. When the news of the repeal reached America, it came six weeks too late. On June 18th an act of Congress had declared the United States at war with Great Britain.

Had Napoleon been able to reap the fruits of the strife which his policy had thus forced on the two English peoples, it is hard to say how Britain could have coped with him. Cut off from her markets alike in east and west, her industries checked and disorganized, a financial crisis added to her social embarrassment, it may be doubted whether she must not have bowed in the end before the pressure of the Continental System. But if that system had thrust her into aggression and ruin, it was as inevitably thrusting the same aggression and ruin on her rival. The moment when the United States entered into the great struggle was a critical moment in the history of mankind.

Six days after President Madison issued his declaration of war, Napoleon crossed the Niemen on his march to Moscow. Successful as his policy had been in stirring up war between England and America, it had been no less successful in breaking the alliance which he had made with the Czar at Tilsit and in forcing on a contest with Russia. On the one hand, Napoleon was irritated by the refusal of Russia to enforce strictly the suspension of all trade with England, though such a suspension would have ruined the Russian landowners. On the other, Alexander saw with growing anxiety the advance of the French Empire which sprang from Napoleon's resolve to enforce his system by a seizure of the northern coasts. In 1811 Holland, the Hanseatic towns, part of Westphalia, and the Duchy of Oldenburg were successively annexed, and the Duchy of Mecklenburg threatened with seizure. A peremptory demand on the part of France for the entire cessation of intercourse with England brought the quarrel to a head; and preparations were made on both sides for a gigantic struggle.

Even before it opened, this new enterprise gave fresh vigor to Napoleon's foes. The best of the French soldiers were drawn from Spain to the frontier of Poland; and Wellington, whose army had been raised to a force of forty thousand Englishmen and twenty thousand Portuguese, profited by the withdrawal to throw off his system of defence and to assume an attitude of attack. Ciudad Rodrigo and Badajoz were taken by storm during the spring of 1812; and at the close of June, three days before Napoleon crossed the Niemen in his march on Moscow, Wellington crossed the Agreda in a march on Salamanca.

After a series of masterly movements on both sides, Marmont with the French Army of the North attacked the English on the hills in the neighborhood of that town on July 22d. While he was marching round the right of the English position his left wing remained isolated; and with a sudden exclamation of "Marmont is lost!" Wellington flung on it the bulk of his force, crushed it, and drove the whole army from the field. The loss on either side was nearly equal, but failure had demoralized the French army; and its retreat forced Joseph to leave Madrid, and Soult to evacuate Andalusia and to concentrate the Southern Army on the eastern coast. While Napoleon was still pushing slowly over the vast plains of Poland, Wellington made his entry into Madrid in August, and began the siege of Burgos. The town, however, held out gallantly for a month, till the advance of the two French armies, now concentrated in the north and south of Spain, forced Wellington, in October, to a hasty retreat on the Portuguese frontier.

Wellington once more left Portugal in May, 1813, with an army which had now risen to ninety thousand men; and overtaking the French forces in retreat at Vitoria on June 21st, he inflicted on them a defeat which drove them in utter rout across the Pyrenees. Madrid was at once evacuated; and Clauzel fell back from Saragossa into France. The victory not only freed Spain from its invaders; it restored the spirit of the allies. The close of the armistice was followed by a union of Austria with the forces of Prussia and the Czar; and in October the final overthrow of Napoleon at Leipsic forced the French army to fall back in rout across the Rhine.

The war now hurried to its close. Though held at bay for a

while by the sieges of San Sebastian and Pampeluna, as well as
by an obstinate defence of the Pyrenees, Wellington succeeded
in the very month of the triumph at Leipsic in winning a victory
on the Bidassoa, which enabled him to enter France. He was
soon followed by the allies. For two months more Napoleon
maintained a wonderful struggle with a handful of raw conscripts against their overwhelming numbers; while in the south
Soult, forced from his intrenched camp near Bayonne and defeated at Orthes, fell back before Wellington on Toulouse.
Here their two armies met in April in a stubborn and indecisive
engagement. But though neither leader knew it, the war was
even then at an end. The struggle of Napoleon himself had
ended at the close of March with the surrender of Paris; and
the submission of the capital was at once followed by the abdication of the Emperor and the return of the Bourbons.

BRAZIL BECOMES INDEPENDENT

A.D. 1808–1822

DANIEL P. KIDDER

In its close connection with the asylum given by Brazil to Portuguese royalty in 1808, the almost bloodless revolution whereby that South American country obtained complete independence presents an unusual instance of national birth. Portuguese colonization in Brazil began as early as 1510. During the next century the colonists lost much of their possessions to the Dutch, but quickly recovered them.

After this the Portuguese in Brazil adopted a policy of restriction and exclusion; and boundary disputes, such as have ever vexed the South American republics, caused serious difficulties. In 1713 the title of Portugal to the Brazilian territory was confirmed by the Peace of Utrecht, and for almost a century the colony existed without disturbance or important event.

Bonaparte's attack upon Portugal, and the events which ensued in that country and her South American colony, form distinct episodes in the history of this period and the years directly following. During the ascendency of Bonaparte in Europe, Portugal upheld the cause of England, with the result that the French dictator despatched an army of punishment against Lisbon, announcing that the "house of Braganza" had ceased to reign.

IN 1807 the French army, under Marshal Junot, invaded Portugal with the design of seizing the royal family. The Prince Regent, Dom John VI, had tried every means, and had submitted to the most humiliating concessions, to avert the impending storm.

But Napoleon had resolved on adding the Peninsula to his empire, and on November 29th the vanguard of his army surmounted the heights of Lisbon. Then, and not till then, the Prince resolved upon emigration to Brazil.

Everything of value that could be transported was hastily embarked with the royal family. The Portuguese fleet consisted of eight ships of the line, four frigates, twelve brigs, and a number of merchantmen.

These, in company with an English squadron, then lying at the mouth of the Tagus, bore away for Brazil. The French took

181

possession of Lisbon the following day. Early in January, 1808, the news of these surprising events reached Rio de Janeiro and excited the most lively interest.

What the Brazilians had scarcely dreamed of as a possible event was now suddenly to be realized. The royal family might be expected to arrive any day, and preparations for their reception occupied the attention of all. The Viceroy's palace was immediately prepared, and all the public offices in the palace square were vacated to accommodate the royal suite. These not being deemed sufficient, proprietors of private houses in the neighborhood were required to leave their residences and send their keys to the Viceroy.

Such were the sentiments of the people respecting the hospitality due to their distinguished guests that nothing seems to have been withheld; while many, even of the less opulent families, voluntarily offered sums of money and objects of value to administer to their comfort.

The fleet having been scattered in a storm, the principal vessels had put into Bahia. But at length they all made a safe entry into the harbor of Rio, on March 7, 1808. In the manifestations of joy upon this occasion the houses were deserted and the hills were covered with spectators. Those who could, procured boats and sailed out to meet the royal squadron. The Prince, immediately after landing, proceeded to the cathedral, publicly to offer up thanks for his safe arrival. The city was illuminated for nine successive evenings.

In order to form an idea of the changes that have occurred in Brazil, it must be remarked that up to the period now under consideration all commerce and intercourse with foreigners had been rigidly prohibited by the narrow policy of Portugal. Vessels of nations allied to the mother-country were occasionally permitted to come to anchor in the ports of this mammoth colony, but neither passengers nor crew were allowed to land, excepting under the superintendence of a guard of soldiers.

To prevent all possibility of trade, foreign vessels, whether they had put in to repair damages or to procure provisions and water, immediately on their arrival were invested with a custom-house guard, and the time for their remaining was fixed by the authorities according to the supposed necessities of the case. As a consequence of these oppressive regulations, a people who were rich in gold and diamonds were unable to procure the essential implements of agriculture and of domestic convenience. A senhor who could display the most rich and massive plate at a festival, might not be able to furnish each of his guests with a knife at table. A single tumbler at the same time might be under the necessity of making repeated circuits through the company. The printing-press had not made its appearance. Books and learning were equally rare. The people were in every way made to feel their dependence; and the spirit of industry and that of enterprise were alike unknown.

On the arrival of the Prince Regent the ports were thrown open. A printing-press was introduced, and a royal gazette was published. Academies of medicine and the fine arts were established. The Royal Library, containing sixty thousand volumes of books, was opened for the free use of the public. Foreigners were invited, and embassies from England and France took up their residence at Rio de Janeiro.

From this period decided improvements were made in the condition and aspect of the city. New streets and squares were added, and splendid residences were arranged on the neighboring islands and hills, augmenting with the growth of the town the picturesque beauties of the surrounding scenery. The sudden and continued influx of Portuguese and foreigners not only showed itself in the population of Rio, but extended inland, causing new ways of communication to be opened with the interior—new towns to be erected, and old ones to be improved. In fact, the whole face of the country underwent great and rapid changes.

The manners of the people also experienced a corresponding change. The fashions of Europe were introduced. From the seclusion and restraints of non-intercourse the people emerged into the festive ceremonies of a court, whose levees and gala days drew together multitudes from all directions. In the mingled society which the capital now offered, the dust of retirement was brushed off, antiquated customs gave way, new ideas and modes of life were adopted, and these spread from circle to circle and from town to town.

Business assumed an aspect equally changed. Foreign commercial houses were opened, and foreign artisans established themselves in Rio and other cities.

This country could no longer remain a colony. A decree was promulgated in December, 1815, declaring it elevated to the dignity of a kingdom, and hereafter to form an integral part of the United Kingdom of Portugal, Algarves, and Brazil. It is scarcely possible to imagine the enthusiasm awakened by this unlooked-for change throughout the vast extent of Portuguese America. Messengers were despatched to bear the news, which was hailed with spontaneous illuminations from the La Plata to the Amazon. Scarcely was this event consummated when the Queen, Donna Maria I, died.

She was mother to the Prince Regent, and had been for years in a state of mental imbecility, so that her death had no influence upon political affairs. Her funeral obsequies were performed with great splendor; and her son, in respect for her memory, delayed the acclamation of his succession to the throne for a year. He was at length crowned with the title of Dom John VI. The ceremonies of the coronation were celebrated with suitable magnificence in the palace square, on February 5, 1818. Amid all the advantages attendant upon the new state of things in Brazil there were many circumstances calculated to provoke political discontent. Mr. Armitage has very appropriately summed up the political condition of Brazil at this period in the following terms:

"A swarm of needy and unprincipled adventurers came over with the royal family, for whom the Government felt constrained to find places. These men took but little interest in the welfare of the country, and were far more eager to enrich themselves than to administer justice or to benefit the public. The rivalry, which had always prevailed between the native Brazilians and the Portuguese, found, in this state of things, a new cause of excitement. Dom John, from his naturally obliging disposition, delighted in rewarding every service rendered to him or to the State; but being straitened for funds, he adopted the cheaper custom of bestowing titulary honors upon those who had merited his favor. To such an extent did he carry this species of liberality that during the period of his administration he distributed more honorary insignia than had been conferred by all the preceding monarchs of the house of Braganza.

"Those merchants and landed proprietors, who, on the arrival of the royal cortège, had given up their houses and advanced their money to do honor to their guests, were decorated with the various honorary orders, originally instituted during the days of chivalry. Individuals were dubbed knights who had never buckled on a spur; and *commendadores* of the Order of Christ were created in the persons of those who were by no means learned in the elementary doctrines of their missals.

"The excitement resulting from such a distribution of honors, in a country where titulary distinctions were hitherto almost unknown and where the veneration for sounding titles and antiquated institutions was as profound as it was unenlightened, could not but be great. These, being now brought apparently within the reach of all, became the great objects of competition to the aspiring; and there was soon no species of petty tyranny which was not put in force, nor any degradation which was not cheerfully submitted to, when these manifestations of royal favor were the objects in view. Success was generally attended with an instantaneous change in the style of living. Knights could no longer descend to the drudgeries of commercial life, but were compelled to live either on resources already acquired or, in default of resources, to solicit employment under the Government.

"Here, however, the difficulties were greater than in the first instance—competition being increased by the numerous emigrants from the mother-country. Even when obtained, the emoluments attached to public offices were too limited to admit of much extravagance on the part of the holders. Opportunities were nevertheless frequently occurring for the sale of favors and exemptions, and the venality of the Brazilians in office became ere long equal to that of their Portuguese colleagues. These things, together with the wretched state of morals that prevailed at court, were calculated to foment those jealousies of foreign dominion which could hardly fail to arise in view of the independence recently achieved by the English colonies of North America, and of the revolutionary struggle in which the neighboring colonies of Spain were already engaged.

"A consciousness of this increasing discontent, and a fear that Brazil would by and by follow the example of her Spanish neighbors, doubtless had a powerful influence in causing the country to be politically elevated to the rank of a kingdom.

"Quietness prevailed for several years; but discontent became gradually disseminated, and was often promoted by the very means used for its suppression. Murmurs, too, were excited, but as yet they found no echo; the only printing-press in the country being under the immediate direction of the royal authorities. Through its medium the public was duly and faithfully informed concerning the health of all the princes in Europe. Official edicts, birthday odes, and panegyrics on the reigning family from time to time illumined its pages, which were unsullied either by the ebullitions of democracy or the exposure of grievances. To have judged of the country by the tone of its only journal, it must have been pronounced a terrestrial paradise, where no word of complaint had ever yet found utterance."

The revolution which occurred in Portugal in 1821, in favor of a constitution, was immediately responded to by a similar one in Brazil. After much excitement and alarm from the tumultuous movements of the people, the King (Dom John VI) conferred upon his son Dom Pedro, Prince Royal, the office of regent and lieutenant to His Majesty in the kingdom of Brazil. He then hastened his departure for Portugal, accompanied by the remainder of his family and the principal nobility who had followed him. The disheartened monarch embarked on board a line-of-battle ship on April 24, 1821, leaving the widest and fairest portion of his dominions to an unlooked-for destiny.

Rapid as had been the political changes in Brazil during the last ten years, greater changes still were to transpire. Dom Pedro was at this period twenty-three years of age. He had left Portugal when a lad, and his warmest aspirations were associated with the land of his adoption. In 1817 he was married to the Archduchess Leopoldina, of the house of Austria, sister to Maria Louisa, ex-Empress of France. The bride arrived at Rio de Janeiro in November of that year.

In the office of prince regent, Dom Pedro certainly found scope for his most ardent ambition; but he also discovered himself to be surrounded with numerous difficulties, political and financial. So embarrassing indeed was his situation that in the course of a few months he begged his father to allow him to resign his office and attributes. The Cortes of Portgual, about this time, becoming jealous of the position of the Prince in Brazil, passed a decree ordering him to return to Europe, and at the same time abolishing the royal tribunals at Rio. This decree was received with indignation by the Brazilians, who immediately rallied around Dom Pedro and persuaded him to remain among them. His consent to do so gave rise to the most enthusiastic demonstrations of joy among both patriots and loyalists. But the Portuguese military soon evinced symptoms of mutiny. The troops, to the number of two thousand men, left their quarters on the evening of January 11, 1822, and, providing themselves with artillery, marched to Castello Hill, which commanded the entire city. Intelligence of this movement was, during the night, made public; and ere the following day dawned the Campo de Santa Anna, a large square in sight of the station occupied by the Portuguese troops, was crowded with armed men.

A conflict seemed inevitable; but the Portuguese commander vacillated in view of such determined opposition, and offered to capitulate on the condition of his soldiers retaining their arms. This was conceded, on their agreeing to retire to Praya Grande, a village on the opposite side of the bay, until transports could be provided for their embarkation to Lisbon, which was subsequently effected. The measure of the Cortes of Portugal, which continued to be arbitrary in the extreme toward Brazil, finally had the effect to hasten, in the latter country, a declaration of absolute independence. This measure had long been ardently desired by the more enlightened Brazilians, some of whom had already urged Dom Pedro to assume the title of emperor. Hitherto he had refused, and reiterated his allegiance to Portugal. But he at length, while on a journey to the Province of São Paulo, received despatches from the mother-country which had the effect to induce him instantly to resolve on independence.

His exclamation, "Independence or death," was enthusiastically reiterated by those who surrounded him, and thenceforward became the watchword of the Brazilian revolution. This declaration was made on September 7th, and was repeated at Rio as soon as the Prince could hasten there by a rapid journey.

The municipality of the capital issued a proclamation on the 21st, declaring their intention to fulfil the manifest wishes of the people, by proclaiming Dom Pedro the constitutional emperor and perpetual defender of Brazil. This ceremony was performed on October 12th following, in the Campo de Santa Anna, in the presence of the municipal authorities, the functionaries of the court, the troops, and an immense concourse of people. His Highness there publicly declared his acceptance of the title conferred on him, from the conviction that he was thus obeying the will of the people. The troops fired a salute, and the city was illuminated in the evening. Jozé Bonifacio de Andrada, prime minister of the Government, had in the mean time promulgated a decree requiring all the Portuguese who were disposed to embrace the popular cause, to manifest their sentiment by wearing the Emperor's motto, "*Independencia ou morte*" upon their arm— ordering also that all dissentients should leave the country within a given period, and threatening the penalties imposed upon high treason against anyone who should thenceforward attack, by word or deed, the sacred cause of Brazil.

The Brazilian revolution was comparatively a bloodless one. The glory of Portugal was already waning; her resources were exhausted and her energies crippled by internal dissensions. That nation made nothing like a systematic and persevering effort to maintain her ascendency over her long depressed but now rebellious colony. The insulting measures of the Cortes were consummated only in their vaporing decrees. The Portuguese dominion was maintained for some time in Bahia and other ports which had been occupied by military forces. But these forces were at length compelled to withdraw and leave Brazil to her own control.

So little contested, indeed, and so rapid was this revolution, that in less than three years from the time independence was declared on the plains of the Ypiranga, Brazil was acknowledged to be independent at the court of Lisbon. In the mean time the Emperor had been crowned as Dom Pedro I, and an assembly of delegates from the provinces had been convoked. A constitution had been framed by this assembly and accepted by the Emperor, and on March 24, 1824, was sworn to throughout the empire.

REVOLUTION IN MEXICO

A.D. 1810

JOEL R. POINSETT

Mexican independence was won from Spain through two revolutions (1810 and 1821) connected by a sustained guerilla warfare which made the struggle a prolonged movement marked by interruptions. This war of independence, although followed by many vicissitudes which greatly disturbed the country, may be regarded as the preparatory stage of its formative era, when many of the elements since at work in its constructive history first actively appeared.

For almost three centuries Mexico was governed by Spanish viceroys, of whom, from 1535 to 1822, there were sixty-four. During the earlier part of their administration, while at home Spain was weakened through misgovernment, Mexico, more wisely and honestly ruled, developed into a stable and peaceful colony. During the War of the Spanish Succession (1701-1714) Mexico remained undisturbed in her domestic affairs. But the great changes wrought in the New World, as well as in Europe, by the French Revolution, affected the Mexican people with the contagion of its ideas, and discontents which had already been shown began to manifest themselves more plainly.

Spain had enforced a law excluding creoles or American-born Spaniards in Mexico from rights given to those who emigrated from the mother-country. This caused irritation between these two classes. The Viceroy showed little consideration for the concerns of the Mexican people, whom he subjected to burdensome exactions, partly to supply the Madrid Government with money needed in the Napoleonic wars. Napoleon's invasion of Spain, in 1807, accelerated a revolution toward which the conduct of that country had been steadily driving her Mexican subjects, and to which the political ideas and events of the age irresistibly impelled them.

Poinsett had unusual advantages as the historian of this movement, having been in Mexico on a diplomatic mission in 1822, and subsequently served as United States minister (1825-1829) to that country.

A FTER the occupation of Madrid by the French (1808), the Viceroy of Mexico, Don José Iturrigaray, received such contradictory orders from the King, from Murat, and from the council of the Indies, that he proposed calling a junta, to be formed by a representation from each province, as the best means of pre-

serving the country from the horrors of anarchy. The Europeans in the capital, who viewed this scheme with great jealousy,
as it was calculated to place the creoles upon an equal footing
with themselves in the government of the country, conspired
against the Viceroy, and, having surprised him in his palace, sent
him and his family prisoners to Spain, and assumed the reins of
government. This act excited universal indignation among all
classes of Americans. Iturrigaray was a just and a good man,
and he is still spoken of with respect by the creoles. The conduct
of the Spaniards on this occasion was highly approved by the
Government in Spain; and his successor, Vanegas, brought with
him rewards and distinctions for those who had been most conspicuous in this revolt against the authority of Iturrigaray.

Shortly after the arrival of the new Viceroy a conspiracy was
formed among the creoles to overthrow his power; it is said to
have been very extensive, and that a great many of the most distinguished citizens throughout the empire were engaged in it.
This conspiracy was disclosed by Iturriaga, a canon of Valladolid, who on his deathbed revealed the whole plan, and the names
of the conspirators, to a priest of Queretaro. In consequence of
this disclosure, the *corregidor* of that city, who was included in the
denunciation, was arrested in the night. This act spread alarm
among the principal conspirators, and hastened the execution of
their plot; and Allende, one of the chiefs, at the head of a small
band, immediately united himself with Hidalgo in Dolores.

Hidalgo was a priest of some talent, an enthusiast in the cause
of independence, and possessing unbounded influence over the
Indians. From Dolores, where they assembled a large body of
men, they marched upon San Miguel el Grande, and pillaged the
houses of the Spaniards. Hidalgo next led his desultory forces
to Zelaya, where he was joined by the troops of that garrison.
Thus reënforced, he marched forward against the populous and
wealthy city of Guanajuato. Here, too, the garrison joined the
insurgents, and the only opposition which was made was by the
intendant, who shut himself up with some of the inhabitants and
a large amount of treasure in the Alhondiga, a large circular
building in the centre of the city, which was used for a granary.
Riana, the intendant, was killed during the first attack, and the
inhabitants soon after surrendered. By this capture Hidalgo

acquired five million dollars, besides the plunder which fell into the hands of his followers.

The Viceroy, Vanegas, took active measures to suppress the insurrection, but the whole country north of Queretaro took up arms and united with Hidalgo. Acting with great policy he abolished the tribute, which gained him friends among the Indians, and they flocked in crowds to his standard. After endeavoring to introduce some order among an army composed of all classes, and armed with pikes, clubs, hatchets, and a few muskets, he left Guanajuato and marched to Valladolid, where he was received with shouts of joy by the Indians and creoles. On October 24, 1810, Hidalgo was proclaimed generalissimo of the Mexican armies, and Allende and several others appointed generals under him. On this occasion he threw aside his priest's robes, and appeared in uniform. From Indaparapeo, where this ceremony took place, the patriot army marched toward the capital, and on October 27th entered Toluca, a town not more than twelve leagues west of the capital. The royal forces were scattered throughout the kingdom, and Mexico was considered in imminent danger. In this extremity, the European authorities resorted to the spiritual weapons of the Church. Hidalgo, his army, and all who espoused the cause of independence were solemnly excommunicated by the archbishop. This act did not produce all the effect that was expected from it upon the immediate followers of Hidalgo. Being a priest himself, he easily persuaded his troops that an excommunication pronounced by their enemies could not avail against them; but the people who were at a distance abandoned a cause to which was attached so dreadful a penalty. After some skirmishing between Toluca and Lerma, the Independents, on October 31st, crowned the heights of Santa Fé. The Royalists, not more than two thousand men, were drawn up to defend the city, when to the astonishment of everyone Hidalgo withdrew his troops, taking the route to Guanajuato. This extraordinary movement was fatal to the cause of the patriots.

This movement was attended with some confusion; and Calleja, at the head of six thousand men, who had been collected by calling in the garrisons of Queretaro and other towns, pursued him so closely as to bring on an action at Aculeo. Hidalgo's troops were defeated with great slaughter, and he retreated with the remains of his forces to Guanajuato. Here Calleja again overtook him, but Hidalgo, leaving Allende to guard the defile of Marfil, evacuated Guanajuato with the main body of his forces, and pursued his march to Guadalajara. Calleja attacked the Independents with his usual impetuosity and success, and after an obstinate resistance Allende retired upon Hidalgo with the remains of his troops. From Calleja's despatches to the Viceroy it appears that he committed the most savage acts of barbarity in Guanajuato, and his example was followed by his subalterns in all the towns and villages of the district.

In the mean time the Royalists, under General Cruz, defeated the Independents at Zamora, and recovered possession of Valladolid, whose inhabitants were treated with great barbarity.

Hidalgo continued his retreat until he reached Guadalajara, when he drew up his army in an advantageous position at the Puente de Calderon, eleven leagues from the city of Guadalajara, and waited the attack of Calleja. Here an obstinate battle was fought on January 17, 1811, which ended in the total defeat and dispersion of the Independents. After remaining a short time at Zacatecas, Hidalgo retreated to San Luis Potosi, intending to retire to Texas and there reorganize his army. He was closely followed by Calleja and by a division of Spanish troops under the command of Ochoa, to intercept Hidalgo's retreat, and, thus hemmed in on all sides, he was betrayed by Bustamante, one of his own officers, and made prisoner with all his staff. They were suddenly attacked at Acatita de Bajan on March 21, 1811, and, being taken by surprise, were easily vanquished. Fifty of his officers were executed on the field of battle. Hidalgo and Allende, with eight or ten others, were removed to Chihuahua, where, after the form of a trial, Hidalgo was shot on June 20, 1811, having been deprived of his priest's orders previous to his execution. Allende and the other officers were executed on June 20th. The death of Hidalgo did not check the progress of the revolution in other parts of the kingdom.

Rayon, a lawyer of great influence, formed a junta at Zitaquaro and endeavored to introduce some order and subordination among the Independents. Calleja, to whose activity and courage the suppression of this formidable revolt is attributed, marched against the forces collected at Zitaquaro, and after an engagement which lasted three hours succeeded in driving the parties from all their posts and in taking this important place. By a solemn decree the property of the inhabitants of this town was confiscated and the town itself razed to the ground.

Notwithstanding these losses, the Independents continued to carry on a desultory warfare. The Junta took refuge in Zultepec, and Morelos, a priest, organized a large force, and was victorious in several actions fought in the south against the Royalists. Calleja marched against him, and at length succeeded in driving him from Quautla-Amilpa, a town which had been strongly fortified by Morelos. Compelled to evacuate this place, by famine, the Independents were harassed in their retreat by Calleja, who says, in his despatches to the Viceroy, that "an extent of seven leagues was covered with the dead bodies of the enemy." The principal sufferers were the unarmed inhabitants of the town, who, warned by the fate of Zitaquaro, were eager to escape from the persecutions and cruelties of the bloodthirsty Calleja.

Such was the spirit of the people that Morelos was soon able to act again offensively. He successively captured the towns of Chilapa, Tehuacan, Orizaba, and Oaxaca, and shortly after Acapulco fell into his power. Guerillas of the Independents under Guadalupe Victoria (an assumed name) extended to the country between Xalapa and Vera Cruz, and occupied all the strongholds there. Don Manuel Teran had a respectable force in the Province of Puebla. Ossourno, with another division, was spreading terror and confusion in the Province of Mexico, while a Doctor Coss, a priest, with Rayon, Bustamante, Liceaga, and other brave officers, occupied a great part of the provinces of Guanajuato, Valladolid, Zacatecas, and New Galicia.

Morelos at this period convened a congress, composed of forty members, which assembled at Apatzinjan, in the Province of Valladolid. A constitution was framed and accepted by the provinces in possession of the Independents, and they shortly after made proposals to suspend hostilities and to enter into a treaty with the Royalists, which were rejected with scorn and insult.

Calleja was appointed viceroy, with the title of Conde de Calderon, and the war was prosecuted against the Independents with vigor and with circumstances of the most barbarous and refined cruelty.

Morelos soon found that by delegating the authority to a congress at this critical period he had very much augmented the difficulties of his situation. No sooner did he or his officers form any military plan, than its merits became a matter of discussion in Congress, and all confidence between the military and civil authorities was destroyed.

Morelos made an unsuccessful attack on Valladolid, and in the retreat, Matamoros, a priest, who had throughout this contest displayed great valor and considerable military talent, was defeated and fell into the hands of the Royalists. Offers and menaces were resorted to by Morelos, to save the life of this officer, but in vain—he was degraded and shot.

Compelled to evacuate the Province of Valladolid, Morelos resolved to transfer his headquarters to the city of Tehuacan, in the Province of Puebla, where Teran had a respectable division. The Congress, together with the most respectable inhabitants of that part of the country, determined to accompany the Independent forces; and the expedition of Morelos is said rather to have resembled the emigration of a vast body of people than the march of an army. The Royalists hovered about this crowd without attacking it, until, learning that Morelos had separated himself from the main body of his army, and with a small division of cavalry lay at a place called Tepecuacuilco, they attacked him on November 5, 1815. After a short combat his troops were defeated and he himself taken prisoner. He was conducted to Mexico, degraded and shot on December 22, 1815, at San Cristobal, in the neighborhood of the capital.

The members of the Mexican Congress, after the capture of Morelos, pursued their route to Tehuacan, where they continued to exercise their doubtful authority, until they were dissolved by Teran. This arbitrary act proved fatal to the cause of the patriots. The military commanders in the different provinces acted from that moment as independent chiefs, and the war was feebly carried on until the arrival of General Mina, who landed at Galveston in November, 1816.

Mina, nephew of the famous guerilla, Mina Espoz, who later so much distinguished himself by his disinterested and devoted attachment to his country, left England with a small expedition in May, 1816, and after touching at the United States, where he received some succors, he landed at Galveston in the month of November of that year; he spent some time there organizing his forces, and did not reach Soto la Marina until April 16th; he entered this place without opposition, and after constructing a small fort, he left his military stores there, under the protection of a small garrison, and on May 24th took up his line of march for the interior of Mexico. At this time his whole force consisted of three hundred eight men, including officers.

On June 8th he encountered a body of the enemy near the town of the Valle del Mais, and after smart skirmishing routed them and took possession of the town. He made no halt in this place, but, anxious to form a junction with the Independents, pushed forward toward the interior. On the night of June 14th he encamped at the hacienda of Peotillas, and the next morning was attacked by a very superior force. His little band defended themselves valiantly, and Mina on this occasion proved himself a brave and skilful officer; the enemy were compelled to abandon the field after sustaining a heavy loss. The ensuing day Mina continued his march into the interior, and on the 18th took by assault the town of Real del Pinos, which was garrisoned with three hundred men. On the 24th he effected a junction with the patriots at Sombrero, after a march of two hundred twenty leagues, which he accomplished in thirty-two days, during which the troops had endured with cheerfulness great fatigue and privations. They had been animated by their gallant leader, who shared their hardships, and who in the hour of danger was distinguished for his valor and presence of mind, and in battle was always to be found leading them on to victory. They arrived at Sombrero, two hundred sixty-nine rank and file.

From Sombrero, Mina sent despatches to the Government setting forth his object of entering the country, and offering his services. He wrote likewise to Padre Torres, who bore the title of commander-in-chief.

Having received information that some forces of the enemy, amounting to seven hundred men, were in the neighborhood, Mina left the fort, which was commanded by Don Pedro Morenc, and marched to meet them. Having been joined by guerillas under Ortiz, his troops amounted to four hundred men. On the 30th they found the enemy drawn up at the hacienda of Los Llanos, about five leagues from San Felipe. The Royalists, unable to withstand the vigorous charge of the patriots, were routed and fled in confusion, leaving more than half their number on the field of battle.

After remaining a few days at Sombrero to refresh his troops, Mina, accompanied by Don Pedro Moreno, made an excursion as far as Xaral, a large hacienda twenty leagues from Guanajuato. This place was taken by surprise, and by its capture the patriots gained an immense booty. They returned to Sombrero, where Mina received accounts of the fall of Soto la Marina; it surrendered on the 15th to the Royalists under General Arredondo.

Soon after the return of Mina from Xaral, a large division of the Royalists invested Sombrero, and after an obstinate defence the Independents were compelled to evacuate the place and to cut their way through the enemy. Fifty only of Mina's troops survived the siege. Mina himself had escaped from the fort some days previous, in hopes of obtaining succors for the besieged from Padre Torres. Finding his application unavailing, he retired to Los Remedios, the headquarters of Torres, where he was joined by the remnant of his forces. Flushed with success, Liñan advanced against Remedios, and on August 31st laid siege to that place. Torres, with some of Mina's officers, remained to defend the fort; while Mina, at the head of a small body of cavalry, advanced toward Guanajuato. He possessed himself successively of the hacienda of Biscocho and the town of San Luis la Paz, and attacked San Miguel el Grande; but learning that a strong body of the enemy were on the march to relieve the place, he thought it prudent to retire to the Valle de Santiago, then in possession of the patriots.

He was here joined by a great many patriots, and soon found himself at the head of one thousand horse. With this force he advanced to relieve Remedios, which was invested by the enemy, but finding his numbers insufficient for such a purpose he retreated to the mountains near Guanajuato, pursued by the Royalists under Orrantia.

The Royalists continued to press the siege of Los Remedios

with great vigor, and Mina to harass them with his cavalry and to cut off their supplies, until at length he was attacked at the hacienda of La Caxa by Orrantia, and completely defeated. He retreated to Puebla Nuevo, a small town about four leagues from the scene of this disaster, where he rallied a few of the fugitives; but of those who escaped, the greater part returned to their respective homes. His only recourse in this state of things was to proceed to Xauxilla, the seat of government of the Independents, in the hope of inducing them to aid his future operations. Here he urged the expediency of attacking Guanajuato, and after some opposition prevailed upon them to adopt his plan. Being furnished with some troops, he proceeded to the Valle de Santiago, where he found a small body of men from Xalapa waiting his arrival. The approach of the division of Orrantia compelled Mina to abandon the Valle, and making a rapid march through the mountains he descended in the rear of the enemy and reached La Caxa.

Here he mustered eleven hundred men, and marching all night across the country he gained an unfrequented spot called La Mina de la Luz, where he was joined by some further reënforcements; and his little army now amounted to fourteen hundred men. With this force and without artillery he had the temerity to attack the city of Guanajuato, and it is not surprising that he failed. After burning the machinery of the mine of Valenciana, Mina retired from Guanajuato, and dismissed his troops to their several stations, retaining only sixty or seventy men. On September 27th Mina was surprised at the *rancho* of Venadito, and fell into the hands of Orrantia. Orders for his immediate execution were despatched by Apodaca, who was then Viceroy of New Spain. He was conducted through Silao to Irrapuato, and finally to the headquarters of Liñan, who commanded the besieging army before Remedios, where, on November 11th, he was shot, pursuant to his sentence. The capture of Mina was considered a matter of so much importance in Spain that Apodaca was created Conde del Venadito, and Liñan and Orrantia received marks of distinction for their services on this occasion.

The siege of Los Remedios was now pressed with renewed vigor, and Torres, finding the place no longer tenable and being without ammunition, resolved to evacuate it. This was effected on the night of January 1, 1818, but was so badly conducted that the greater part of the garrison perished, and the unarmed inhabitants, women and children, were involved in one indiscriminate massacre. The death of Mina and the fall of Los Remedios enabled the Royalists to take active measures to reduce the Independents. The fortress of Xauxilla, where the Government resided, was invested by a body of one thousand men under Don Matias Martin y Aguirre. The garrison defended the place with great courage during three months, but were finally obliged to surrender.

The revolutionary Government, compelled to remove from Xauxilla, established itself in the Province of Valladolid. In the month of February, 1818, they were surprised by a party of the enemy, and the President made prisoner. The form of government, however, continued to be kept up, although the members were obliged to move from place to place. Padre Torres, who since his disaster at Los Remedios had rendered himself odious by his capricious and tyrannical conduct, was formally deposed from the chief command, and Don Juan Arago, a French officer, who arrived in the country with Mina, appointed to fill his place. The padre resisted this decree of the Government, and both parties had recourse to arms. The contest between them was terminated only by the advance of a division of Royalists under Donallo; Torres was compelled to submit, and to place himself under the protection of the Government.

From this time, July, 1819, the war languished everywhere. The Royalists occupied all the strong places and every town. General Guerrero, who was distinguished for his courage and enterprise, continued at the head of a formidable guerilla force in the Tierra Caliente of the Province of Valladolid. Arago roamed over the mountains of Guanajuato. Bradburn, another of Mina's officers, organized a small force in the Cañadas de Huango, but was overtaken by a division of the Royalists under Lara, and his party cut to pieces. Guadalupe Victoria, after maintaining himself a long time in the Province of Vera Cruz, had been compelled to disband his troops, and to retire to the mountains for refuge. The chiefs and leaders were dispersed throughout the country, waiting until the cause of independence should assume a more favorable aspect.

The termination of the first revolution is principally to be attributed to the opposition of the clergy. The cry of liberty raised by Hidalgo and his brave companions-in-arms was echoed with exultation by all classes of people and from the remotest parts of the empire; and notwithstanding their want of concert, the strenuous opposition of the clergy alone prevented success being secured by a general rising of the Mexican people.

They were exhorted to persevere in their loyalty to the mother-country; anathemas were thundered out against the disaffected; the rites of the Church were denied them; and the Inquisition, that powerful instrument of despotism, by denouncing and perse-cuting the friends of liberty, by alarming the conscientious scru-ples of some, and by exciting the fears of others, checked the progress of the revolution and aided the arms of the Royalists. By these means the patriots were divided and weakened; creoles were armed against creoles, and despotism triumphed.

The contest for independence, although conducted feebly and unsuccessfully, was protracted for many years, and produced some good effects. The creoles and Indians, who continued firm in the cause of liberty, were soon taught to attribute their ill suc-cess to the true causes—their own want of discipline, and the in-experience of their commanders—rather than to the spiritual weapons of their adversaries.

The revolution in Spain was viewed with dread by the clergy of Mexico; and no sooner had the decrees of the Cortes, confis-cating the estates, and reducing and reforming some of the higher orders of the clergy, reached America, than the indignation of the Church burst out against the mother-country. They declared from the pulpit that these tyrannical acts must be resisted, that the yoke was no longer to be borne, and that the interests of the Catholic religion, nay, its very existence in America, demanded that Mexico should be separated from Spain.

The influence of the clergy, although in some measure dimin-ished, was still powerful, and had for years controlled the wishes of a vast majority of the nation. To have withdrawn their oppo-sition would have been sufficient to have occasioned a general movement of the people. They did more: they encouraged the people to resist the tyranny of Spain, and took an active part in organizing the plan of operation by which the revolution was successfully effected. They were aided in their plans by the wealthy Europeans, who were anxious to preserve this kingdom in the pureness of despotism, that it might serve as a refuge to Ferdinand VII from the persecution of the Cortes and from the Constitution of Spain.

Don Augustin Iturbide was fixed upon as a proper agent to carry their plans into effect. Although a creole, he had been an active and a zealous officer to the King, and had fought valiantly and successfully against the friends of liberty. The Europeans considered him as attached to their party and interests; the clergy relied upon his maintaining them in all their privileges and immunities; and all parties knew that he would be opposed to a liberal form of government. They were ignorant of the projects of personal aggrandizement which he is said to have entertained even at that period. Iturbide had been appointed by the Viceroy to command the army destined to crush the remnant of the insurgent forces. This enabled him to act promptly and efficiently. The priests and Europeans furnished him with some money, and on his march toward the south he seized on a convoy of specie belonging to the Manila merchants. He soon formed a junction with Guerrero, who commanded the patriots in that quarter; an event which, in order to deceive the Viceroy, he attributed to the good policy of his administration, in offering a pardon to all who would claim the protection of the Government within a certain period.

Emissaries had been despatched by the Revolutionists in the capital to every part of the empire, and by the time the armies reached Iguala the people were everywhere ready to declare in favor of independence. On February 24, 1822, Iturbide proposed to the chiefs the plan of Iguala, which was unanimously adopted by them, and was immediately transmitted to the Viceroy and to all the governors of provinces. The plan provides: First, for the protection and preservation of the holy Catholic religion; secondly, for the intimate union of Europeans and creoles; and thirdly, for the independence of Mexico. It declares that the constitution of the empire shall be that of a limited monarchy, and offers the crown, first to Ferdinand VII, and then to the other members of his family, in regular succession, provided that he or they shall agree to reside in Mexico, and shall take an oath to maintain the constitution which shall be established by a congress to be assembled for that purpose.

It further provides for the protection of the persons and property of the citizens, and for the preservation of the privileges and immunities of the secular and regular clergy. It declares all the inhabitants of New Spain, without distinction of persons—Europeans, Africans, and Indians, and their descendants—to be citizens of the monarchy, and to be eligible to all offices according to their merits and virtues: and to carry this plan into effect, an army, called the "Army of the Three Guarantees," is to be raised, which is to preserve the Catholic, Apostolic, and Roman religion, to effect the independence of the empire, and to maintain the union of the Americans and Europeans in Mexico.

The first intimation received by the Viceroy Apodaca of the defection of Iturbide and of the force under his command was the promulgation of the plan of Iguala, and he used every means in his power to frustrate the revolutionists and to prepare for defence; but the Royalists, either believing that he wanted sufficient energy of character for such a crisis or dissatisfied with his measures, deposed him and placed an officer of artillery, Don Francisco Novella, at the head of the Government.

The Europeans were startled by the establishment of the Cortes, and the avowal of an intention to control the monarch, but they were informed that such a provision was necessary to reconcile the creoles to the place; and as the clergy were satisfied, they were compelled to submit.

On March 1st Iturbide assembled the officers of his army and submitted to them this plan. He exposed his views, and laid before them the resources and means he possessed of carrying them into effect; and after assuring them that they were at liberty to act as they might think proper, he urged them to give their opinions. He was interrupted by shouts and *vivas* from the officers, who not only approved the plan, but insisted upon creating him lieutenant-general, that he might lead them at once to the capital and enforce its observance. Iturbide declined the promotion, and recommended to them the greatest moderation, declaring it to be his intention not to proceed to hostilities until he had tried every means of negotiation.

On the ensuing day, the army took an oath to maintain the

plan of Iguala; and on that occasion Iturbide addressed them in the following words: "Soldiers, you have this day sworn to preserve the Catholic, Apostolic, and Roman religion; to protect the union of Europeans and Americans; to effect the independence of this empire; and, on certain conditions, to obey the King. This act will be applauded by foreign nations; your services will be gratefully acknowledged by your fellow-citizens; and your names will be inscribed in the temple of immortality. Yesterday I refused the title of lieutenant-general, which you would have conferred upon me, and now I renounce this distinction (tearing from his sleeves the bands of lace which distinguished a colonel in the Spanish service). To be ranked as your companion fills all my ambitious desires."

The subsequent conduct of this chief shows how very insincere were these professions. Few creoles approved the plan of Iguala. Most of them objected to pledge themselves to receive a prince of the house of Bourbon or even to adopt a monarchical form of government. They were told that Hidalgo, Albude, and others had used the same language, and at the commencement of the revolution had declared their only object in taking up arms to be the preservation of America for Ferdinand VII; that a prince of the house of Bourbon would unite all parties and prevent anarchy and civil war; that he, being a stranger without influence and without resources, surrounded only by a small body of his personal dependents, might be compelled to observe the constitution. Notwithstanding these arguments, they yielded only because they had not the power of dictating other terms. It is not probable, however, that either party considered the plan as binding on them, but that all believed that a congress elected by the people would possess the power of altering or modifying it, so as to suit the circumstances of the country, or of adopting any form of government most pleasing to the majority of the nation.

On the part of the Royalists there was a show of resistance in some of the provinces; but the public opinion, no longer restrained by the opposition of the clergy, manifested itself so powerfully as to effect the revolution in every part of the empire without bloodshed and almost without a struggle. From Iguala, Iturbide crossed over to the Baxio, that rich and fertile country situated between Guanajuato and the capital. Here he was joined by several general officers and governors of provinces. Guadalupe Victoria, who had resisted the Royalists to the last, and who, since the dispersion of his forces, had been concealed in the mountains of Vera Cruz, united himself with Iturbide at San Juan del Rio. His presence gave confidence to the revolutionists and added strength to the cause of independence. He had been distinguished from the beginning of the revolution by his devotion to the cause of freedom and by his valor, activity, and disinterested generosity; and he had won the hearts of the people by the strictest observance of the forms of the Catholic religion.

The Army of the Three Guarantees marched upon Queretaro, which from its position may be considered the military key of the interior provinces, and gained immediate possession of that place. Here the army was formed into two divisions. One, commanded by Guadalupe Victoria, marched toward the capital, while the commander-in-chief made a rapid movement upon Puebla. This place too was given up as soon as he appeared before it.

Things were in this state when General O'Donoju arrived at Vera Cruz, to take the command of the country as captain-general and political chief of Mexico. Finding, as he himself declares, the empire possessing forces sufficient to secure the independence it had proclaimed, the capital besieged, and the legitimate authorities deposed; the places of Vera Cruz and Acapulco alone in the possession of the European Government; without garrisons, and without the means of defending themselves against a protracted and well-directed siege—he proposed to treat with Iturbide on the basis of the plan of Iguala. This proposal was readily acceded to, and the parties met at Cordova, and soon agreed upon the terms of negotiation. It was stipulated that New Spain should be considered a sovereign and independent nation, that commissioners should be sent to Spain to offer the crown to Ferdinand VII and that in the mean time a governing junta and a regency should be appointed, and that a cortes should be immediately elected and convened for the purpose of framing a constitution.

General O'Donoju engaged to use his influence with the commander and officers of the European troops, to persuade them to evacuate the capital; but when he applied to them, they refused to yield to his request. At the same time they expressed their readiness to submit to the authority with which he was vested by the King, and to obey whatever orders he, as commander-in-chief, might think proper to extend to the garrison of Mexico. In consequence of this, he agreed upon terms of capitulation with Iturbide, and the garrison marched out of the capital with the honors of war, and were quartered at Toluca, there to remain until the transports were ready to convey them to Spain.

As soon as the revolutionists took possession of the capital, a junta, composed of thirty-six members, was appointed; by them, a regency, consisting of five persons, was chosen, of which Iturbide was made president. He was at the same time appointed admiral and generalissimo of the navy and army, and assigned a yearly salary of one hundred twenty thousand dollars.

UPRISING IN SOUTH AMERICA

CAREER OF BOLIVAR, THE LIBERATOR

A.D. 1810

ALFRED DÉBÉRLE

Three great periods have been marked in the history of the South American countries—that of discovery and conquest, chiefly by Spain and Portugal; that of colonization; and the period of revolution in which the Spanish colonies became independent. In these colonies the kings of Spain at first established a single viceroyal government, that of Peru. Later, separate viceroys were sent to New Granada and Buenos Aires, and captains-general to Caracas (Venezuela) and Chile. These governments were despotisms modelled on that of Madrid, but administered with colonial license and caprice.

The population included European Spaniards; their children born in America, who were called creoles; mestizos, children of mixed blood, white and Indian; mulattoes, children of European and negro parentage; zambos, children of negroes and Indians; African negroes, and the native Indians. This admixture of races led to social jealousies and class hatred, which complicated political troubles whenever they arose. The European Spaniards, there as elsewhere, looked with contempt upon the creoles, who returned the feeling with violent animosity. The native Indians were mere slaves under the other classes, and subject to outrageous abuse.

By a policy of ruinous imposts, oppression, and violence, the Spanish kings at last wore out the patience of their South American colonists. Not only were the persecuted Indians provoked to open mutiny; the creoles also rebelled; and when at last, early in the nineteenth century, the rapacious rulers sought to save themselves by some show of reform, they found that they were too late. The Revolution of the United States and that of France had had their influence upon the intelligent patriots of South America, and the work of deliverance was soon to begin. In 1808 Napoleon set his brother, Joseph Bonaparte, upon the Spanish throne, and while the latter, during his short-lived rule, was vainly endeavoring to cope with insurrection in Spain, the South American colonies continued their revolutionary preparations.

For the history of South America, from its discovery to the present day, there is no authority to be preferred to Débérle, whose recent work, from which the following narrative is taken, is based upon those of the best previous authors, and verified from authentic documents—many of them never before published—in archives and public and private libraries, in America and Spain.

THE third period of the history of the South American colonies, in relation to their respective mother-countries, we may say begins for the Spanish possessions with the events in Caracas and Buenos Aires (1810), and for the Portuguese with the "declaration of independence" of Brazil, which was converted in 1822 into a constitutional empire.

To the cruelty of the conduct of Spain at the end of the eighteenth century, and to her obstinate persistence in refusing to listen to counsels that would have been profitable to her, may be attributed the fact that the idea of an insurrection spread everywhere. It soon became general, and seems fully justifiable on the impartial ground of history.

The revolution in Spain itself brought matters to a head. The Spanish people had dethroned the feeble Carlos IV (1808), that King who, occupying himself only in the pleasures of the chase and the care of his stables, had placed all his authority in the hands of Godoy. When Ferdinand VII, the evil son of an imbecile father, assumed the crown of Spain, numerous quarrels broke out between these degenerate Bourbon kings whose influence Napoleon was, at the same time, endeavoring to undermine at all costs. Determining causes of the rupture with the South Americans may also be found in the imprisonment of the unfortunate Bourbons at Valençay; in their exchanging their rights for certain pensions; in the imposition of the Napoleonic dynasty, and the want of tact of the political parties who were disputing for power. All these facts gave the colonies a secret right, as it were, to rebel against the mother-country and throw off what to them was equivalent to the heavy yoke of slavery. South Americans would no longer participate in the fate of conquered Spain, which, even in the midst of her misfortunes, endeavored to exact from them a strict obedience. They could not know whom to obey, since decrees and proclamations arrived simultaneously from Carlos IV, Ferdinand VII, and even from the puppet king, Joseph Bonaparte; neither could they tell which junta to respect, since they received, in addition to these, conflicting orders from those of Cadiz, Seville, and Asturias, each claiming to be the only legitimate source of authority; and, at the same time, they received orders from the Council of Regency. A ray of hope was seen in this kind of anarchy, and the idea of independence began to germinate in the minds of the colonists.

The movement, begun in 1809 at Quito, in the northwest of the Department of Ecuador, in the Province of Colombia, was repressed for the time—two of its promoters having paid for it with their lives—but a year had not elapsed before it was successfully carried out.

Between 1808 and 1810 it might have been thought that the mother-country was about to make laudable endeavors to retain these territories by taking away every pretext for rebellion. The colonies received at that time considerable favors and subsidies, and the justly demanded reforms were attempted. The royal decree of January 22, 1809, had declared that the South American provinces were not considered like the colonies of other nations, but as an integral part of the monarchy, and consequently ought to have a direct and immediate representation in the Spanish Cortes. Moreover the Junta of Seville sent in 1810 to the Spanish-Americans to say: "At last you are raised to the dignity of free men! The time has passed in which, under the weight of an insupportable yoke, you were the victims of absolutism, ambition, and ignorance. Bear in mind that, electing your representatives to the Cortes, your destiny will no longer depend on ministers, kings, or governors, but is in your own hands." After this explicit declaration of the manner in which Spain had governed her colonies the decree was published by the terms of which those representatives were to be elected. There was to be one for each capital, chosen by lot from three individuals designated by the municipalities, according to the formalities that the Viceroy would be pleased to prescribe.

When the Regency of Cadiz came to replace the central Junta, the ordinances of 1809 on the liberty of commerce, which they had reëstablished, were abolished, the immediate consequence of such an extraordinary measure being to arouse men's minds, especially in the Province of Caracas, where the principles of liberty and equality had grown with greater vigor than in the other South American colonies. The municipal council formed itself into a supreme junta of government, April 19, 1810, and at the same time that it recognized Ferdinand VII as king it rebelled against the decrees of the Regency.   The formation of this junta coincided with the arrival of certain agents who went to demand the oath of fidelity to Joseph, and who were received with the shout of "Long live Ferdinand!" since the hatred against Napoleon and all his partisans (who were called *afrancesados*) was as general in the colonies as at home.   The Viceroy of Nueva Granada, accused of intending to deliver America into Napoleon's hands, was exiled to Cartagena, and almost simultaneously the Provinces of Cundinamarca, Pamplona, and Socorro, as well as those of the north—Tunja, Casanare, Antioquia, Choco, Neiva, and Mariquita, rose, and the Province of Quito attempted a second revolt at the mere rumor that the French troops were threatening Nueva Granada.   The viceroyalty having disappeared from the latter, each provincial capital desired to be the seat of the Junta without heeding the claims of the others; but as union was absolutely necessary to attain the end proposed it was eventually fixed in Santa Fé de Bogota, and recognized Ferdinand VII as sovereign ruler, and invited Caracas to follow its example. But this province, which obeyed General Miranda, an old companion-in-arms of Washington, would not accept the invitation, replying that the representatives of the united provinces of Venezuela were going to found a free government—which in fact they afterward did—intending to form part of the Republic of Colombia by a declaration of the deputies of Caracas, Varinas, Barcelona, Cumana, Margarita, Merida, and Trujillo, but later (in 1830), they declared themselves an independent state.

The insurrection had taken alarming proportions in various other parts of America.   Buenos Aires and Montevideo maintained a war against the English from 1804 to 1807, the ports of La Plata having to support continuous and formidable blockades. Jacques de Liniers, a Frenchman by birth, in the service of Spain, by reanimating the courage of the colonists had succeeded in raising the blockade.   These inexperienced soldiers, proud of their success, and allowing themselves to be led by the advice of such men as Moreno, Castelli, Belgrano, and Valcarcel—all imbued with ideas imported from the United States and France—formed the nucleus of the army of the insurrection; so that, in a short time, Buenos Aires was prepared to sustain the struggle in a formal and decisive manner.   An assembly of about six hundred notables of the country deprived the Viceroy, Baltasar de Cisneros, of power in 1810, and the movement that was directed by Castelli and Belgrano went on gaining ground daily and overcame all opposition in spite of the reënforcements that the wife of John VI sent from Portugal and the formation of an army corps under the command of the Viceroy of Peru. Victory remained with the men of Buenos Aires after a few days' contest, and many Spanish officers were made prisoners after being deserted by their soldiers. Montevideo served as a refuge for the Royalists, where they established their headquarters, no doubt, with the intention of making another attempt to overcome the Independents, but very soon, in Montevideo as in all the provinces of Paraguay, supreme juntas were formed and the revolution became general.

The Chileans revolted in 1810 and were also victorious. This was the more remarkable, as the Chileans, having a very small quantity of arms, had to manufacture their cannon out of the trunks of trees, and these could be discharged only four times before they became useless. Some battalions had only agricultural instruments for weapons. To fight and conquer under such conditions could be done only by a people who rose at the sacred call of liberty.

The cause of independence presented a different aspect among the Peruvians, for, although Upper Peru struggled with rare heroism, Lower Peru remained loyal, and this afforded a strong base of operations to the Spaniards. The revolution having broken out in May, 1809, in Charcas and La Paz, a small army corps from Buenos Aires had marched to them in order to support the movement, and, having been joined by many revolutionists, they had succeeded at length in entering Potosi, guided by Castelli and Valcarcel. The victories gained by the Government of Lima were not of any permanent benefit, since, being obliged to divide their forces to oppose the insurgents of Quito, Upper Peru, and Chile, their effectiveness was very much reduced. In the capital, a beautiful and indolent city, the movement was not taken up with equal enthusiasm by all classes of the population. It was supported everywhere by the members of the lower order of the clergy; but, on the other hand, the high dignitaries of the Church, the nobility, and the families and dependents of the public officers rejected it. Referring to the former, a letter of *Morillo to his Government*, published in the *Revolutions of Spanish America*, says that they were very discontented; not a single one appearing devoted to the Government of the King of Spain.

The younger members of the upper classes gave great support to the cause of the revolution, since their admirable sentiments of patriotism made them submit to the exigencies of the conscription wherever it was established (as in Venezuela), while it was necessary to take men of the lower ranks to the army by force. The negroes and Indians, brutalized by slavery, allowed themselves to be dragged away as often by those who defended as by those who attacked the insurrection that was to give them their liberty. In various places, and especially in Buenos Aires, some tribes took advantage of the movement to renew their raids, which carried terror and misfortune into many districts. Everywhere the cause of independence suffered alternations—events being sometimes favorable to it and sometimes adverse. If, at that time, Spain had had a man of sufficient practical knowledge to advise her, perhaps it might have been easy to preserve the extensive districts in the rich colonies which still remained loyal to the mother-country, thus allowing them to retain—by means of prudent reforms in their administration—the conquests which had cost them so much to secure.

The South American insurrection, like all great social upheavals, produced extraordinary men, of whom Simon Bolivar, the idolized hero of the Spanish-Americans, may be reckoned the chief. That Titanic struggle for liberty, which was to last for fifteen years, found in him a second Arminius. His country has given him the name of "Liberator," and one of the States that owe their liberty to him bears his name.

Simon Bolivar was born in Caracas in 1785. He was the youngest of the four children of Juan Vicente Bolivar y Ponte, colonel of the militia of the plains of Aragua, a rich and respected man. An orphan from the age of six, and master to an immense fortune, Simon was sent, while still a youth, to Madrid to finish his education in the family of his uncle, the Marques de Palacios, and after travelling for some time in Europe, at the age of eighteen he married his cousin, the daughter of the Marques de Toro. He took her back to Caracas with him, but had the misfortune to lose her within five months of their arrival, the victim of a violent attack of yellow fever. After so great and irreparable a loss he returned to Europe, where he remained visiting various capitals until 1809, passing on his return through the United States. During his stay in France he had an opportunity, after the apotheosis of Napoleon, to observe the energy of a whole nation which had freed itself by a supreme effort of its will; and in the United States, to admire the honored and illustrious Washington.

After his return to his estates in Aragua, the revolution which demanded his services came suddenly upon him, and having been deputed to go to England with Luis Lopez y Mendez to solicit her protection they set out for London, where they were received very coolly, because the English Government, making common cause with the Spanish Cortes against the French domination, could not support a movement contrary to the nation to which they were bound by previous engagements.

Bolivar being obliged to return to America, took with him a small quantity of arms, and General Miranda, an old and valiant soldier, also a native of Caracas, who had always striven to give liberty to his country, and who, being expatriated for his well-known labors in favor of independence, had been going about the world for twenty-five years in search of resources for the cause. Miranda had served with Dumouriez in France, and with Washington in the United States, and weary of hoping, and relying only on his own resources and those of a few friends, had already organized an expedition that had disembarked at Ocumare, and afterward at Coro, but which had had an unfortunate termination from the ill-reception that his compatriots had given him on that occasion. When he joined Bolivar, although at an advanced age, he offered his services to his country with the same faith that he had in his youth, and he was rewarded by being placed at the head of the movement.

In 1812, on Holy Thursday, a terrible earthquake overthrew nine-tenths of the houses in Caracas. The clergy, taking advantage of the terror that such a catastrophe caused among the inhabitants, attributed it to the effect of God's anger, and thus a certain reaction set in in favor of the Spanish arms, which caused them to gain some ground. General Monteverde, a man of rough manners and great severity, succeeded in recovering

Venezuela at the head of the Royalist troops and obliged Miranda to capitulate, with the promise of an amnesty in favor of the rebels—a promise that was not kept—and the unfortunate general, the victim of the reactionary rule that was established through this feat of arms, was sent by Monteverde to Cadiz, where he died in one of the dungeons in 1816, after having had the grief of seeing Bolivar among his enemies. Monteverde succeeded in spreading terror through those provinces which saw their prisons filled; the horrible instruments of torture laid out every moment, the fields covered with unfortunate wretches cast out of the city after having had their noses, ears, or cheeks cut off, or having suffered other cruel tortures. The cause of independence was then passing through its supreme crisis in Venezuela as well as in Nueva Granada.

The position of the revolutionists in Chile was not much more satisfactory, since the reaction was gaining advantages in Quito while they were waiting for the brave Mariño, who came, at length, at the head of a new expedition and wrested that country again out of the hands of the Spaniards. By good fortune La Plata was now completely emancipated, and the armies of Artiga and Lopez held the Spaniards in check on the frontiers of Chile and Peru, the cause of Spain being considered completely lost in the last-named State.

Bolivar had taken refuge in Curaçao with his cousin, Felix Ribas, where he collected all the refugees in order to take them to Cartagena, a province that had been able to preserve its freedom. He there laid his plan before the Congress. This consisted in making use of all the resources that they might be able to give them, in order to liberate Venezuela and save Nueva Granada at one and the same time. His petition having been considered, the Congress furnished him with money, arms, and provisions, and Manuel Castillo sent to him five hundred men; these, united with the three hundred Venezuelans who followed him, formed a small army corps under his command of eight hundred men, the second in command being the above-named Ribas. The expedition left Cartagena in January, 1813, and Castillo wanted to march immediately on his own account, advancing toward the east, while Bolivar received orders from the Congress to occupy and hold Barancas, a town on the banks of the Magdalena. Bolivar, who did not wish to remain inactive, resolved to disobey these orders, promising himself to obtain pardon for this fault by covering himself with glory.

He first seized Teneriffe, a town situated on the right bank of the Magdalena, then Mompos, and lastly Ocaña, dividing, beating, and dispersing the enemy. When he entered Venezuela, Nueva Granada was already free. The cruelties of Monteverde saved the revolution, obliging the moderates to throw themselves into the arms of the patriots. Recruits arrived from all parts; and already followed by more than two thousand men when he penetrated the Andes in the environs of Pamplona, Bolivar saw many thousands of volunteers united under his banner after he had succeeded in joining Ribas in the territory of Venezuela. Six hundred Granadinos sent by the Congress of Tunja had come with Ribas at the same time that Colonel Briceno, detached in Guadalito, arrived with a body of cavalry. Without loss of time, Bolivar attacked the Royalists at La Grita and afterward at Merida, making himself master of the district of that name; with the same rapidity he occupied the Province of Varinas. In the mean while Marino, that young student who after passing all the military grades in a few months was already named as one of the firmest supports of the revolution, defeated Monteverde, made himself master of the Provinces of Cumana and Barcelona, and took the title of general-in-chief and dictator of the Eastern Provinces of Venezuela.

Favored by these successes, which, however, were an obstacle to his views of unity, Bolivar divided his army into two parts; taking command of one, he placed Ribas in command of the other, and, pursuing the Spaniards closely, beat them in Niquitas, Betioca, Caracha, Barquisimeto, and Varinas, at last reaching Monteverde, whom he totally defeated; he then marched to Caracas, into which capital he made his entry (August 4, 1813) in a carriage drawn by twelve handsome young men; the enthusiasm with which the man, who was henceforth saluted by the title of "Liberator," was received was indescribable. In a few months he had gone over one hundred fifty leagues and fought fifteen battles besides numerous smaller actions. His glory would have been complete if, in this memorable campaign, he had not retaliated by sanguinary executions of the Spaniards against the horrible cruelties inflicted by Monteverde, whose barbaric acts were no justification of his own.

The liberation of Venezuela appeared to be completely assured, since Bolivar occupied almost half of the captaincy-general and Mariño the rest. The Spaniards held only a few unimportant points, Monteverde being blockaded in Puerto Cabello; it was difficult to foresee that Fortune would turn her back on the South Americans.

Bolivar, who had taken the title of "Dictator of the Western Provinces of Venezuela," did not think of reëstablishing the civil government—the only conditions under which democracies can live without danger; but the echoes of public opinion which reached him gave him to understand clearly the error that he had committed, and he hastened to convoke an assembly to which he gave an account of his operations and plans and tendered his resignation. This was not accepted, the dictatorship being conferred on him until Venezuela should be able to unite with Nueva Granada.

The Royalists, who had not lost all hope, armed the slaves, under a promise of giving them their liberty, the vagabonds, and all who had no visible means of subsistence whom they could meet with. At the head of these bloodthirsty bands was the ferocious Puy, who, after seizing Varinas, shot five hundred patriots there; Puy was lieutenant of Bover, the most dreaded of the adversaries of Bolivar. This Bover, a Castilian by origin, who had been successively sailor, coast-guard, and pedler, and had been imprisoned for his misdeeds, had come to America seeking an asylum from justice. Although his motive is unknown, he enlisted in the Royalist ranks, in which he held the rank of captain at the time of the defeats of the Spaniards. He made an appeal to the idlers, the fugitives from justice, the negroes and the mulattoes, and with these organized a body of troops which, from their ferocity, deserved the name of the "Infernal Legion," in which were many *llaneros*, barbarians from the plains, herdsmen, and slaughterers accustomed to tame the wildest horses and unrivalled as horsemen. These men of the plains despised the mountaineer who lowered himself by going on foot, as well as the European who could not endure a gallop continued for sixteen hours. They ride bareback and have no other dress than a sort of short breeches or drawers. Stretched out over their horses, with lance in rest and a lasso in the other hand, they fall upon the enemy, and wound and destroy with the rapidity of lightning. No regular cavalry can resist the onset of these Cossacks of the Colombian steppes, who always leave behind them such terrible trails. The cupidity of these nomads had been excited by the promise to distribute the lands of the conquered among them, and thus Bover succeeded very quickly in getting together an army of eight thousand men.

From the moment that he appears on the theatre of war it acquired such a character of ferocity and barbarity that both sides rivalled each other in committing atrocities. Nevertheless, it is right to confess that it was Bover who began it by beheading in one day twelve hundred prisoners. The energy of Bover was more than once paralyzed by the carelessness of the Spanish generals, and Bolivar succeeded in defeating him several times, as well as his lieutenants, the mulatto Roseta, and the guerilla chief Yañez. The Dictator had the imprudence to risk himself with all his forces on the vast plains, where he was surprised and destroyed by the cavalry of Bover. Mariño, beaten almost at the same time, was driven back toward Cumana. The conqueror entered Caracas with such precipitation that the Dictator had only sufficient time to get on board a ship, trusting the safety of the republic to the mercy of the elements. Ribas collected the dispersed patriot forces and continued the campaign, but he was finally defeated in the Battle of Erisa by Bover, who, receiving a spear wound, died on the field of battle. His ferocious soldiers made him a funeral worthy of his person: women, children, and old men, all were put to the sword; and Ribas, who had been taken prisoner, was shot, and his head was sent to Caracas to be publicly exposed (December, 1814).

Bolivar had been able to reach Cartagena, which, with the Province of Santa Marta, had been formed into a republic of which Torrices was president. Nueva Granada was very much divided. It will be remembered that a provisional junta had been formed in Bogota since July, 1810. The provincial deputies assembled in Congress had drawn up an act of federation which had not succeeded in obtaining the approbation of all the provinces, the dissidents selecting a junta called the "Junta of

Cundinamarca." In 1812 this assembly published its plan of a constitution, which was no better received than the preceding. Anarchy reigned everywhere. A third Congress assembled in Tunja (September, 1814), to which Bolivar offered his services. These were accepted, and, being ordered to march against Bogota and its dictator Alvarez, he obtained the formal promise that the dissident provinces would join the confederation, although in exchange the old capital should be the seat of government. The Congress being installed in Bogota immediately set about preparing means to repulse the Spaniards, who were expected to appear very shortly. Napoleon had fallen; Ferdinand VII already occupied the throne of his fathers, and very soon news arrived that he was sending a squadron with ten thousand men under the command of Morillo to succor the Royalists. The speedy arrival of this important reënforcement had been communicated to all the viceroys. The Madrid Government, thinking no doubt that they still had to do with the Indians of Cortés and Pizarro, had conceived the hope that on this news alone the rebels, seized with terror, would immediately submit in a body; this was reckoning too much on the prestige of the Spanish arms which, it was already known, were not invincible. These events coincided on the other hand with the capitulation of Montevideo, the last refuge of the mother-country in the old viceroyalty of Buenos Aires, which was converted from that moment into an independent state. The new republic formed a squadron and its seamen had beaten the Spanish fleet. Although it is certain that, by the capitulation of Montevideo and the five thousand five hundred men who defended it, Spain lost the only territory that remained to her on the east coast of South America, it is not less so that these misfortunes had been partly counterbalanced by successes in Chile, which in 1814 had again fallen under the yoke of the Spaniards, who gave themselves up to all the horrors of the most sanguinary repression. The guerilla chief Rodriguez, nevertheless, constantly harassed the Royalists of Chile, while, yielding to the suggestions of Belgrano, and the Government of Buenos Aires, the Provinces of Cuzco, Huamanga, and Arequipa in Peru, which had hitherto continued tranquil, declared for the cause of independence, and the Royalists were able to retain Lima only with great difficulty.

The Granadine and Venezuelan chiefs had united; Castillo, Cabal, and Urdaneta acted for Nueva Granada, Bolivar and Mariño for Venezuela. Troops were sent to the south to support the Government of Quito, and Urdaneta marched toward the east, charged to restrain the devastating incursions of Puy. Bolivar, appointed Captain-General of Nueva Granada and Venezuela, descended through the Province of Magdalena at the head of three thousand men, surprised Mompos, where he shot four hundred prisoners, and demanded reënforcements that the latter obstinately refused him, thinking it more important to uphold the independence of Cartagena with respect to Bogota than to repel the enemy. Bolivar wished to force President Torrices to give him the troops which he required, and, instead of continuing his march, returned to Cartagena, thus losing precious time. In the mean while the enemy was approaching, and the common danger averted a fratricidal struggle. He joined his troops to those that were in Cartagena and embarked for Jamaica, whence he hoped to bring succor, and, when he had obtained this and was preparing to return, he received news that Cartagena had surrendered after a heroic resistance of four months. Morillo entered Cartagena on December 6, 1815; the city was nothing but a heap of ruins, since the whole strength of the enemy had been directed against it, and it thus expiated, very cruelly certainly, its refusal to assist the common cause. With the taking of this fortified town, Nueva Granada was again opened to the enemy, and the second period of the war of independence terminated still more unfortunately than the first had done.

At first Morillo appeared to be animated by pacific intentions, but almost immediately, yielding to the suggestions of Morales, he gave orders that with respect to the rebels "all considerations of humanity" should be set aside. Summary executions, wholesale deportations, imprisonments, forced contributions, and sequestration of property began everywhere. In the mean time the patriots were masters of the plain, which they defended with fierce obstinacy. After an important victory at Puente (February 16, 1816) Morillo allowed himself to be defeated by Urdaneta and Torrices, his position becoming very critical for a time. Five hundred Spaniards went over to the patriots; the corsairs captured his convoys, blowing up one of his ships; Brion, that rich

Dutch merchant of Cartagena whom Caracas had made captain of a frigate and afterward an admiral, brought to Bolivar Mariño and fifteen hundred resolute men, with one thousand negroes furnished by Pétion.

Morillo's bad faith, his tyrannical measures, and his inhuman proceedings threw into the ranks of the rebellion very many men who were convinced that the capitulations and promises of pardon were nothing more than deceptions. A good example of this is what occurred in Bogota, which opened its gates to the Royalists after a formal treaty in which the most complete amnesty was accorded to the inhabitants; a treaty that Morillo did not hesitate to violate by executing Torres, Lozano, Torrices, Cabal, Pombo, Caldas, and two hundred other patriots, exiling their families and confiscating their property. This man, endowed with incontestable military qualities, was nevertheless very far from having those necessary for pacifying a country. By exasperating the vanquished he rendered their submission impossible; and to him alone, who came to reconquer America, must his country impute its loss. He believed in the efficiency of the odious and arbitrary measures adopted by him, the execution of which he had intrusted to a permanent council of war, a council of purification, a committee of sequestrations, and courts-martial.

As we have said before, the Spanish flag floated over all the territory of Nueva Granada, and this fortunate success blinded Morillo, who, exaggerating his power and considering it as stable as it was invincible, was preparing to carry his system of terror to Peru. Bolivar undertook to dissipate his illusions. Having secretly set sail from Cayes, he put himself at the head of an expedition composed of two ships of war and thirteen transports, fitted out for the most part at the expense of Brion. On May 2d Brion defeated the Spanish flotilla, taking two vessels; on the 3d Bolivar disembarked on the island of Margarita, which had fallen into the hands of the mulatto Arismendi, and the insurgents, in a general assembly four days later, proclaimed the Republic of Venezuela, one and indivisible, and Bolivar head of the same. Arismendi presented to the Dictator a gold-headed cane, "emblem of the supreme authority in a country that can bend under the blast of adversity, but never break."

The Scotchman, Macgregor, at the head of six hundred men

was ordered to go to the succor of Mariño and Piar, who were holding out in Guiana, while Paez, taking the province of Apure as the base of his operations, ejected Morillo from it. The Indian Paez, who had passed his youth among the llaneros, proposed to draw his old companions from the reactionary party, uniting them to the cause of independence; a thing that was not difficult for him inasmuch as the Spanish Government, proceeding with the greatest ingratitude and thinking they had no further need of their services, had contemptuously disbanded them without giving them the slightest remuneration. They passed over, then, to serve the cause of the revolution, of which they were the most efficacious instruments. Paez, by his loyal and generous character, had become the idol of these untamed natures. The brave deeds of Paez, as numerous as they are surprising, are those of a legendary hero; it is asserted that he repulsed the Spanish infantry by letting wild oxen loose against them; that he arrested pursuit by setting fire to the steppes; that he seized the Royalist gunboats in the waters of the Apure by swimming; that with his terrible lance he killed as many as forty enemies in the fight, and when he fell upon a flying division he completed the rout by his powerful voice and the fear that he inspired. Endowed with herculean strength and unconquerable energy, he took part in the amusements and the dangers of his men. At the head of the ferocious llaneros of the plains of the Apure, he began those brilliant exploits that were later to make him the terror of the Spanish armies.

Bolivar, deserted by fortune, found himself obliged to beat a retreat once more. He took refuge in Jamaica, where his life was seriously threatened by the poniards of the Royalists; but nothing could abate his courage; active, resolute, and fertile in resources, the moment had arrived when after having fallen to the bottom of the abyss he was to rise and issue from it. The disobedience of some chiefs, his rivals, had been very fatal to the cause of independence and would have been much more so if on their part the Spanish chiefs had not been so divided, since Morillo had taken the extreme step of arresting two general officers, Morales and Real. After many conferences, Arismendi, Via, Paez, Rojas, Monagas, Sedeno, and Bermudez agreed to recognize him as generalissimo. He called together a general congress in the island of Margarita, and the provisional government, of which he took the direction with the title of "President of the Republic of Venezuela," was established in Barcelona; but some months later, after sanguinary combats, this city was recovered by the Royalists (April 7, 1817), who in a short time were once again masters of almost all the coast.

The position of the Republicans was critical and perplexing, and in order to draw them from it Bolivar conceived the daring project of transferring the insurrection to Guiana, which until then had remained loyal. This campaign was well directed by the "Liberator," seconded by Piar and Brion, and its success was so great that in less than three months that vast and rich province was subdued by the Republican army, which entered its capital, Angostura, July 17th. During this bold and distant expedition of the Generalissimo, numerous and brilliant victories had been gained in other parts. General Morillo, who came in person to besiege the island of Margarita, was defeated, his camp falling into the hands of the besieged, who on the other hand obliged the Spanish squadron to leave their coast after miraculously escaping complete destruction. Insurrectionary movements increased in Nueva Granada, and guerilla bands were numerous in the Provinces of Antioquia, Quito, and Popayan; Paez with his cavalry gained two important victories over Morillo.

Before the termination of the year 1817 the seat of government was transferred to the capital of Guiana, and Bolivar, who had established his headquarters there, prepared to divide the lands among the Independent soldiers as a recompense for their sacrifices. The campaign of 1818, although it gave the Republican generals opportunities of showing proofs of their courage and military knowledge, had no decisive result, the Republicans only obtaining possession of San Fernando; but other events of immense importance occurred to awaken the general enthusiasm. The very great popularity that Bolivar enjoyed, not only on the American continent but also in Europe itself, attracted to his banner many volunteers from England, France, and the United States, with whom he organized a model legion; at the same time, in Washington and in London, *chargés d'affaires* of Venezuela were received, which was equivalent to recognizing her existence. In England, Lopez Mendez, charged to contract loans and enlist men, had seen money and men, arms and munitions flow in;

so that besides the resources necessary to the prosecution of the war the new republic at the end of 1818 relied upon nine thousand foreign combatants. Despairing of conquering the Liberator they attempted to assassinate him; twelve men armed with daggers penetrated one night into the tent, from which he escaped half-dressed.

At the end of the year 1818 the Republicans were in an excellent position; the Spaniards on the contrary found themselves reduced to the last extremity, having to face on all sides regular armies and the guerilla bands which fell upon them suddenly. Bolivar, who remained in Angostura, after having occupied himself in the regulation of the administration, of agriculture and commerce, assembled in that city the National Congress, which he opened in person on February 15, 1819, laying before it a draft constitution and resigning the dictatorship with which he had been invested. At the request of the Congress, Bolivar accepted the Presidency of the republic, of which Zea was appointed Vice-President, until the new constitution was promulgated.

The Liberator, desirous of consolidating the independence, thought the time had arrived to go in search of Morillo, whom he succeeded in putting on the wrong track, moving his troops in different directions and pretending to operate in view of Caracas, while he marched, as he had intended, toward the south of Nueva Granada, of which the Spaniards had been in tranquil possession for two years. After many battles, in which the Republicans were always victorious, Bolivar, not without much fatigue, succeeded in joining Santander and taking him with him. Both armies being united continued their march across the plains inundated by continuous rains, crossed rivers that had overflowed their banks, penetrated deserts where they suffered the torments of thirst, and woods whose trees, of a prodigious height, intercepted the light of day and dropped with continuous rain; scaled the scarped Andes of Tunja, and at length, after undergoing the greatest sufferings for seventy days, and losing a large part of their baggage and all their horses, they arrived at Paya on June 27th. Four days after, Bolivar met in the valley of Sagamoso three thousand five hundred Spaniards, and, without heeding the inferiority of his forces or their reduced condition, routed them, and the same night Tunja fell into his hands. Other actions followed, and the Republicans, by victory after victory, arrived at the bridge of Boyaca, where they gained a decisive victory over the partisans of Spain. When the news of this battle had spread throughout the province the insurrection broke out in all parts with such violence that the Spanish authorities saw no other means of escape than a precipitate flight. Bogota opened its gates to the Independents on August 10, 1819, Santander being instantly appointed President of the Provisional Government.

During this time the squadron of Margarita, commanded by Admiral Brion, took by assault the fort and city of Barcelona (July 18th), while the Spanish squadron had to return to La Guaira after a fruitless attempt against Margarita. The triumph of the Republicans was as complete as it was decisive. Bolivar having returned to Angostura amid the victorious shouts of the people, the Congress, in accord with public opinion, and after mature deliberation, carried out the favorite project of the Liberator by sanctioning the fusion of the two Provinces of Nueva Granada and Venezuela, which, in honor of Christopher Columbus, received, on December 17, 1819, the glorious name of "The Republic of Colombia."

MASSACRE OF THE MAMELUKES

A.D. 1811

ANDREW A. PATON

From 1250 to 1517 the Mamelukes, a military organization created from a body of slaves sold to the Sultan of Egypt, ruled in that country. Under the line of sultans springing from them the land suffered from almost constant strife, intrigue, murder, and rapine. These sultans were overthrown in 1517 by the Ottoman Sultan Selim, who made a complete conquest of Egypt, but the Mamelukes remained as a famous cavalry corps in the Egyptian army until, in 1811, they were treacherously destroyed by Mehemet Ali, as related below.

At the Battle of the Pyramids, July 21, 1798, the Mamelukes, under Murad Bey, were defeated by Napoleon. For several years the French occupied Egypt; and upon their expulsion by the English, Mehemet Ali rose to power as Turkish commander and (1805) viceroy of the country. The English having withdrawn from Egypt, he prepared to establish his authority. This he did after a ruthless suppression of the Mameluke beys, who made a struggle for their provincial governorships.

By a show of clemency and conciliation toward the Mamelukes, Mehemet Ali secured an appearance of tranquillity in Egypt. This policy, however, was only a preparation for " the act of consummate treachery which finally uprooted the Mameluke power."

BEING free from the English, Mehemet Ali began to develop his plans for taking firm root in Egypt. He saw that, by extracting large revenues, he could maintain his influence by rich presents to Constantinople. His military position in Egypt was improved, and the increasing and advancing power of the Wahhabees (Mahometan reformers) rendered him more than ever necessary to the Porte. With the interior of the country tranquil and freed from civil war, an interval of prosperity, however brief, might have been expected. Such, however, was not the case. An act of spoliation—unaccompanied, to be sure, by bloodshed— but of a grasp more comprehensive and ruinous than anything that had been done by the predecessors of Mehemet Ali, was shortly consummated.

It was in the years 1808–1810 that Mehemet Ali effected a

revolutionary transfer of landed property in Egypt. Not content with greatly increasing the taxes on the soil, he ordered an inspection to be made of all title-deeds; and, on one pretext or another, his agents objected to their validity, contesting the legitimacy of the successions, imposing additions to the land-tax, and in a great multitude of instances retaining the title-deeds, which were burned. A few influential sheiks were spared; but, wherever the Government chose, the land, for want of titles, gradually lapsed to the *miri;* so that in a few years the Pacha became landlord of nearly the whole of the soil of Egypt, some insignificant annuities being granted in compensation. Mehemet Ali's elevation to power was founded on public opinion; but his first acts, after the consolidation of his rule, were the most flagrant defiance of public opinion and of the sacred rights of private property in the modern annals of Egypt. The Mamelukes, the French, and the intervening pachas had overwhelmed the people with exactions; but no attempt had been made to tear up by the very roots the pacific and legal possession of property.

The commotion which these proceedings caused was violent in the extreme, and society was agitated to its inmost depths. Even the women and the children crowded the mosques, and made the *azhar* resound with their wailings. Classes and individuals, utter strangers to politics and political discussion, stood aghast at an event which rendered reasoning superfluous and precipitated all the rights of property into a common abyss. The sheiks met in assembly, and used every resource, both of representation and petition to the Pacha and the Porte; but Mehemet Ali was firm in his purpose. The vehement representations of the sheiks against the additional land-taxes, and even the persevering refusals of Said Omar Mekrum, the *nackeeb* of the *sherifs,* to go near the divan of the Pacha were declared by him to savor of a stiff-necked and rebellious spirit which must be repressed. And, throughout this curious struggle, the firm defence of the indefeasible rights of property was conveniently characterized by a lawless governor as an aggression and an invasion of the supreme authority. Said Omar Mekrum was exiled to Damietta. The military governors of provinces arbitrarily collected contributions without the intervention of the Coptic clerks; and thenceforth began that direct grinding of the peasantry

which, before the death of Mehemet Ali, greatly reduced them in
number and impoverished them almost to the minimum of possible human existence.

At this period (1809) events in Arabia were preparing a triumph for Mehemet Ali and an extension of his political power.
This vast country, the cradle of Islamism, was now overrun by
the Wahhabee reformers, who, from small beginnings, had mastered both Mecca and Medina, and, although without the science of European warfare, made up for their deficiencies by an
enthusiastic and undaunted bravery in action, as well as by great
powers of endurance in the arduous campaigns of that torrid
region. Their peculiar doctrines were based on the self-denial
of the early Moslems, which made them avoid both those stimu-
lants which expend the nervous and muscular energies and those
lethargic habits which are alternately the effect and the cause of
inaction.

The barren shores of the Red Sea being in a great measure
devoid of ports and of navigation, and the trade of Suez having
sunk into insignificance, it was not easy to transport an army
from Egypt to Arabia. By a series of most painful efforts, wood,
cordage, and other materials for shipbuilding were carried from
the ports of Turkey to Egypt, and across the desert, on the backs
of camels to Suez. Numbers of men and of those useful beasts
of burden perished in the attempt; but at length, after incredible
efforts, eighteen vessels were launched in the space of less than a
year, and fitted up for the conveyance of troops and provisions.
A baptism of blood accompanied their launch; for the better
solemnization of the departure from Cairo of the troops destined
for the Arabian expedition this time was chosen for the final
massacre of the Mamelukes. The infirmities of Ibrahim Bey
had shown the Mamelukes that they could no longer hope for
any revival of their supremacy; the remaining head men were
therefore disposed toward a passive and luxurious existence, giving no further umbrage to the Porte or to Mehemet Ali, and
contenting themselves with as large a share as they could grasp
of the produce of Egypt. Mehemet Ali, on his side, was not displeased to patch up an accommodation with these turbulent bar-
ons of Eastern feudalism so as to have more elbow room to carry
out his designs of a virtual sovereignty under the mask of zeal

for the service of the Porte, and at the same time to have them more securely in his power when the convenient moment came for getting entirely rid of them.

Shahin Bey, the elected successor of Elfy Bey, had made his submission to Mehemet Ali, and signed an arrangement the conditions of which were advantageous to him. From the Pyramids up the left bank of the Nile, to beyond Beni-Suef, and including the Faioum, was assigned to him as an appanage; and, on his presenting himself for investiture to Mehemet Ali at Cairo, he was loaded with rich gifts of shawls, pelisses, and diamond-mounted daggers. The other Mamelukes, even although jealous of Shahin Bey, were also gradually obliged to yield. The beys at Siut on the upper Nile wished at first to refuse tribute. But the Mamelukes, being no longer a corps united under an Ali Bey, or a Murad, as in former times, were fain to yield on finding that Mehemet Ali himself had come to Siut with an army of several thousand men to collect the tribute. After this there was not even the shadow of a rising. Many of the Mamelukes came to Cairo and sank completely into sloth and sensuality, passing from the wild to the tame state like beasts fatted for slaughter.

In February, 1811, the chiefs destined by Mehemet Ali to extirpate the Wahhabee reformers, and restore Arabia to the Caliph of Constantinople, went to encamp at Kubbet el Azab, on the desert near Cairo. Here four thousand men were united under the orders of Toussun Pacha, the son of Mehemet Ali, who was destined to command the expedition. On the following Friday the youthful general was to receive the pelisse of investiture and thereafter to proceed to the camp by the "Gate of Victory"—the astrologers having fixed on this day as propitious to the success of the enterprise. All the civil and military authorities and the principal people of the country were informed of the approach of the ceremony; and on the night before, the Mameluke chiefs were invited to take part in full costume. A simple invitation to the Mamelukes in a mass, on any other occasion, would have been received with the habitual Oriental mistrust of such hospitality; but, with a skill in the way of evil worthy of a better cause, Mehemet Ali so managed that the obvious motive of the departure of an army, and the association of the Mamelukes with all the other authorities of the country, not only lulled their suspicions, but even flattered their self-love.

On March 1, 1811, all the principal men of Cairo flocked to the citadel. Shahin Bey appeared there at the head of his household, having come with the other beys to pay his respects to Mehemet Ali, who received them in the great hall. Coffee was then served and conversation took place. When all those who were to take part in the procession were assembled, the signal for departure was given, each person taking the place that was assigned him by the master of the ceremonies. A corps of *delis*, commanded by Oozoon Ali, opened the march; then came the *waly* or municipal governor of Cairo, the *aga* of the janizaries, with Turkish troops; then came the Albanians, especially devoted to Mehemet Ali, under the immediate command of Saleh Khosh. The regular troops came last, and the Mamelukes had their places assigned between the infantry and cavalry at the rear and the Albanians, who marched in front of them. The plateau of the citadel, on which are situated the chief buildings, is elevated high above the level of the city. Down on the lower level, and close to the public place of the Roumeyleh, is the gate of Azaba—a picturesque object flanked with round towers, painted in stripes of red and white. Between the high courtyard and this gate was the old access to the plateau—not the modern macadamized slope, but a steep winding passage with sharp angles, and cut in the rock.

Down this road came the procession, and no sooner were the *delis* and *agas* out than Saleh Khosh ordered the gates to be shut, and communicated the order he had received, to exterminate the Mamelukes, to his Albanians, who immediately turned about, and, jumping aside or leaping up the rock, began to fire on the horsemen. To charge down the steep rock was useless or impossible, for the gates were shut and exit barred; and on the sloping or angular rocks the heavily mounted Mamelukes, though powerful on the plains of Egypt, had no chance with the Albanians, whose home is only the mountainside. Behind the Mamelukes were the infantry troops closing the procession, whose advantage was still more decided; for they poured volleys of musketry down on these devoted men from the parapets above.

The Mamelukes now wished to return by another road into the citadel, but not being able to manage their horses on account of the unfavorable ground, and seeing that many of their people were killed and wounded, they alighted, and abandoning their horses and upper clothes, remounted the road, sabre in hand, but were fired on from the windows of the citadel above. Shahin Bey fell pierced with balls before the gates of the palace of Saladin. Solyman Bey, another Mameluke, ran, half-naked and frightened, to implore the protection of the harem of the Viceroy, according to Oriental usage, but in vain. He was conducted to the palace, where he was decapitated. Others went to beg for mercy from Toussun Pacha, who took no part in the events of the day.

The troops had orders to arrest the Mamelukes wherever they might be found. Those taken were conducted to Kiahia Bey, and instantaneously decapitated. Many persons not Mamelukes were also killed. The citadel flowed with blood, and the dead filled up the passages. The dead body of Shahin Bey was, with barbarous brutality, dragged about with a cord round the neck. On every side were seen horses expensively caparisoned, stretched by the side of their masters, and the richest dresses saturated with blood; for gold embroidery and the most costly cloth stuffs, with elaborately finished and decorated arms and caparisons, were what the Mamelukes mostly delighted in; and all these became the booty of the bloodthirsty soldiery. Of four hundred sixty Mamelukes who had mounted that morning to the citadel, not one escaped. A few French Mamelukes, in the service of Mehemet Ali, who had remained behind after the departure of Menou, and had been locked up by Kiahia Bey in a room adjoining his own, were saved. A bey of the house of Elfy had three French Mamelukes in his service, but they did not mount on horseback on that day.

Amyn Bey, another Mameluke, was saved by accident. Being prevented by pressing business from arriving in time, he found himself outside the gate just as the head of the procession was issuing from under the arch. He waited a little until they were gone out, but seeing that the gate was suddenly closed, and then hearing the musketry, he put spurs to his horse, and never stopped until he found his way across the desert into Syria.

Scarcely had the procession begun to move when Mehemet Ali showed signs of agitation, which increased when he heard the first discharge of musketry. He grew pale, fearing lest his orders might not have been properly executed, and that some struggle might ensue fatal to himself and his party. When he saw the prisoners and the trunkless heads he grew calm. Soon after, his physician, a Genoese, entered, and said with the sickening gayety of sycophancy: "The affair is over; this is a *fête* for Your Highness." To this Mehemet Ali gave no answer, and only asked for a draught to quench his thirst.

Meanwhile the crowds of citizens in the town were waiting to see the procession, and expectation was succeeded by surprise when only the delis forming its head were seen to pass, followed by grooms hurrying away in silence. This sudden movement caused an agitation among the spectators, and then the cry having arisen, "Shahin Bey is killed!" all the shops were shut, which was invariably the case when turbulence, bloodshed, and their concomitant, rapine, were apprehended. The streets became deserted, and only bands of lawless soldiery were seen, who rushed to pillage the houses of the Mamelukes, violating their women, and committing every atrocity.

The Turks, who could only marry women of an inferior class, saw with displeasure that those of a higher rank, disdaining their alliance, displayed eagerness to marry Mamelukes, and therefore took care to avenge themselves. The houses of the beys were full of valuables. Several of these cavaliers were making preparations for marriage, decorating their apartments, and purchasing rich clothes, cashmeres, and jewels. Not only the houses of these persons were pillaged, but others besides. Cairo appeared like a place taken by assault, the inhabitants not showing themselves in the streets, but awaiting indoors what destiny had in store for them.

The murder and pillage continuing on the following day, Mehemet Ali descended from the citadel to reëstablish order and stop bloodshed. He was in full dress and accompanied by a large armed force. At each police post he reprimanded the officer in charge for having permitted such disorders. Mehemet Ali himself had only taken the lives of the Mamelukes: he had only massacred a political party addicted to cashmeres, diamond-mounted pipes, and enamelled pistols, as well as to sharing the political power with the agents of the Porte. He himself had laid the axe to the very root of Mameluke appropriation, and therefore all mangling of the branches excited his just reprobation as a superfluous expenditure of labor. Near Bab Zueileh the Pacha met a Mogrebbin who complained of the pillage of his house, protesting that he was neither soldier nor Mameluke, on which Mehemet Ali stopped his horse, and sent an armed force, who arrested a Turk and a fellah, whose heads they cut off. Advancing toward the quarter of Kakeen, he was informed that the sheiks were assembled with the intention of complimenting him; but the Pacha answered that he would himself go to receive their felicitations, on which he proceeded to the house of Sheik Abdullah el Sherkawy, and after having passed an hour with him he returned to the citadel.

The following day Toussun Pacha went through the town, followed by a numerous guard, causing those who were found pillaging to be decapitated; for more than five hundred houses had been sacked on this occasion. Meanwhile the Mamelukes were diligently sought after. Even the old ones, who in all the troubles had never quitted Cairo, were unmercifully killed. Many made their escape by changing their costume for that of delis; others dressed as women escaped to Upper Egypt.

In the citadel, the dead bodies were thrown pell-mell into pits dug for them, the relations of the murdered being so overwhelmed as not to be able to bury them decently. The mother of the Emir Merzouk, son of Ibrahim Bey, was, however, allowed his dead body, which was found after two days' search. Protection was also given to the widows of the Mamelukes by Mehemet Ali, who allowed his own men to marry them.

The secret of this sanguinary affair had been confided to only four persons on whom the Pacha could rely; but he had at the same time written, through his secretary, to the commanders of the different provinces ordering them to arrest and put to death all the Mamelukes they could lay their hands upon. This order was mercilessly executed, and their heads were sent to Cairo and exposed there.

NAPOLEON'S RUSSIAN CAMPAIGN

A.D. 1812

CHARLES A. FYFFE   **FRANÇOIS P. G. GUIZOT**

While Napoleon was busy in Spain, Austria again rose in arms against him, a rebellion it might almost be called, considering to what subjection the once proud domain of the Hapsburgs had been reduced. She was defeated in the conqueror's last successful war, and her princess, Maria Louisa, became Napoleon's bride (1810). This family alliance between France and Austria marred the fraternal relations which had existed with Russia. Czar Alexander had not profited all he had hoped from the famous Treaty of Tilsit, and moreover he found his interests repeatedly neglected and even directly injured by the French Emperor. Napoleon's commercial policy of closing the ports of Europe against England had almost ruined the merchants of every country where it prevailed. Finally, in December, 1810, the Czar deliberately abandoned his agreement with France and opened his ports to British ships.

Napoleon prepared solemnly for war. The other European states no longer dared oppose him, and unwillingly supplied him troops. All the year 1811 was employed in gathering the largest army Europe had ever known. Not only Frenchmen, but Prussians, Austrians, and other Germans, Italians also and even a few Spaniards, were gathered on the Russian frontier. The Poles were promised freedom, and joined enthusiastically in the attack. Kings and emperors surrounded Napoleon in Dresden to wish him godspeed, and on June 23, 1812, with more than four hundred thousand men he crossed the River Niemen and began his spectacular advance into the Russian wastes.

The Russians under General Barclay de Tolly retreated before him, more perhaps from necessity than design, and the vastness of the country became the invaders' chief enemy. His troops fell by the roadside, they perished of exhaustion, and Barclay seeing the success of his Fabian policy persisted in it. The Czar protested and finally supplanted Barclay with the Russian general, Kutusoff, who risked a decisive battle and met complete defeat at Borodino. Napoleon entered Moscow in triumph and waited for the Czar to come to him as other sovereigns had come to entreat for mercy. But Alexander and his generals had learned at last that their country would fight their battles for them better than they. Instead of offering peace they left the conquerors to the fangs of the Russian winter.

CHARLES A. FYFFE

THE French steadily advanced; the Russians retreated to
Moscow, and evacuated the capital when their generals decided that they could not encounter the French assault. The
holy city was left undefended before the invader. But the departure of the army was the smallest part of the evacuation.
The inhabitants, partly of their own free will, partly under the
compulsion of the governor, abandoned the city in a mass. No
gloomy or excited crowd, as at Vienna and Berlin, thronged the
streets to witness the entrance of the great conqueror, when
on September 14th Napoleon took possession of Moscow. His
troops marched through silent and deserted streets. In the soli-
tude of the Kremlin Napoleon received the homage of a few foreigners, who alone could be collected by his servants to tender
to him the submission of the city.

But the worst was yet to come. On the night after Napoleon's entry, fires broke out in different parts of Moscow. They
were ascribed at first to accident; but when on the next day the
French saw the flames gaining ground in every direction, and
found that all the means of extinguishing fire had been removed
from the city, they understood the doom to which Moscow had
been devoted by its own defenders. Count Rostoptchin, the governor, had determined on the destruction of Moscow, without
the knowledge of the Czar. The doors of the prisons were thrown
open. Rostoptchin gave the signal by setting fire to his own palace, and let loose his bands of incendiaries over the city. For
five days the flames rose and fell; and when, on the evening of
the 20th, the last fires ceased, three-fourths of Moscow lay in
ruins.

Such was the prize for which Napoleon had sacrificed two
hundred thousand men, and engulfed the weak remnant of his
army six hundred miles deep in an enemy's country. Throughout all the terrors of the advance Napoleon had held fast to the
belief that Alexander's resistance would end with the fall of his
capital. The events that accompanied the entry of the French
into Moscow shook his confidence; yet even now Napoleon
could not believe that the Czar remained firm against all thoughts
of peace. His experience in all earlier wars had given him con-

fidence in the power of one conspicuous disaster to unhinge the
resolution of kings. His trust in the deepening impression made
by the fall of Moscow was fostered by negotiations begun by
Kutusoff for the very purpose of delaying the French retreat.
For five weeks Napoleon remained at Moscow as if spellbound,
unable to convince himself of his powerlessness to break Alexander's determination, unable to face a retreat which would display to all Europe the failure of his arms and the termination of
his career of victory.

At length the approach of winter forced him to action. It
was impossible to provision the army at Moscow during the
winter months, even if there had been nothing to fear from the
enemy. Even the mocking overtures of Kutusoff had ceased.
The frightful reality could no longer be concealed. On October
19th the order for retreat was given. It was not the destruction
of Moscow, but the departure of its inhabitants, that had brought
the conqueror to ruin. Above two thousand houses were still
standing; but whether the buildings remained or perished made
little difference; the whole value of the capital to Napoleon was
lost when the inhabitants, whom he could have forced to procure supplies for his army, disappeared. Vienna and Berlin had
been of such incalculable service to Napoleon because the whole
native administration placed itself under his orders, and every
rich and important citizen became a hostage for the activity of
the rest. When the French gained Moscow, they gained nothing beyond the supplies which were at that moment in the city.
All was lost to Napoleon when the class who in other capitals
had been his instruments fled at his approach. The conflagration of Moscow acted upon all Europe as a signal of inextin-
guishable national hatred; as a military operation, it neither
accelerated the retreat of Napoleon nor added to the miseries
which his army had to undergo.

The French forces which quitted Moscow in October numbered about one hundred thousand men. Reënforcements had
come in during the occupation of the city, and the health of the
soldiers had been in some degree restored by a month's rest.
Everything now depended upon gaining a line of retreat where
food could be found. Though but a fourth part of the army
which entered Russia in the summer, the army which left Mos-

cow was still large enough to protect itself against the enemy, if allowed to retreat through a fresh country; if forced back upon the devastated line of its advance it was impossible for it to escape destruction. Napoleon therefore determined to make for Kaluga, on the south of Moscow, and to endeavor to gain a road to Smolensk far distant from that by which he had come. The army moved from Moscow in a southern direction. But its route had been foreseen by Kutusoff. At the end of four days' march it was met by a Russian corps at Yaroslavitz. A bloody struggle left the French in possession of the road: they continued their advance; but it was only to find that Kutusoff, with his full strength, had occupied a line of heights farther south, and barred the way to Kaluga.

The effort of an assault was beyond the powers of the French. Napoleon surveyed the enemy's position, and recognized the fatal necessity of abandoning the march southward and returning to the wasted road by which he had advanced. The meaning of the backward movement was quickly understood by the army. From the moment of quitting Yaroslavitz, disorder and despair increased with every march. Thirty thousand men were lost upon the road before a pursuer appeared in sight. When, on November 2d, the army reached Viazma, it numbered no more than sixty-five thousand men.

Kutusoff was unadventurous in pursuit. The necessity of moving his army along a parallel road south of the French, in order to avoid starvation, diminished the opportunities for attack; but the General himself disliked risking his forces, and preferred to see the enemy's destruction effected by the elements. At Viazma, where, on November 3d, the French were for the first time attacked in force, Kutusoff's own delay alone saved them from total ruin. In spite of heavy loss the French kept possession of the road, and secured their retreat to Smolensk, where stores of food had been accumulated, and where other and less exhausted French troops were at hand.

Up to November 6th the weather had been sunny and dry. On the 6th the long-delayed terrors of Russian winter broke upon the pursuers and the pursued. Snow darkened the air and hid the last traces of vegetation from the starving cavalry trains. The temperature dropped at times to 40° of frost. Death came, sometimes in the unfelt release from misery, sometimes in horrible forms of mutilation and disease. Both armies were exposed to the same sufferings; but the Russians had at least such succor as their countrymen could give: where the French fell, they died. The order of war disappeared under conditions which made life itself the accident of a meal or of a place by the camp-fire. Though most of the French soldiery continued to carry their arms, the Guard alone kept its separate formation; the other regiments marched in confused masses. From November 9th to the 13th these starving bands arrived one after another at Smolensk, expecting that here their sufferings would end. But the organization for distributing the stores accumulated in Smolensk no longer existed. The perishing crowds were left to find shelter where they could; sacks of corn were thrown to them for food.

It was impossible for Napoleon to give his wearied soldiers rest, for new Russian armies were advancing from the north and the south to cut off their retreat. From the Danube and from the Baltic Sea troops were pressing forward to their meeting-point upon the rear of the invader. Wittgenstein, moving southward at the head of the army of the Dwina, had overpowered the French corps stationed upon that river, and made himself master of Vitebsk. The army of Bucharest, which had been toiling northward ever since the beginning of August, had advanced to within a few days' march of its meeting-point with the army of the Dwina upon the line of Napoleon's communications. Before Napoleon reached Smolensk he sent orders to Victor, who was at Smolensk with some reserves, to march against Wittgenstein and drive him back upon the Dwina. Victor set out on his mission.

During the short halt of Napoleon in Smolensk, Kutusoff pushed forward to the west of the French, and took post at Krasnoi, thirty miles farther along the road by which Napoleon had to pass. The retreat of the French seemed to be actually cut off. Had the Russian General dared to face Napoleon and his Guards, he might have held the French in check until the arrival of the two auxiliary armies from the north and south enabled him to capture Napoleon and his entire force. Kutusoff, however, preferred a partial and certain victory to a struggle with Napoleon for life or death. He permitted Napoleon and the Guard to pass by unattacked, and then fell upon the hinder divisions of the French army (November 17th).

These unfortunate troops were successively cut to pieces. Twenty-six thousand were made prisoners. Ney, with a part of the rear-guard, only escaped by crossing the Dnieper on the ice. Of the army that had quitted Moscow there now remained but ten thousand combatants and twenty thousand followers. Kutusoff himself was brought to such a state of exhaustion that he could carry the pursuit no further, and entered into quarters upon the Dnieper.

It was a few days after the battle at Krasnoi that the divisions of Victor, coming from the direction of the Dwina, suddenly encountered the remnant of Napoleon's army. Though aware that Napoleon was in retreat, they knew nothing of the calamities that had befallen him, and were struck with amazement when, in the middle of a forest, they met with what seemed more like a miserable troop of captives than an army upon the march. Victor's soldiers of a mere auxiliary corps found themselves more than double the effective strength of the whole army of Moscow. Their arrival again placed Napoleon at the head of thirty thousand disciplined troops, and gave the French a gleam of victory in the last and seemingly most hopeless struggle in the campaign. Admiral Tchitchagoff, in command of the army marching from the Danube, had at length reached the line of Napoleon's retreat, and established himself at Borisov, where the road through Poland crosses the river Beresina. The bridge was destroyed by the Russians, and Tchitchagoff opened communication with Wittgenstein's army, which lay only a few miles to the north.

It appeared as if the retreat of the French was now finally intercepted, and the surrender of Napoleon inevitable. Yet even in this hopeless situation the military skill and daring of the French worked with something of its ancient power. The army reached the Beresina; Napoleon succeeded in withdrawing the enemy from the real point of passage; bridges were thrown across the river, and after desperate fighting a great part of the army made good its footing upon the western bank (November 28th). But the losses even among the effective troops were enormous. The fate of the miserable crowd that followed them, torn by the cannon-fire of the Russians, and precipitated into the river by the breaking of one of the bridges, has made the passage of the Beresina a synonyme for the utmost degree of human woe.

This was the last engagement fought by the army. The Guards still preserved their order; Marshal Ney still found soldiers capable of turning upon the pursuer with his own steady and unflagging courage; but the bulk of the army struggled forward in confused crowds, harassed by the Cossacks, and laying down their arms by thousands before the enemy. The frost, which had broken up on November 19th, returned on the 30th with even greater severity. Twenty thousand fresh troops which joined the army between the Beresina and Vilna scarcely arrested the process of dissolution. On December 3d Napoleon quitted the army. Vilna itself was abandoned with all its stores; and when at length the fugitives reached the Niemen, they numbered little more than twenty thousand. Here, six months earlier, three hundred eighty thousand men had crossed with Napoleon. A hundred thousand more had joined the army in the course of its retreat. Of all this host, not the twentieth part reached the Prussian frontier. A hundred seventy thousand remained prisoners in the hands of the Russians; a greater number had perished. Of the twenty thousand men who now beheld the Niemen, probably not seven thousand had crossed with Napoleon.

In the presence of a catastrophe so overwhelming and so unparalleled the Russian generals might well be content with their own share in the work of destruction. Yet events proved that Kutusoff had done ill in failing to employ every effort to capture or annihilate his foe. Not only was Napoleon's own escape the pledge of continued war, but the remnant that escaped with him possessed a military value out of all proportion to its insignificant numbers. The best of the army were the last to succumb. Out of those few thousands who endured to the end, a very large proportion were veteran officers, who immediately took their place at the head of Napoleon's newly raised armies, and gave to them a military efficiency soon to be bitterly proved by Europe on many a German battle-field.

FRANÇOIS P. G. GUIZOT

The solitary consolation left to the army was that which the Emperor had himself presented to Europe—the presence of Napoleon; his physical and mental energy and vigor. His flight from Smorgoni deprived the soldiers of this last resource of their confidence; from that day, as soon as the report spread, despair seized upon the strongest hearts. Nothing is more enduring than the instinctive courage which resists pain and death, because it becomes a man to strive to the last. All the ties of discipline, military fraternity, and ordinary humanity were broken together. I borrow from the recollections of the Duke Fezensac, then colonel of the Fourth of the line, the following picture of the horrors which he saw, and of which he has given the story with a touching and manly simplicity:

"It is useless at the present day to tell the details of every day's march; it would merely be a repetition of the same misfortunes. The cold, which seemed to have become milder only to make the passage of the Dnieper and the Beresina more difficult, again set in more keenly than ever. The thermometer fell, first, to 6° below zero, and then to 24° below (Fahrenheit), and the severity of the season completed the exhaustion of men who were already half dead with hunger and fatigue. I shall not undertake to depict the spectacle which we looked upon. You must imagine plains as far as the horizon covered with snow, long forests of pines, villages half-burned and deserted; and through those pitiful districts an endless column of wretches, nearly all without arms, marching in disorder, and falling at every step on the ice, near the carcasses of horses and the bodies of their companions. Their faces bore the impress of utter exhaustion or despair, their eyes were lifeless, their features convulsed, and quite black with dirt and smoke. Sheepskins and pieces of cloth served them for shoes; their heads were wrapped with rags; their shoulders covered with horse-cloths, women's petticoats, and half-burned skins. Also, when one fell from fatigue, his comrades stripped him before he was dead, in order to clothe themselves with his rags. Each bivouac seemed next day like a battle-field, and men found dead at their side those beside whom they had gone to sleep the night before. An officer of the

Russian advance-guard, who was a witness of those scenes of horror—which the rapidity of our flight prevented us from carefully observing—has given a description of them to which nothing need be added:

"'The road which we followed,' says he, 'was covered with prisoners who required no watching, and who underwent hardships till then unheard of. Several still dragged themselves mechanically along the road, with their feet naked and half frozen; some had lost the power of speech, others had fallen into a kind of savage stupidity, and wished, in spite of us, to roast dead bodies in order to eat them. Those who were too weak to go to fetch wood stopped near the first fire which they found, and sitting upon one another they crowded closely round the fire, the feeble heat of which still sustained them, the little life left in them going out at the same time as it did. The houses and farms which the wretches had set on fire were surrounded with dead bodies, for those who went near had not the power to escape the flames which reached them; and soon others were seen, with a convulsive laugh, rushing voluntarily into the midst of the burning, so that they were consumed also.'"

I hasten to avoid the spectacle of so many sufferings. Yet it is right and proper that children should know what was endured by their fathers. In proportion as the last survivors of the generations who saw and suffered so many evils disappear, we who have in our turn undergone other disasters owe it to them to recount both their glory and their misery. The time will soon come when our descendants in their turn will include in the annals of history the great epochs through which we have lived, struggled, and suffered.

Napoleon crossed Germany like an unknown fugitive, and his generals also made haste to escape. They had at last reached Vilna, alarming Lithuania by their rout, and themselves terror-struck during the halt on ascertaining the actual numbers of their losses, and the state of the disorderly battalions which were being again formed in the streets of the hospitable town. For a long time the crowd of disbanded soldiers, deserters, and those who had fallen behind were collected together at the gates of Vilna in so dense a throng that they could not enter. Scarcely had the hungry wretches begun to take some food and taste a moment's rest, when the Russian cannon was heard, and Platov's Cossacks appeared at the gates.

The King of Naples, heroic on the battle-field, but incapable of efficient command in a rout, took refuge in a suburb, in order to set out from it at break of day. Marshal Ney, the old Marshal Lefebvre, and General Loyson, with the remains of the division which he recently brought back from Poland, kept back the Cossacks for some time, and left the army time to resume its deplorable flight. A large number of exhausted men fell into the hands of the enemy; the fragments of our ruined regiments disappeared piecemeal. At Ponare, where the road between Vilna and Kovno rises, the baggage which they had with great difficulty dragged so far, the flags taken from the enemy, the army-chest, the trophies carried off from Moscow, all remained scattered at the foot of the icy hill. The pillagers quarrelled over the gold and silver in the coffers, on the snow, in the ditches. Then the Cossacks coming upon them, some of the French fired in defence of treasures they were no longer able to carry.

When the ruins of the main army at last reached Kovno, where they found supplies of food and ammunition, they were no longer able to make use of it, or to resist the pursuit of the Russians. The generals held a council. In weariness and despair some gave vent to complaints against Napoleon, and Murat's words were susceptible of a more sinister meaning.

Marshal Davoust, honorable and unconquerable, though still strongly prejudiced against the King of Naples, boldly expressed his indignation against the falling off of the lieutenants whom the Emperor had made kings. All with one accord handed over to Ney the command of the rear-guard, and that defence of Kovno which was for a few minutes longer to protect the retreat. General Gerard alone remained faithful to this last despairing effort. When at last he crossed the Niemen with General Ney, on December 14, 1812, they were abandoned by all: their soldiers had fled, either scattering before the enemy or stealing away during the night from a useless resistance. When, in Koenigsberg, he overtook the remnant of the staff, Marshal Ney, with haggard looks and clad in rags, entered alone into their room. "Here comes the rear-guard of the great army!" said he bitterly.

WAR ON THE CANADIAN BORDER

A.D. 1812–1814

AGNES M. MACHAR   **JAMES GRAHAME**

A peculiar and remarkable feature of the War of 1812 is the fact that in the treaty designating its diplomatic close nothing was said about its principal cause, which nevertheless the events of the struggle removed. The war brought about no radical changes in the relations of England and the United States; it ended with mutual concessions; and its most important result was that it taught the supreme desirability of settling their future disagreements without appealing to arms. This, in spite of some grave misunderstandings, they have ever since succeeded in doing.

The war grew out of irritations which wise policies should easily have avoided. During the French Revolution, although a formal neutrality was observed by the United States, popular sympathy with France was strongly expressed. This was the more pronounced because England's refusal, after the peace of 1783, to give up Western posts to the United States involved the latter country in a long and costly Indian war. In 1807 Great Britain published decrees known as "Orders in Council," prohibiting neutral trade with France or her allies. Similar decrees were issued by France. Great injury resulted to American commerce. Every American ship on the seas became liable to capture.

England also claimed the right to search American vessels and take from them any English seamen found on board. In a single year several hundred seizures were made. This was really the exciting cause of the War of 1812. The practice was discontinued, not through the articles of peace, but as a result of the victories gained in the war by the American navy. In 1807 Congress, by way of reprisal, laid an embargo or prohibition forbidding American vessels to leave United States ports, but this measure only reacted unfavorably, adding to the injury against which it was directed.

At Madison's inauguration in 1809, these difficulties with England were not settled; they continued to increase the feeling of hostility, especially on the part of the United States; and at last Congress, by a large majority, declared war against Great Britain, although great opposition to such a war was manifested by many of the American people. The first military operations of the war were directed against Canada, and are here described by a Canadian historian, whose distinctly partisan account of the salient events is then balanced by that of Grahame, who, though a native of Scotland, is eminently fair in his treatment of the United

States.   The difference between the two is striking and instructive.   The patriots of each side accuse the opposing government of juggling with numbers.

AGNES M. MACHAR[1]

THE actual declaration of war could not but spread a thrill of dismay in a comparatively defenceless and sparsely populated colony.   The population of Upper Canada was only about eighty thousand; that of the whole colony did not exceed three hundred thousand.   To defend a frontier of one thousand seven hundred miles, threatened by several powerful armies, they had but four thousand four hundred fifty regular troops of all arms, only about one thousand five hundred of whom were in Upper Canada.   It is little wonder if the task of resisting so powerful a neighbor seemed at first almost a hopeless one, and if, for a short time, some despondency prevailed.   But the spirit of the old Spartans lived in the breasts of the hardy Canadian yeomen, many of whom had already sacrificed so much to their loyal love for the British flag; and the confidence of the people in their brave General Brock acted as a rallying-point of hope and courage.   The militia justified the expectations the General had expressed of "the sons of a loyal and brave band of veterans"; and troops of volunteers poured into all the garrison towns, ready "to do, and die," if necessary, rather than yield to the invader.

As soon as the declaration of war was ascertained beyond a doubt, General Brock's measures were prompt and energetic. He called a meeting of the Legislature, established his headquarters at Fort George, requested reënforcements from the Lower Province, which, however, could not be granted till the arrival of more troops from England; appointed a day of fasting and prayer in recognition of the great ever-present "Help in time of trouble"; looked to the condition of the frontier forts and outposts, and paid especial attention to the securing of the allegiance of the Indians, and the equipping, drilling, and organizing the militia.   Of arms, however, there was a great scarcity, and many brave volunteers, who poured into York (now Toronto), Kingston, and other places, had to retire, disappointed, for lack of weapons; some indeed supplying the deficiency from their implements of husbandry.

[1] By permission of the author.

On July 12th General Hull, with an army of two thousand five hundred men, crossed to Canada from Detroit, issuing from Sandwich a proclamation, doubtless emanating from Washington, in which he informed the Canadians that he did not ask their aid, because he came with a force that must overpower all opposition, and which was, moreover, only the vanguard of a far greater one. He offered the Canadians, in exchange for the tyranny under which they were supposed to groan, "the invaluable blessings of civil, political, and religious liberty" (it is to be remembered that the slave-holding States were the chief instigators and supporters of the war!). He ended his proclamation by expressing the hope that "He who holds in his hand the fate of nations may guide you to a result the most compatible with your rights and interests, your peace and prosperity." This hope the Canadians, at least, deemed fulfilled in their being led to refuse the bribe of a personal ease and security purchased by the sacrifice of their sense of right and duty—of their loyalty to the country whose noble traditions they claimed as their own—to the flag which, notwithstanding the occasional shortcomings of its standard-bearers, they still regarded as the time-honored defender of "civil, political, and religious liberty."

The preceding May, General Brock had sent a detachment of the Forty-first Regiment to Amherstburg or Fort Malden, some eighteen miles from Sandwich, to be in readiness to defend that frontier. On hearing of the landing of General Hull, he despatched Colonel Proctor thither with a further reënforcement of the Forty-first. It was time to take energetic measures, for the fact that the enemy had been able to establish a footing in the country had excited alarm and gloom, and endangered the adherence of the Indians of that region. Even General Brock could hardly resist the feeling that without speedy reënforcements, and unless the enemy could be speedily driven from Sandwich, the ruin of the country was imminent. Indeed had Hull pressed on at once, it is impossible to say what the result might have been. Happily for Canada, however, he delayed his advance till there were troops enough on the spot to embarrass him, with the assistance of the militia and Indians, until Brock himself could arrive.

The tidings of the capture of the American trading-post of Mi chilimackinac (Mackinac), with its garrison, stores and furs, by Captain Roberts, with some thirty regular soldiers and a band of French *voyageurs* and Indians, came as a gleam of brightness to relieve the gloom.   Then came the gallant encounter at Tarontee in the western marshes, where a small British force held a strong American one at bay, and two privates of the Forty-first "kept the bridge" with a valor and tenacity worthy of the "brave days of old."   At the same time, the capture of a provision convoy of Hull's, by the Shawnee chief, Tecumseh, with his Indians, seriously embarrassing the American General—who had to draw his supplies from distant Ohio, over roads which were no roads— induced him to "change his base of operations," and, recrossing the river, to retire to Detroit.   Proctor followed him up, and endeavored to intercept another convoy escorted by a strong force, but this attempt was unsuccessful, and in an action at Brownstown the Americans were the victors.   But Brock was at hand.   On August 13th he arrived at Amherstburg at the head of a small force of regulars and militia, about seven hundred in all; of these, four hundred were militiamen disguised in red coats.   The journey had been a most fatiguing one; a toilsome march through the wilderness from Burlington Heights to Long Point, and then four days and nights of hard rowing along the dangerous coast of Lake Erie, through rainy and tempestuous weather, in such clumsy open boats as the neighboring farmers could supply.   To the cheerfulness and endurance of the troops during the trying journey, Brock bore most honorable testimony.   Their mettle deserved the success they so honorably achieved.

Arrived at Amherstburg, General Brock met Tecumseh, the Shawnee chief already referred to, one of the heroes of the war. Quickly recognizing in Brock the characteristics of a brave and noble leader, Tecumseh and his Indians were at his service at once, and together they concerted plans against Hull and Fort Detroit.   By a happy inspiration, General Brock saw that promptitude and resolution were the qualities to gain the day, and General Hull was startled, first by a summons for the immediate surrender of Fort Detroit, and next by the crossing of the British force—General Brock, "erect in his canoe, leading the way to battle."   Tecumseh and his Indians were disposed in readiness to attack in flank and rear, while the British force first drove the Americans from a favorable position back on the fort, and then prepared to assault it. To their surprise, however, a flag of truce anticipated the attack, and the garrison capitulated, surrendering to the British the Michigan territory, Fort Detroit, thirty-three pieces of cannon, a vessel of war, the military chest, a very large quantity of stores, and about two thousand five hundred troops with their arms, which latter were a much appreciated boon for arming the Canadian militia. General Brock was himself surprised at the ease of this brilliant success, which, at one stroke, revived the drooping spirits of the Canadians, rallied the hestitating, fixed the adhesion of wavering Indian tribes, encouraged the militia, who had now tried their strength in action, and made Brock deservedly the idol of the people. On his return to York (Toronto), he was greeted with the warmest acclamations, as befitted a leader who in such trying circumstances had organized the military protection of the Province, met and advised with the Legislature, accomplished a trying journey of three hundred miles in pursuit of a force more than double his own—had gone, had seen, and had conquered!

It was now his ardent desire to proceed, amid the prestige of victory and in the first flush of success, to sweep the Niagara frontier of the last vestige of the invading enemy. It seems most probable that he could have done so, and thus might, at this early stage of the war, have nipped the invasion in the bud, and saved both countries a protracted and harassing struggle. But his hands were, at this critical moment, fatally tied by an armistice agreed to by the Governor-General, Sir George Prevost, probably in the hope that the revocation of the British "Orders in Council," which took place almost simultaneously with the American declaration of war, would evoke a more pacific spirit. This was not the case, however; things had gone too far; the people were too eager for conquest to be easily persuaded to recede. The sole effect of this most ill-timed armistice was to give the Americans time to recover from the effect of their reverses, to increase their forces, and to prepare for subsequent successes on the lakes, by building vessels on Lake Erie, under the very eyes of General Brock, who, eager to act, had to remain passively watching the augmentation of the enemy's force and the equipment of their boats, without being able to fire a shot to prevent it.

The first-fruits of this enforced passiveness was the surprise and capture, on October 9th, of the brig-of-war Detroit and the private brig Caledonia, both laden with arms and spoils from Detroit. The former, however, grounded, and was destroyed by its captor, Captain Elliott, who was then fitting out an armed schooner at Black Rock, with a strong force of American seamen under his command.

This stroke of success greatly stimulated the eagerness of the American force under Van Rensselaer—now increased to six thousand men—to engage in action. General Brock expected this, and issued particular directions to all the outposts where landing might be effected. On October 11th a crossing at Queenston was attempted, but failed through unfavorable weather and lack of boats. Before daybreak on the 13th, however, a crossing was effected, and the advance-guard of the American force, protected by a battery commanding every spot where they could be opposed by musketry, had gained the Canadian shore. On landing, they were gallantly opposed by the small outpost force of militia and regulars, aided by the fire of an eighteen-pounder on the heights and another gun a mile below; a part of the defending force meeting the enemy as they landed, the remainder firing down from the heights above. Both assault and resistance were resolute and brave.

General Brock, at Fort George, having risen, as usual, before daylight, heard the cannonade, and galloped up to the scene of action, where he found himself at once in the midst of a desperate hand-to-hand combat, a detachment of the enemy, who had landed higher up, having gained unobserved a spur of the heights by a secluded and circuitous path. Brock led his men with his usual unflinching valor, unmindful of the circumstance that his height, dress, and bearing made him too conspicuous a mark for the American riflemen. A ball, well and deliberately aimed, struck him down, with the words, "Push on the brave York Volunteers," on his lips. Stung by their loss, his regiment raised a shout of "Avenge the General!" and by a desperate onset, the regulars and militia drove the enemy from the vantage ground they had gained. But the latter, being strongly reënforced, the little British force of about three hundred was compelled to retire toward the village while awaiting the reënforcements that were

on their way, hastened by the tidings of the calamity that had befallen the nation. General Sheaffe, Brock's old comrade-in-
arms in other fields, ere long came up, with all the available troops,
volunteers and Indians, eager to avenge the death of their commander. By an admirable arrangement of his forces he outflanked the enemy and surrounded them in their dangerous position, from which a determined and successful onset forced them
to a headlong and fearful retreat—many being dashed to pieces
in descending the precipitous rocks or drowned in attempting to
cross the river. The surviving remnant of the invading force,
which had numbered about one thousand five hundred, to eight
hundred on the British side, mustered on the brink of the river,
and surrendered themselves unconditionally, with their General,
Wadsworth, as prisoners of war.

The day had been won, indeed, and won gallantly, but the
sacrifice of Brock's valuable life took away all the exultation from
the victory, and turned gratulation into mourning. It was a
blow which the enemy might well consider almost a fatal one to the
Canadian people, and which gave some color of truth to the American representation of the battle of Queenston Heights as "a
success." Three days after the engagement the deceased General was interred—temporarily, at Fort George—in a bastion just
finished under his own superintendence, amid the tears of his
soldiers, the mourning of the nation, while the minute-guns of the
American Fort Niagara fired shot for shot with those of Fort
George, "as a mark of respect due to a brave enemy." He died
"Sir" Isaac Brock, though he knew it not, having been knighted
in England for his brilliant services at Detroit. But he had a
higher tribute in the love and mourning of the Canadian people,
who have gratefully preserved and done honor to his memory as
one of the heroes of its history. Queenston Heights, where his
death occurred, and where his memorial column stands, is, no
less than the Plains of Abraham, one of Canada's sacred places,
where memories akin to those of Thermopylæ and Marathon
may well move every Canadian who has a heart to feel them.

The American navy had been so wonderfully improved during the last few years that, though still of course vastly smaller
than the British, its first-class men-of-war were individually much
better equipped. In the naval engagements of 1812 this was

speedily seen.   The British frigates Guerrière and Macedonian and the sloop-of-war Frolic were successively attacked and taken by the American Constitution, United States, and Wasp, of equal nominal, but much greater actual, strength.   Then the guns of the Constitution took a second prize in the Java, a fine frigate commanded by a promising officer, Captain Lambert, who fell, with most of her crew.   And, as the final disaster of the year, the "American Hornet," as Colonel Coffin has it, "stung to death the British Peacock."   The tide was not turned till the following June, when Captain Broke, of the Shannon, took a splendid prize in the Chesapeake, of unfortunate memory.   In the mean time, of course, these successes kept up the warlike spirit of the Americans.

Early in 1813 hostilities recommenced with a Canadian success in the Far West.   There General Harrison, who had succeeded Hull, still threatened Proctor with a formidable army of sturdy Kentucky forest rangers and Ohio sharpshooters, and sent on Winchester with a brigade of his army to drive the British and Indians from Frenchtown, one of their outposts.   The latter had to retire upon Brownstown, but Proctor pushed forward, attacked Winchester, and, with the assistance of his Indian allies, completely routed him and captured all his surviving force, with stores and ammunition.   For this success—securing Detroit for the present—Proctor was made a brigadier-general and also received the thanks of the Legislature.

In the St. Lawrence, while the ice still held the river, a brilliant demonstration was made at Ogdensburg, or Oswegatchie, against Fort La Presentation, by the gallant Highland Glengarries, under Colonel Macdonnell.   They took the enemy by surprise, drove them from each successive position, stormed and carried the battery, burned four armed vessels in the harbor, and captured eleven pieces of cannon and a large amount of military stores.   The achievement was an important one, putting a stop to border forays from the American side on that frontier during the rest of the winter.

Hardly any reënforcements had as yet been received from the mother-country, a deficiency, however, made up by the gallant conduct of the militia, worthy of the best regular troops.   A formidable campaign was now opening before them.   The American

plan of operations was, that Harrison and his army should recover Michigan and threaten the West; that Commodore Chauncey, aided by General Pike's land force, should invest York
and the Niagara frontier; and that, after succeeding in Western Canada, the two armies should combine with the large
force under Dearborn, and make a descent upon Kingston and
Montreal.

Sir George Prevost had in the mean time arrived at Kingston, and was endeavoring to hasten the equipment of two vessels
in preparation there and at York, but men and stores were lack-
ing; Sir James Yeo and his English seamen not arriving until
May. Before anything of importance could be done, Chauncey
had made his memorable descent upon York, now Toronto—
then, as now, the capital of the Upper Province—with only too
much success. The attack was not unexpected, but the town
was defenceless so far as military works were concerned, owing,
it is said, to the negligence of Sheaffe. On the evening of April
26th the ominous sound of the alarm-gun was heard, startling
the citizens with the dreaded signal of the enemy's approach.
Such defence as could be made was made. Sheaffe was there on
his way from Newark [Niagara] to Kingston with two companies
of the Eighth; and the enemy, on landing a little west of the town,
met with a brave but ineffectual resistance from both regulars and
volunteers.

After a sharp contest the British troops were obliged to retire
from the unequal struggle—doubly unequal since the fleet was
about to attack the town in front. Sheaffe accordingly retired
toward Kingston, and the defenceless town fell into the hands of
the enemy, whose advance column, on reaching the fort, was
nearly destroyed by the explosion of the powder-magazine, fired
by a sergeant named Marshall. The American general, Zebu-
lon Pike, lost his life in the catastrophe. The ship then building, the dockyard, and a quantity of marine stores had been destroyed or removed by the British before deserting the town; and
the Americans, previous to evacuating it on May 2d, completed
the work of destruction by burning the public buildings and
plundering the church and the library.

If this harassing war is, comparatively, little known to fame,
it certainly extended over an area far wider than that of many

a world-renowned European campaign. Along a frontier one thousand seven hundred miles in length, border frays of varying importance and success were harassing the country. Far to the west, among the rich alluvial forests and tangled jungles of the Detroit district, Proctor, aided by Tecumseh and his Indians, was waging an unequal and somewhat ineffectual struggle with Harrison and his "Army of the West," while near him, on the waters of Lake Erie, Captain Barclay was doing all he could to aid him in naval encounters with Commodore Perry. On the Niagara frontier, within sight of the spray of the Falls, attacks and reprisals were going on as just described. On the broad bosom of Lake Ontario, Chauncey and Yeo were fighting a naval duel, with some success to the latter, while the former made a second descent upon York, just then undefended, and completed the devastation previously begun, demolishing barracks and boats, throwing open the jail, and ill-treating and plundering a number of the inhabitants.

Among the picturesque windings of the Thousand Islands, in the mazes of the blue St. Lawrence, American attacking parties were intercepting convoys of batteaux, carrying provisions for Western garrisons—a serious misfortune in days when, in our now rich and fertile Canada, not only the regular troops, but the militia and the Indian allies, had to be fed on the Irish mess pork, and "hard-tack" from Portsmouth, all stores having to be laboriously carried westward from Montreal. Amid the landlocked, mountain-girdled bays of the beautiful Lake Champlain, hostilities, chiefly in the shape of naval encounters, were proceeding, an American fleet attempting to surprise Isle-aux-Noix, and, in return, destructive reprisals being made by the British upon Plattsburg, Burlington, Scranton, and Champlain town; while far out on the misty Atlantic, British and American men-of-war were "storming with shot and shell," the British Pelican taking the American Argus, and the American Enterprise and Decatur —with great advantage of guns and numbers—taking respectively the Dominica and the Boxer. In the early part of the year, Sir John Borlase, as a prudential measure, had established a vigilant blockade of the American coast, which hemmed in most of the American frigates in their ports, sending their officers and crews to the service of the lakes, harassed the maritime towns and naval arsenals, and, by keeping the merchantmen idle in the harbors, intercepted the coasting trade, ruined the commerce, and diminished the national revenue by two-thirds.

As the autumn of 1813 approached, the American leaders began to make more urgently threatening movements, apparently determined to make some decisive use of their masses of collected troops. Hampton, on the eastern frontier, at the head of nearly five thousand men, crossed Lake Champlain to Plattsburg, in advance on Montreal. At Sackett's Harbor, Wilkinson threatened Kingston with a force of ten thousand men. And General Harrison, in the West, was only awaiting the naval success of Captain Perry, on Lake Erie, in order to advance upon Proctor with an army of six thousand men.

Notwithstanding the difficulty of procuring facilities for ship-building in that far inland region, Captain Barclay had been doing his utmost, by fitting out the Detroit, a larger vessel than his little squadron had hitherto possessed, to keep from Perry the command of the lake. But Perry was well armed and well supplied, while Barclay was driven to the greatest straits for lack of the supplies which it was impossible for him to procure. He succeeded, however, in blockading Perry for a time in the harbor of Presqu'île, where the water on the bar was too shallow to allow his ships to float out with heavy guns on board. But, a gale driving Barclay away, Perry got out, and established his position between the land force and the vessels acting as their store-ships. It became absolutely necessary, at last, to fight the enemy in order to enable the fleet to get supplies, there being, in Barclay's own words, "not a day's flour in the store, and the squadron being on half allowance of many things."

A desperate engagement took place, in the course of which Barclay reduced the Lawrence, Perry's flag-ship, to an unmanageable hulk; and the mixed crews of seamen, militia, and soldiers, in the proportion of one of the first to six of the last, fought as true Britons fight, till, overpowered by superior numbers and heavier metal, aided by a favoring breeze, Barclay's squadron was forced to surrender, only, however, when every vessel had become unmanageable, every officer had been killed or wounded, and a third of the crews put *hors de combat*. Barclay himself, when, some months later, mutilated and maimed, he appeared before the Admiralty, presented a spectacle which moved stern warriors to tears, and drew forth a just tribute to his patriotism and courage.

But that defeat was a fatal one for General Proctor. It destroyed his last hope, and retreat or ruin lay before him. Without supplies, deprived of the arms and ammunition of which Fort Malden had been stripped in order to supply the fleet, his prospects seemed gloomy indeed. Retreat across the wilderness behind him in rainy autumn weather might be arduous and ruinous enough, yet it seemed the only escape from hopeless surrender. And so, despite the earnest and eloquent remonstrances of Tecumseh,[1] who thought he should have held his ground, and who, doubtless, remembered the bold and victorious advance of General Brock at the head of his little force one year before, he abandoned and dismantled Fort Detroit, crossed over to Sandwich, whither he transported his guns, and commenced his retreat upon Burlington Heights with a force of eight hundred thirty men. The faithful Tecumseh, grieved and indignant as he was at the General's determination to retreat, adhered to the fortunes of his British allies with noble constancy, and accompanied Proctor with his band of three hundred Indian followers.

The English General did not expect to be immediately followed up by Harrison, knowing the difficulties in the way of his progress. But the Kentucky "mounted infantry," or forest rangers—each carrying, wherever practicable, a foot soldier behind him—proved capital bush-warriors. Harrison's army of three thousand five hundred men came up with the little retreating force before it could have been supposed possible, surprised

[1] Extract from Tecumseh's despairing appeal to General Proctor: "We are astonished to see our Father giving up everything and preparing to run away without letting his red children know what his intentions are. You always told us you would never draw your foot off British ground. But now, Father, we see you are drawing back, and we are sorry to see our Father doing so without seeing the enemy. We must compare our Father's conduct to a fat dog that carries his tail upon his back, but when affrighted it drops it between its legs and runs off. Father! you have got the arms and ammunition which our great Father sent for his red children. If you have an idea of going away, give them to us, and you may go and welcome. Our lives are in the hands of the Great Spirit. We are determined to defend our lands, and if it be his will we wish to leave our bones upon them."

Proctor's rear-guard, captured his stores and ammunition and one hundred prisoners. Thus brought to bay, the British General, apparently stunned and bewildered by accumulated misfortunes, felt compelled to risk an almost hopeless fight. His little band of footsore and weary men—dejected, hopeless, exhausted by a harassing and depressing retreat, weakened by the effects of exposure and fatigue, and by the ravages of fever and ague, insufficiently clothed, scantily fed, and further disintegrated by the want of harmony and the relaxed discipline which unfortunately characterized Proctor's command — were faced about to strike one last desparing blow. The position taken by Proctor at Moravian Town, on the Thames, seems to have been a good one, but the General seems to have lost all energy and foresight. No protective breastwork was thrown up—no sharp watch kept on the enemy's advance. The latter, having reconnoitred carefully the British position, opened a skilful and vigorous attack, and in a short time the exhausted and hopeless troops were totally routed, Proctor and a remnant of his troops effecting a wretched retreat to Burlington Heights, while a number of the captured British soldiers were taken in triumph to "grace a Roman holiday," some of them, instead of being treated honorably as prisoners of war, being consigned to penitentiary cells.

Tecumseh, with his band of Indians, had taken up a position in the swamp to the right of the British force. His last words, as he shook hands with Proctor before the engagement, were, "Father, have a big heart!" It was indeed the thing that Proctor most needed and most lacked just then. Tecumseh was to make his onset on the discharge of a signal gun. But the gun was never fired, and Tecumseh found himself deserted by his English allies and surrounded by the enemy. Attacked by the dismounted riflemen in the swamp, like a lion in the toils, Tecumseh and his "braves" fought on till the noble chieftain fell—as courageous a warrior and faithful an ally as ever fought under the union jack.

Proctor survived, but his military career was closed forever, and the dishonor of its termination fatally tarnishes the glory of his earlier success. The catastrophe of Moravian Town, giving the Americans complete possession of Lakes Erie and Huron, and undisturbed range of the Western frontier, striking a blow at the British ascendency, and giving renewed hopes of success to the Americans, though it awoke a spirit of more intense and dogged resolution in the Canadians, was the saddest reverse of the war, and is said to be "unparalleled in the annals of the British army."

But it did not come singly. On the very day of Proctor's defeat, a body of two hundred fifty soldiers, proceeding from York to Kingston in two schooners, without convoy, were captured on Lake Ontario. These accumulated disasters, added to the knowledge that the Americans were concentrating their forces on Montreal and Kingston, with the probability of the advance of Harrison's army toward the Niagara frontier, compelled General Vincent to raise the blockade of Fort George, on which Prevost had made another of his undecided and ineffectual demonstrations, and retire to Burlington Heights. The unfavorable aspect of affairs, indeed, spread such consternation at headquarters that Prevost issued orders to abandon the Upper Province west of Kingston. In the face of this order, however, a council of war, held at Burlington Heights, decided at all hazards to maintain the defence of the Western Peninsula. The American Government, sure apparently that the British forces would make good their retreat, recalled their victorious General to Detroit just at the time when his advance would have been most disastrous to the small British force on the Niagara frontier.

The force with which it was now expected, under Wilkinson and Hampton, to make an easy conquest of Lower Canada, amounted to twenty-one thousand men, opposed to three thousand British regulars in Lower Canada—strongly supported, however, by a gallant and enthusiastic French-Canadian militia, who proved themselves in the day of trial no less loyal and unflinching than their Upper Canadian brothers. Wilkinson's concerted attack upon Kingston from Sackett's Harbor was averted by the timely throwing of two thousand troops into the Kingston garrison, which changed Wilkinson's plans, and sent him down the St. Lawrence to join Hampton—followed, however, by British schooners and gunboats, and by a corps of observation, under Colonel Morrison, which made a descent upon him at Chrysler's Farm on the Canadian shore of the river—midway between Kingston and Montreal—and forced him to retreat, completely routed, though numbering two to ¦one of the British force, the scattered American force precipitately taking to their boats and hastening down the river.

Amid these scenes of devastation the campaign of 1813 closed. The next year a large American force, under General Brown, harassed the Niagara frontier.   An incursion on Port Dover took place, and the entire village was burned down without the slightest provocation.   In July Fort Erie surrendered, without firing a shot, to two strong brigades under Generals Scott and Ripley, Major Buck, then in command, thinking it would be a useless sacrifice of life to hold out with a garrison of one hundred seventy against four thousand assailants.   On the whole frontier there were only one thousand seven hundred eighty British troops, opposed to a strong American force.   General Riall, however, the British commander on the frontier, was determined to check the enemy's advance by a vigorous resistance.

A strong American force, led by General Brown, marched down the river to Chippewa, the extreme right of the British position.   Notwithstanding the greatly superior numbers of the Americans—double those of the British troops—and the strong position which Brown had taken up, Riall, having received reënforcements from Toronto, resolved to attack the enemy.   Again and again his columns gallantly charged against the solid American line, but were forced back by their formidable fire; and Riall, after suffering severe loss, had to order a retreat toward Niagara. The unsuccessful attempt was, at least, sufficiently demonstrative of British and Canadian pluck, and seems to have had the effect of deterring the enemy from following up his success even so far as to molest the retreating force.   His army, however, advanced leisurely, and occupied Queenston—his light infantry and Indians making marauding incursions in every direction, burning the village of St. David's and plundering and destroying the property of the unhappy colonists whom the Americans had been so benevolently desirous to free from British tyranny.

General Brown, disappointed in his expectation of being assisted to take Fort George and Fort Niagara by Chauncey's fleet—now effectually held in check by Commodore Yeo, and finding the garrison on the *qui vive*—retreated to Chippewa, followed by Riall, who took up a position close to the American force at Lundy's Lane. General Drummond having heard at Kingston of Brown's advance and the defeat of Chippewa, hastened to Niagara, where, finding that Riall had gone on before him, he sent Colonel Tucker, on the American side of the river, against a detachment at Lewiston, while he himself pushed on to Queenston. From thence, the enemy having disappeared from Lewiston, he sent Tucker back to Niagara, and moved on with eight hundred regulars to Lundy's Lane, where he found that Riall had commenced a retreat; Scott, who had advanced to the Falls, having sent for Brown to come on with the rest of his force to join him.

The retreat was speedily countermanded by Drummond, who with one thousand six hundred men, found himself confronted with an American force of five thousand, part of which had already arrived within six hundred yards when the British General arrived—the engagement commencing almost before he had completed his formation—and established a battery on the slight eminence now crowned by an observatory. From thence, on a summer's day, the eye can take in a large expanse of sunny, peaceful country, rich green woods, peach orchards and vineyards, tranquil homesteads, and fields of the richest, softest green. But on that July afternoon, as evening drew on, the peaceful landscape was clouded by heavy sulphurous smoke, the sweet summer air was filled with the dull boom of artillery, the rattle of volleys of musketry, the sharp crack of the rifle, the shout of the charge, and the groans of the dying—all blending strangely with the solemn, unceasing roar of the great cataract close by. The combat—the most sanguinary and most fiercely contested of the war—raged with terrible carnage and desperate obstinacy till the summer darkness closed over the scene, and the moon rose to cast a dim and uncertain light over the bloody field.

At one time the enemy had captured several of the British cannon, but they were speedily recovered, with one of the enemy's guns in addition. In the darkness strange mistakes occurred, pieces of artillery being exchanged during the charges made after nightfall. About nine a brief lull in the fighting occurred, while the rear guard of the American force under General Brown took the place of Scott's brigade, which had suffered severely. Riall's retiring division now came up—with two guns and four hundred militia—one thousand two hundred strong, and between the two forces thus strengthened, the fierce contest was renewed. "Nothing," says an eye-witness, "could have been more terrible, nor yet more solemn, than this midnight contest." The desperate charges of the enemy were succeeded by a deathlike silence, interrupted only by the groans of the dying and the dull sound of the Falls of Niagara, while the adverse lines were now and then dimly discerned through the moonlight by the gleam of their arms.

These anxious pauses were succeeded by a blaze of musketry along the lines, and by a repetition of the most desperate charges from the enemy, which the British regulars and militia received with the most unshaken firmness. At midnight, Brown, having unsuccessfully tried for six hours, with his force of five thousand against half that number, to force the British from their position, retreated to Chippewa with a loss of nine hundred thirty—that on the British side amounting to eight hundred seventy. Generals Scott and Brown were severely wounded, as was also General Drummond, though he retained his command, notwithstanding, to the end of the action. Next day a fresh demonstration was planned but abandoned, and Brown, on the 27th, having burned Street's mills, destroyed the bridge over the Chippewa Creek, and thrown his *impedimenta* and provisions into the river, retired on Fort Erie, Drummond's light infantry, cavalry, and Indians following in pursuit.

General Drummond having followed up and invested the American troops in Fort Erie, daringly attempted to storm the fort, and nearly succeeded; indeed, a portion of his columns actually succeeded in penetrating the fort—the centre of the intrenched camp—but were driven thence by the accidental explosion of a powder-magazine, which made the assailants retreat in dismay. This disastrous repulse cost the British and Canadians some five hundred men—the American loss being scarcely one hundred; and a simultaneous attack by Colonel Tucker on Black Rock was not more successful. Notwithstanding this, however, Drummond, being reënforced by the Sixth and Eighty-second regiments, was able to maintain his position and keep the American force blockaded in Fort Erie.

The cessation of the general war in Europe, early in 1814, had left Britain free to turn her chief attention to America, and the effects of this were soon felt. The whole American seaboard, from Maine to Mexico, was subject to the inroads of British squadrons, whose descents forced the recall of much of the land force sent to Canada. In Maine, Sir John Sherbrooke, Lieutenant-Governor of Nova Scotia, made successful inroads carrying one place after another, till the whole border, from Penobscot to New Brunswick, was under British rule, and so continued till the ratification of peace. Further south, General Ross landed at Benedict, ascended the Patuxent to Washington, dispersed its defenders and burned the Capitol, the Arsenal, the Treasury, the War-Office, the President's Mansion, and the great bridge across the Potomac, the conflagration being aided by the explosion of magazines fired by the retreating Americans. The devastation at Washington was a severe though unexpected retribution for York left in ashes by the Americans during the preceding year.

An attempt on Baltimore did not terminate so successfully, for the English General Ross being killed, the British force, finally giving up the attempt, returned to their ships. In Florida, the British forces established themselves for some time, and the army of General Pakenham assaulted New Orleans (January 8, 1815), with about eight thousand men, but they were repulsed by a vigorous defence, and compelled to retreat. Pakenham was killed. In August, 1814, British and American envoys had met at Ghent to consider terms of pacification.

In that same month of August, however, occurred an unfortunate British reverse in Canada. Sixteen hundred men of the Duke of Wellington's army had arrived at Quebec, and Sir George Prevost sent a portion of this body to Upper Canada, directed against Sackett's Harbor, while he concentrated eleven thousand on the Richelieu frontier to attack the American position on Lake Champlain, aided by a small and very badly equipped naval force.

General Izzard's departure with four thousand men to assist the still blockaded American troops at Fort Erie left the American force on Lake Champlain very inadequate, and Prevost's army, meeting with no opposition, advanced against Plattsburg, defended by two blockhouses and a chain of field-works, and garrisoned by one thousand five hundred troops and militia under

General Macomb. Three successive days were employed in bringing up the heavy artillery, and Prevost waited for the advance of the fleet, still in a very backward state of preparation, before proceeding to the attack. The result, however, was a repetition of the inglorious affair of the preceding summer at Sackett's Harbor. Prevost allowed the right moment for the joint attack to pass, and, instead of moving his columns at once to joint action with the fleet, he waited till the fleet had been defeated by the greatly superior squadron opposed to them, and then irresolutely put his troops in motion. But, meeting with some discouragement, he immediately ordered a retreat, without even attempting to carry works which it seemed were quite within his power to capture.

The indignation of the disappointed troops, thus compelled to an inglorious retreat, was uncontrollable, and many of the officers broke their swords, declaring that they would never serve again. The retiring force withdrew unmolested. Opinions seemed to differ as to whether Prevost's conduct was pusillanimity or prudence.

Taking into consideration the events of the preceding year, appearances seem to favor the former view. Yet Prevost was said to be personally brave in action, his chief lack seeming to be that of decision in command. He was to have been tried by court-martial, but died before this could take place, so that his military reputation still rests under a cloud.

At Fort Erie the disaster on Lake Champlain encouraged the blockaded garrison to make a vigorous sortie on September 17th. At first partially successful, they were soon driven back, and pursued to the very glacis of the fort, with a loss of five hundred, the British having lost six hundred, half of these being made prisoners in the trenches at the beginning of the sortie. Hearing of Izzard's advance, Drummond thought it prudent to withdraw to Chippewa his small force, thus reduced and much enfeebled by sickness.

On Lake Ontario, however, Yeo, having constructed a flagship carrying one hundred guns, effectually vindicated the British supremacy. In October, Chauncey withdrew into Sackett's Harbor, and was blockaded therein. This secured abundant facility for conveying troops and provisions to the Niagara frontier, and though Izzard had now eight thousand men at Fort Erie, he saw the fruitlessness of prosecuting the invasion any farther, blew up the works, and recrossed with his troops to American territory, leaving the long disturbed frontier to repose.   With the exception of a western border foray by some mounted Kentucky brigands, this concluded the hostilities of the long and harassing war, and "burst the bubble of the invasion of Canada."   The peace ratified by the Treaty of Ghent, concluded December 24, 1814, terminated the protracted war, which had been so unjustifiable, so disastrous, and so absolutely fruitless to both countries—a war which had desolated large tracts of fertile territory, sacrificed many valuable lives, and kept up a spirit of hatred between two Christian nations, which should have been endeavoring in unison to advance the liberty and the highest interests of the human race.

JAMES GRAHAME

The American Congress, in 1811, while continuing the preparations for war, still cherished the hope that a change of policy in Europe would render unnecessary an appeal to arms till May in the following year.   Toward the close of that season, the Hornet arrived from London, bringing information that no prospect existed of a favorable change.   On June 1st the President sent a message to Congress, recounting the wrongs received from Great Britain, and submitting the question, whether the United States should continue to endure them or resort to war?   The message was considered with closed doors.   On the 18th an act was passed declaring war against Great Britain; and the next day a proclamation was issued.   Against this declaration, however, the Representatives belonging to the Federal party presented a solemn protest, which was written with great ability.

At the time of the declaration of war, General Hull was also Governor of the Michigan Territory, of which Detroit was the capital.   On July 12, 1812, with two thousand regulars and volunteers, he crossed the river dividing the United States from Canada, apparently intending to attack Malden, and thence to proceed to Montreal.   Information was, however, received that Mackinac, an American post above Detroit, had surrendered to a large body of British and Indians, who were rushing down the river in numbers sufficient to overwhelm the American forces.

Panic-struck, General Hull hastened back to Detroit. General Brock, the commander at Malden, pursued him and erected batteries opposite Detroit. The next day, meeting with no resistance, General Brock resolved to march directly forward and assault the fort. The American troops awaited the approach of the enemy, and anticipated victory; but, to their dismay, General Hull opened a correspondence, which ended in the surrender of the army and of the Territory of Michigan. An event so disgraceful, occurring in a quarter where success was confidently anticipated, caused the greatest mortification and amazement throughout the Union.

General Van Rensselaer, of the New York militia, had the command of the troops which were called the "Army of the Centre." His headquarters were at Lewiston on the river Niagara, and on the opposite side was Queenston, a fortified British post. The militia displaying great eagerness to be led against the enemy, the General determined to cross the river at the head of about one thousand men; though successful at first, he was compelled, after a long and obstinate engagement, to surrender. General Brock, the British commander, fell in rallying his troops.

The Army of the North, which was under the immediate command of General Dearborn, was stationed at Greenbush, near Albany, and at Plattsburg, on Lake Champlain. From the latter post a detachment marched a short distance into Canada, surprised a small body of British and Indians, and destroyed a considerable quantity of public stores. Other movements were anxiously expected by the people; but after the misfortunes of Detroit and Niagara, the General deemed it inexpedient to engage in any important enterprise.

The scene of the campaign of 1813 was principally in the north, toward Canada. Brigadier-General Winchester, of the United States army, and nearly five hundred men, officers and soldiers, were made prisoners at Frenchtown, by a division of the British army from Detroit, with their Indian allies, under Colonel Proctor. Colonel Proctor leaving the Americans without a guard, the Indians returned, and deeds of horror followed. The wounded officers were dragged from the houses, killed, and scalped in the streets. The buildings were set on fire. Some who attempted to escape were forced back into the flames, while others were put to death by the tomahawk, and left shockingly mangled in the highway. The infamy of this butchery does not fall upon the perpetrators alone, but extends to those who were able, and were bound by a solemn engagement, to restrain them. The battle and massacre at Frenchtown clothed Kentucky and Ohio in mourning. Other volunteers, indignant at the treachery and cruelty of their foes, hastened to the aid of Harrison. He marched to the rapids of the Miami, where he erected a fort, which he called Fort Meigs, in honor of the Governor of Ohio. On May 1st it was invested by a large number of Indians, and by a party of British troops from Malden, the whole commanded by Colonel Proctor. An unsuccessful attempt to raise the siege was made by General Clay, at the head of twelve hundred Kentuckians; but the fort continued to be defended with bravery and skill. The Indians, unaccustomed to sieges, became weary and discontented; and on May 8th they deserted their allies. The British, despairing of success, then made a precipitate retreat.

On the northern frontier a body of troops had been assembled under the command of General Dearborn, at Sackett's Harbor, and great exertions were made by Commodore Chauncey to build and equip a squadron on Lake Ontario sufficiently powerful to contend with that of the British. By April 25th the naval preparations were so far completed that the General and seventeen thousand troops were conveyed across the lake to the attack of York (Toronto), the capital of Upper Canada. On the 27th an advanced party, commanded by Brigadier-General Pike, who was born in a camp, and bred a soldier from his birth, landed, although opposed at the water's edge by a superior force. After a short but severe conflict, the British were driven to their fortifications. The rest of the troops having landed, the whole party pressed forward, carried the first battery by assault, and were moving toward the main works, when the English magazine blew up, with a tremendous explosion, hurling upon the advancing troops immense quantities of stone and timber. Numbers were killed; the gallant Pike received a mortal wound; the troops halted for a moment, but, recovering from the shock, again pressed forward, and soon gained possession of the town. Of the British troops, one hundred were killed, nearly three hundred were wounded, and the same number made prisoners.

The object of the expedition attained, the squadron and troops returned to Sackett's Harbor, and subsequently sailed to Fort George, situated at the head of the lake. After a warm engagement, the British abandoned the fort and retired to the heights at the head of Burlington Bay.

While the greater part of the American army was thus employed, the British made an attack upon the important post of Sackett's Harbor. On May 27th their squadron appeared before the town. Alarm guns instantly assembled the citizens of the neighborhood. General Brown's force amounted to about one thousand men; a slight breastwork was hastily thrown up at the only place where the British could land, and behind this he placed the militia; the regulars, under Colonel Backus, forming a second line. On the morning of the 29th one thousand British troops landed from the squadron and advanced toward the breastwork; the militia gave way, but by the bravery of the regulars under the skilful arrangement of General Brown the British were repulsed, and reëmbarked so hastily as to leave behind most of their wounded.

While each nation was busily employed in equipping a squadron on Lake Erie, General Clay remained inactive at Fort Meigs. About the last of July a large number of British and Indians appeared before the fort, hoping to entice the garrison to a general action in the field. After waiting a few days without succeeding, they decamped, and proceeded to Fort Stephenson, on the river Sandusky. This fort was little more than a picketing, surrounded by a ditch, and the garrison consisted of but one hundred sixty men, who were commanded by Major Croghan, a youth of twenty-one. The force of the assailants was estimated at about four hundred in uniform, and as many Indians; they were repulsed, and their loss in killed, wounded, and prisoners is supposed to have exceeded one hundred fifty; those of the remainder who were not able to escape were taken off during the night by the Indians. The whole loss of Major Croghan during the siege was one killed and seven slightly wounded. About three the next morning the British sailed down the river, leaving behind them a boat containing clothing and considerable military stores.

By the exertions of Captain Perry, an American squadron

had been fitted out on Lake Erie early in September. It consisted of nine small vessels, in all carrying fifty-four guns. A
British squadron had also been built and equipped, under the
superintendence of Commodore Barclay. It consisted of six
vessels, mounting sixty-three guns. Commodore Perry, immediately sailing, offered battle to his adversary, and on September
10th the British commander left the harbor of Malden to accept
the offer. In a few hours the wind shifted, giving the Americans
the advantage. Perry, forming the line of battle, hoisted his
flag, on which were inscribed the words of the dying Lawrence,
"Don't give up the ship." Loud huzzas from all the vessels
proclaimed the animation which this motto inspired. About
noon the firing commenced; and after a short action two of the
British vessels surrendered, and, the rest of the American squadron now joining in the battle, the victory was rendered decisive
and complete. The British loss was forty-one killed and ninety-
four wounded. The American loss was twenty-seven killed
and ninety-six wounded, of which number twenty-one were
killed and sixty-two wounded on board the flag-ship Lawrence,
whose whole complement of able-bodied men before the action
was about one hundred. The Commodore gave intelligence of
the victory to General Harrison in these words: "We have met
the enemy, and they are ours! Two ships, two brigs, one schooner,
and one sloop." The Americans were now masters of the
lake; but the Territory of Michigan was still in the possession of
Colonel Proctor. The next movements were against the British
and Indians at Detroit and Malden. General Harrison had previously assembled a portion of the Ohio militia on the Sandusky
River; and on September 7th four thousand from Kentucky, the
flower of the State, with Governor Shelby at their head, arrived
at his camp. With the cooperation of the fleet, it was determined
to proceed at once to Malden. On the 27th the troops were received on board, and reached Malden on the same day; but the
British had, in the mean time, destroyed the fort and public
stores, and had retreated along the Thames toward the Moravian villages, together with Tecumseh's Indians amounting to
twelve or fifteen hundred. It was now resolved to proceed in
pursuit of Proctor. On October 5th a severe battle was fought
between the two armies at the River Thames, and the British army

was defeated by the Americans. In this battle Tecumseh was killed and the Indians fled. The British loss was nineteen regulars killed, and fifty wounded, and about six hundred prisoners. The American loss, in killed and wounded, amounted to upward of fifty. Proctor made his escape up the Thames. On September 29th the Americans took possession of Detroit, which, on the approach of Harrison's army, had been abandoned by the British. Preparations were now made for subduing Upper Canada and taking Montreal; but owing to the difficulties attending the concentration of the troops, and perhaps also to the want of vigor in the commanders, that project was abandoned, and the army under Wilkinson, marching to French Mills, there encamped for the winter.

The pacification in Europe in 1814 offered to the British a large disposable force, both naval and military, and with it the means of giving to the war in America a character of new and increased activity and extent. The friends of the Administration anticipated a severer conflict, and prepared for greater sacrifices and greater sufferings. Its opposers, where difficulties thickened and danger pressed, were encouraged to make vigorous efforts to wrest the reins of authority from men who, they asserted, had shown themselves incompetent to hold them. The President deemed it advisable to strengthen the line of the Atlantic, and therefore called on the executives of several States to organize and hold in readinesss for immediate service a corps of ninety-three thousand five hundred men.

The hostile movements on the northern frontier were now becoming vigorous and interesting. In the beginning of July General Brown, who had been assiduously employed in disciplining his troops, crossed the Niagara with about three thousand men, and took possession, without opposition, of Fort Erie. In a strong position at Chippewa, a few miles distant, was intrenched an equal number of British troops, commanded by General Riall. On the 4th General Brown approached their works; and the next day, on the plains of Chippewa, an obstinate and sanguinary battle was fought, which compelled the British to retire to their intrenchments. In this action, which was fought with great judgment and coolness on both sides, the loss of the Americans was about four hundred men, that of the British was upward of five hundred. Soon afterward, General Riall, abandoning his works, retired to the heights of Burlington. Here Lieutenant-General Drummond, with a large reënforcement, joined him, and assuming the command, led back the army toward the American camp. On the 25th was fought the Battle of Bridgewater [Lundy's Lane], which began at four in the afternoon and continued until midnight. After a desperate conflict the British troops were withdrawn, and the Americans left in possession of the field.

The loss on both sides was severe and nearly equal. Generals Brown and Scott having both been severely wounded, the command developed upon General Ripley. He remained a few hours upon the hill, collected the wounded, and then returned unmolested to the camp. This battle was fought near the cataract of Niagara, whose roar was silenced by the thunder of cannon and the din of arms, but was distinctly heard during the pauses of the fight. The American General found his force so much weakened that he deemed it prudent again to occupy Fort Erie. On August 4th it was invested by General Drummond with five thousand troops. In the night between the 14th and 15th the besiegers made a daring assault upon the fort, which was repelled with conspicuous gallantry by the garrison, the former losing more than nine hundred men, the latter but eighty-four. The siege was still continued. On September 2d General Brown, having recovered from his wounds, threw himself into the fort, and took command of the garrison. For their fate great anxiety was felt by the nation, which was, however, in some degree removed by the march from Plattsburg of five thousand men to their relief. After an hour of close fighting they entered the fort, having killed, wounded, and taken one thousand of the British. The loss of the Americans was also considerable, amounting to more than five hundred. On September 21st the forty-ninth day of the siege, General Drummond withdrew his forces.

The march of the troops from Plattsburg having left that post almost defenceless, the enemy determined to attack it by land, and, at the same time, to attempt the destruction of the American flotilla on Lake Champlain. On September 3d Sir George Prevost, the Governor-General of Canada, at the head of fourteen thousand men, entered the territories of the United States.   On the 6th they arrived at Plattsburg.   It is situated near Lake Champlain, on the northern bank of the small river Saranac. On their approach the American troops, who were posted on the opposite bank, tore up the planks on the bridges, with which they formed slight breastworks, and prepared to dispute the passage of the stream.   The British employed themselves for several days in erecting batteries, while the American forces were daily augmented by the arrival of volunteers and militia.   Early in the morning of the 11th the British squadron, commanded by Commodore Downie, appeared off the harbor of Plattsburg, where that of the United States, commanded by Captain Macdonough, lay at anchor prepared for battle.   At nine o'clock the action commenced.   Seldom has there been a more furious encounter than the bosom of this transparent and peaceful lake was now called to witness.   During the naval conflict the British on land began a heavy cannonade upon the American lines, and attempted at different places to cross the Saranac; but as often as the British advanced into the water they were repelled by a destructive fire from the militia.   At half past eleven the shout of victory heard along the American lines announced the result of the battle on the lake.   Thus deprived of naval aid, in the afternoon the British withdrew to their intrenchments, and in the night they commenced a precipitate retreat.   Upon the lake the American loss was one hundred ten; the British one hundred ninety-four, besides prisoners.   On land, the American loss was one hundred nineteen; that of the British has been estimated as high as two thousand five hundred.

PERRY'S VICTORY ON LAKE ERIE

A.D. 1813

THEODORE ROOSEVELT[1]

At the beginning of the War of 1812 most of the leaders of the American war party in Congress were anticipating a contest mainly on the land, where they confidently looked for successes and territorial conquests. They appear to have thought and expected little of the navy, notwithstanding its brilliant services in, the Revolution. So little faith had the Administration in the power of the navy that it was determined to lay up the frigates in some safe port, to prevent their capture or destruction. But Captains William Bainbridge and Charles Stewart hastened to Washington and persuaded the President to reverse that decision and let the battle-ships take part in the war. The navy was destined to play the leading part, and none of its performances did more to increase its prestige than the victory of Perry on Lake Erie. Already there had been notable successes of the navy in the war, such as the capture of the British ship Alert by the Essex, of the Guerrière by the Constitution (the famous "Old Ironsides"), of the Frolic by the Wasp, and of the Macedonian by the United States. But the triumph of Perry was of even greater consequence than these.

The war had begun on the New York frontier, and the Great Lakes and the St. Lawrence River region became a most important part of this theatre. As soon as this fact was recognized, Commodore Isaac Chauncey, who had served in the Tripolitan War, was placed in command in those waters, and he detailed a young naval officer, Captain Oliver Hazard Perry, of Rhode Island, to take charge of a flotilla to act against a British fleet on Lake Erie. Perry was born in 1785, became a midshipman in 1799, and, like Chauncey, had served with credit in the Tripolitan War.

Theodore Roosevelt's spirited account of this action is not only interesting as a historical narrative, but is also of special value for its critical analysis and comparative estimate of an exploit that for almost a century has been regarded as one of the chief glories of the United States Navy.

CAPTAIN OLIVER HAZARD PERRY had assumed command of Erie and the upper lakes, acting under Commodore Chauncey. With intense energy he at once began creating a naval force which should be able to contend successfully with

[1] From Theodore Roosevelt's *Naval War of 1812* (G. P. Putnam's Sons), by permission.

the foe. The latter in the beginning had exclusive control of Lake Erie; but the Americans had captured the Caledonia brig, and purchased three schooners, afterward named the Somers, Tigress, and Ohio, and a sloop, the Trippe. These at first were blockaded in the Niagara, but after the fall of Fort George and the retreat of the British forces Captain Perry was enabled to get them out, tacking them up against the current by the most arduous labor. They ran up to Presqu'île (now called Erie), where two twenty-gun brigs were being constructed under the directions of the indefatigable captain. Three other schooners, the Ariel, Scorpion, and Porcupine, were also built.

The harbor of Erie was good and spacious but had a bar on which there was less than seven feet of water. Hitherto this had prevented the enemy from getting in; now it prevented the two brigs from getting out. Captain Robert Heriot Barclay had been appointed commander of the British forces on Lake Erie; and he was having built at Amherstburg a twenty-gun ship. Meanwhile he blockaded Perry's force, and as the brigs could not cross the bar, with their guns in, or except in smooth water, they of course could not do so in his presence. He kept a close blockade for some time; but on August 2d he disappeared. Perry at once hurried forward everything; and on the 4th, at 2 P.M., one brig, the Lawrence, was towed to that point of the bar where the water was deepest. Her guns were whipped out and landed on the beach, and the brig got over the bar by a hastily improvised "camel."

"Two large scows, prepared for the purpose, were hauled alongside, and the work of lifting the brig proceeded as fast as possible. Pieces of massive timber had been run through the forward and after ports, and when the scows were sunk to the water's edge the ends of the timbers were blocked up, supported by these floating foundations. The plugs were now put in the scows, and the water was pumped out of them. By this process the brig was lifted quite two feet, though when she was got on the bar it was found that she still drew too much water. It became necessary, in consequence, to cover up everything, sink the scows anew, and block up the timbers afresh. This duty occupied the whole night."

Just as the Lawrence had passed the bar, at 8 A.M. on the

5th, the enemy reappeared, but too late; Captain Barclay exchanged a few shots with the schooners and then drew off. The Niagara crossed without difficulty. There were still not enough men to man the vessels, but a draft arrived from Ontario, and many of the frontiersmen volunteered, while soldiers also were sent on board. The squadron sailed on the 18th in pursuit of the enemy, whose ship was now ready. After cruising about some time the Ohio was sent down the lake, and the other ships went into Put-in Bay. On September 9th Captain Barclay put out from Amherstburg, being so short of provisions that he felt compelled to risk an action with the superior force opposed. On September 10th his squadron was discovered from the masthead of the Lawrence in the northwest. Before going into details of the action we will examine the force of the two squadrons, as the accounts vary considerably.

The tonnage of the British ships, as already stated, we know exactly; they having been all carefully appraised and measured by the builder, Mr. Henry Eckford, and two sea captains. We also know the dimensions of the American ships. The Lawrence and Niagara measured 480 tons apiece. The Caledonia brig was about the size of the Hunter, or 180 tons. The Tigress, Somers, and Scorpion were subsequently captured by the foe, and were then said to measure respectively 96, 94, and 86 tons; in which case they were larger than similar boats on Lake Ontario. The Ariel was about the size of the Hamilton; the Porcupine and Trippe about the size of the Asp and Pert. As for the guns, Captain Barclay in his letter gives a complete account of those on board his squadron. He has also given a complete account of the American guns, which is most accurate, and, if anything, underestimates them. At least Emmons in his *History* gives the Trippe a long 32, while Barclay says she had only a long 24; and Lossing in his *Field Book* says (but I do not know on what authority) that the Caledonia had three long 24's, while Barclay gives her two long 24's and one 32-pound carronade; and that the Somers had two long 32's, while Barclay gives her one long 32 and one 24-pound carronade. I shall take Barclay's account, which corresponds with that of Emmons; the only difference being that Emmons puts a 24-pounder on the Scorpion and a 32 on the Trippe, while Barclay reverses this. I shall also follow

Emmons in giving the Scorpion a 32-pound carronade instead of a 24.

It is more difficult to give the strength of the respective crews. James says the Americans had 580, all "picked men." They were just as much picked men as Barclay's were, and no more; that is, the ships had "scratch" crews. Lieutenant Emmons gives Perry 490 men; and Lossing says he "had upon his muster-roll 490 names." In Volume xiv, page 566, of the *American State Papers*, is a list of the prize moneys owing to each man (or to the survivors of the killed), which gives a grand total of 532 men, including 136 on the Lawrence and 155 on the Niagara, 45 of whom were volunteers—frontiersmen. Deducting these we get 487 men, which is pretty near Lieutenant Emmons's 490. Possibly Lieutenant Emmons did not include these volunteers; and it may be that some of the men whose names were down on the prize list had been so sick that they were left on shore. Thus Lieutenant Yarnall testified before a court of inquiry in 1815 that there were but 131 men and boys of every description on board the Lawrence in the action; and the Niagara was said to have had but 140.

Lieutenant Yarnall also said that "but 103 men on board the Lawrence were fit for duty"; as Captain Perry in his letter said that 31 were unfit for duty, this would make a total of 134. So I shall follow the prize-money list; at any rate the difference in number is so slight as to be immaterial. Of the 532 men whose names the list gives, 45 were volunteers, or landsmen from among the surrounding inhabitants; 158 were marines, or soldiers (I do not know which, as the list gives marines, soldiers, and privates, and it is impossible to tell which of the two former heads includes the last); and 329 were officers, seamen, cooks, pursers, chaplains, and supernumeraries. Of the total number there were on the day of action, according to Perry's report, 116 men unfit for duty, including 31 on board the Lawrence, 28 on board the Niagara, and 57 on the small vessels.

All the later American writers put the number of men in Barclay's fleet precisely at 502, but I have not been able to find the original authority. James (*Naval Occurrences*, page 289) says the British had but 345, consisting of 50 seamen, 85 Canadians, and 210 soldiers. But the letter of Adjutant-General E.

Bayne, November 24, 1813, states that there were 250 soldiers aboard Barclay's squadron, of whom 23 were killed, 49 wounded, and the remainder (178) captured; and James himself on a previous page (284) states that there were 102 Canadians on Barclay's vessels, not counting the Detroit, and we know that Barclay originally joined the squadron with 19 sailors from the Ontario fleet, and that subsequently 50 sailors came up from the Dover. James gives at the end of his *Naval Occurrences* some extracts from the court-martial held on Captain Barclay. Lieutenant Thomas Stokes, of the Queen Charlotte, there testified that he had on board "between 120 and 130 men, officers and all together," of whom "16 came up from the Dover three days before." James (on page 284) says her crew already consisted of 110 men; adding these 16 gives us 126—almost exactly "between 120 and 130." Lieutenant Stokes also testified that the Detroit had more men on account of being a larger and heavier vessel; to give her 150 is perfectly safe, as her heavier guns and larger size would at least need 24 men more than the Queen Charlotte. James gives the Lady Prevost 76, Hunter 39, Little Belt 15, and Chippeway 13 men, Canadians and soldiers, a total of 143; supposing that the number of British sailors placed on them was proportional to the amount placed on board the Queen Charlotte, we could add 21. This would make a grand total of 440 men, which must certainly be near the truth. This number is corroborated otherwise: General Bayne, as already quoted, says that there were aboard 250 soldiers, of whom 72 were killed or wounded. Barclay reports a total loss of 135, of whom 63 must therefore have been sailors or Canadians, and if the loss suffered by these bore the same proportion to their whole number as in the case of the soldiers, there ought to have been 219 sailors and Canadians, making in all 469 men. It can thus be said with certainty that there were between 440 and 490 men aboard, and I shall take the former number, though I have no doubt that this is too small. But it is not a point of very much importance, as the battle was fought largely at long range, where the number of men, provided there were plenty to handle the sails and guns, did not much matter.

The superiority of the Americans in long-gun metal was nearly as three is to two, and in carronade metal greater than two to one. The chief fault to be found in the various American accounts is that they sedulously conceal the comparative weight of metal, while carefully specifying the number of guns. Thus, Lossing says, "Barclay had 35 long guns to Perry's 15, and possessed greatly the advantage in action at a distance"; which he certainly did not. The tonnage of the fleets is not so very important. It is, I suppose, impossible to tell exactly the number of men in the two crews. Barclay almost certainly had more than the 440 men I have given him, but in all likelihood some of them were unfit for duty, and the number of his effectives was most probably somewhat less than Perry's. As the battle was fought in such smooth water, and part of the time at long range, this, as already said, does not much matter. The Niagara might be considered a match for the Detroit, and the Lawrence and Caledonia for the five other British vessels; so the Americans were certainly very greatly superior in force.

At daylight on September 10th Barclay's squadron was discovered in the northwest, and Perry at once got under weigh; the wind soon shifted to the northeast, giving us the weather-gage, the breeze being very light. Barclay lay to in a close column, heading to the southwest, in the following order: Chippeway, Master's Mate J. Campbell; Detroit, Captain R. H. Barclay; Hunter, Lieutenant G. Bignell; Queen Charlotte, Captain R. Linnis; Lady Prevost, Lieutenant Edward Buchan; and Little Belt, by whom commanded is not said. Perry came down with the wind on his port beam, and made the attack in column ahead, obliquely. First in order came the Ariel, Lieutenant John H. Packet; and Scorpion, Sailing-Master Stephen Champlin, both being on the weather bow of the Lawrence, Captain O. H. Perry; next came the Caledonia, Lieutenant Daniel Turner; Niagara, Captain Jesse D. Elliott; Somers, Lieutenant A. H. M. Conklin; Porcupine, Acting Master George Serrat; Tigress, Sailing-Master Thomas C. Almy, and Trippe, Lieutenant Thomas Holdup.[1]

[1] The accounts of the two commanders tally almost exactly. Barclay's letter is a model of its kind for candor and generosity. Letters of Capt. R. H. Barclay to Sir James Yeo, September 2, 1813; of Lieut. Inglis to Captain Barclay, September 10th; of Captain Perry to the Secretary of the Navy, September 10th and September 13th, and to Gen-

As, amid light and rather baffling winds, the American squadron approached the enemy, Perry's straggling line formed an angle of about fifteen degrees with the more compact one of his foes. At 11.45 the Detroit opened the action by a shot from her long 24, which fell short; at 11.50 she fired a second, which went crashing through the Lawrence, and was replied to by the Scorpion's long 32. At 11.55 the Lawrence, having shifted her port bow-chaser, opened with both the long 12's, and at meridian began with her carronades, but the shot from the latter all fell short. At the same time the action became general on both sides, though the rearmost American vessels were almost beyond the range of their own guns, and quite out of range of the guns of their antagonists. Meanwhile the Lawrence was already suffering considerably as she bore down on the enemy. It was twenty minutes before she succeeded in getting within good carronade range, and during that time the action at the head of the line was between the long guns of the Chippeway and Detroit, throwing 123 pounds, and those of the Scorpion, Ariel, and Lawrence, throwing 104 pounds. As the enemy's fire was directed almost exclusively at the Lawrence, she suffered a great deal.

The Caledonia, Niagara, and Somers were meanwhile engaging, at long range, the Hunter and Queen Charlotte, opposing from their long guns 96 pounds to the 39 pounds of their antagonists, while from a distance the three other American gun-vessels engaged the Prevost and Little Belt. By 12.20 the Lawrence had worked down to close quarters, and at 12.30 the action was going on with great fury between her and her antagonists, within canister range. The raw and inexperienced American crews committed the same fault the British so often fell into on the ocean, and overloaded their carronades. In consequence, that of the Scorpion upset down the hatchway in the middle of the action, and the sides of the Detroit were dotted with marks from shot that did not penetrate. One of the Ariel's long 12's also burst. Barclay fought the Detroit exceedingly well, her guns being most excellently aimed, though they actu-

eral Harrison, September 11th and September 13th. I have relied mainly on Lossing's *Field Book of the War of 1812;* on Commander Ward's *Naval Tactics*, page 76, and on Cooper's *Naval History*.

ally had to be discharged by flashing pistols at the touchholes, so deficient was the ship's equipment.

Meanwhile the Caledonia came down too, but the Niagara was wretchedly handled, Elliott keeping at a distance which prevented the use either of his carronades or of those of the Queen Charlotte, his antagonist; the latter, however, suffered greatly from the long guns of the opposing schooners, and lost her gallant commander, Captain Linnis, and first lieutenant, Mr. Stokes, who were killed early in the action. Her next in command, Provincial Lieutenant Irvine, perceiving that he could do no good, passed the Hunter and joined in the attack on the Lawrence, at close quarters. The Niagara, the most efficient and best manned of the American vessels, was thus almost kept out of the action by her captain's misconduct. At the end of the line, the fight went on at long range between the Somers, Tigress, Porcupine, and Trippe on one side, and Little Belt and Lady Prevost on the other; the Lady Prevost making a very noble fight, although her 12-pound carronades rendered her almost helpless against the long guns of the Americans. She was greatly cut up, her commander, Lieutenant Buchan, was dangerously, and her acting first lieutenant, Mr. Roulette, severely, wounded, and she began falling gradually to leeward.

The fighting at the head of the line was fierce and bloody to an extraordinary degree. The Scorpion, Ariel, Lawrence, and Caledonia, all of them handled with the most determined courage, were opposed to the Chippeway, Detroit, Queen Charlotte, and Hunter, which were fought to the full as bravely. At such close quarters the two sides engaged on about equal terms, the Americans being superior in weight of metal and inferior in number of men. But the Lawrence had received such damage in working down as to make the odds against Perry. On each side almost the whole fire was directed at the opposing large vessel or vessels; in consequence the Queen Charlotte was almost disabled, and the Detroit was also frightfully shattered, especially by the raking fire of the gunboats, her first lieutenant, Mr. Garland, being mortally wounded, and Captain Barclay so severely injured that he was obliged to quit the deck, leaving his ship in the command of Lieutenant George Inglis. But on board the Lawrence matters had gone even worse, the combined fire of her adversaries having made the grimmest carnage on her decks. Of the 103 men who were fit for duty when she began the action, 83, or over four-fifths, were killed or wounded. The vessel was shallow, and the wardroom, used as a cockpit to which the wounded were taken, was mostly above water, and the shot came through it continually, killing and wounding many men under the hands of the surgeon.

The first lieutenant, Yarnall, was three times wounded, but kept to the deck through all; the only other lieutenant on board, Brooks of the marines, was mortally wounded. Every brace and bowline was shot away, and the brig almost completely dismantled; her hull was shattered to pieces, many shot going completely through it, and the guns on the engaged side were by degrees all dismounted. Perry kept up the fight with splendid courage. As the crew fell one by one, the Captain called down through the skylight for one of the surgeon's assistants; and this call was repeated and obeyed till none was left; then he asked, "Can any of the wounded pull a rope?" and three or four of them crawled up on deck to lend a feeble hand in placing the last guns. Perry himself fired the last effective heavy gun, assisted only by the purser and the chaplain. A man who did not possess his indomitable spirit would then have struck. Instead, although failing in the attack so far, Perry merely determined to win by new methods, and remodelled the line accordingly.

Turner, in the Caledonia, when ordered to close, had put his helm up, run down on the opposing line, and engaged at very short range, though the brig was absolutely without quarters. The Niagara had thus become the next in line astern of the Lawrence, and the sloop Trippe, having passed the three schooners in front of her, was next ahead. The Niagara now, having a breeze, steered for the head of Barclay's line, passing over a quarter of a mile to windward of the Lawrence on her port beam. She was almost uninjured, having so far taken very little part in the combat, and to her Perry shifted his flag. Leaping into a rowboat, with his brother and four seamen, he rowed to the fresh brig, where he arrived at 2.30, and at once sent Elliott astern to hurry up the three schooners. The Trippe was now very near the Caledonia. The Lawrence, having but fourteen sound men left, struck her colors, but could not be taken possession of before the action recommenced. She drifted astern, the Caledonia passing between her and her foes. At 2.45, the schooners having closed up, Perry in his fresh vessel bore up to break Barclay's line.

The British ships had fought themselves to a standstill. The Lady Prevost was crippled and sagged to leeward, though ahead of the others. The Detroit and Queen Charlotte were so disabled that they could not effectually oppose fresh antagonists. There could thus be but little resistance to Perry, as the Niagara stood down and broke the British line, firing her port guns into the Chippeway, Little Belt, and Lady Prevost, and the starboard ones into the Detroit, Queen Charlotte, and Hunter, raking on both sides. Too disabled to tack, the Detroit and Charlotte tried to wear, the latter running up to leeward of the former; and, both vessels having every brace and almost every stay shot away, they fell foul. The Niagara luffed athwart their bows, within half-pistol-shot, keeping up a terrific discharge of great guns and musketry, while on the other side the British vessels were raked by the Caledonia and the schooners so closely that some of their grapeshot, passing over the foe, rattled through Perry's spars. Nothing further could be done, and Barclay's flag was struck at 3 P.M., after three and a quarter hours' most gallant and desperate fighting. The Chippeway and Little Belt tried to escape, but were overtaken and brought-to respectively by the Trippe and Scorpion, the commander of the latter, Mr. Stephen Champlin, firing the last, as he had the first shot of the battle. "Captain Perry has behaved in the most humane and attentive manner, not only to myself and officers, but to all the wounded," writes Captain Barclay.

The victory of Lake Erie was most important, both in its material results and in its moral effect. It gave us complete command of all the upper lakes, prevented any fears of invasion from that quarter, increased our prestige with the foe and our confidence in ourselves, and insured the conquest of Upper Canada; in all these respects its importance has not been over-rated. But the "glory" acquired by it most certainly *has* been estimated at more than its worth. Most Americans, even the well educated, if asked which was the most glorious victory of the war, would point to this battle. Captain Perry's name is more widely known than that of any other commander. Every schoolboy reads about *him*, if of no other sea captain; yet he certainly stands on a lower grade than either Hull or Macdonough, and not a bit higher than a dozen others. On Lake Erie our seamen displayed great courage and skill; but so did their antagonists. The simple truth is that, where on both sides the officers and men were equally brave and skilful, the side which possessed the superiority in force, in the proportion of three to two, could not well help winning. The courage with which the Lawrence was defended has hardly ever been surpassed and may fairly be called heroic; but equal praise belongs to the men on board the Detroit, who had to discharge the great guns by flashing pistols at the touchholes, and yet made such a terribly effective defence. Courage is only one of the many elements which go to make up the character of a first-class commander; something more than bravery is needed before a leader can be really called great.

There happened to be circumstances which rendered the bragging of our writers over the victory somewhat plausible. Thus they could say with an appearance of truth that the enemy had 63 guns to our 54, and outnumbered us. In reality, as well as can be ascertained from the conflicting evidence, he was inferior in number; but a few men more or less mattered nothing. Both sides had men enough to work the guns and handle the ships, especially as the fight was in smooth water and largely at long range. The important fact was that, though we had nine guns less, yet at a broadside they threw half as much metal again as those of our antagonist. With such odds in our favor it would have been a disgrace to have been beaten. The water was too smooth for our two brigs to show at their best; but this very smoothness rendered our gunboats more formidable than any of the British vessels, and the British testimony is unanimous that it was to them the defeat was primarily due.

The American fleet came into action in worse form than the hostile squadron, the ships straggling badly, either owing to Perry having formed his line badly or else to his having failed to train the subordinate commanders how to keep their places. The Niagara was not fought well at first, Captain Elliott keeping her at a distance that prevented her from doing any damage to the vessels opposed, which were battered to pieces by the gun-boats without the chance of replying. It certainly seems as if the small vessels at the rear of the line should have been closer up and in a position to render more effectual assistance; the attack was made in too loose order, and, whether it was the fault of Perry or of his subordinates, it fails to reflect credit on the Americans. Cooper as usual praises all concerned, but in this instance not with very good judgment. He says the line of battle was highly judicious, but this may be doubted. The weather was peculiarly suitable for the gunboats, with their long, heavy guns; and yet the line of battle was so arranged as to keep them in the rear and let the brunt of the assault fall on the Lawrence with her short carronades. Cooper again praises Perry for steer-ing for the head of the enemy's line, but he could hardly have done anything else.

In this battle the firing seems to have been equally skilful on both sides, the Detroit's long guns being peculiarly well served; but the British captains manœuvred better than their foes at first, and supported one another better, so that the disparity in damage done on each side was not equal to the disparity in force. The chief merit of the American commander and his followers was indomitable courage and determination to not be beaten. This is no slight merit; but it may well be doubted if it would have insured victory had Barclay's force been as strong as Perry's. Perry made a headlong attack; his superior force—whether through his fault or his misfortune can hardly be said—being brought into action in such a manner that the head of the line was crushed by the inferior force opposed. Being literally hammered out of his own ship, Perry brought up its powerful twin sister, and the already shattered hostile squadron was crushed by sheer weight. The manœuvres which marked the close of the battle, and which insured the capture of all the op-posing ships, were unquestionably very fine.

The British ships were fought as resolutely as their antago-nists, not being surrendered till they were crippled and helpless, and almost all the officers, and a large proportion of the men placed *hors de combat*. Captain Barclay handled his ships like a first-rate seaman. It was impossible to arrange them so as to be superior to his antagonist, for the latter's force was of such a nature that in smooth water his gunboats gave him a great advantage, while in any sea his two brigs were more than a match for the whole British squadron. In short our victory was due to our heavy metal.

As regards the honor of the affair, in spite of the amount of boasting it has given rise to, I should say it was a battle to be looked upon as in an equally high degree creditable to both sides. Indeed, if it were not for the fact that the victory was so complete, it might be said that the length of the contest and the trifling disparity in loss reflected rather the most credit on the British. Captain Perry showed indomitable pluck and readiness to adapt himself to circumstances; but his claim to fame rests much less on his actual victory than on the way in which he prepared the fleet that was to win it. Here his energy and activity deserve all praise, not only for his success in collecting sailors and vessels, and in building the two brigs, but above all for the manner in which he succeeded in getting them out on the lake. On *that* occasion he certainly outgeneralled Barclay; indeed, the latter committed an error that the skill and address he subsequently showed could not retrieve.

UPRISING OF GERMANY

BATTLE OF THE NATIONS AT LEIPSIC

A.D. 1813

WOLFGANG MENZEL

Any man but Napoleon would have been crushed by the extermination of his great army in Russia. The Prussians rose in eager passion against the remnants of French garrisons left among them. The Russian armies, strong, compact, and triumphant, advanced from their impregnable fastnesses. Sweden joined Russia and Prussia, and Austria threatened to do the same. In Spain Wellington defeated the weakened French forces at Vitoria. But Napoleon by tremendous efforts raised another army from almost exhausted France, and in the spring of 1813 reappeared in Germany, defiant and apparently unconquerable as ever. He even defeated the Russians and Prussians in two fierce battles.

But it was not merely the German princes who were fighting now; it was the German *people*, roused at last by the tyranny and arrogance of the French. When defeated, the Prussian armies no longer scattered and disappeared; they rallied and fought again, striving desperately with clubbed muskets. Napoleon arranged an armistice, his first sign of weakness. Austria joined the allies against him, and once more he confronted united Europe in the great " Battle of the Nations " at Leipsic.

THE King of Prussia had suddenly abandoned Berlin, which was still in the hands of the French, for Breslau, whence he declared war against France. A conference also took place between him and Emperor Alexander at Kalisch, and, on February 28, 1813, an offensive and defensive alliance was concluded between them. The hour for vengeance had at length arrived. The whole Prussian nation, eager to throw off the hated yoke of the foreigner, to obliterate their disgrace in 1806, to regain their ancient name, cheerfully hastened to place their lives and property at the service of the impoverished Government. The whole of the able-bodied population was put under arms. The standing army was increased: to each regiment were appended troops of volunteers, *jaegers*, composed of young men belonging to the

281

higher classes, who furnished their own equipments. A numerous *landwehr*, a sort of militia, was, as in Austria, raised besides the standing army, and measures were even taken to call out, in case of necessity, the heads of families and elderly men remaining at home, under the name of the *landsturm*.[1]

When news of these preparations reached Davoust he sent serious warning to Napoleon, who contemptuously replied, "Pah! Germans never can become Spaniards!" With his customary rapidity he levied in France a fresh army three hundred thousand strong, with which he so completely awed the Rhenish Confederation as to compel it to take the field once more with thousands of Germans against their brother-Germans. The troops, however, obeyed reluctantly, and even the traitors were but lukewarm, for they doubted of success. Mecklenburg alone sided with Prussia. Austria remained neutral.

A Russian corps under General Tettenborn had preceded the rest of the troops and reached the coasts of the Baltic. As early as March 24, 1813, it appeared in Hamburg and expelled the French authorities from the city. The heavily oppressed people of Hamburg, whose commerce had been totally annihilated by the Continental System, gave way to the utmost demonstrations of delight, received their deliverers with open arms, revived their ancient rights, and immediately raised a Hanseatic corps, destined to take the field against Napoleon. As the army advanced, Baron von Stein was nominated chief of the Provisional Government of the still unconquered provinces of Western Germany.

The first Russian army, seventeen thousand strong, under Wittgenstein, pushed forward to Magdeburg, and, at Moeckern, repulsed forty thousand French, who were advancing upon Berlin. The Prussians, under their veteran general, Blucher, entered Saxony and garrisoned Dresden, on March 27, 1813; an arch of the fine bridge across the Elbe having been uselessly blown up by the French. Blucher, whose gallantry in the former wars had gained for him the general esteem, and whose kind and generous disposition had won the affection of the soldiery, was nominated generalissimo of the Prussian forces, but subordinate in command to Wittgenstein, who replaced Kutusoff[2] as generalis-

---

[1] Literally, the general levy of the people.—ED.
[2] Kutusoff had recently died.—ED.

simo of the united forces of Russia and Prussia. The Emperor of Russia and the King of Prussia accompanied the army and were received with loud acclamations by the people of Dresden and Leipsic. The allied army was merely seventy thousand strong, and Blucher had not formed a junction with Wittgenstein when Napoleon invaded the country by Erfurt and Merseburg at the head of one hundred sixty thousand men.

On the eve of the bloody engagement of May 2d the allied cavalry attempted a general attack in the dark, which was unsuccessful on account of the superiority of the enemy's forces. The allies had, nevertheless, captured some cannon; the French, none. The most painful loss was that of the noble Scharnhorst, who was mortally wounded. Buelow had, on the same day, stormed Halle with a Prussian corps, but was now compelled to resolve upon a retreat, which was conducted in the most orderly manner by the allies. At Koldiz the Prussian rearguard repulsed the French van in a bloody engagement on May 5th.

Napoleon attacked the allies at Bautzen from May 19th to the 21st, but was gloriously repulsed by the Prussians under Kleist, while Blucher, who was in danger of being completely surrounded, undauntedly defended himself on three sides. The French had suffered an immense loss; eighteen thousand of their wounded were sent to Dresden. Napoleon's favorite, Marshal Duroc, and General Kirchner, a native of Alsace, were killed, close to his side, by a cannon-ball. The allied troops, forced to retire after an obstinate encounter, neither fled nor dispersed, but withdrew in close column and repelling each successive attack. The whole of the lowlands of Silesia now lay open to the French, who entered Breslau on June 1st.

Napoleon remained at Breslau awaiting the arrival of reënforcements, and to rest his unseasoned troops, mostly conscripts. In the mean time he demanded an armistice, to which the allies, whose force was still incomplete and to whom the decision of Austria was of equal importance, gladly assented. On this celebrated armistice, concluded June 4, 1813, at the village of Pleisswitz, the fate of Europe was to depend. Napoleon's power was still terrible; fresh victory had obliterated the disgrace of his flight from Russia; he stood once more an invincible leader on

German soil.   The French were animated by success and blindly
devoted to their Emperor.   Italy and Denmark were prostrate at
his feet.   The Rhenish Confederation was also faithful to his
standard.   The declaration of the Emperor of Austria in favor
of his son-in-law, Napoleon, who was lavish of promises, and,
among other things, offered to restore Silesia, was consequently,
at the opening of the armistice, deemed certain.

Austria, at first, instead of aiding the allies, allowed the Poles
to range themselves beneath the standard of Napoleon, whom she
overwhelmed with protestations of friendship, which served to
mask her real intentions, and meanwhile gave her time to arm
herself to the teeth and to make the allies sensible of the fact of
their utter impotency against Napoleon unless aided by her.   The
interests of Austria favored her alliance with France, but Napoleon, instead of confidence, inspired mistrust.   Austria, notwithstanding the marriage between him and Maria Louisa, was, as
had been shown at the Congress of Dresden, treated merely as a
tributary to France, and Napoleon's ambition offered no guarantee to the ancient imperial dynasty.   There was no security that
the provinces bestowed in momentary reward for her alliance
must not, on the first occasion, be restored.   Nor was public
opinion entirely without weight.   Napoleon's star was on the
wane, whole nations stood like to a dark and ominous cloud
threatening on the horizon, and Count Metternich prudently
chose rather to attempt to guide the storm ere it burst than trust
to a falling star.

Austria had, as early as June 27, 1813, signed a treaty, at
Reichenbach in Silesia, with Russia and Prussia, by which she
bound herself to declare war against France in case Napoleon
had not before July 20th accepted the terms of peace about to
be proposed to him.   Already the sovereigns and generals of Russia and Prussia had sketched—during a conference held with the
Crown Prince of Sweden, July 11th, at Trachenberg—the plan
for the approaching campaign, and, with the permission of Austria, assigned to her the part she was to take as one of the allies
against Napoleon, when Count Metternich visited Dresden, in
person, for the purpose of repeating his assurances of amity—for
the armistice had but just commenced—to Napoleon.

The French Emperor had an indistinct idea of the transac-

tions then passing, and bluntly said to the Count, "As you wish
to mediate, you are no longer on my side." He hoped partly to
win Austria over by redoubling his promises, partly to terrify her
by the dread of the future ascendency of Russia, but, perceiving
how Metternich evaded him by his artful diplomacy, he suddenly
asked, "Well, Metternich, how much has England given you in
order to engage you to play this part toward me?" This trait of
insolence toward an antagonist of whose superiority he felt conscious, and of the most deadly hatred masked by contempt, was
peculiarly characteristic of the Corsican, who, besides the qualities of the lion, fully possessed those of the cat. Napoleon let his
hat drop in order to see whether Metternich would raise it. He
did not, and war was resolved upon.

A pretended congress for the conclusion of peace was again
arranged by both sides; by Napoleon, in order to elude the re-
proach cast upon him of an insurmountable and eternal desire
for war, and by the allies, in order to prove to the whole world
their desire for peace. Each side was, however, fully aware that
the palm of peace was alone to be found on the other side of the
battlefield. Napoleon was generous in his concessions, but delayed granting full powers to his envoy, an opportune circumstance for the allies, who were by this means able to charge him
with the whole blame of procrastination. Napoleon, in all his
concessions, merely included Russia and Austria to the exclusion
of Prussia.

But neither Russia nor Austria trusted to his promises, and
the negotiations were broken off on the termination of the armistice, when Napoleon sent full powers to his plenipotentiary.
Now, it was said, it is too late! The art with which Metternich
passed from the alliance with Napoleon to neutrality, to mediation, and finally to the coalition against him, will, in every age, be
acknowledged a masterpiece of diplomacy. Austria, while co-
alescing with Russia and Prussia, in a certain degree assumed a
rank conventionally superior to both. The whole of the allied
armies was placed under the command of an Austrian general,
Prince von Schwarzenberg, and if the proclamation published at
Kalisch had merely summoned the people of Germany to assert
their independence, the manifesto of Count Metternich spoke
already in the tone of the future regulator of the affairs of Europe.

Austria declared herself on August 12, 1813, two days after the termination of the armistice.

Immediately after this—for all had been previously arranged —the monarchs of Russia and Prussia passed the Riesengebirge with a division of their forces into Bohemia, and joined the Emperor Francis and the great Austrian army at Prague. The celebrated general, Moreau, who had returned from America, where he had hitherto dwelt incognito, in order to take up arms against Napoleon, was in the train of the Czar. His example, it was hoped, would induce many of his countrymen to abandon Napoleon.

The plan of the allies was to advance with their main body, under Schwarzenberg, consisting of one hundred twenty thousand Austrians and seventy thousand Russians and Prussians, through the Erzgebirge to Napoleon's rear. A lesser Prussian force, principally Silesian landwehr, under Blucher, eighty thousand strong, besides a small Russian corps, was meanwhile to cover Silesia, or, in case of an attack by Napoleon's main body, to retire before it and draw it farther eastward. A third division, under the Crown Prince of Sweden, principally Swedes, with some Prussian troops, mostly Pomeranian and Brandenburg landwehr under Buelow, and some Russians, in all ninety thousand men, was destined to cover Berlin, and in case of a victory to form a junction in Napoleon's rear with the main body of the allied army. A still lesser and equally mixed division under Wallmoden, thirty thousand strong, was destined to watch Davoust in Hamburg, while an Austrian corps of twenty-five thousand men under Prince Reuss watched the movements of the Bavarians, and another Austrian force of forty thousand, under Hiller, those of the Viceroy, Eugene, in Italy.

Napoleon had concentrated his main body, that still consisted of two hundred fifty thousand men, in and around Dresden. Davoust received orders to advance with thirty thousand men from Hamburg upon Berlin; in Bavaria, there were thirty thousand men under Wrede; in Italy, forty thousand under Eugene. The German fortresses were, moreover, strongly garrisoned with French troops. Napoleon took up a defensive position with his main body at Dresden, whence he could watch the proceedings and take advantage of any indiscretion on the part of his opponents. A body of ninety thousand men under Oudinot meantime acted on the offensive, being directed to advance, simultaneously with Davoust from Hamburg and with Girard from Magdeburg, upon Berlin, and to take possession of that metropolis. Napoleon hoped, when master of the ancient Prussian provinces, to be able to suppress German enthusiasm at its source, and to induce Russia and Austria to conclude a separate peace at the expense of Prussia.

In August, 1813, the tempest of war broke loose on every side, and all Europe prepared for a decisive struggle. About this time, the whole of Northern Germany was visited for some weeks, as was the case on the defeat of Varus in the Teutoburg forest, with heavy rains and violent storms. The elements seemed to combine their efforts, as in Russia, with those of man against Napoleon. There his soldiers fell victims to frost and snow, here they sank into the boggy soil and were carried away by the swollen rivers. In the midst of the uproar of the elements, bloody engagements continually took place, in which the bayonet and the butt end of the firelock were used, the muskets being rendered unserviceable by the water.

The first engagement of importance was that of August 21st between Wallmoden and Davoust at Vellahn. A few days later, Karl Theodor Koerner, the youthful poet and hero, fell in a skirmish between the French and Wallmoden's outpost at Gadebusch. Oudinot advanced close upon Berlin, which was protected by the Crown Prince of Sweden. A murderous conflict took place, on August 23d, at Grossbeeren between the Prussian division under General von Buelow and the French. The Swedes, a troop of horse artillery alone excepted, were not brought into action, and the Prussians, unaided, repulsed the greatly superior forces of the French. The almost untrained peasantry comprising the landwehr of the Mark and of Pomerania rushed upon the enemy, and, unaccustomed to the use of the bayonet and firelock, beat down entire battalions of the French with the butt end of their muskets. After a frightful massacre, the French were utterly routed and fled in wild disorder, but the gallant Prussians vainly expected the Swedes to aid in the pursuit. The Crown Prince, partly from a desire to spare his troops and partly from a feeling of shame—he was also a Frenchman—remained motionless. Oudinot, nevertheless, lost two thousand four hundred, taken prisoner. Davoust, from this disaster, returned once more to Hamburg. Girard, who had advanced with eight thousand men from Magdeburg, was, on the 27th, put to flight by the Prussian landwehr under General Hirschfeld.

Napoleon's plan of attack against Prussia had completely failed, and his sole alternative was to act on the defensive. But on perceiving that the main body of the allied forces under Schwarzenberg was advancing to his rear, while Blucher was stationed with merely a weak division in Silesia, he took the field with immensely superior forces against the latter, under an idea of being able easily to vanquish his weak antagonist and to fall back again in time upon Dresden. Blucher cautiously retired, but, unable to restrain the martial spirit of the soldiery, who obstinately defended every position whence they were driven, lost two thousand of his men on August 21st.

Napoleon had pursued Blucher as far as the Katzbach near Goldberg, when he returned and boldly resolved to cross the Elbe above Dresden, to seize the passes of the Bohemian mountains, and to fall upon the rear of the main body of the allied army. Vandamme's *corps d'armée* had already set forward with this design, when Napoleon learned that Dresden could no longer hold out unless he returned thither with a division of his army, and, in order to preserve that city and the centre of his position, he hastily returned thither in the hope of defeating the allied army and of bringing it between two fires, as Vandamme must meanwhile have occupied the narrow outlets of the Erzgebirge with thirty thousand men and by that means cut off the retreat of the allied army.

The plan was on a grand scale, and, as far as related to Napoleon in person, was executed, to the extreme discomfiture of the allies, with his usual success. Schwarzenberg, with true Austrian procrastination, had allowed August 25th to pass in inaction, when, as the French themselves confess, Dresden, in her then ill-defended state, might have been taken almost without a stroke. When he attempted to storm the city on the 26th, Napoleon, who had meanwhile arrived, calmly awaited the onset of the thick masses of the enemy in order to open a murderous discharge of grape upon them on every side. They were repulsed after suffering a frightful loss. On the following day, destined to end in still more terrible bloodshed, Napoleon assumed the offensive, separated the retiring allied army by well-combined sallies, cut off its left wing, and made an immense number of prisoners, chiefly Austrians. The unfortunate Moreau had both his legs shot off in the very first encounter. His death was an act of justice, for he had taken up arms against his fellow-countrymen.

The main body of the allied army retreated on every side; part of the troops disbanded, the rest were exposed to extreme hardship owing to the torrents of rain that fell without intermission, and the scarcity of provisions. Their annihilation must have inevitably followed had Vandamme executed Napoleon's commands and blocked up the mountain passes, in which he was unsuccessful, being defeated and, with his whole division, taken prisoner near Culm (August 29, 1813).

On August 26th a signal victory was gained by Blucher in Silesia. After having drawn Macdonald across the Katzbach and the foaming Neisse, he drove him, after a desperate and bloody engagement, into those rivers, which were greatly swollen by the incessant rains. The muskets of the soldiery had been rendered unserviceable by the wet, and Blucher, drawing his sabre from beneath his cloak, dashed forward exclaiming, "Forward!" Several thousand of the French were drowned or fell by the bayonet, or beneath the heavy blows dealt by the landwehr with the butt ends of their firelocks. Blucher was rewarded with the title of Prince von der Wahlstadt, but his soldiers surnamed him Marshal "Vorwaerts" (Forward). The French lost one hundred three guns, eighteen thousand prisoners, and a still greater number in killed; the loss on the side of the Prussians amounted to one thousand men. Macdonald returned almost totally unattended to Dresden and brought the melancholy intelligence to Napoleon.

The Crown Prince of Sweden and Buelow had meanwhile pursued Oudinot's retreating corps in the direction of the Elbe. Napoleon despatched Ney against them, but he met with the fate of his predecessor, at Dennewitz, on September 6th. The Prussians, on this occasion, again triumphed, unaided by their confederates. Buelow and Tauenzien, with twenty thousand men, defeated the French army, seventy thousand strong. The French

lost eighteen thousand men and eighty guns. The rout was complete. The rear-guard, consisting of the Wurtembergers under
Franquemont, was again overtaken at the head of the bridge at
Zwittau, and, after a frightful carnage, driven in wild confusion
across the dam to Torgau.

Napoleon's generals had been thrown back in every quarter,
with immense loss, upon Dresden, toward which the allies now
advanced, threatening to enclose it on every side. Napoleon
manœuvred until the beginning of October with the view of executing a *coup de main* against Schwarzenberg and Blucher; the
allies were, however, on their guard, and he was constantly reduced to the necessity of recalling his troops, sent for that purpose into the field, to Dresden. The danger in which he now
stood of being completely surrounded and cut off from the Rhine
at length rendered retreat his sole alternative. Blucher had already crossed the Elbe on October 5th, and, in conjunction with
the Crown Prince of Sweden, had approached the head of the
main body of the allied army under Schwarzenberg, which was
advancing from the Erzgebirge.

On October 7th Napoleon quitted Dresden, leaving a garrison of thirty thousand French under St. Cyr, and removed his
headquarters to Duben, on the road leading from Leipsic to Berlin, in the hope of drawing Blucher and the Swedes once more on
the right side of the Elbe, in which case he intended to turn unexpectedly upon the Austrians; Blucher, however, eluded him,
without quitting the left bank. Napoleon's plan was to take advantage of the absence of Blucher and of the Swedes from Berlin
in order to hasten across the defenceless country, for the purpose
of inflicting punishment upon Prussia, of raising Poland, etc.
But his plan met with opposition in his own military council.
His ill success had caused those who had hitherto followed his
fortunes to waver. The King of Bavaria declared against him
on October 8th, and the Bavarian army under Wrede united
with, instead of opposing, the Austrian army, and was sent to the
Maine in order to cut off Napoleon's retreat. The news of this
defection speedily reached the French camp and caused the rest
of the troops of the Rhenish Confederation to waver in their
allegiance; while the French, wearied with useless manœuvres,
beaten in every quarter, opposed by an enemy greatly their supe-

rior in number and glowing with revenge, despaired of the event and sighed for peace and their quiet homes. All refused to march upon Berlin, nay, the very idea of removing farther from Paris almost produced a mutiny in the camp.

Four days, from October 11th to the 14th, were passed by Napoleon in a state of melancholy irresolution, when he appeared as if suddenly inspired by the idea of there still being time to execute a *coup de main* upon the main body of the allied army under Schwarzenberg before its junction with Blucher and the Swedes. Schwarzenberg was slowly advancing from Bohemia and had already allowed himself to be defeated before Dresden. Napoleon intended to fall upon him on his arrival in the vicinity of Leipsic, but it was already too late—Blucher was at hand. On October 14th[1] the flower of the French cavalry, headed by the King of Naples, encountered Blucher's and Wittgenstein's cavalry at Wachau, not far from Leipsic. The contest was broken off, both sides being desirous of husbanding their strength, but terminated to the disadvantage of the French notwithstanding their numerical superiority, besides proving the vicinity of the Prussians. This was the most important cavalry fight that took place during this war.

On October 16th, while Napoleon was merely awaiting the arrival of Macdonald's corps, that had remained behind, before proceeding to attack Schwarzenberg's Bohemian army, he was unexpectedly attacked on the right bank of the Pleisse, at Liebertwolkwitz, by the Austrians, who were, however, compelled to retire before a superior force. The French cavalry under Latour-Mauborg pressed so closely upon the Emperor of Russia and the King of Prussia that they merely owed their escape to the gallantry of the Russian, Orloff Denisoff, and to Latour's fall. Napoleon had already ordered all the bells in Leipsic to be rung, had sent the news of his victory to Paris, and seems to have expected a complete triumph when joyfully exclaiming, "*Le monde tourne pour nous!*" ("The world [everything] changes for us!")

But his victory had been only partial, and he had been unable

---

[1] On the evening of October 14th (the anniversary of the Battle of Jena) a hurricane raged in the neighborhood of Leipsic, where the French lay, carrying away roofs and uprooting trees, while, during the whole night, the rain fell in torrents.

to follow up his advantage, another division of the Austrian army, under General Meerveldt, having simultaneously occupied him and compelled him to cross the Pleisse at Dolnitz; and, although Meerveldt had been in his turn repulsed with severe loss and been himself taken prisoner, the diversion proved of service to the Austrians by keeping Napoleon in check until the arrival of Blucher, who threw himself upon the division of the French army opposed to him at Moeckern by Marshal Marmont. Napoleon, while thus occupied with the Austrians, was unable to meet the attack of the Prussians with sufficient force. Marmont, after a massacre of some hours' duration in and around Moeckern, was compelled to retire with the loss of forty guns. The second Prussian brigade lost, either in killed or wounded, all its officers except one.

The battle had, on October 16th, raged around Leipsic; Napoleon had triumphed over the Austrians, whom he had solely intended to attack, but had, at the same time, been attacked and defeated by the Prussians, and now found himself opposed and almost surrounded by the whole allied force—one road for retreat alone remaining open. He instantly gave orders to General Bertrand to occupy Weissenfels during the night, in order to secure his retreat through Thuringia; but, during the following day, October 17th, he neither seized that opportunity to retreat nor to make a last attack upon the allies—whose forces were not yet completely concentrated—ere the circle had been fully drawn around him. The Swedes, the Russians under Bennigsen, and a large Austrian division under Colloredo had not yet arrived.

Napoleon might with advantage have again attacked the defeated Austrians under Schwarzenberg or have thrown himself with the whole of his forces upon Blucher. He had still an opportunity of making an orderly retreat without any great exposure to danger. But he did neither. He remained motionless during the whole day, which was also passed in tranquillity by the allies, who thus gained time to receive fresh reënforcements. Napoleon's inactivity was caused by his having sent his prisoner, General Meerveldt, to the Emperor of Austria, whom he still hoped to induce, by means of great assurances, to secede from the coalition and to make peace. Not even a reply was vouchsafed. On the very day, thus futilely lost by Napoleon, the allied army was reintegrated by the arrival of the masses commanded by the Crown Prince, by Bennigsen and Colloredo, and was consequently raised to double the strength of that of France, which now merely amounted to one hundred fifty thousand men.

On the 18th a murderous conflict began on both sides. Napoleon long and skilfully opposed the fierce onset of the allied troops, but was at length driven off the field by their superior weight and persevering efforts. The Austrians, stationed on the left wing of the allied army, were opposed by Oudinot, Augereau, and Poniatowsky; the Prussians, stationed on the right wing, by Marmont and Ney; the Russians and Swedes in the centre, by Murat and Regnier. In the hottest of the battle two Saxon cavalry regiments went over to Blucher, and General Normann, when about to be charged at Taucha by the Prussian cavalry under Buelow, also deserted to him with two Wurtemberg cavalry regiments, in order to avoid an unpleasant reminiscence of the treacherous ill-treatment of Luetzow's corps. The whole of the Saxon infantry, commanded by Regnier, shortly afterward went, with thirty-eight guns, over to the Swedes, five hundred men and General Zeschau alone remaining true to Napoleon. The Saxons stationed themselves behind the lines of the allies, but their guns were instantly turned upon the enemy.

In the evening of this terrible day the French were driven back close upon the walls of Leipsic.[1] On the certainty of victory being announced by Schwarzenberg to the three monarchs, who had watched the progress of the battle, they knelt on the open field and returned thanks to God. Napoleon, before nightfall, gave orders for full retreat; but, on the morning of the 19th, recommenced the battle and sacrificed some of his *corps d'armée* in order to save the remainder. He had, however, foolishly left but one bridge across the Elster open, and the retreat was consequently retarded. Leipsic was stormed by the Prussians, and, while the French rear-guard was still battling on that side of the bridge, Napoleon fled, and had no sooner crossed the bridge than it was blown up with a tremendous explosion, owing to the inad-

[1] The city was in a state of utter confusion. The noise caused by the passage of the cavalry, carriages, etc., and by the cries of the fugitives through the streets exceeded that of the most terrific storm. The earth shook, the windows clattered with the thunder of artillery.

vertence of a subaltern, who is said to have fired the train too hastily.

The troops engaged on the opposite bank were irremediably lost. Prince Poniatowsky plunged on horseback into the Elster in order to swim across, but sank in the deep mud. The King of Saxony, who to the last had remained true to Napoleon, was among the prisoners. The loss during this battle, which raged for four days, and in which almost every nation in Europe stood opposed to each other, was immense on both sides. The total loss in dead was computed at eighty thousand. The French lost, moreover, three hundred guns and a multitude of prisoners— in the city of Leipsic alone twenty-three thousand sick, without reckoning the innumerable wounded. Numbers of these unfortunates lay bleeding and starving to death during the cold October nights on the field of battle, it being found impossible to erect a sufficient number of *lazaretti* for their accommodation.

Napoleon made a hasty and disorderly retreat with the remainder of his troops, but was overtaken at Freiburg on the Unstrut, where the bridge broke and a repetition of the disastrous passage of the Beresina occurred. The fugitives collected into a dense mass, upon which the Prussian artillery played with murderous effect. The French lost forty of their guns. At Hanau, Wrede, Napoleon's former favorite, after taking Wuerzburg, watched the movements of his ancient patron, and, had he occupied the pass at Gelnhausen, might have annihilated him. Napoleon, however, furiously charged his flank, and, on October 20th, succeeded in forcing a passage and in sending seventy thousand men across the Rhine.

Wrede was dangerously wounded. On November 9th the last French corps was defeated at Hochheim and driven back upon Mainz. In the November of this ever memorable year, 1813, Germany, as far as the Rhine, was completely freed from the French.

THE BURNING OF WASHINGTON

A.D. 1814

RICHARD HILDRETH   GEORGE R. GLEIG

This event, while it had no decisive result, stands out prominently in the history of the War of 1812. Washington was selected as the site of the United States capital in 1790, and ten years later the Government was removed from Philadelphia to its new seat, where at the period of the war it occupied public buildings which, if not all of great importance in themselves, were yet sufficient for governmental purposes. The destruction of some of them by the British, of which two accounts follow—one by a candid American historian, the other that of a British officer (Gleig) who took part in the affair—proved to be but an incident in the development of those architectural features which now form a chief attraction of the national capital.

In 1814 the war had entered upon a stage requiring increased defensive measures on the part of the United States Government. There were threats of attack upon New York and the Chesapeake, as well as upon Washington. President Madison ordered the militia of the States to be ready for instant service, and a new military district, including Maryland, the District of Columbia, and a part of Northern Virginia, was erected.

General W. H. Winder, a tried officer, lately released from long detention in Canada as a prisoner of war, took command of the district in June. The defences of Washington were very weak—no forts nor guns, and only a few hundred men. Such additional preparations as could be made were wholly inadequate. Meanwhile the British were marshalling their forces for a movement against the capital.

THE forces assigned to Winder, on taking the command of his new military district, were some fragments of regulars, less than 500, mostly raw recruits in and about Washington, including the garrison of the fort of that name below Alexandria; the militia of the District of Columbia, some 2000 strong; and an authority, in case of actual or menaced invasion, to call upon the State of Maryland for 6000 militia, the whole of her lately assigned quota, upon Virginia for 2000, and upon Pennsylvania for 5000. Winder proposed to call out at once a part of this militia, and to place them in a central camp, whence they might march to Washington, Annapolis, or Baltimore, either of which might be approached so near by water as to be liable to be struck at before a force could be collected. The President seemed inclined to this plan, but it was opposed by Armstrong, who objected to it that militia were always the most effective when first called out. Baltimore, he thought, could defend itself; Washington he did not believe would be attacked.

Calls for militia were freely made to garrison Buffalo and Sackett's Harbor, and thereby to sustain Brown's invasion of Canada, but Armstrong hesitated at the additional expense of the calls proposed by Winder; and, in the existing state of the finances, not without reason. Of the loan of twenty-five million dollars, sole resource for conducting the campaign, the Government had yet asked for but ten million. This amount had been subscribed at the former rate of 88 per cent., not without difficulty, and a condition, as to half of it, that the contractors should participate in any more favorable terms granted to any future lenders. Even on these terms there had been failures of payment by the contractors to the extent of two million dollars, so that Armstrong's hesitation on the score of expense is not so remarkable. Winder, being thus left to his own responsibility, and cautioned besides to avoid unnecessary calls for militia, of course made none till the emergency became unquestionable. Nor was this reluctance of Armstrong the only difficulty. The Governor of Maryland, on receiving the President's proclamation, hesitated, at this moment of danger, to ask volunteers from the eastern shore. He doubted if, under the militia law of the State, a draft would be effectual, and the War Department finally agreed to accept, in lieu of the quota to be detached by Maryland, the troops already called out by the State authority for the defence of Baltimore, thus reducing the quota of that State to less than three thousand men.

The Governor of Virginia had already ordered twenty regiments of militia to hold themselves in constant readiness for the field; and a correspondence backward and forward, as to whether these orders did not substantially meet the proclamation, consumed the time which ought to have been employed in having the quota ready to march. The Legislature of Pennsylvania, at their last session, had passed an act for the reorganization of the militia, which vacated all existing commissions after August 1st, but, strange to say, without any provision for completing the proposed reorganization before the end of October; thus leaving the State for two months without any legal militia at all, and rendering it impossible to make the detachment which the President had ordered.

So things stood when news reached Washington that a new and large British fleet had arrived in the Chesapeake. This was Cochrane, from Bermuda, with General Ross on board, and a division, some four thousand strong, of Wellington's late army. To this fleet Cockburn's blockading squadron soon joined itself, adding to Ross's force a thousand marines, and a hundred armed and disciplined negroes, deserters from the plantations bordering on the Chesapeake. As the ships passed the Potomac some of the frigates entered that river, but the main fleet, some sixty vessels in all, stood on for the Patuxent, which they ascended to Benedict, where the frith begins to narrow. There, some fifty miles from Washington, the troops were landed without a sign of opposition, though there were several detachments of Maryland militia, under State orders, at points not far distant. As Ross had no horses, his men, some four thousand five hundred in all, were organized into a light infantry corps. Three pieces of light artillery were dragged along by a hundred sailors. As many more transported munitions. The soldiers carried at their backs eighty rounds of ammunition and three days' provisions.

Enervated as the troops had been by the close confinement of the voyage, and wilting under the burning sun of that season, it was with difficulty, at first, that they staggered along. Nothing but the constant efforts of their officers prevented them from dissolving into a long train of stragglers. The felling of a few trees, where the road crossed the frequent streams and swamps, would have seriously delayed, if not effectually have stopped, them. But in that part of Maryland, a level region of cornfields and pine forests, the slave population exceeded the whites, and the frightened planters thought of little except to save their own throats from insurgent knives, and their human property from English seduction.

In the slaves the British had good friends and sure means of information. With the trained negroes in front, they advanced cautiously, the first day only six miles, but still without encountering the slightest opposition, feeling their way up the left bank of the Patuxent—a route which threatened Barney's squadron in front, Alexandria and Washington on the left, and Annapolis and Baltimore on the right. Cockburn accompanied the army, and from his dashing, buccaneering spirit, and long experience in that neighborhood, became the soul of the enterprise.

At the first alarm of the appearance of the British fleet, Winder had sent off his requisitions for militia; but, even had the quotas of Virginia and Pennsylvania been embodied and ready to march, and had the swiftest expresses been employed instead of the slow course of the mail, it was already too late for effectual aid from that quarter. The District militia, summoned to arms, marched to a point some eight miles east of Washington, where they were joined by the regulars, who fell back from a more advanced position which they had occupied for some time at Marlborough.

As the British column, on the third day of its uninterrupted advance, approached Barney's flotilla, the boats, agreeably to an order from Armstrong, were blown up, Barney himself hastening with his men, some five hundred in number, to Winder's camp, where some pieces of heavy artillery from the navy-yard were placed under his command. That camp presented a scene of noise and confusion more like a racecourse or a fair than the gathering of an army about to fight for the national capital. About midnight, the President, with Armstrong, Jones of the Navy Department, and Rush, the Attorney-General, arrived. Monroe was there already; Campbell, the Secretary of the Treasury, was busy with contrivances for replenishing the exhausted finances, proposals having been made out that very day for a loan of six million dollars, of the getting of which there was, however, but very little prospect.

The President, full of doubts and alarms, and disturbed by a thousand contradictory rumors, reviewed, the next morning, an army of three thousand two hundred men, with seventeen pieces of artillery, but as doubtful, hesitating, and consciously incapable as himself. Shortly after, Winder departed to reconnoitre; from the length of his absence it was feared that he had fallen into the hands of the enemy, but toward evening he returned, and, dreading a night attack, which was probable, as the British, now but a few miles off, had struck into the Alexandria road, as if to gain his right, he ordered a retreat.

This was made in great haste and disorder, by the bridges over the Eastern Branch, his troops encamping near the navy-yard, where they received the alarming news that the enemy's ships in the Potomac had already passed the shoals by which their ascent had been stopped the year before. That same night some six hundred Virginia militia reached Washington, but without arms or accoutrements, which Armstrong told the commanding officer it would be time enough to serve out the next morning. About four hundred fifty other Virginia militia, stationed on the Maryland side of the Potomac, opposite Alexandria, as a covering party for Fort Washington, remained there, distracted by contradictory orders, and taking no part in the general movement.

Meanwhile another force had mustered for the defence of the capital. Stansbury's brigade of Maryland drafted militia, fourteen hundred strong, marching from the neighborhood of Baltimore, had encamped the previous evening, just in advance of Bladensburg, six miles north of Washington; and the next day, while the President was reviewing the District army, they were joined by a regiment esteemed the flower of the Baltimore city militia, by some companies of artillery, and by a battalion of city riflemen, led by Pinckney, the late minister to London. This Maryland army amounted to some two thousand one hundred men; but the city part, that most relied upon, had little experience in field service, having suddenly changed the comforts of their homes for the bare ground and rations of bad salt beef and musty flour, which they did not even know how to cook.

Stansbury's forces had already once turned out on a false alarm, when, about two in the morning, he received information from Winder of his (Winder's) retreat, and orders to fight should the enemy, as was probable, approach Washington in that direction. A council of war, immediately summoned, not pleased with the idea of being thus put forward to encounter ten thousand British veterans—for to that number report had by this time swelled the enemy—began to retire over Bladensburg bridge; and, but for new orders from Winder to stop, and, if the enemy approached by Bladensburg, to fight, the retreat, it is probable, would have continued to Washington.

In the morning, Winder still remaining uncertain what direction the British might take, the President repaired to the navy-yard, where a consultation was had as to the best means of destroying the public property there. Monroe and Rush spent the forenoon in riding to and fro between Washington and Bladensburg. Armstrong remained quietly at the war office, not even yet able to believe that the enemy would venture an attack. But, toward noon authentic information came that the British, who had encamped the previous night near the ground lately occupied by Winder, were marching on Bladensburg. Winder thereupon put his forces in motion, except the newly arrived Virginians left behind to complete their equipments, which a very careful clerk still delayed by scrupulously counting out their flints one by one. Barney was to have remained to superintend the blowing up of the bridges over the Eastern Branch, but his remonstrances finally extorted from the President, after a consultation with the heads of departments, all of whom were present on horseback, liberty to march with his guns for the field.

Campbell moodily retired, having first lent the President his duelling pistols—the same, probably, with which a few years before, in a quarrel about the embargo, he had shot Gardinier through the body on the very ground of the approaching battle. With the provision of ways and means on his hands, he had, indeed, a sufficiently arduous task of his own, without aiding in military movements. Armstrong, by permission of the President, on Campbell's suggestion that his military knowledge might be of use there, had already ridden to the field. The President, Monroe, and Rush, who soon followed, were prevented only by an accidental piece of information from riding straight into Bladensburg, where the enemy had already arrived. The President, on reaching the field, revoking the permission lately given, directed Armstrong to leave to the commanding general the array of the battle.

The Eastern Branch of the Potomac, deep enough opposite Washington to float a frigate, dwindles at Bladensburg to a shallow stream. A few houses occupy the eastern bank. Stansbury, abandoning the village and the bridge, had posted his men on an

eminence on the Washington side of the river, with his right on
the Washington road, in which were planted two pieces of artillery, to sweep the bridge. Pinckney's riflemen lined the bushes
which skirted the river-bank. The Baltimore regiment had been
originally posted nearest the bridge, but, by Monroe's orders, who
rode up just before the battle began, they were thrown back behind an orchard, leaving Stansbury's drafted men to stand the
first brunt of attack. As Winder reached the front, other military amateurs were busy in giving their advice, the enemy's column just then beginning to show itself on the opposite bank.
Another Maryland regiment, which had marched that morning
from Annapolis, but by a route which avoided the British army,
appeared just at this moment on the field, and occupied a commanding eminence. The forces from Washington, as they arrived, were drawn up in the rear of the Maryland line. Barney,
with his sailors, and Miller, of the marines, arrived last, and
planted four heavy guns in a position to sweep the road, with the
advantage, also, of being flanked by the Annapolis regiment.

The British soldiers, by the time they reached Bladensburg,
were almost ready to drop, so excessive was the heat; and so
formidable was the appearance of the American army that Ross
and his officers, reconnoitring from one of the highest houses of
the village, were not a little uneasy as to the result. But it was
now too late to hesitate. The British column, again in motion
after a momentary check, dashed across the bridge. Some dis-
charges of Congreve rockets put the Maryland drafted militia
to flight. They were followed by the riflemen, Pinckney getting
a broken arm in the tumult, and by the artillerymen, whose pieces
had scarcely been twice discharged; and as the British came up,
the Baltimore regiment fled also, sweeping off with them General
Winder, the President, and the Cabinet officers. Encouraged by
this easy victory, the enemy pushed rapidly forward, till Barney's artillery opened upon them with severe effect. After several
vain efforts, during which many fell, to advance in face of this
fire, advantage was taken of the shelter of a ravine to file off by
the right and left. Those who emerged on the left encountered
the Annapolis regiment, which fled after a single fire. Those on
the right fell in with some detachments of regulars, forming an
advanced portion of the second line. They retired with equal

promptitude, as did the militia behind them; and the enemy having thus gained both flanks, the sailors and marines were obliged to fly, leaving their guns and their wounded commanders in the enemy's hands.

Such was the famous Battle of Bladensburg, in which very few Americans had the honor to be either killed or wounded, not more than fifty in all; and yet, according to the evidence subsequently given before a Congressional committee of investigation, everybody behaved with wonderful courage and coolness, and nobody retired except by orders or for want of orders. The British loss was a good deal larger, principally in the attack on the sailors and marines. Several had dropped dead with heat and fatigue; and the whole force was so completely exhausted that it was necessary to allow them some hours' rest before advancing on Washington.

The Maryland militia, as they fled, dispersed in every direction, and soon ceased to exist as an embodied force. The District militia kept more together; the Virginians had at last obtained their flints; and Winder had still at his command some two thousand men and several pieces of artillery. Two miles from Washington a momentary stand was made, but the retreating troops soon fell back to the Capitol. Armstrong wished to occupy the two massive, detached wings of that building (the central rotunda and porticos having not then been built), and to play the part of the British in Chew's house[1] at the Battle of Germantown. But, if able to withstand an assault, how long could they hold out without provisions or water? It was finally decided to abandon Washington, and to rally on the heights of Georgetown. Simultaneously with this abandonment of their homes by an army that retired but did not rally, fire was put at the navy-yard to a frigate on the stocks, to a sloop-of-war lately launched, and to several magazines of stores and provisions, for the destruction of which ample preparations had been made; and by the light of this fire, made lurid by a sudden thunderbolt, Ross, toward evening, advanced into Washington, then a straggling village of some eight thousand people, but, for the moment, almost deserted by the male part of the white inhabitants.

[1] The British during the action occupied the Chew house as a fortress, and its stone walls still show the marks left by American shot.—ED.

From Gallatin's late residence, one of the first considerable houses which the British column passed, a shot was fired which killed Ross's horse, and which was instantly revenged by setting fire to the house. After three or four British volleys at the Capitol, the two detached wings were set on fire. The massive walls defied the flames, but all the interior was destroyed, with many valuable papers, and the library of Congress—a piece of vandalism alleged to be in revenge for the burning of the Parliament House at York. An encampment was formed on Capitol Hill; but meanwhile a detachment marched along Pennsylvania Avenue to the President's house, of which the great hall had been converted into a military magazine, and before which some cannon had been placed. These cannon, however, had been carried off, and Mrs. Madison, having first stripped from its frame and provided for the safety of a valuable portrait of Washington, which ornamented the principal room, had also fled, with her plate and valuables loaded into a cart, obtained not without difficulty.

The President's house, and the offices of the Treasury and State Departments near by, were set on fire, Ross and Cockburn, who had forced themselves as unbidden guests upon a neighboring boarding-house woman, supping by the light of the blazing buildings. By the precaution of Monroe, the most valuable papers of the State Department had been previously removed; yet here, too, some important records were destroyed. The next morning the War Office was burned. The office of the *National Intelligencer* was ransacked, and the type thrown into the street, Cockburn himself presiding with gusto over this operation, thus revenging himself for the severe strictures of that journal on his proceedings in the Chesapeake. The arsenal at Greenleaf's Point was also fired, as were some rope-walks near by.

Several private houses were burned, and some private warehouses broken open and plundered; but, in general, private property was respected, the plundering being less on the part of the British soldiers than of the low inhabitants, black and white, who took advantage of the terror and confusion to help themselves. The only public building that escaped was the General Post Office and Patent Office, both under the same roof, of which the burning was delayed by the entreaties and remonstrances of the superintendent, and finally prevented by a tremendous tornado which passed over the city and for a while completely dispersed the British column, the soldiers seeking refuge where they could, and several being buried in the ruins of the falling buildings.

A still more serious accident at Greenleaf's Point, where near a hundred British soldiers were killed or wounded by an accidental explosion, added to the anxiety of the British commander, otherwise ill enough at ease. He naturally imagined, though as it happened without any occasion for it, that an army of indignant citizen-soldiers was mustering on the heights of Georgetown. An attack was also apprehended from the south, to guard against which the Washington end of the Potomac bridge was set on fire by the British, while at the same moment a like precaution was taken at the Alexandria end to keep them from crossing. No news came of the British ships in the Potomac, which Ross anxiously expected; and that same night, leaving his severely wounded behind, and his camp-fires burning, he silently retired, and, after a four days' uninterrupted march, arrived again at Benedict, where the troops were reëmbarked, diminished, however, by a loss in killed, wounded, and deserters of several hundred men. Yet while Ross, on his part, thus stealthily withdrew, so great was the terror which he left behind him that some sixty British invalids, left in charge of the wounded, continued in undisturbed possession of Capitol Hill for more than twenty-four hours after his departure, till at last the citizens mustered courage to disarm them.

GEORGE R. GLEIG

While the two brigades which had been engaged at Bladensburg remained upon the field to recover their order, the third, which formed the reserve, and was consequently unbroken, took the lead, and pushed forward at a rapid rate toward Washington. As it was not the intention of the British Government to attempt permanent conquest in this part of America, and as General Ross was well aware that with a handful of men he could not pretend to establish himself for any length of time in the enemy's capital, he determined to lay it under contribution and to return quietly to the shipping. Nor was there anything unworthy of the character of a British officer in this determination. By all the customs of war, whatever public property may chance to be in a captured town becomes confessedly the just spoil of the conqueror; and in thus proposing to accept a certain sum of money in lieu of that property, he was showing mercy rather than severity to the vanquished.

Such being the intention of General Ross, he did not march the troops immediately into the city, but halted them upon a plain in its vicinity while a flag of truce was sent in with terms. But whatever his proposal might have been, it was not so much as heard; for scarcely had the party bearing the flag entered the street than they were fired upon from the windows of one of the houses, and the horse of the General himself, who accompanied them, killed. All thoughts of accommodation were instantly laid aside; the troops advanced forthwith into the town, and having first put to the sword all who were found in the house from which the shots were fired, and reduced it to ashes, they proceeded without a moment's delay to burn and destroy everything in the most distant degree connected with the Government.

In this general devastation were included the Senate House, the President's official residence, an extensive dockyard and arsenal, barracks for two or three thousand men, several large storehouses filled with naval and military stores, some hundreds of cannon of different kinds, and nearly twenty thousand stand of small arms. There were also two or three public rope-works which shared in the same fate; a fine frigate, pierced for sixty guns, and just ready to be launched; several gun-brigs and armed schooners, with a variety of gunboats and small craft. The powder-magazines were of course set on fire, and exploded with a tremendous crash, throwing down many houses in their vicinity, partly by pieces of the walls striking them and partly by the concussion of the air; while quantities of shot, shell, and hand-grenades, which could not otherwise be rendered useless, were thrown into the river.

All this was as it should be; and had the arm of vengeance been extended no further there would not have been room given for so much as a whisper of disapprobation. But unfortunately it did not stop here. A noble library, several printing-offices, and all the public archives were likewise committed to the flames, which, though undoubtedly the property of the Government, might better have been spared.

I need scarcely observe that the consternation of the inhabitants was complete and that to them this was a night of terror. So confident had they been in the success of their troops that few of them had dreamed of quitting their houses or abandoning the city. Nor was it till the fugitives from the battle began to rush in that the President himself thought of providing for his safety. That gentleman, as I was informed, had gone forth in the morning with the army, and had continued among his troops till the British forces began to make their appearance. Having ridden through the ranks and exhorted every man to do his duty, he hurried back to his own house, that he might prepare a feast for the entertainment of his officers when they should return victorious. For the truth of this I will not be answerable; but this much I know, that the feast was actually prepared, though, instead of being eaten by American officers, it went to satisfy the less delicate appetites of a party of English soldiers.

When the detachment sent out to destroy President Madison's house entered his dining-parlor, they found a dinner-table spread and covers laid for forty guests. Several kinds of wine, in handsome cut-glass decanters, were cooling on the sideboard; plate-holders stood by the fireplace, filled with dishes and plates; knives, forks, and spoons were arranged for immediate use. In short, everything was ready for the entertainment of a ceremonious party. Such were the arrangements in the dining-room, while in the kitchen were others answerable to them in every respect. Spits, loaded with joints of various sorts, turned before the fire; pots, saucepans, and other ordinary utensils, upon the grate; and all the other requisites for an elegant and substantial repast were exactly in a state which indicated that they had been lately and precipitately abandoned. It may be readily imagined that these preparations were beheld by a party of hungry soldiers with no indifferent eyes. An elegant dinner, even though considerably overdressed, was a luxury to which few of them, at least for some time back, had been accustomed, and which after the dangers and fatigues of the day, appeared peculiarly inviting. They sat down to it, therefore, not indeed in the most orderly manner, but with countenances which would not have

disgraced a party of aldermen at a civil feast; and having satisfied their appetites and partaken pretty freely of the wines,
they finished by setting fire to the house which had so liberally
entertained them.

But as I have observed, this was a night of dismay to the inhabitants of Washington. They were taken completely by surprise; nor could the arrival of the Flood be more unexpected to
the natives of the antediluvian world than the arrival of the British army to them. The first impulse, of course, tempted them to
fly, and the streets were in consequence crowded with soldiers
and Senators, men, women, and children; horses, carriages, and
carts loaded with household furniture, all hastening toward a
wooden bridge which crosses the Potomac. The confusion thus
occasioned was terrible, and the crowd upon the bridge was such
as to endanger its safety. But President Madison, having escaped among the first, was no sooner safe on the opposite bank
of the river than he gave orders that the bridge should be broken
down; which being obeyed, the rest were obliged to return and
to trust to the clemency of the victors.

In this manner was the night passed by both parties, and at
daybreak the next morning the light brigade moved into the city,
while the reserve fell back to a height about half a mile in the rear.
Little, however, now remained to be done, because everything
marked out for destruction was already consumed. Of the Senate House, the President's mansion, the barracks, the dockyard,
etc., nothing could be seen except heaps of smoking ruins; and
even the bridge, a noble structure upward of a mile in length, was
almost wholly demolished. There was, therefore, no further occasion to scatter the troops, and they were accordingly kept together as much as possible on Capitol Hill. But it was not alone
on account of the completion of their destructive labors that this
was done. A powerful army of Americans already began to
show themselves upon some heights at the distance of two or
three miles from the city; and as they sent out detachments of
horse even to the very suburbs, for the purpose of watching our
motions, it would have been unsafe to permit more straggling
than was absolutely necessary. The army which we had overthrown on the day before, though defeated, was far from annihilated, and having by this time recovered from its panic, began to

concentrate itself in our front, and presented quite as formidable an appearance as ever. We learned also that it was joined by a considerable force from the back settlements, which had arrived too late to take part in the action, and the report was that both combined amounted to nearly twelve thousand men.

Whether or not it was their intention to attack, I cannot pretend to say, because it was noon before they showed themselves; and soon after, when something like a movement could be discerned, the sky grew suddenly dark, and the most tremendous hurricane ever remembered by the oldest inhabitants of the place came on. When the hurricane had blown over, the camp of the Americans appeared to be in as great a state of confusion as our own, nor could either party recover themselves sufficiently during the rest of the day to try the fortune of a battle. Of this General Ross did not fail to take advantage. He had already attained all that he could hope, and perhaps more than he originally expected to attain; consequently, to risk another action would only be to spill blood for no purpose. Whatever might be the issue of the contest, he could derive from it no advantage. If he were victorious, it would not destroy the necessity which existed for evacuating Washington; if defeated, his ruin was certain. To avoid fighting was therefore his object; and perhaps he owed its accomplishment to the fortunate occurrence of the storm. Be that, however, as it may, a retreat was resolved upon; and we now only waited for night to put the resolution into practice.

As soon as darkness had come on, the Third Brigade, which was posted in the rear of our army, began its retreat. Then followed the guns; afterward the Second, and last of all the Light Brigade; exactly reversing the order which had been maintained during the advance. It being a matter of great importance to deceive the enemy, and to prevent pursuit, the rear of the column did not quit its ground upon the Capitol Hill till a late hour. During the day an order had been issued that none of the inhabitants should be seen in the streets after eight o'clock; and as fear renders most men obedient, this order was punctually attended to. All the horses belonging to different officers had likewise been removed to drag the guns, nor was anyone allowed to ride, lest a neigh or even the trampling of hoofs should excite suspicion. The fires were trimmed and made to blaze bright, and fuel was left to keep them many hours; and finally, about half past nine o'clock, the troops formed in marching order and moved off in the most profound silence. Not a word was spoken nor a single individual permitted to step one inch out of his place; and thus they passed along the streets perfectly unnoticed, and cleared the town without any alarm being given.

THE CONGRESS OF VIENNA

A.D. 1814

HENRY M. STEPHENS

This famous Congress was a sequel of the wars of Napoleon, and its decrees had a most important effect in determining the character of a new epoch in European history. Napoleon never recovered his ascendency in Europe after the Battle of Leipsic (October 16-19, 1813), in which he was overthrown by the great alliance of nations. On March 31, 1814, the allies entered Paris. Napoleon was compelled to abdicate (April 11th), and was banished to the island of Elba.

The Bourbons, having promised a constitutional government, were recalled, and with Louis XVIII began the ascendency of the Legitimist party in France. But Louis returned to the odious ways of the ancient monarchy. His constitution failed to satisfy the people, and, such as it was, Louis violated it, to the indignation of the French, many of whom, including the army, welcomed the return of Napoleon, who expelled Louis in March, 1815.

Meanwhile, soon after the capture of Paris, representatives of the great powers met at the Congress of Vienna, for the purpose of settling European affairs. The original object was to restore the map of Europe as it was before the Napoleonic wars. The Congress (September, 1814, to June, 1815) at first could make no headway, owing to the conflicting interests presented; but when Napoleon renewed the war in 1815, the powers saw that they must come to an agreement. The decisions finally adopted by the Congress remained effective among the signatory powers for more than forty years.

ON November 1, 1814, the diplomatists who were to resettle Europe as arranged by the definitive Treaty of Paris (May, 1814), met at Vienna. But many of the monarchs most concerned felt that they could not give their entire confidence to any diplomat, however faithful or distinguished, and they therefore came to Vienna in person to support their views. The final decision of disputes obviously lay in the hands of the four powers (England, Russia, Prussia, and Austria) which by their union had conquered Napoleon. These four powers solemnly agreed to act in harmony and to prepare all questions privately and then lay them before the Congress. In fact, they intended to impose their will upon the smaller states of Europe just as Napoleon had done. That they did not succeed and that their concert was broken were due to the extraordinary ability of Talleyrand, the first French plenipotentiary. The history of the Congress is the history of Talleyrand's skilful diplomacy, and the resettlement of Europe which it effected was therefore largely the work of France.

Emperor Francis of Austria acted as host to his illustrious guests. The royalties present were Emperor Alexander of Russia, with the Empress; the Grand Duke Constantine, and his sisters the Grand Duchesses Marie of Saxe-Weimar, and Catherine of Oldenburg; the King of Prussia, with his nephew Prince William; the King and Queen of Bavaria; the King and Crown Prince of Wurtemberg; the King of Denmark; the Prince of Orange; the Grand Dukes of Baden, Saxe-Weimar, and Hesse-Cassel; the Dukes of Brunswick, Nassau, and Saxe-Coburg. The King of Saxony was a prisoner of war and absent.

The plenipotentiaries of Russia were Count Razumovski, Count von Stackelberg, and Count Nesselrode, who were assisted by Stein, the former Prussian minister and one of Alexander's most trusted advisers; by Pozzo di Borgo, the Corsican, now appointed Russian ambassador to Paris; by Count Capo d'Istria, the future President of Greece; by Prince Adam Czartoryski, one of the most patriotic Poles; and by some of the most famous Russian generals, such as Chernishev and Wolkonski. The Austrian plenipotentiaries were Prince Metternich, the State Chancellor; the Baron von Wessenberg-Ampfingen; and Friedrich von Gentz, who was appointed to act as secretary to the Congress.

England was represented by Lord Castlereagh, Lord Cathcart, Lord Clancarty, and Lord Stewart, Castlereagh's brother, who as Sir Charles Stewart had played so great a part in the negotiations in 1813, and who had been created a peer for his services. The English plenipotentiaries were also aided by Count von Hardenberg and Count von Muenster, who were deputed to represent the Hanoverian interests. The Prussian plenipotentiaries were Prince von Hardenberg, the State Chancellor, and William von Humboldt, who in military matters were advised by General von Knesebeck. The French representatives, whose part was to be so important, were Talleyrand, Prince of Benevento; the Duc de Dalberg, nephew of the Prince Primate; the Marquis de la Tour du Pin, and the Comte Alexis de Noailles. These were the representatives of the great powers.

Among the representatives of the lesser powers may be noted, from the importance of their action, Cardinal Consalvi, who represented the Pope (Pius VII), the Count of Labrador for Spain, Count Palmella for Portugal, Count Bernstorf for Denmark, Count Loewenhielm for Sweden, the Marquis de Saint-Marsan for Sardinia, the Duke di Campo-Chiaro for Murat, King of Naples; Ruffo for Ferdinand, King of the Two Sicilies; Prince von Wrede for Bavaria, Count Wintzingerode for Wurtemberg, and Count von Schulemburg for Saxony. In addition to these representing powers of the first and second rank, were innumerable representatives of petty principalities, deputies for the free cities of Germany, and even agents for petty German princes mediatized by Napoleon in 1806.

When Talleyrand with the French legation arrived in Vienna he found, as has been said, that the four great powers had formed a close union in order to control the Congress. His first step, therefore, was to set France forth as the champion of the second-rate states of Europe. The Count of Labrador, the Spanish representative, strongly resented the conduct of the great powers in pretending to arrange matters, as they called it, for the Congress. Talleyrand skilfully made use of Labrador, and, through him and Palmella, Bernstorf and Loewenhielm managed to upset the preconcerted ideas of the four allies, and insisted on every matter being brought before the Congress as a whole, and being prepared by small committees specially selected for that purpose. His next step was to sow dissension among the great powers. As the champion of the smaller states he had already made France of considerable importance, and he then claimed that she, too, had a right to be treated as a great power and not as an enemy. His argument was that Europe had fought Napoleon and not France; that Louis XVIII was the legitimate monarch of France; and that any disrespect shown to him or his ambassadors would recoil on the heads of all other legitimate monarchs. He claimed that France had as much right to make her voice heard in the resettlement of Europe as any other country, because the allied monarchs had distinctly recognized that she was only to be thrust back into her former limits and not to be expunged from the map of Europe.

Having made his claim good on the right of legitimacy of his master to speak for France as a great power equal in all respects to the others, he proceeded to sow dissension among the representatives of the four allied monarchs. This was not a difficult thing to do, for the seeds of dissension had long existed. The difference he introduced was that in speaking as a fifth great power, and as the champion of the smaller states, France became the arbiter in the chief questions before the Congress.

The division between the great powers was caused by the desire of Russia and Prussia for the aggrandizement of their territories. The Emperor Alexander wished to receive the whole of Poland. His idea, which was inspired by his friend, Prince Adam Czartoryski, was to form Poland into an independent kingdom, ruled, however, by himself as emperor of Russia. The Poles were to have a new constitution based on that propounded in 1791, and the Czar of Russia was to be also King of Poland, just as in former days the electors of Saxony had been kings of Poland, but he was to be a hereditary, not an elected, sovereign. To form once more a united Poland, Austria and Prussia were to surrender their gains in the three partitions of Poland. Austria was to receive compensation for her loss of Galicia in Italy; Prussia was to be compensated for the loss of Prussian Poland, by receiving the whole of Saxony. As it had been already arranged that Prussia was to receive the bulk of the Rhenish territory on the left bank of the Rhine in addition to her great extensions of 1803, the result would be to make Prussia by far the greatest power in Germany.

Talleyrand was acute enough to perceive that Lord Castlereagh did not approve of the extension of the influence of Russia, and that Metternich was equally indisposed to allow Prussia to obtain such a wholesale aggrandizement. Saxony had been the faithful ally of France to the very last, and Talleyrand felt that it would be an indelible stain on the French name if it were thus sacrificed. He was cordially supported in this view by his new master, for though the King of Saxony had been the faithful ally of Napoleon, Louis XVIII did not forget that his own mother was a Saxon princess. Working, therefore, on the feelings of Castlereagh and Metternich, he induced England and Austria to declare against the scheme of Russia and Prussia.

The Emperor Alexander and Frederick William blustered loudly; they declared that they were in actual military possession of Poland and of Saxony, and that they would hold those states by force of arms against all comers. In answer, Talleyrand, Castlereagh, and Metternich signed a treaty of mutual alliance between France, England, and Austria, on January 3, 1815. By this secret treaty the three powers bound themselves to resist by arms the schemes of Russia and Prussia, and in the face of their determined opposition the Emperor Alexander gave way. Immediately Napoleon returned from Elba he found the draft treaty between the three powers on the table of Louis XVIII and at once sent it to Alexander. That monarch, confronted with the danger threatened by Napoleon's landing in France, contented himself with showing the draft to Metternich and then threw it in the fire. The whole of this strange story is of the utmost interest; it proves not only the ability of Talleyrand, but the inherent strength of France. It is most significant that within a few months after the occupation of Paris by the allies for the first time France should again be recognized as a great power and form the main factor in breaking up the cohesion of the alliance which had been formed against her.

The result of Talleyrand's skilful policy was thus to unite England, Austria, and France, supported by many of these secondary states, such as Bavaria and Spain, against the pretensions of Prussia and Russia. Powerful armies were immediately set on foot. France in particular raised her military forces from one hundred thirty thousand to two hundred thousand men, and her new army was in every way superior to that with which Napoleon had fought his defensive campaigns in 1814, for it contained the veteran soldiers who had been blockaded in the distant fortresses or had been prisoners of war. England too was enabled to make adequate preparations, for on December 24, 1814, a treaty had been signed at Ghent between the United States and England which put an end to the war which had been proceeding ever since 1812 on account of England's naval pretensions.

Bavaria also promised to put in the field thirty thousand men for every one hundred thousand supplied by Austria.

The determined attitude of the opposition caused the Emperor Alexander to give way. It was decided that instead of the whole of Saxony, Prussia should only receive the district of Lusatia, including the towns of Torgau and Wittenberg, a territory which embraced half the area of Saxony and one-third of its population. The King of Saxony, who had been treated as a prisoner of war, and whom the Emperor of Russia had even threatened to send to Siberia, was released from captivity, and induced by the Duke of Wellington, who succeeded Lord Castlereagh as English plenipotentiary in February, 1815, to agree to these terms. The salvation of Saxony was a matter of great gratification to Louis XVIII, who remembered that though the King had been the faithful ally of Napoleon, he was also his own near relative.

Since Prussia was obliged to give up the whole of her claim to Saxony, Russia also had to withdraw from her scheme of uniting the whole of Poland. Nevertheless, Russia retained the lion's share of the grand duchy of Warsaw; in 1774 her frontier had reached the Dwina and the Dnieper; in 1793 she obtained half of Lithuania and touched the Niemen and the Bug; in 1809 Napoleon had granted her the territory containing the sources of the Bug; and now in 1815 her borders crossed the Vistula, and by the annexation of the grand duchy of Warsaw, including that city, penetrated for some distance between Eastern Prussia and Galicia. Prussia received back its share of the two first partitions of Poland, with the addition of the province of Posen and the city of Thorn, but lost Warsaw and its share in the last partition; while Austria received Cracow, which was to be administered as a free city. Alexander was deeply disappointed by the frustration of his Polish schemes, but he nevertheless kept his promise to Prince Adam Czartoryski and granted a representative constitution and a measure of independence to Russian Poland.

Though the great diplomatic struggle arose over the combined question of Saxony and Poland, the most important work of the Congress was not confined to it alone. Committees were appointed to make new arrangements for Germany, Switzerland, Italy, and to settle other miscellaneous questions. Of these committees the most important was that which reorganized Germany. It had been arranged by the secret articles of the Treaty of Paris that a Germanic Confederation should take the place of the Holy Roman Empire. The example of Napoleon in his institution of the Confederation of the Rhine was followed and developed. Instead of the hundreds of small states which had existed at the commencement of the French Revolution, Germany, apart from Austria and Prussia, was organized into only thirty-eight states. These were the four kingdoms of Hanover, Bavaria, Wurtemberg, and Saxony; the seven grand duchies of Baden, Oldenburg, Mecklenburg-Schwerin, Mecklenburg-Strelitz, Hesse-Cassel, Hesse-Darmstadt, and Saxe-Weimar; the nine duchies of Nassau, Brunswick, Saxe-Gotha, Saxe-Coburg, Saxe-Meiningen, Saxe-Hildburghausen, Anhalt-Dessau, Anhalt-Bernburg, and Anhalt-Koethen; eleven principalities; two of Schwarzburg, two of Hohenzollern, two of Lippe, two of Reuss, Hesse-Homburg, Lichtenstein, and Waldeck; and the four free cities of Hamburg, Frankfort, Bremen, and Lubeck. The number of thirty-eight was made up by the duchies of Holstein and Lauenburg, belonging to the King of Denmark, and the grand duchy of Luxemburg, granted to the King of the Netherlands. In its organization the Germanic Confederation resembled the Confederation of the Rhine. The Diet of the Confederation was to be always presided over by Austria and was to consist of two chambers. The Ordinary Assembly was composed of seventeen members, one for each of the larger states, one for free cities combined, one for Brunswick, one for Nassau, one for the four duchies of Saxony united, one for the three duchies of Anhalt united, and one for the smaller principalities. This Assembly was to sit permanently at Frankfort and to settle all ordinary matters. In addition there was to be a General Assembly to be summoned intermittently for important subjects, consisting of sixty-nine members returned by the different states in proportion to their size and population. Each state was to be supreme in internal matters, but private wars against each other were forbidden as well as external wars by individual states on powers outside the limits of the Confederacy. In the territorial arrangements of the new Confederation, the most important point is the disappearance of all ecclesiastical states. The prince-primacy, which Napoleon had established in his Confederation of the Rhine, was not maintained, and Dalberg, who had filled that office throughout the empire, was restricted to his ecclesiastical functions.

The most difficult problem to be decided was the final disposition of the districts on the left bank of the Rhine, which had been ruled by France ever since 1794. It had been settled by the secret articles at Paris that these dominions should be used for the establishment of strong powers upon the borders of France. The main difficulty was as to the disposition of the important border fortresses of Mayence and Luxemburg. Prussia laid claim to both these places, but was strongly resisted by Austria, France, and the smaller states of Germany. It was eventually resolved that Prussia should receive the northern territory on the left bank of the Rhine, from Elten to Coblentz, including Duesseldorf and Cologne, Treves, and Aix-la-Chapelle.

In compensation for the Tyrol and Salzburg, which she was forced to return to Austria, and in recognition of her former sovereignty in the Palatinate, Bavaria was granted a district from the Prussian borders to Alsace, including Mayence, which was designated Rhenish Bavaria. Finally Luxemburg was formed into a grand duchy, and given as a German state to the house of Orange. It was not united to the new kingdom of the Netherlands, which was formed out of Holland and Belgium, but was to retain its independence under the sovereignty of the King of the Netherlands. The union of the provinces of the Netherlands was one of the favorite schemes of England, and was carried into effect in spite of the well-known feeling of opposition between the Catholic provinces of Belgium and the Protestant provinces of Holland.

As in its reorganization of Germany, so in the settlement of Switzerland, the Congress of Vienna followed the example set by Napoleon. The Emperor had quite given up the idea which had fascinated the French Directory of forming Switzerland into a republic, one and indivisible. He had yielded to the wishes of the Swiss people themselves, and organized them on the basis of a confederation of independent cantons. The Congress of

Vienna continued Napoleon's policy of forbidding the existence
of subject cantons in spite of the protests of the Canton of Bern.
Napoleon's cantons of Argau, Thurgau, St. Gall, the Grisons,
the Ticino, and the Pays de Vaud were maintained, but the
number of the cantons was raised from nineteen to twenty-two by
the formation of the three new cantons of Geneva, the Valais,
and Neuchâtel, which had formed part of the French empire.
The Canton of Bern received in reply to its importunities the
greater part of the former bishopric of Basel. The Swiss Confederation as thus constituted was placed under the guarantee
of the great powers and declared neutral forever. The Helvetic
Constitution, which was promulgated by a Federal act dated
April 17, 1815, was not quite so liberal as Napoleon's constitution.

Greater independence was secured in that the constitutions
of the separate cantons and organic reforms in them had not to
be submitted to the Federal Diet. The prohibition against internal custom-houses was removed. The presidency of the Diet
was reserved to Zurich, Bern, and Lucerne alternately, and the
Helvetic Diet became a congress of delegates like the Germanic
Diet rather than a legislative assembly. It is to be noted that in
spite of the declaration of the Congress of Vienna, Prussia refused to renounce her claims on her former territory of Neuchâtel, the independence of which as a Swiss canton was not
recognized by her until 1857.

The resettlement of Italy presented more than one special
problem. The most difficult of these to solve was caused by the
engagements entered into by the allies with Murat in 1814. Talleyrand, on behalf of the King of France, insisted on the de-
thronement and expulsion of Murat, while Metternich, from
friendship for Caroline Murat, wished to retain him in his kingdom. The Emperor Alexander, who ever prided himself on his
fidelity to his engagements, wished to protect Murat, and had
at Vienna struck up a warm friendship with Eugène de Beau-
harnais, Napoleon's Viceroy of Italy. Murat, ungrateful though
he was personally toward Napoleon, had yet imbibed his master's ideas in favor of the unity and independence of Italy. During the campaign of 1814 he had led his army to the banks of
the Po, and he persisted in remaining there after the Congress

of Vienna had met. But the diplomatists at Vienna had no wish to accept the great idea of Italian unity. Murat's aspirations in this direction were most annoying to them, and it was with real pleasure that they heard, after the landing of Napoleon from Elba, that Murat had by an indiscreet proclamation given them an excuse for an open declaration of war.

The Duke di Campo-Chiaro, Murat's representative at Vienna, had kept him informed of the differences between the allied powers, and an indiscreet note asking whether he was to be considered as at peace or at war with the house of Bourbon gave the plenipotentiaries their opportunity. War was immediately declared against him; an Austrian army defeated him at Tolentino on May 3, 1815, and he was forced to fly from Italy. The acceptance of Murat's ambassador, who spoke in his name as King of the Two Sicilies, made it difficult for the Congress to know how to treat with Ruffo, who had been sent as ambassador by Ferdinand, the Bourbon King of the Two Sicilies, who had maintained his power in the island of Sicily through the presence of the English garrison. Acting on the ground of legitimacy, it was difficult to reject Ferdinand's claims, which were warmly supported by France and Spain, but Murat's ill-considered behavior solved the difficulty, and after his defeat Ferdinand was recognized as King of the Two Sicilies. Murat, later in the year, landed in his former dominions, but he was taken prisoner and promptly shot.

Another Italian question which presented considerable difficulty was the disposal of Genoa and the surrounding territory. When Lord William Bentinck occupied that city, he had in the name of England promised it independence and even hinted at the unity of Italy. Castlereagh unfortunately felt it to be his duty to disavow Bentinck's declaration, and Genoa was united to Piedmont as part of the kingdom of Sardinia. The third difficult question was the creation of a state for the Empress Marie Louise. An independent sovereignty had been promised to her. She was naturally supported by her father, the Emperor Francis of Austria, and was ably represented at Vienna by her future husband, Count Neipperg. It was eventually resolved that she should receive the duchies of Parma, Piacenza, and Guastalla, but the succession was not secured to her son, the King of Rome, but was granted to the rightful heir, the King of Etruria, who, until the succession fell in, was to rule at Lucca. The other arrangements in Italy were comparatively simple. Austria received the whole of Venetia and Lombardy, in the place of Mantua and the Milanese, which she had possessed before 1789. The grand duchy of Tuscany, with the principality of Piombino, was restored to the Grand Duke Ferdinand, the uncle of the Emperor Francis of Austria, with the eventual succession to the duchy of Lucca. The Pope received back his dominions, including the legations of Bologna and Ferrara, and Duke Francis, the grandson of Hercules III, was recognized as Duke of Modena, to which duchy he would have succeeded had not Napoleon absorbed it in his kingdom of Italy. The arrangements with regard to the other states of Europe made at the Congress of Vienna were comparatively unimportant and did not present the same difficult problems as the resettlement of Germany, Switzerland, and Italy. Norway, in spite of its disinclination, was definitely ceded to Sweden, but Bernadotte had to restore to France the West Indian island of Guadelupe, which had been handed over to him by England in 1813 as part of the price of his alliance. Denmark had by the Treaty of Kiel with Bernadotte been promised Swedish Pomerania in the place of Norway. This promise was not kept. Denmark, like Saxony, had been too faithful an ally of Napoleon not to be made to suffer. Swedish Pomerania was given to Prussia, and Denmark received only the small duchy of Lauenburg. By these arrangements both Sweden and Denmark were greatly weakened, and the Scandinavian states, by the loss of Finland and Pomerania, surrendered to their powerful neighbors, Prussia and Russia, the command of the Baltic Sea.

Spain, owing to the ability of the Count of Labrador and the support of Talleyrand, not only lost nothing except the island of Trinidad, which had been conquered by England, but was allowed to retain the district round Olivenza, which had been ceded to her by Portugal in 1801. The desertion of Portugal by England in this particular is the chief blot on Lord Castlereagh's policy at Vienna. The Portuguese army had fought gallantly with Wellington, and there was no reason why she should have been forced to consent to the definite cession of Olivenza to

THE CONGRESS OF VIENNA

THE CONGRESS OF VIENNA 321
Spain when other countries were winning back their former
borders. Portugal was also made to surrender French Guiana
and Cayenne to France. England, though she had borne the
chief pecuniary stress of the war—had been more instrumental
than any other power in overthrowing Napoleon—received less
compensation than any other country. She kept Malta, thus
settling the question which led to the rupture of the Peace of
Amiens; she received Heligoland, which was ceded to her by
Denmark, as commanding the mouth of the Elbe, and she was
also granted the protectorate of the Ionian Islands, which enabled her to close the Adriatic.

Among colonial possessions England took from France the
Mauritius, Tobago, and St. Lucia, but she returned Martinique
and the Isle of Bourbon, and forced Sweden and Portugal to
restore Guadelupe and French Guiana. With regard to Holland, England retained Ceylon and the Cape of Good Hope,
but she restored Java, Curaçao, and the other Dutch possessions.
In the West Indies, also, she retained, as has been said, the
former Spanish island of Trinidad.

One reason for Castlereagh's moderation at Vienna is to be
found in the pressure that was exerted upon him in England to
secure the abolition of the slave trade. It is a curious fact that
while the English plenipotentiary was taking such an important
share in the resettlement of Europe, the English people were
mainly interested in the question of the slave trade. The great
changes which were leading to new combinations in Europe, the
aggrandizement of Prussia, the reconstitution of Germany, the
extension of Austria, all passed without notice, but meetings, in
Lord Castlereagh's own words, were held in nearly every village
to insist upon his exerting his authority to abolish the trade in
negro slaves. Castlereagh, therefore, lent his best efforts, in
obedience to his constituents, to this end.

The other ambassadors could not understand why he troubled so much about what seemed to them a trivial matter. They
suspected a deep design, and thought that the reason of England's humanity was that her West Indian colonies were well
stocked with negroes, whereas the islands she was restoring were
empty of them. The plenipotentiaries of other powers possessing colonies in the tropics therefore refused to comply with Cas-

tlereagh's request, and it was eventually settled that the slave trade should be abolished by France after five and by Spain after eight years. Castlereagh had to be content with this concession, but to satisfy his English constituents he got a declaration condemning the slave trade assented to by all the powers at the Congress. Another point of great importance which was settled at the Congress of Vienna was with regard to the navigation of rivers which flow through more than one state. It had been the custom for all the petty sovereigns to impose such very heavy tolls on river traffic that such rivers as the Rhine were made practically useless for commerce. This question was discussed by a committee at the Congress, and a code for the international regulation of rivers was drawn up and generally agreed to.

These matters took long to discuss, and might have taken longer had not the news arrived at the beginning of March, 1815, that Napoleon had left Elba and become once more undisputed ruler of France. In the month of February the Duke of Wellington had succeeded Lord Castlereagh as English representative at Vienna, for the latter nobleman had to return to London to take his place in Parliament. At the news of the striking event of Napoleon's being once more at the head of a French army all jealousies at Vienna ceased for a time. The Duke of Wellington was taken into consultation by the allied monarchs, and it was resolved to carry into effect the provisions of the Treaty of Chaumont. The great armies which had been prepared for a struggle among themselves were now turned by the allies against France. A treaty of alliance was signed at Vienna between Austria, Russia, Prussia, and England on March 25, 1815, by which those powers promised to furnish one hundred eighty thousand men each for the prosecution of war, and stipulated that none of them should lay down arms until the power of Napoleon was completely destroyed. It was arranged that three armies should invade France: the first of two hundred fifty thousand Austrians, Russians, and Bavarians under Schwarzenburg across the Upper Rhine; the second of one hundred fifty thousand Prussians under Blucher across the Lower Rhine; and the third of one hundred fifty thousand English, Hanoverians, and Dutch from the Netherlands. Subsidies to the extent of eleven millions of pounds were promised by England to the allies. These arrangements made, the allied monarchs and their ministers left Vienna. But the final general act of the Congress was not drawn up and signed until June 8, 1815, ten days before the Battle of Waterloo.

The final overthrow of Napoleon and his exile to St. Helena allowed the new system for the government of Europe as laid down by the Congress of Vienna to be tried. That system may be roughly designated as the system of the Great Powers. Before 1789, certain states, such as France and England and Spain, were, from fortuitous circumstances or the course of their history, larger, more united, and therefore more fitted for war than others, but the greater part of the Continent was split up into small, and in the case of Germany into very small, states. Several of these small states, such as Sweden and Holland, had at different times exercised a very considerable influence, and the policy of Frederick the Great had added another to them, in the military state of Prussia. At the Congress of Vienna the tendency was to diminish the number and power of the secondary states and to destroy minute sovereignties. Sweden and Denmark were relegated to the rank of third-rate powers; the petty principalities of Germany were built up into third-rate states. Austria and Prussia were established as great powers, but the increase of their territory brought with it dissimilar results. Prussia became the preponderant state of Germany, while Austria, whose imperial house had so long held the title of Holy Roman Emperor, became less German, and now depended for its strength on its Italian, Magyar, and Slavonic provinces. The irruption of Russia into the European comity of nations was another significant feature. By its annexation of the greater part of the grand duchy of Warsaw, Russia thrust itself between Prussia and Austria territorially, while its leading share in the overthrow of Napoleon made its place as a European power unassailable. It may be doubted if the policy of Peter the Great and the Empress Catherine was thus carried out. The tendency of those rulers was to make the Baltic and the Black Sea Russian lakes, and to build up an empire of the East; affairs in Central Europe interested them only in so far as they prevented interference with their Eastern designs, and did not lead to the erection of powerful states on the Russian border.

Nothing is more remarkable in the settlement of Europe by

the Congress of Vienna than the entire neglect of the principle of nationality. Yet it was the sentiment of national patriotism which had enabled France to repulse Europe in arms, and had trained the soldiers with whom Napoleon had given the law to the Continent and had overthrown the mercenary armies of his opponents. It was the principle of nationality which had crippled Napoleon's finest armies in Spain, and which had produced his expulsion from Russia. It was the feeling of intense national patriotism which had made the Prussian army of 1813, and enabled Prussia after its deepest humiliation to take rank as a first-class power. But the diplomatists at Vienna treated the idea as without force. They had not learned the great lesson of the French Revolution, that the first result of rousing a national consciousness of political liberty is to create a spirit of national patriotism. The Congress of Vienna trampled such notions under foot. The partition of Poland was consecrated by Europe; Italy was placed under foreign rulers; Belgium and Holland, in spite of the hereditary opposition of centuries, were united under one king. The territories on the left bank of the Rhine, which were happy under French rule, and had been an integral part of France for twenty years, were roughly torn away, and divided between Prussia, Bavaria, and the house of Orange, under the fancied necessity induced by the exploded notion of maintaining the balance of power in Europe, of building up a bulwark against France. Such short-sighted policy was certain to be undone. Holland and Belgium separated; Italy became united, Poland maintained the consciousness of her national unity, and has more than once endeavored to regain her independence; France has never ceased to yearn after her natural frontier, the Rhine; the states of Germany have developed a national German patriotism which has led to the creation of the modern German Empire. This feeling of conscious nationality was the result of the French Revolution and the wars of Napoleon; its existence is the strength of England, France, Russia, and Germany; its absence is the weakness of Austria. In so far as the spirit of nationality was neglected at the Congress of Vienna, its work was but temporary; in its resurrection, which has filled the history of the present century, the work of the French Revolution has been permanent.

But after all, the growth of the spirit of nationality is only a secondary result of the French Revolution upon Europe; it did not arise in France until foreign powers attempted to interfere with the development of the French people after their own fashion; it did not arise in Europe until Napoleon began to interfere with the development of other nations. The primary results of the French Revolution—the recognition of individual liberty, which implied the abolition of serfdom and of social privileges; the establishment of political liberty, which implied the abolition of despots, however benevolent, and of political privileges; the maintenance of the doctrine of the sovereignty of the people, which implied the right of the people, through their representatives, to govern themselves—have also survived the Congress of Vienna.

When Europe tried to interfere, the French people sacrificed these great gains to the spirit of nationality, and bowed before the despotism of the Committee of Public Safety and of Napoleon; they have since regained them. The French taught these principles to the rest of Europe, and the history of Europe since 1815 has been the history of their growth side by side with the idea of nationality. How the two—liberty and nationality—can be preserved in harmony is the great problem of the future.

THE HARTFORD CONVENTION

PROTESTS AGAINST THE WAR OF 1812

A.D. 1814

SIMEON E. BALDWIN   JOHN S. BARRY

Although this gathering of New England men long since became mainly a subject of "academic" discussion among historical critics, it was nevertheless an event of much political significance at the time when such a strong protest was uttered against the war policy of President Madison, so disastrous to New England commerce. As shown in the following accounts, the principal question raised for historians by the action of the convention concerns its attitude regarding a possible dissolution of the Union.

The Hartford Convention (so called from the place of its meeting, Hartford, Connecticut) was held December 15, 1814, to January 5, 1815. It was composed of twelve delegates from Massachusetts, seven from Connecticut, four from Rhode Island, two from New Hampshire, and one from Vermont. The conditions that led to the calling of the convention, its proceedings, which were carried on in secret, and the grounds upon which have rested the suspicions of its "treasonable" designs, are clearly and impartially set forth below.

SIMEON E. BALDWIN

THE last days of the Federalists were not their best days. The vigor with which they carried through the adoption of the Constitution, and the dignity with which they at first administered the government, seemed to desert them as they approached what Jefferson and his friends used to call the "Revolution of 1800." Personal rivalries and misunderstandings among their leaders, unworthy intrigues, if not to make C. C. Pinckney President instead of Adams, yet certainly to make Burr President instead of Jefferson; bitterness in opposition, which almost overcame love of country—these make up the miserable chapter which closes the history of a great party.

It is now many years since John Quincy Adams brought forward the charge that some leading Federalists of Massachusetts were and had long been plotting the secession from the Union of the Northern or at least the New England States. The many additions, of late, to American political biography, and the growing frankness and unreserve with which the private letters of a public man are now published, almost before the grave has closed over him, have placed the present generation in a position to judge intelligently of the truth of this accusation. That it was not without some foundation is now plain, but that it was pressed too far seems hardly less so.

The person most active in pushing the scheme for a separation seems to have been Timothy Pickering. Soured by political disappointments and pecuniary embarrassments, when he found himself in 1803 returned by Massachusetts to the Senate of the United States, he could not bear the sight of Jefferson in power.

"Apostasy and original depravity," he writes to George Cabot in January, 1804, "are the qualifications for official honors and emoluments while men of sterling worth are displaced and held up to popular contempt and scorn. And shall we sit still, until this system shall universally triumph; until even in the Eastern States the principles of genuine Federalism shall be overwhelmed? This is a delicate subject.

"The principles of our Revolution point to the remedy—a separation. That this can be accomplished, and without spilling one drop of blood, I have little doubt. One thing I know, that the rapid progress of innovation, of corruption, of oppression, forces the idea upon many a reflecting mind. The people of the East cannot reconcile their habits, views, and interests with those of the South and West. The latter are beginning to rule with a rod of iron. Some Connecticut gentlemen—and they are all well informed and discreet—assure me that, if the leading Democrats in that State were to get the upper hand—which would be followed by a radical change in their unwritten constitution—they should not think themselves safe, either in person or property, and would therefore immediately quit the State. I do not believe in the practicability of a long-continued union. A Northern confederacy would unite congenial characters and present a fairer prospect of public happiness; while the Southern States, having a similarity of habits, might be left 'to manage their own affairs in their own way.' If a separation were to take place, our mutual wants would render a friendly and commercial intercourse inevitable.

"I believe, indeed, that if a Northern confederacy were forming, our Southern brethren would be seriously alarmed, and probably abandon their virulent measures; but I greatly doubt whether prudence should suffer the connection to continue much longer. The proposition would be welcomed in Connecticut; and could we doubt of New Hampshire? But New York must be associated; and how is her concurrence to be obtained? She must be made the centre of the confederacy. Vermont and New Jersey would follow of course, and Rhode Island of necessity. Who can be consulted and who will take the lead?"

Many were consulted, but no one was found ready to lead who was able to lead. Cabot sent this letter of Pickering to Fisher Ames, and talked it over with Chief Justice Parsons and Stephen Higginson; but it met with sympathy rather than approval. In Connecticut, apparently, the project was received with greater favor than in Massachusetts. Judge Reeve, the founder of the Litchfield Law School, and a brother-in-law of Aaron Burr, committed himself to it unreservedly.

"I have seen many of our friends," he writes to Senator Tracy in February, 1804, "and all that I have seen, and most that I have heard from, believe that we must separate, and that this is the most favorable moment. The difficulty is, how is this to be accomplished? I have heard of only three gentlemen as yet who appear undecided upon this subject."

Burr was understood to entertain similar sentiments, as also did Governor Griswold of Connecticut and Senator Plumer of New Hampshire. Griswold writes at length to Oliver Wolcott in March, 1804, on the subject of Burr's views; looking to him as probably the best man around whom to rally the "Northern interest," but complaining that he found his expression of his purposes rather Delphic. "I have no hesitation myself," he adds, "in saying that there can be no safety to the Northern States without a separation from the Confederacy. The balance of power under the present Government is decidedly in favor of the Southern States; nor can that balance be changed or destroyed. The question, then, is, Can it be safe to remain un-

der a government in whose measures we can have no effective
agency?

"With these views I should certainly deem it unfortunate
to be compelled to place any man at the head of the Northern
interest who would stop short of the object, or would only use
his influence and power for the purpose of placing himself at the
head of the whole Confederacy as it now stands. If gentlemen
in New York should entertain similar opinions, it must be very
important to ascertain what the ultimate objects of Colonel
Burr are. If we remain inactive, our ruin is certain. Our
friends will make no attempts alone. By supporting Mr. Burr
we gain some support, although it is of a doubtful nature and of
which, God knows, we have cause enough to be jealous. In
short I see nothing else left for us. The project which we had
formed was to induce, if possible, the legislatures of the three
New England States who remain Federal to commence measures which should call for a reunion of the Northern States.
The extent of those measures, and the rapidity with which they
shall be followed up, must be governed by circumstances."

But the great men of the party looked coldly on the project
of breaking up the Union, which they had done so much to form.
The Adamses were scarcely approached, and Hamilton, when
consulted, gave it no encouragement, although he probably
agreed to attend a private meeting of the leaders at Boston, which,
but for his own death, would have been held in the winter of
1804. Not a few regarded an ultimate separation as probable
and perhaps as not very distant, but believed that it would come
only after great suffering had been found to result from the
measures inspired by Southern influences.

"If," wrote Cabot to Pickering in reply to the letter of January, 1804, from which we have quoted, "we should be made
to feel a very great calamity from the abuse of power by the national Administration, we might do almost anything, but it would
be idle to talk to the deaf, to warn the people of distant evils.
By this time you will suppose I am willing to do nothing but
submit to fate. I would not be so understood. I am convinced
we cannot do what is wished; but we can do much if we work
with Nature—or the course of things—and not against her. A
separation is now impracticable, because we do not feel the ne-

cessity or utility of it. The same separation then will be unavoidable when our loyalty to the Union is generally perceived to
be the instrument of debasement and impoverishment. If it be
prematurely attempted, those few only will promote it who discern what is hidden from the multitude; and to those may be
addressed

> "'Truths would you teach, or save a sinking land,
> All fear, none aid you, and few understand.'"

Fisher Ames writes to him a few weeks later in the same
vein: "Nothing is to be done rashly; but mature counsels and
united efforts are necessary in the most forlorn case. The fact is
our people know little of the political dangers; the best men, at
least, ought to be made to know them, and to digest at least the
general outlines of a system." Referring, playfully and possibly with an allusion to the personal hazards which might attend
the prosecution of Pickering's plans, to his failing health, he
says that it is "not wholly to be despaired of. If Jacobinism
makes haste, I may yet live to be hanged."

Similar letters came back to Plumer from New Hampshire;
and Hillhouse at least seems not to have pushed the movement
further in Connecticut. The plan of a Northern confederacy,
when deliberately examined, could have looked feasible only to
the knot of politicians in the excitement of Washington life with
whom it originated. The sober thought of men at home condemned it as impracticable, if not undesirable. Such a venture
might seem attractive to the audacity of Burr or the heated par-
tisanship of some better men, who were fighting a hopeless
battle in opposition; but there were few to support it who had
much to lose if it were tried and failed. The following of
Colonel Pickering must have been mainly of the kind which went
down after David to the cave of Adullam; and the whole movement was over and forgotten in a twelvemonth.

The proposition does not seem to have been communicated
even to a majority of the Federalists in Congress. Among the
Connecticut delegation of that day, Baldwin, Davenport, God-
dard, Smith, and Tallmadge afterward publicly denied any
knowledge of it whatever: and Senator Hillhouse made a guarded
statement, to the effect that he never knew of any combination

or plot among Federal members of Congress to dissolve the Union or to form a Northern or Eastern confederacy. Senator Plumer, however, on learning of this statement (in 1829), wrote that he was much surprised at it, for, says he, "I recollect, and am certain that, on returning early one evening from dining with Aaron Burr, this same Mr. Hillhouse, after saying to me that New England had no influence in the Government, added, in an animated tone, 'The Eastern States must and will dissolve the Union, and form a separate government of their own; and the sooner they do this, the better.'" As this story is corroborated by an entry in Mr. Plumer's diary, made twenty years earlier, it is probably correct, but the remark reported may well be imputed to the warmth of an after-dinner conversation among old friends, and has not at all the sound of a conspirator's declarations or even of an allusion to any formed and definite plan.

From Washington down, indeed, all the founders of the Republic had looked for its permanency more with hope than with assurance. We should do injustice to the tone of the political correspondence and conversation of the times, if we applied to it the standard of loyalty of the present generation. Both parties regarded the Constitution of 1787—like that of 1781, or those which France was still forming and rejecting with such rapidity —as an experiment in government-making. The right of a State to repudiate a law of the Union, which it deemed unconstitutional, whether the courts of the Union upheld it or not, had been emphatically asserted by Virginia and Kentucky, under the lead of Madison and Jefferson, and, this granted, the right of secession seems necessarily to follow.

In writing to Doctor Priestly in 1804, Jefferson alludes to the questions arising from the purchase of Louisiana, and then says: "Whether we remain in one confederacy or form into Atlantic and Mississippi confederacies, I believe not very important to the happiness of either part. Those of the Western confederacy will be as much our children and descendants as those of the Eastern, and I feel myself as much identified with that country in future time as with this."

It was not strange that some of the Federalists should learn a lesson from their opponents. Colonel Pickering thought that the embargo of 1807 presented a proper occasion for the application of the principles of the Virginia resolutions at the North. A letter sent from his seat in the Senate to the Governor of Massachusetts, for communication to the Legislature, looked so plainly to concerted resistance in New England to laws deemed unconstitutional, which were ruining its commerce, that the Governor declined to give it the publicity desired.

Adams was at this time Pickering's colleague in the Senate, and was no stranger to his views on the question of separation. After resigning his seat, Adams, in November, 1808, writes thus from Boston to Ezekiel Bacon, one of the Massachusetts Representatives in Congress: "A war with England would probably soon, if not immediately, be complicated with a civil war and with a desperate effort to break up the Union, the project for which has been several years preparing in this quarter, and which waits only for a possible chance of popular support to explode. That this project has been in serious contemplation of those whom you describe as being called in England 'Colonel Pickering's Party,' for several years, I know by the most unequivocal evidence, though it be not evidence provable in a court of law. To this project, as matured, a very small part of the Federal party is privy; the great proportion of them do not even believe in its existence."

A few years later, in 1811, Josiah Quincy of Massachusetts declared upon the floor of the House of Representatives that should Louisiana be admitted as a State, it would be so flagrant a disregard of the Constitution as virtually to dissolve the Union, "freeing the States composing it from their moral obligation of adhesion to each other, and making it the right of all, as it would become the duty of some, to prepare definitely for separation—amicably if they might, violently if they must." The Speaker ruled the concluding portion of the remarks out of order, but the House reversed his decision by a close vote, in which the majority was chiefly made up of Federalists. Many of Quincy's political friends, and among them John Adams and Harrison Gray Otis, wrote to him in general commendation of the sentiments of this speech, though without alluding particularly to the threat of secession. It was probably little more than a rhetorical flourish, intended to impress upon the administration party the idea that the North was in earnest when it demanded that the balance of power be left unchanged. In a familiar letter to his wife, a few days afterward, Quincy writes: "You have no idea how these Southern demagogues tremble at the word 'separation' from a Northern man; and yet they are riding the Atlantic States like a nightmare. I shall not fail to make their ears tingle with it whenever they attempt, as in this instance, grossly to violate the Constitution of my country."

The Washington Government was regarded at this time by a large part of New England much as a foreign conqueror is looked upon by the vanquished community. Its policy was unfavorable, almost destructive, to New England interests; and the leaders on both sides had nothing but distrust and dislike for each other. "New England," said a Baltimore newspaper, "is the Vendée of the United States." We shall look in vain, however, for any direct menace of secession in the action of any of her legislatures.

"The people of New England," said the Senate of Massachusetts in 1809, in answer to the inaugural speech of Governor Lincoln, in which he had intimated that rumors of an intended separation were afloat, "perfectly understand the distinction between the Constitution and the Administration. They are as sincerely attached to the Constitution as any portion of the United States. They may be put under the ban of the empire, but they have no intention of abandoning the Union."

The War of 1812 increased the general sense of injustice and wrong, but legislative protests were still kept within bounds. In the address of the House of Representatives of Massachusetts to the people of that State, adopted immediately after the declaration of war, and under the pressure of strong feeling, they explicitly denounce as unworthy of notice "the insinuations and assertions, so lavishly made, of a plot to dismember the Union"; and, while declaring that "the National Government has been induced to believe that your fears and dissensions, combined with your sober habits, and natural aversion from the appearance of opposition to the laws, are sufficient pledges for your tame acquiescence in the abandonment of your local interests, and for your supporting at the expense of your blood and treasure a war, unnecessary, unjustifiable, and impolitic, which, under the pretence of vindicating the independence of our country against a nation which does not threaten it, must too probably consign your liberties to the care of a tyrant who has blotted every vestige of independence from the Continent of Europe"; and that "when a great people find themselves oppressed by the measures of their government, when their just rights are neglected, their interests overlooked, their opinions disregarded, and their respectful petitions received with supercilious contempt, it is impossible for them to submit in silence," they propose and indeed admit of no other remedy, than a general resolution to let all party distinctions vanish, and unite as a "peace party," in order by constitutional methods "to displace those who have abused their power and betrayed their trust."

The General Assembly of Connecticut at the same time adopted a declaration even more unequivocal. After stating their belief that the Constitution will be "found competent to the objects of its institution, in all the various vicissitudes of our affairs," they add, "These sentiments of attachment to the Union and to the Constitution are believed to be common to the American people; and those who express and disseminate distrust of their fidelity to both or either we cannot regard as the most discreet of their friends."

The charge, however, that secession was really meditated by the Federalist leaders in Massachusetts and particularly in Boston, which had received a colorable support from the "Henry letters," which President Madison thought worth paying fifty thousand dollars for from the secret service fund, and making the subject of a special message to Congress in March, 1812, was too valuable as a party cry to be readily abandoned; and it found new credit when the Hartford Convention was called together.

Doctor Webster has shown clearly that the plan of such a convention originated, not in Boston, but in Northampton, and we have his testimony, as one of its original promoters, that "the thought of dissolving the Union never entered into the head of any of the projectors or of the members of the convention." But although the resolutions finally adopted by that body speak only of a temporary alliance for defence on the part of the Northern States, and that by the consent of Congress, the declaration by which they are prefaced makes no scruple of discussing the possibility of disunion.

"Finally," is its language, "if the Union be destined to dissolution by reason of the multiplied abuses of bad administration, it should if possible be the work of peaceable times and deliberate consent. Some new form of confederacy should be substituted among those States which shall intend to maintain a federal relation to each other; but a severance from the Union by one or more States, against the will of the rest, and especially in a time of war, can be justified only by absolute necessity. These are among the principal objections against precipitate measures tending to dissolve the States, and, when examined in connection with the farewell address of the Father of his Country, they must, it is believed, be deemed conclusive."

The not unnatural implication from such expressions was that absolute necessity—described as likely to proceed from "implacable combinations of individuals or of States, to monopolize power and office and to trample without reserve upon the rights and interests of commercial sections of the Union"—might justify secession, even during the pending war; and the provision for holding another convention at Boston within five months in case the recommendations of the present one should fail of effect upon Congress, "with such powers and instructions as the exigency of a crisis so momentous may require," was quite an intelligible menace of future possibilities.

JOHN S. BARRY

The citizens of Massachusetts, impressed with the dangers which threatened them, and heavily burdened with the expenses of the War of 1812, were urgent that means should be adopted by the Executive toward persuading the General Government to negotiate a peace, or to assist the State in defending its borders, without compelling it to rely entirely upon its own resources. His Excellency concurred in these views; but not choosing, it would seem, to assume the responsibility, he concluded, by the unanimous advice of the Council, to summon a special meeting of the General Court. To this body, when assembled, a message was sent informing them of his proceedings since their adjournment, and of the reasons which had induced him to call them together.

"The situation of the State," he observed in concluding his

address, "is dangerous and perplexing. We have been led, by the terms of the Constitution, to rely on the General Government to provide the means of defence; and to that government we have resigned the resources of the State. It has declared war against a powerful maritime nation, whose fleet can approach every part of our extended coast; and we are disappointed in the expectation of a national defence. But, though we may believe the war was unnecessary, and has been prosecuted without any useful or practicable object against a province of the enemy, while the seacoast of this State has been left almost wholly defenceless; and though in such a war we may not afford voluntary aid to any of the offensive operations, there can be no doubt of our right to defend our possessions and dwellings against any hostile attacks."

The joint committee to whom this message was referred, and of which Harrison Gray Otis was chairman, reported in favor of the Governor's recommendations and observed: "The state of the national treasury requires a great augmentation of existing taxes; and if, in addition to these, the people of Massachusetts, deprived of their commerce, and harassed by a formidable enemy, are compelled to provide for self-defence, it will soon be impossible for them to sustain the burden. There remains to them no alternative but submission to the enemy, or the control of her own resources to repel his aggressions. It is impossible to hesitate in making the election. This people are not ready for conquest or submission. But being ready and determined to defend themselves, and having no other prospect of adequate means of defence, they have the greatest need of all those resources derivable from themselves, which the National Government has thought proper to employ elsewhere.

"But, while your committee think that the people of this Commonwealth ought to unite, and that they will unite, under any circumstances, at the hazard of all which is dear, in repelling an invading foe, it is not believed that this solemn obligation imposes silence upon their just complaints against the authors of the national calamities. It is, on the contrary, a sacred duty to hold up to view on all occasions the destructive policy by which a state of unparalleled national felicity has been converted into one of humiliation, of danger, and distress; believing that, unless an almost ruined people will discard the men and change the measures which have induced this state of peril and suffering, the day of their political salvation is passed.

"It is not to be forgotten that this disastrous state of affairs has been brought upon Massachusetts, not only against her consent, but in opposition to her most earnest protestations. Of the many great evils of war, especially in the present state of Europe, the national rulers were often warned by the people of Massachusetts, whose vital interests were thus put in jeopardy. But the General Government, deaf to their voice, and listening to men distinguished in their native State only by their disloyalty to its interests, and the enjoyment of a patronage bestowed upon them as its price, have affected to consider the patriotic citizens of this great State as tainted with disaffection to the Union, and with predilections for Great Britain, and have lavished the public treasure in vain attempts to fasten the odious imputation."

The resolutions which followed this report, and which were adopted by the Legislature, were quite significant. These were: "That, the calamities of war being now brought home to the territory of this Commonwealth—a portion of it being in the occupation of the enemy; our seacoasts and rivers invaded in several places, and in all exposed to immediate danger, the people of Massachusetts are impelled by the duty of self-defence and by all the feelings and attachments which bind good citizens to their country, to unite in the most vigorous means for defending the State and repelling the invader; and that no party feelings or political dissensions can ever interfere with the discharge of this exalted duty;"

"That a number of men be raised, not exceeding ten thousand, for twelve months, to be organized and officered by the Governor, for the defence of the State;"

"That the Governor be authorized to borrow, from time to time, a sum not exceeding one million of dollars, and that the faith of the Legislature be pledged to provide funds for the payment of the same."

And finally: "That twelve persons be appointed, as delegates from this Commonwealth, to meet and confer with delegates from the other States of New England upon the subject of their public grievances and concerns; upon the best means of preserving our resources, and of defence against the enemy; and to devise and suggest for adoption, by those respective States, such measures as they may deem expedient; and also to take measures, if they shall think it proper, for procuring a convention of delegates from all the United States in order to revise the Constitution thereof and more effectually to secure the support and attachment of all the people by placing all upon the basis of fair representation."

The adoption of the last of these resolutions by a vote of twenty-two to twelve in the Senate and of two hundred sixty to ninety in the House shows how largely the popular sentiment was enlisted against the war. Only about a half of the House, it is true, appear to have actively participated in the passage of this resolve, and, perhaps, had the other half voted, the majority in its favor might have been lessened. But of this there is no certain proof; and it might perhaps be affirmed on the other side that, had all voted, the majority would have been increased. As the case stands, however, nearly two to one in the Senate and three to one in the House voted in favor of the resolution; and it can hardly be doubted, when all the circumstances are considered, that the vote of the Legislature reflected quite faithfully the wishes of the people.

Nor did the General Court attempt to conceal their transactions from the scrutiny of the whole nation or to withhold from the other States a coöperation in their measures; for the day after the passage of this resolution the presiding officers of the Senate and House were directed to make their proceedings known as speedily as possible, and letters were written to be sent to the different governments, inviting them to join in such measures as might be "adapted to their local situation and mutual relations and habits, and not repugnant to their obligations as members of the Union."

The adoption of the report of the committee of the Legislature, and the calling of the convention, which assembled shortly after in Hartford, Connecticut, was censured severely by the Democratic party, at the head of which stood Levi Lincoln, Jr.; and for many years' accusations were "thrown broadcast upon the members of that body, and renewed at every election," charging them with a studied design to subvert the Government and destroy the Union. The delegates from Massachusetts, however, as well as from the other States, were gentlemen of the highest respectability and talent, and, "as far as their professions can be considered as sincere; as far as their votes and proceedings afford evidence of their designs," so far their conduct has been adjudged to be defensible.

As has been well observed, "It is not to be supposed, without proof, that their object was treason or disunion; and their proceedings unite with their declarations and the sentiments entertained by those who appointed them to show that they neither purposed nor meditated any other means of defence than such as were perfectly justifiable, pacific, and constitutional." Indeed, such men as George Cabot, of Boston, the president of the convention, not a politician by profession, yet "a man of so enlightened a mind, of such wisdom, virtue, and piety, that one must travel far, very far, to find his equal;" Nathan Dane, father of the Ordinance of 1787 for the government of the Northwest Territory, and the author of a digest of the common law, eminent for his services in the State and National Legislatures, and possessing the esteem and respect of all who knew him; William Prescott, of Boston, father of the historian of that name, a Councillor, a Senator, and a Representative from that town, subsequently a member of the Convention for the Revision of the Constitution, and the president of the Common Council of Boston as a city; Harrison Gray Otis, for two years succeeding this convention a member of the Legislature, and afterward a Senator in the Congress of the United States, a gentleman of fine talents, fascinating manners, and great legislative experience; Timothy Bigelow, of Medford, a member and the Speaker of the House, and afterward a Councillor; Joshua Thomas, of Plymouth, an upright, popular, and honored judge of probate to the time of his death; Joseph Lyman, of Northampton, the sheriff of Hampshire County, and a member of the Convention for Revising the Constitution; Daniel Waldo, of Worcester, a member of the Senate, respected by his townsmen, as by all others who knew him; Hodijah Baylies, of Taunton, aide-de-camp to a distinguished officer during the Revolution, and long judge of probate for the County of Bristol; George Bliss, of

Springfield, a member of the State Government and of the Convention for Revising the Constitution; Samuel S. Wilde, of Newburyport, also a member of the State Convention, and a judge of the Supreme Judicial Court, beloved and respected by a wide circle of acquaintances, and possessing the confidence and attachment of the people; Stephen Longfellow, Jr., father of the distinguished professor and poet—such men, by the most violent partisan, could hardly be suspected of deliberately "plotting a conspiracy against the National Government, of exciting a civil war, of favoring a dissolution of the Union, of submitting to an allegiance to George III." Their character and standing at the period of their choice and to the day of their death are a sufficient refutation of all such charges, even if made; and if they were unworthy the confidence of the public, upon whom could reliance be more safely placed?

On the appointed day twenty-four delegates took their seats, and the convention was organized by the choice of George Cabot as president and Theodore Dwight as secretary. Each session of this body was opened with prayer; and, after its sessions had continued for three weeks, it was adjourned. The report of the committee, appointed at an early stage, suggested the following topics for the consideration of the convention: "The powers claimed by the Executive of the United States to determine conclusively in respect to calling out the militia of the States into the service of the United States, and the dividing the United States into military districts, with an officer of the army in each thereof, with discretionary authority from the Executive of the United States to call for the militia, to be under the command of such officer; the refusal of the Executive of the United States to supply or pay the militia of certain States, called out for their defence, on the ground of their not having been, by the Executive of the State, put under the command of the commander over the military district; the failure of the Government of the United States to supply and pay the militia of the States, by them admitted to have been in the United States service; the report of the Secretary of War to Congress on filling the ranks of the army, together with a bill or act on that subject; the bill before Congress providing for classing and drafting the militia; the expenditure of the revenue of the nation in offensive operations on the neighboring provinces of the enemy; the failure of the Government of the United States to provide for the common defence, and the consequent obligations, necessity, and burdens devolved on the several States to defend themselves; together with the mode, the ways, and the means in their power for accomplishing the object."

The report thus made was accepted and approved; and at a subsequent date, upon the report of a new committee which had been appointed, several amendments to the Federal Constitution were proposed, to be recommended to the several State legislatures for approval or rejection. These amendments, as in the published report, were: "(1) Representatives and direct taxes shall be apportioned among the several States which may be included within this Union according to their respective number of free persons, including those bound to serve for a term of years, and excluding Indians not taxed and all others. (2) No new State shall be admitted into the Union by Congress, in virtue of the power granted by the Constitution, without the concurrence of two-thirds of both Houses. (3) Congress shall not have power to lay any embargo on the ships or vessels of the citizens of the United States in the ports and harbors thereof, for more than sixty days. (4) Congress shall not have power, without the concurrence of two-thirds of both Houses, to interdict the commercial intercourse between the United States and any foreign nation or the dependencies thereof. (5) Congress shall not make or declare war or authorize acts of hostility against any foreign nation, without the concurrence of two-thirds of both Houses, except such acts of hostility be in defence of the territories of the United States when actually invaded. (6) No person who shall hereafter be naturalized shall be eligible as a member of the Senate or House of Representatives of the United States, nor capable of holding any civil office under the authority of the United States. (7) The same person shall not be elected President of the United States a second time; nor shall the President be elected from the same State two terms in succession."

Such was the "treason" of the Hartford Convention — a "treason" with which Anti-Federalists had once largely sympathized; for the very amendments proposed by this convention were substantially such as had been agitated at the time of the adoption of the Constitution, and deemed necessary by its opponents to prevent the encroachments of the Federal Government. But time often changes the opinions of men, or at least induces forgetfulness of once favorite measures.

THE BATTLE OF NEW ORLEANS

END OF THE WAR OF 1812

A.D. 1815

JAMES PARTON

General Jackson's triumph over the British at New Orleans was one of the chief military events of the earlier period in United States history. The greatest American successes in the War of 1812 had been won by the Navy; therefore Jackson's brilliant defence of New Orleans, against a much superior force, stands out the more conspicuously among the actions on land.

An unusual feeling of regret mingles even with the natural patriotic pride of the victorious country in the strength of her defenders, because, unhappily, the battle was fought after peace had been signed; the opposing forces not having received information of the Treaty of Ghent (December 24, 1814).

In October, 1814, the Americans learned that twelve or fifteen thousand British troops had been ordered to leave Ireland for New Orleans and Mobile. Early in December it was known that this force had been joined by another at Jamaica, and that all were ready to sail for the mouths of the Mississippi. Monroe, Secretary of War, ordered the hastening of militia from Southern States to New Orleans. The British forces arrived and anchored between the Mississippi River and Mobile Bay. Troops were landed on a small island, from which (December 23d) a detachment reached the Mississippi at a point within nine miles of New Orleans. The object of this movement was to get possession of the mouth of the Mississippi and hold it as British territory after the war should end.

Meanwhile General Jackson, who had been placed in command at New Orleans, had made timely preparations for the defence. Many of the volunteers who came to him were expert riflemen. Breastworks of cotton-bales were built to protect the Americans. After some demonstrations on each side, the British commander, General Pakenham, brought up heavy guns from the fleet. As Jackson's cotton-bales were not proof against cannon, when the British attacked him with these guns the Americans replied effectively with artillery, and Pakenham found that his only hope of success lay in storming his enemy's lines. This movement he attempted to execute on January 8, 1815, in the manner and with the result here recorded.

A T one o'clock on the morning of this memorable day, on a couch in a room of the M'Carty mansion-house, General Jackson lay asleep, in his worn uniform. Several of his aids slept upon the floor in the same apartment, all equipped for the field, except that their sword-belts were unbuckled and their swords and pistols laid aside. A sentinel paced the adjacent passage. Sentinels moved noiselessly about the building, which loomed up large, dim, and silent in the foggy night, among the darkening trees. Most of those who slept at all that night were still asleep, and there was as yet little stir in either camp.

Commodore Patterson was not among the sleepers that night. Soon after dark, accompanied by his faithful aid, Shepherd, he took his position on the western bank of the river, directly opposite to where Colonel Thornton was struggling to launch his boats into the stream, and there he watched and listened till nearly midnight. He could hear almost everything that passed, and could see, by the light of the camp-fires, a line of redcoats drawn up along the levee. He heard the cries of the tugging sailors, as they drew the boats along the shallow, caving canal, and their shouts of satisfaction as each boat was launched with a loud splash into the Mississippi. From the great commotion and the sound of so many voices he began to surmise that the main body of the enemy were about to cross, and that the day was to be lost or won on his side of the river. There was terror in the thought, and wisdom too; and if General Pakenham had been indeed a general the Commodore's surmise would have been correct. Patterson's first thought was to drop the ship Louisiana down upon them. But no; the Louisiana had been stripped of half her guns and all her men, and had on board, above water, hundreds of pounds of powder: for she was then serving as powder-magazine to the western bank. To man the ship, moreover, would involve the withdrawal of all the men from the river batteries; which, if the main attack were on Jackson's side of the river, would be of such vital importance to him.

Revolving such thoughts in his anxious mind, Commodore Patterson hastened back to his post, again observing and lamenting the weakness of General Morgan's line of defence. All that he could do in the circumstances was to despatch Mr. Shepherd across the river to inform General Jackson of what they had seen and what they feared, and to beg an immediate reënforcement. Informing the captain of the guard that he had important intelligence to communicate, Shepherd was conducted to the room in which the General was sleeping.

"Who's there?" asked Jackson, raising his head, as the door opened. Mr. Shepherd gave his name and stated his errand, adding that General Morgan agreed with Commodore Patterson in the opinion that more troops would be required to defend the lines on the western bank.

"Hurry back," replied the General, as he rose, "and tell General Morgan that he is mistaken. The main attack will be on this side, and I have no men to spare. He must maintain his position at all hazards." Shepherd recrossed the river with the General's answer, which could not have been very reassuring to Morgan and his inexperienced men.

Jackson looked at his watch. It was past one. "Gentlemen," said he to his dozing aids, "we have slept enough. Rise. The enemy will be upon us in a few minutes. I must go and see Coffee."

The order was obeyed very promptly. Sword-belts were buckled, pistols resumed, and in a few minutes the party were ready to begin the duties of the day. There was little for the American troops to do but to repair to their posts. By four o'clock in the morning, along the whole line of works, every man was in his place and everything was ready. A little later General Adair marched down a reserve of a thousand Kentuckians to the rear of General Carroll's position, and, halting them fifty yards from the works, went forward himself to join the line of men peering over the top of the embankment into the fog and darkness of the morning. The position of the reserve was most fortunately chosen. It was almost directly behind that part of the lines which a deserter from Jackson's army had yesterday told General Pakenham was their weakest point. And the deserter was half right. He had deserted on Friday, before there had been any thought of the reserve, and he forgot to mention that Coffee and Carroll's men, over two thousand in number, were the best and coolest shots in the world. What a terrible trap his half-true information led a British column into!

Not long after the hour when the American general had been roused from his couch, General Pakenham, who had slept an hour or two at the Villeré mansion, also rose, and rode immediately to the bank of the river, where Thornton had just embarked his diminished force. He learned of delay and difficulty that had occurred there, and lingered long upon the spot listening for some sound that should indicate the whereabouts of Thornton. But no sound was heard, as the swift Mississippi had carried the boats far down out of hearing. Surely Pakenham must have known that the vital part of his plan was, for that morning, frustrated. Surely he will hold back his troops from the assault until Thornton announces himself. The doomed man had no such thought.

Before four o'clock the British troops were up and in the several positions assigned them. Let us note, as accurately as possible, the distribution of the British forces. The official statements of the General aid us little here; for, as an English officer observed, nothing was done on this awful day as it was intended to be done. The actual positions of the various corps at four o'clock in the morning were as follows:

First, and chiefly. On the borders of the cypress swamp, half a mile below that part of the lines where Carroll commanded and Adair was ready to support him, was a powerful column of nearly three thousand men, under the command of General Gibbs. This column was to storm the lines where they were supposed to be weakest, keeping close to the wood, and as far as possible from the enfilading fire of Commodore Patterson's batteries. This was the main column of attack. It consisted of three entire regiments, the Fourth, the Twenty-first, and the Forty-fourth, with three companies of the Ninety-fifth Rifles. The Forty-fourth, an Irish regiment, which had seen much service in America, was ordered to head this column and carry the fascines and ladders, which, having been deposited in a redout near the swamp over night, were to be taken up by the Forty-fourth as they passed to the front.

Secondly, and next in importance. A column of light troops, something less than a thousand in number, under the brave and energetic Colonel Rennie, stood upon the highroad that ran along the river. This column, at the concerted signal, was to

spring forward and assail the strong river end of Jackson's lines.
That isolated redout, or horn-work, lay right in their path. We
shall soon see what they did with it.

Third. About midway between these two columns of attack
stood that magnificent regiment of praying Highlanders, the
Ninety-third, mustering that morning about nine hundred fifty
men, superbly appointed, and nobly led by Colonel Dale. Here
General Keane, who commanded all the troops on the left,
commanded in person. His plan was, or seems to have been, to
hold back his Highlanders until circumstances should invite or
compel their advance, and then to go to the aid of whichever column should appear most to need support.

Fourth. There was a corps of about two hundred men, consisting of some companies of the Ninety-fifth Rifles and some of
the Fusileers, who had been employed at the battery all night,
and were now wandering, lost, and leaderless in the fog. They
were to support the Highlanders, but never found them.

Fifth. One of the "black regiments," totally demoralized
by cold and hardship, was posted in the wood on the very skirts
of the swamp, for the purpose of "skirmishing," says the British
official paper; to amuse General Coffee, let us say. The other
black corps was ordered to carry the ladders and fascines for
General Keane's division, and fine work they made of it.

Sixth. On the open plain, eight hundred fifty yards from
Dominguez's post in the American lines, was the English battery, mounting six eighteen-pounders, and containing an abundant supply of Congreve rockets.

Seventh. The reserve corps consisted of the greater part of
the newly arrived regiments, the Seventh and the Forty-third,
under the officer who accompanied them, General Lambert.
This column was posted behind all, a mile from the lines.

The older soldiers augured ill of the coming attack. Colonel
Mullens, of the Forty-fourth, openly expressed his dissatisfaction.
"My regiment," said he, "has been ordered to execution. Their
dead bodies are to be used as a bridge for the rest of the army to
march over." And, what was worse, in the dense darkness of
the morning he had gone by the redout where were deposited the
fascines and ladders, and marched his men to the head of the
column without one of them. Whether this neglect was owing

to accident or design concerns us not.   For that and other military sins Mullens was afterward cashiered.

Colonel Dale, too, of the Ninety-third Highlanders, a man of far different quality from Colonel Mullens, was grave and depressed.   "What do you think of it?" asked the physician of the regiment, when word was brought of Thornton's detention. Colonel Dale made no reply in words.   Giving the doctor his watch and a letter, he simply said: "Give these to my wife; I shall die at the head of my regiment."

Soon after four, General Pakenham rode away from the bank of the river, saying to one of his aids, "I will wait my own plans no longer."   He rode to the quarters of General Gibbs, who met him with another piece of ominous intelligence.   "The Forty-fourth," Gibbs said, "had not taken the fascines and ladders to the head of the column," but he had sent an officer to cause the error to be rectified, and he was then expecting every moment a report from that regiment.   General Pakenham instantly despatched Major Sir John Tylden to ascertain whether the regiment could be got into position in time.   Tylden found the Forty-fourth just moving off from the redout, "in a most irregular and unsoldierlike manner, with the fascines and ladders.   I then returned," adds Tylden, in his evidence, "after some time, to Sir Edward Pakenham, and reported the circumstance to him; stating that by the time which had elapsed since I left them they must have arrived at their situation in column."

This was not half an hour before dawn.   Without waiting to obtain absolute certainty upon a point so important as the condition of the head of his main column of attack, the impetuous Pakenham commanded, to use the language of one of his own officers, "that *the fatal, ever-fatal rocket* should be discharged as a signal to begin the assault on the left."   A few minutes later a second rocket whizzed aloft—the signal of attack on the right.

If there was confusion in the column of General Gibbs, there was uncertainty in that of General Keane.   But the suspense was soon over.   Daylight struggled through the mist.   About six o'clock both columns were advancing at the steady, solid British pace to the attack; the Forty-fourth nowhere, straggling in the rear with the fascines and ladders.   The column soon came up with the American outposts, who at first retreated slowly before it, but soon quickened their pace, and ran in, bearing their great news and putting every man in the works intensely on the alert, each commander anxious for the honor of first getting a glimpse of the foe and opening fire upon him.

Lieutenant Spotts, of battery Number Six, was the first man in the American lines who descried through the fog the dim red line of General Gibbs's advancing column, far away down the plain, close to the forest. The thunder of his great gun broke the dread stillness. Then there was silence again; for the shifting fog or the altered position of the enemy concealed him from view once more. The fog lifted again, and soon revealed both divisions, which, with their detached companies, seemed to cover two-thirds of the plain, and gave the Americans a splendid military spectacle. Three cheers from Carroll's men. Three cheers from the Kentuckians behind them. Cheers continued from the advancing column, not heard yet in the American lines.

Steadily and fast the column of General Gibbs marched toward batteries numbered Six, Seven, and Eight, which played upon it, at first with but occasional effect, often missing, sometimes throwing a ball right into its midst and causing it to reel and pause for a moment. Promptly were the gaps filled up; bravely the column came on. As they neared the lines the well-aimed shot made more dreadful havoc, "cutting great lanes in the column from front to rear," and tossing men and parts of men aloft, or hurling them far on one side. At length, still steady and unbroken, they came within range of the small arms, the rifles of Carroll's Tennesseeans, the muskets of Adair's Kentuckians, four lines of sharpshooters, one behind the other. General Carroll, coolly waiting for the right moment, held his fire till the enemy were within two hundred yards, and then gave the word "Fire!"

At first with a certain deliberation, afterward in hottest haste, always with deadly effect, the riflemen plied their terrible weapon. The summit of the embankment was a line of spouting fire, except where the great guns showed their liquid, belching flash. The noise was peculiar and altogether indescribable; a rolling, bursting, echoing noise, never to be forgotten by a man that heard it. Along the whole line it blazed and rolled; the British batteries showering rockets over the scene; Patterson's batteries on the other side of the river joining in the hellish concert.

The column of General Gibbs, mowed by the fire of the riflemen, still advanced, Gibbs at its head. As they caught sight of the ditch some of the officers cried out: "Where is the Forty-fourth? If we get to the ditch, we have no means of crossing and scaling the lines!"

"Here come the Forty-fourth! Here come the Forty-fourth!" shouted the General, adding, in an undertone, for his own private solace, that if he lived till to-morrow he would hang Mullens on the highest tree in the cypress wood. Reassured, these heroic men again pressed on, in the face of that murderous, slaughtering fire. But this could not last. With half its number fallen, and all its commanding officers disabled except the General, its pathway strewed with dead and wounded, and the men falling ever faster and faster, the column wavered and reeled—so the American riflemen thought—like a red ship on a tempestuous sea. At about a hundred yards from the lines the front ranks halted, and so threw the column into disorder, Gibbs shouting in the madness of vexation for them to re-form and advance. There was no re-forming under such a fire. Once checked, the column could not but break and retreat in confusion.

Just as the troops began to falter, General Pakenham rode up from his post in the rear toward the head of the column. Meeting parties of the Forty-fourth running about distracted, some carrying fascines, other firing, others in headlong flight, their leader nowhere to be seen, Pakenham strove to restore them to order and to urge them on the way they were to go.

"For shame," he cried bitterly; "recollect that you are British soldiers. *This* is the road you ought to take!" pointing to the flashing and roaring hell in front. Riding on, he was soon met by General Gibbs, who said, "I am sorry to have to report to you that the troops will not obey me. They will not follow me."

Taking off his hat, General Pakenham spurred his horse to the very front of the wavering column, amid a torrent of rifle balls, cheering on the troops by voice, by gesture, by example. At that moment a ball shattered his right arm, and it fell powerless to his side. The next, his horse fell dead upon the field. His aid, Captain McDougal, dismounted from his black creole pony; and Pakenham, apparently unconscious of his dangling arm, mounted again, and followed the retreating column, still calling upon them to halt and re-form.   A few gallant spirits ran in toward the lines, threw themselves into the ditch, plunged across it, and fell scrambling up the sides of the soft and slippery breast-work.

Once out of the reach of those terrible rifles, the column halted and regained its self-possession.   Laying aside their heavy knapsacks, the men prepared for a second and more resolute advance.   They were encouraged, too, by seeing the superb Highlanders marching up in solid phalanx to their support with a front of a hundred men, their bayonets glittering in the sun, which had then begun to pierce the morning mist.   Now for an irresistible onset!   At a quicker step, with General Gibbs on its right, General Pakenham on the left, the Highlanders in clear and imposing view, the column again advanced into the fire.   Oh the slaughter that then ensued!   There was one moment when that thirty-two pounder, loaded to the muzzle with musket-balls, poured its charge directly, at point-blank range, right into the head of the column, literally levelling it with the plain; laying low, as was afterward computed, two hundred men.   The American line, as one of the British officers remarked, looked like a row of fiery furnaces!

The heroic Pakenham had not far to go to meet his doom. He was three hundred yards from the lines when the real nature of his enterprise seemed to flash upon him; and he turned to Sir John Tylden and said, "Order up the reserve."   Then, seeing the Highlanders advancing to the support of General Gibbs, he, still waving his hat, but waving it now with his left hand, cried out, "Hurrah! brave Highlanders!"

At that moment a mass of grape-shot, with a terrible crash, struck the group of which he was the central figure.   One of the shots tore open the General's thigh, killed his horse, and brought horse and rider to the ground.   Captain McDougal caught the General in his arms, removed him from the fallen horse, and was supporting him upon the field when a second shot struck the wounded man in the groin, depriving him instantly of conscious-ness.   He was borne to the rear and placed in the shade of an old live-oak, which still stands; and there, after gasping a few minutes, yielded up his life without a word, happily ignorant of the sad issue of all his plans and toils.

A more painful fate was that of General Gibbs. A few moments after Pakenham fell Gibbs received his death wound and was carried off the field writhing in agony and uttering fierce imprecations. He lingered all that day and the succeeding night, dying in torment on the morrow. Nearly at the same moment General Keane was painfully wounded in the neck and thigh, and was also borne to the rear. Colonel Dale, of the Highlanders, fulfilled his prophecy, and fell at the head of his regiment. The Highlanders, under Major Creagh, wavered not, but advanced steadily, and too slowly, into the very tempest of General Carroll's fire, until they were within one hundred yards of the lines. There, for cause unknown, they halted and stood, a huge and glittering target, until five hundred forty-four of their number had fallen, then broke and fled in horror and amazement to the rear. The column of General Gibbs did not advance after the fall of their leader. Leaving heaps of slain behind them, they, too, forsook the bloody field, rushed in utter confusion out of the fire, and took refuge at the bottom of wet ditches and behind trees and bushes on the borders of the swamp.

But not all of them! Major Wilkinson, followed by Lieutenant Lavack and twenty men, pressed on to the ditch, floundered across it, climbed the breastwork, and raised his head and shoulders above its summit, upon which he fell riddled with balls. The Tennesseeans and Kentuckians defending that part of the lines, struck with admiration at such heroic conduct, lifted his still breathing body and conveyed it tenderly behind the works. "Bear up, my dear fellow," said Major Smiley, of the Kentucky reserve; "you are too brave a man to die."

"I thank you from my heart," whispered the dying man. "It is all over with me. You can render me a favor; it is to communicate to my commander that I fell on your parapet, and died like a soldier and a true Englishman." Lavack reached the summit of the parapet unharmed, though with two shot-holes in his cap. He had heard Wilkinson, as they were crossing the ditch, cry out: "Now, why don't the troops come on? The day is our own."

With these last words in his ears, and not looking behind him, he had no sooner gained the breastwork than he demanded the swords of two American officers, the first he caught sight of in the lines. "Oh, no," replied one of them, "you are alone, and therefore ought to consider yourself *our* prisoner." Then Lavack looked around and saw, what is best described in his own language:

"Now conceive my indignation, on looking round, to find that the two leading regiments had vanished as if the earth had opened and swallowed them up!"

The earth had swallowed them up, or was waiting to do so, and the brave Lavack was a prisoner. Lieutenant Lavack further declared that when he first looked down behind the American lines he saw the riflemen "flying in a disorderly mob," which all other witnesses deny. Doubtless there was some confusion there, as every man was fighting his own battle, and there was much struggling to get to the rampart to fire, and from the rampart to load. Moreover, if the lines had been surmounted by the foe, a backward movement on the part of the defenders would have been in order and necessary. Thus, then, it fared with the attack on the weakest part of the American position. Let us see what success rewarded the enemy's efforts against the strongest.

Colonel Rennie, when he saw the signal rocket ascend, pressed on to the attack with such rapidity that the American outposts along the river had to run for it—Rennie's vanguard close upon their heels. Indeed, so mingled seemed pursuers and pursued that Captain Humphrey had to withhold his fire for a few minutes for fear of sweeping down friend and foe. As the last of the Americans leaped down into the isolated redout, British soldiers began to mount its sides. A brief hand-to-hand conflict ensued within the redout between the party defending it and the British advance. In a surprisingly short time the Americans, overpowered by numbers, and astounded at the suddenness of the attack, fled across the plank and climbed over into safety behind the lines. Then was poured into the redout a deadly and incessant fire, which cleared it of the foe in less time than it had taken them to capture it, while Humphrey, with his great guns, mowed down the still advancing column, and Patterson, from the other side of the river, added the fire of his batteries.

Brief was the unequal contest. Colonel Rennie, Captain Henry, Major King, three only of this column, reached the summit of the rampart near the river's edge. "Hurrah, boys!" cried Rennie, already wounded, as the three officers gained the breastwork, "Hurrah, boys! the day is ours." At that moment Beale's New Orleans sharpshooters, withdrawing a few paces for better aim, fired a volley, and the three noble soldiers fell headlong into the ditch.

That was the end of it. Flight, tumultuous flight—some running on the top of the levee, some under it, others down the road; while Patterson's guns played upon them still with terrible effect.

A pleasant story, connected with the advance of Colonel Rennie's column, is related by the same author. "As the detachments along the road advanced, their bugler, a boy of fourteen or fifteen, climbing a small tree within two hundred yards of the American lines, straddled a limb, and continued to blow the charge with all his power. There he remained during the whole action, while the cannon-balls and bullets ploughed the ground around him, killed scores of men, and tore even the branches of the tree in which he sat. Above the thunder of the artillery, the rattling fire of musketry, and all the din and uproar of the strife the shrill blast of the little bugler could be heard, and even when his companions had fallen back and retreated from the field he continued true to his duty, and blew the charge with undiminished vigor. At last, when the British had entirely abandoned the ground, an American soldier, passing from the lines, captured the little bugler and brought him into camp."

The reserve, under General Lambert, was never ordered up. Major Tylden obeyed the last order of his general, and General Lambert had directed the bugler to sound the advance. A chance shot struck the bugler's uplifted arm, and the instrument fell to the ground. The charge was never sounded. General Lambert brought forward his division far enough to cover the retreat of the broken columns and to deter General Jackson from attempting a sortie. The chief command had fallen upon Lambert, and he was overwhelmed by the unexpected and fearful issue of the battle.

How long a time, does the reader think, elapsed between the

fire of the first American gun and the total rout of the attacking columns? Twenty-five minutes! Not that the American fire ceased, or even slackened, at the expiration of that period. The riflemen on the left and the troops on the right continued to discharge their weapons into the smoke that hung over the plain for two hours. But in the space of twenty-five minutes the discomfiture of the enemy in the open field was complete. The battery alone still made resistance. It required two hours of a tremendous cannonade to silence its great guns and drive its defenders to the rear.

The scene behind the American works during the fire can be easily imagined. One half of the army never fired a shot. The battle was fought at the two extremities of the lines. The battalions of Planché, Dacquin, and Lacoste, the whole of the Forty-fourth Regiment, and one-half of Coffee's Tennesseeans had nothing to do but to stand still at their posts and chafe with vain impatience for a chance to join in the fight. The batteries alone at the centre of the works contributed anything to the fortunes of the day. Yet, no; that is not quite correct. "The moment the British came into view, and their signal rocket pierced the sky with its fiery train, the band of the Battalion D'Orléans struck up *Yankee Doodle;* and thenceforth throughout the action it did not cease to discourse all the national and military airs in which it had been instructed."

When the action began, Jackson walked along the left of the lines, speaking a few words of good cheer to the men as he passed the several corps. "Stand to your guns. Don't waste your ammunition. See that every shot tells." "Give it to them, boys. Let us finish the business to-day." As the battle became general, he took a position on ground slightly elevated, near the centre, which commanded a view of the scene. There, with mien composed and mind intensely excited, he watched the progress of the strife. When it became evident that the enemy's columns were finally broken, Major Hinds, whose dragoons were drawn up in the rear, entreated the General for permission to dash out upon them in pursuit. It was a tempting offer to such a man as Jackson. In the intoxication of such a moment, most born fighters could not but have said, "Have at them, then!" But prudence prevailed, and the request was refused.

At eight o'clock, there being no signs of a renewed attack, and no enemy in sight, an order was sent along the lines to cease firing with the small arms. The General, surrounded by his staff, then walked from end to end of the works, stopping at each battery and post and addressing a few words of congratulation and praise to their defenders. It was a proud, glad moment for these men, when, panting from their two hours' labor, blackened with smoke and sweat, they listened to the General's burning words and saw the light of victory in his countenance. With particular warmth he thanked and commended Beale's little band of riflemen, the companies of the Seventh, and Humphrey's artillerymen, who had so gallantly beaten back the column of Colonel Rennie. Heartily, too, he extolled the wonderful firing of the divisions of General Carroll and General Adair; not forgetting Coffee, who had dashed out upon the black skirmishers in the swamp and driven them out of sight in ten minutes.

This joyful ceremony over, the artillery, which had continued to play upon the British batteries, ceased its fire for the guns to cool and the dense smoke to roll off. The whole army crowded to the parapet and looked over into the field. What a scene was gradually disclosed to them! That gorgeous and imposing military array, the two columns of attack, the Highland phalanx, the distant reserve, all had vanished like an apparition. Far away down the plain, the glass revealed a faint red line still receding. Nearer to the lines, "we could see," says Nolte, "the British troops concealing themselves behind the shrubbery or throwing themselves into the ditches and gullies. In some of the latter indeed they lay so thickly that they were only distinguishable in the distance by the white shoulder-belts, which formed a line along the top of their hiding-place."

Still nearer, the plain was covered and heaped with dead and wounded, as well as with those who had fallen paralyzed by fear alone. "I never had," Jackson would say, "so grand and awful an idea of the resurrection as on that day. After the smoke of the battle had cleared off somewhat, I saw in the distance more than five hundred Britons emerging from the heaps of their dead comrades, all over the plain rising up, and still more distinctly visible as the field became clearer, coming forward and surrendering as prisoners of war to our soldiers. They had fallen at our first fire upon them, without having received so much as a scratch, and lay prostrate as if dead, until the close of the action."

The American army, to their credit be it repeated, were appalled and silenced at the scene before them. The writhings of the wounded, their shrieks and groans, their convulsive and sudden tossing of limbs, were horrible to see and hear. Seven hundred killed, fourteen hundred wounded, five hundred prisoners, were the dread result of that twenty-five minutes' work. Jackson's loss, as all the world knows, was eight killed and thirteen wounded.

"The field," says Mr. Walker, "was so thickly strewn with the dead that from the American ditch you could have walked a quarter of a mile to the front on the bodies of the killed and disabled. The space in front of Carroll's position, for an extent of two hundred yards, was literally covered with the slain. The course of the column could be distinctly traced in the broad red line of the victims of the terrible batteries and unerring guns of the Americans. They fell in their tracks: in some places, whole platoons lay together, as if killed by the same discharge. Dressed in their gay uniforms, cleanly shaved and attired for the promised victory and triumphal entry into the city, these stalwart men lay on the gory field, frightful examples of the horrors of war. Strangely, indeed, did they contrast with those ragged, unshorn, begrimed and untidy, strange-looking, long-haired men who, crowding the American parapet, surveyed and commented upon the terrible destruction they had caused.

"There was not a private among the slain whose aspect did not present more of the pomp and circumstance of war than any of the commanders of the victors. In the ditch there were no less than forty dead and at least a hundred who were wounded or who had thrown themselves into it for shelter. On the edge of the woods there were many who, being slightly wounded or unable to reach the rear, had concealed themselves under the brush and in the trees. It was pitiable, indeed, to see the writhings of the disabled and mutilated, and to hear their terrible cries for help and water, which arose from every quarter of the plain. As this scene of death, desolation, bloodshed, and suffering came into full view of the American lines, a profound and melancholy silence pervaded the victorious army.

"No sounds of exultation or rejoicing were now heard. Pity and sympathy had succeeded to the boisterous and savage feelings which a few minutes before had possessed their souls. They saw no longer the presumptuous, daring, and insolent invader, who had come four thousand miles to lay waste a peaceful country; they forgot their own suffering and losses, and the barbarian threats of the enemy, and now only perceived humanity, fellow-creatures in their own form, reduced to the most helpless, miserable, and pitiable of all conditions of suffering, desolation, and distress. Prompted by this motive, many of the Americans stole without leave from their positions, and with their canteens proceeded to assuage the thirst and render other assistance to the wounded. The latter, and those who were captured in the ditch, were led into the lines, where the wounded received prompt attention from Jackson's medical staff. Many of the Americans carried their disabled enemies into the camp on their backs, as the pious Æneas bore his feeble parent from burning Troy."

General Jackson had no sooner finished his round of congratulations, and beheld the completeness of his victory on the eastern bank, than he began to cast anxious glances across the river, wondering at the silence of Morgan's lines and Patterson's guns. They flashed and spoke, at length. Jackson and Adair, mounting the breastwork, saw Thornton's column advancing to the attack, and saw Morgan's men open fire upon them vigorously. All is well, thought Jackson.

"Take off your hats and give them three cheers!" shouted the General, though Morgan's division was a mile and a half distant. The order was obeyed, and the whole army watched the action with intense interest, not doubting that the gallant Kentuckians and Louisianians, on that side of the river, would soon drive back the British column, as they themselves had just driven back those of Gibbs and Rennie. These men had become used to seeing British columns recoil and vanish before their fire. Not a thought of disaster on the western bank crossed their minds.

Yet Thornton carried the day on the western bank. Even while the men were in the act of cheering, General Jackson saw, with mortification and disgust, never forgotten by him while he drew breath, the division under General Morgan abandon their position and run in headlong flight toward the city. Clouds of smoke soon obscured the scene. But the flashes of the musketry advanced *up* the river, disclosing the humiliating fact that their comrades had not rallied, but were still in swift retreat before the foe. In a moment the elation of General Jackson's troops was changed to anger and apprehension.

Fearing the worst consequences, and fearing them with reason, the General leaped down from the breastwork, and made instant preparations for sending over a powerful reënforcement. At all hazards the western bank must be regained. All is lost if it be not. Let but the enemy have free course up the western bank, with a mortar and a twelve-pounder, and New Orleans will be at their mercy in two hours! Nay, let Commodore Patterson but leave one of his guns unspiked, and Jackson's lines, raked by it from river to swamp, are untenable! All this, which was immediately apparent to the mind of General Jackson, was understood also by all of his army.

The story of the mishap is soon told. At half past four in the morning Colonel Thornton stepped ashore on the western bank at a point about four miles below General Morgan's lines. By the time all his men were ashore and formed the day had dawned, and the flashing of guns on the eastern bank announced that General Pakenham had begun his attack. At double-quick step Thornton began his march along the levee, supported by three small gunboats in the river, that kept abreast of his column. He came up first with a strong outpost consisting of a hundred twenty Louisianians, under Major Arnaud, who had thrown up a small breastwork in the night and then fallen asleep, leaving one sentinel on guard. A shower of grape-shot from one of the gunboats roused Arnaud's company from their ill-timed slumber. These men, taken by surprise, made no resistance, but awoke only to fly toward the main body. And this was right. There was nothing else for them to do.

Thornton next descried Colonel Davis's two hundred Kentuckians—the Kentuckians who were to be immortalized by an act of hasty injustice. These men, worn out by hunger and fatigue, reached Morgan's lines about the hour of Colonel Thornton's landing. Immediately, without rest or refreshment, they were ordered to march down the river until they met the enemy; then engage him; defeat him if they could; retreat to the lines if they could not. This order, ill-considered as it was, was obeyed by them to the letter. Meeting the men of Major Arnaud's command running breathlessly to the rear, they still kept on, until, seeing Thornton's column advancing, they halted and formed in the open field to receive it. Upon being attacked, they made a better resistance than could have been reasonably expected. The best armed among them fired seven rounds upon the enemy; the worst armed, three rounds. Effectual resistance being manifestly impossible, they obeyed the orders they had received, and fell back (in disorder, of course) to the lines, having killed and wounded several of the enemy, and for a few minutes checked his advance. On reaching the lines they were ordered to take post on the right, where the lines consisted merely of a ditch and of the earth that had been thrown out of it, a work which left them exposed to the enemy's fire from the waist upward.

Colonel Thornton having now arrived within seven hundred yards of General Morgan's position, halted his force for the purpose of reconnoitring and making his last preparations for the assault. He saw at once the weakness of that part of the lines which the Kentuckians defended. And not only that. Beyond the Kentuckians there was a portion of the swampy wood, practicable for troops, wholly undefended. The result of his reconnoitring, therefore, was a determination, as Thornton himself says in his despatch, "to turn the right of the enemy's position." Observe his words: "I accordingly detached two divisions of the Eighty-fifth, under Brevet Lieutenant-Colonel Gubbins, to effect that object" (of turning the right); "while Captain Money, of the royal navy, with one hundred sailors, threatened the enemy's left, supported by the division of the Eighty-fifth, under Captain Schaw." The brunt of the battle was therefore to be borne by our defenceless Kentuckians, while the strong part of the lines was to be merely "threatened" with a squad of sailors and a part of the Eighty-fifth.

The result was precisely what Thornton expected and what was literally inevitable. The bugle sounded the charge. Under a shower of screaming rockets the British troops and sailors advanced to the attack. A well-directed fire of grape-shot from Morgan's guns made great havoc among the sailors on the right and compelled them first to pause and then recoil, Captain

Money, their commander, falling wounded. But Colonel Gubbins, with the main strength of Thornton's force, marched toward the extreme left, firing upon the Kentuckians and turning their position, according to Thornton's plan. At the same moment Thornton in person, rallying the sailors, led them up to the battery. The Kentuckians, seeing themselves about to be hemmed in between two bodies of the enemy, and exposed to a fire both in front and rear, fired three rounds and then took to flight. Three minutes more and they would have been prisoners. Armed as they were, and posted as they were, the defence of their position against three hundred perfectly armed and perfectly disciplined troops was a moral impossibility and almost a physical one. They fled, as raw militia generally fly, in wild panic and utter confusion, and never stopped running until they had reached an old mill-race two miles up the river, where they halted and made a show of forming.

The flight of the Kentuckians was decisive upon the issue of the action. The Louisianians held their ground until they saw that the enemy, having gained the abandoned lines, were about to attack them in the rear. Then, having fired eight rounds and killed or wounded a hundred of the enemy, they had no chance but to join in the retreat. In better order than the Kentuckians, they fell back to a point near which the Louisiana was anchored, half a mile behind the lines, where they halted and assisted the sailors to tow the ship up the stream.

Commodore Patterson, in his battery on the levee, three hundred yards in the rear of Morgan's position, witnessed the flight of the Kentuckians and the retreat of the Louisianians with fury. As he had retained but thirty sailors in his battery, just enough to work the few guns that could be pointed down the road, the retreat of Morgan's division involved the immediate abandonment of his own batteries—the batteries of which he had grown so fond and so proud and which had done so much for the success of the campaign. In the rage of the moment he cried out to a midshipman standing near a loaded gun with a lighted match, "Fire your piece into the cowards!"

The youth was about to obey the order when the Commodore recovered his self-possession and arrested the uplifted arm. With admirable calmness he caused every cannon to be spiked, threw all his ammunition into the river, and then walked to the rear with his friend Shepherd, now cursing the Kentuckians, now the British—the worst-tempered commodore then extant.

Colonel Thornton, severely wounded in the assault, yet had strength enough to reach Morgan's redout; but there, overcome by the anguish of his wound, he was compelled to give up the command of the troops to Colonel Gubbins. Ignorant as yet of General Pakenham's fall, he sent over to him a modest despatch announcing his victory, and soon after was obliged to recross the river and go into the hospital.

And thus, by ten o'clock, the British were masters of the western bank, although, owing to the want of available artillery, their triumph, for the moment, was a fruitless one. On one of the guns captured in General Morgan's lines the victors read this inscription: "Taken at the surrender of Yorktown, 1781." In a tent behind the lines they found the ensign of one of the Louisiana regiments, which still hangs in Whitehall, London, bearing these words: "Taken at the Battle of New Orleans, Jan. 8th, 1815."

General Lambert, stunned by the events of the morning, was morally incapable of improving this important success. And it was well for him and for his army that he was so. Soldiers there have been who would have seen in Thornton's triumph the means of turning the tide of disaster and snatching victory from the jaws of defeat. But General Lambert found himself suddenly invested with the command of an army which, besides having lost a third of its effective force, was almost destitute of field officers. The mortality among the higher grade of officers had been frightful. Three major-generals, eight colonels and lieutenant-colonels, six majors, eighteen captains, fifty-four subalterns, were among the killed and wounded. In such circumstances, Lambert, instead of hurrying over artillery and reënforcements, and marching on New Orleans, did a less spirited, but a wiser thing: he proposed an armistice and at once sent an order to Colonel Gubbins to abandon the works and to recross the river with his whole command.

THE BATTLE OF WATERLOO

WOLFGANG MENZEL   WILLIAM SIBORNE   VICTOR HUGO

Having overthrown Napoleon and occupied Paris, the allied monarchs of Europe permitted the defeated Emperor to retire to the Island of Elba off the Italian coast and retain his sovereignty over this tiny domain. Seeing that they had begun quarrelling among themselves and that the new French King, Louis XVIII, was but little welcome to France, Napoleon resolved on a sudden, dashing effort to regain his power.

Leaving Elba without warning, he landed with a few followers at Cannes, March 1, 1815, and was hailed with joy by the people. Even his former marshal, Ney, who was sent by Louis XVIII to suppress the uprising, went over to Napoleon instead. Within a month of his reëntry into the country the Emperor was in Paris with as full control of all France as ever before. Unfortunately for him, the troops raised against him by Europe had been only partly disbanded and were very rapidly regathered. The ensuing war upon the French border, with its culminating "struggle of the giants" at Waterloo, has been very bitterly discussed, very passionately argued. British opinion upon the subject is irreconcilable with Prussian. The French naturally agree with neither. Three narratives are therefore presented : the first by the German author, Menzel; the second by Captain Siborne, generally regarded by Englishmen as the fairest and most accurate description of the battle ; and the third Hugo's celebrated and impassioned picture, giving the French aspect of the tragic struggle.

WOLFGANG MENZEL

WHEN Napoleon returned from Elba, the allied sovereigns were still assembled at Vienna, and at once allowed every dispute to drop in order to form a fresh and closer coalition. They declared the Emperor an outlaw, a robber, proscribed by all Europe, and bound themselves to bring a force more than a million strong into the field against him. All Napoleon's cunning attempts to bribe and set them at variance were treated with scorn, and the combined powers speedily came to an understanding on points hitherto strongly contested.

The lion, thus driven at bay, turned upon his pursuers for a last and desperate struggle. The French were still faithful to Napoleon, who, with a view of reinspiring them with the enthusiastic spirit that had rendered them invincible in the first days of the Republic, again called forth the old Republicans, nominated them to the highest appointments, reëstablished several Republican institutions, and, on June 1st, presented to his dazzled subjects the magnificent spectacle of a field of May, as in the times of Charlemagne and in the beginning of the Revolution, and then led a numerous and spirited army to the Dutch frontiers against the enemy.

Here stood a Prussian army under Blucher, and an Anglo-German one under Wellington, comprehending the Dutch under the Prince of Orange, the Brunswickers under their Duke, the recruited Hanoverian legion under Wallmoden. These *corps d'armée* most imminently threatened Paris. The main body of the allied army, under Schwarzenberg, then advancing from the south, was still distant. Napoleon consequently directed his first attack against the two former. His army had gained immensely in strength and spirit by the return of his veteran troops from foreign imprisonment. Wellington, ignorant at what point Napoleon might cross the frontier, had followed the old and ill-judged plan of dividing his forces; an incredible error, the allies having simply to unite their forces and to take up a firm position in order to draw Napoleon to any given spot. Wellington, moreover, never imagined that Napoleon was so near at hand, and was amusing himself at a ball at Brussels, when Blucher, who was stationed in and around Namur, was attacked on June 14, 1815.

Napoleon afterward observed in his memoirs that he had attacked Blucher first because he well knew that Blucher would not be supported by the over-prudent and egotistical English commander, but that Wellington, had he been first attacked, would have received every aid from his high-spirited and faithful ally. Wellington, after being repeatedly urged by Blucher, collected his scattered corps, but neither completely nor with sufficient rapidity; and on Blucher's announcement of Napoleon's arrival, exerted himself on the following morning so far as to make a reconnoissance. The Duke of Brunswick, with im-

patience equalling that of Blucher, was the only one who had
quitted the ball during the night and had hurried forward against
the enemy. Napoleon, owing to Wellington's negligence, gained
time to throw himself between him and Blucher and to prevent their junction; for he knew the spirit of his opponents.
He consequently opposed merely a small division of his army
under Ney to the English, and turned with the whole of his main
body against the Prussians.

The veteran Blucher perceived his intentions and in consequence urgently demanded aid from the Duke of Wellington,
who promised to send him a reënforcement of twenty thousand
men by four o'clock on the 16th. But this aid never arrived;
Wellington, although Ney was too weak to obstruct the movement, making no attempt to perform his promise. Wellington
retired with superior forces before Ney at Quatre-Bras, and allowed the gallant and unfortunate Duke William of Brunswick
to fall a futile sacrifice. Blucher meanwhile yielded to the overwhelming force brought against him by Napoleon at Ligny, also
on June 16th.

Vainly did the Prussians rush to the attack beneath the murderous fire of the French, vainly did Blucher in person head the
assault and for five hours continue the combat hand to hand in
the village of Ligny. Numbers prevailed, and Wellington sent
no relief. The infantry being at length driven back, Blucher led
the cavalry once more to the charge, but was repulsed and fell
senseless beneath his horse, which was shot dead. His adju-
tant, Count Nostitz, alone remained at his side. The French
cavalry passed close by without perceiving them, twilight and
a misty rain having begun to fall. The Prussians fortunately
missed their leader, repulsed the French cavalry, which again
galloped past him as he lay on the ground, and he was at length
drawn from beneath his horse. He still lived, but only to behold
the complete defeat of his army.

Blucher, although a veteran of seventy-three, and wounded
and shattered by his fall, was not for a moment discouraged.
Ever vigilant, he assembled his scattered troops with wonderful
rapidity, inspirited them by his cheerful words, and had the generosity to promise aid, by the afternoon of June 18th, to Wellington, who was now in his turn attacked by the main body of

the French under Napoleon. What Wellington on the 16th, with a fresh army, could not perform, Blucher now effected with troops dejected by defeat, and put the English leader to the deepest shame—by keeping his word. He consequently fell back upon Wavre in order to remain as close as possible in Wellington's vicinity, and also sent orders to Buelow's corps, which was then on the advance, to join the English army, while Napoleon, with the idea that Blucher was falling back upon the Meuse, sent Grouchy in pursuit with a body of thirty-five thousand men.

Napoleon, far from imagining that the Prussians, after having been, as he supposed, completely annihilated or panic-stricken by Grouchy, could aid the British, wasted the precious moments, and instead of hastily attacking Wellington spent the whole of the morning of the 18th in uselessly parading his troops, possibly with a view of intimidating his opponents and of inducing them to retreat without hazarding an engagement. His well-dressed lines glittered in the sunbeams; the infantry raised their shakos on their bayonet points, the cavalry their helmets on their sabres, and gave a general cheer for their Emperor. The English, however, preserved an undaunted aspect. At length, about midday, Napoleon gave orders for the attack, and, furiously charging the British right wing, drove it from the village of Hougomont. He then sent orders to Ney to charge the British centre. At that moment a dark spot was seen in the direction of St. Lambert. Was it Grouchy? A reconnoitring party was despatched and returned with the news of its being the Prussians under Buelow. The attack upon the British centre was consequently countermanded, and Ney was despatched with a considerable portion of his troops against Buelow.

Wellington now ventured to charge the enemy with his right wing, but was repulsed and lost the farm of La Haye Sainte, which commanded his position on this side as Hougomont did on his right. His centre, however, remained unattacked, the French exerting their utmost strength to keep Buelow's gallant troops back at the village of Planchenoit, where the battle raged with the greatest fury, and a dreadful conflict of some hours' duration ensued hand to hand. But about five o'clock, the left wing of the British being completely thrown into confusion by a fresh attack on the enemy's side, the whole of the French cavalry, twelve thousand strong, made a furious charge upon the British centre, bore down all before them, and took a great number of guns. The Prince of Orange was wounded. The road to Brussels was already thronged with the fugitive English troops, and Wellington, scarcely able to keep his weakened lines together, was apparently on the brink of destruction, when the thunder of artillery was suddenly heard in the direction of Wavre. "It is Grouchy!" joyfully exclaimed Napoleon, who had repeatedly sent orders to that general to push forward with all possible speed. But it was not Grouchy, it was Blucher.

The faithful troops of the veteran Marshal (the old Silesian army) were completely worn out by the battle, by their retreat in the heavy rain over deep roads, and by the want of food. The distance from Wavre, whence they had been driven, to Waterloo, where Wellington was then in action, was not great, but was rendered arduous owing to these circumstances. The men sometimes fell down from extreme weariness, and the guns stuck fast in the deep mud. But Blucher was everywhere present, and notwithstanding his bodily pain ever cheered his men forward, with "indescribable pathos," saying to his disheartened soldiers: "My children, we must advance; I have promised it; do not cause me to break my word!" While still distant from the scene of action, he ordered the guns to be fired in order to keep up the courage of the English, and at length, between six and seven in the evening, the first Prussian corps in advance, that of Zieten, fell furiously upon the enemy. "Bravo!" cried Blucher, "I know you, my Silesians; to-day we shall see the backs of these French rascals!"

Zieten filled up the space still intervening between Wellington and Buelow. Exactly at that moment Napoleon had sent his Old Guard forward in four massive squares in order to make a last attempt to break the British lines, when Zieten fell upon their flank and dealt fearful havoc among their close masses with his artillery. Buelow's troops, inspirited by this success, now pressed gallantly forward and finally regained the long-contested village of Planchenoit from the enemy. The whole of the Prussian army, advancing at the double and with drums beating, had already driven back the right wing of the French, when the English, regaining courage, advanced.

Napoleon was surrounded on two sides, and the whole of his troops, the Old Guard under General Cambronne alone excepted, were totally dispersed and fled in complete disorder. The Old Guard, surrounded by Buelow's cavalry, nobly replied, when challenged to surrender, "*La Garde meurt, et ne se rend pas*" ["The Guard dies, and never surrenders"]; and in a few minutes the veteran conquerors of Europe fell beneath the righteous and avenging blows of their antagonists. At the farm of La Belle Alliance, Blucher offered his hand to Wellington. "I will sleep to-night in Bonaparte's last night's quarters," said Wellington. "And I will drive him out of his present ones!" replied Blucher.

The Prussians, fired by enthusiasm, forgot the fatigues they had for four days endured, and, favored by a moonlight night, so zealously pursued the French that an immense number of prisoners and a vast amount of booty fell into their hands, and Napoleon himself narrowly escaped being taken prisoner. At Genappe, where the bridge was blocked by fugitives, the pursuit was so close that he was compelled to abandon his carriage, leaving his sword and hat behind him. Blucher, who reached the spot a moment afterward, took possession of the booty, sent Napoleon's hat, sword, and star to the King of Prussia, retained his cloak, telescope, and carriage for his own use, and gave up everything else, including a quantity of the most valuable jewelry, gold, and money, to his brave soldiery. The whole of the army stores, two hundred forty guns, and an innumerable quantity of arms thrown away by the fugitives, fell into his hands.

WILLIAM SIBORNE

The night of June 17, 1815, was one of heavy and incessant rain, accompanied by thunder and lightning. Amid such a storm the troops of two mighty armies lay down within cannon-shot of each other. The allied forces under Wellington were posted on the field of Waterloo, about twelve miles from Brussels, with the forest of Soigne, eight miles in width, intervening. Their position extended a little more than two miles, from a ridge on the road to Wavre, to a series of heights in the rear of the château of Hougomont. From the summit of the ridge the ground sloped backward, so as to hide the reserves, and keep the front itself concealed till the moment for action had arrived. In front of the left stood the farm of La Haye Sainte, abutting upon the road from Charleroi to Genappe, and on the right the château of Hougomont—both places being formidable posts in advance.

The army of Napoleon was formed in two lines, with a reserve. The first consisted of infantry flanked by cavalry, with five batteries, comprising eight guns in each, ranged along the front of this line, with a sixth, of twelve-pounders, in support; while six guns of horse artillery were posted on the right of Jacqueminot's cavalry. The second line consisted entirely of cavalry, with the exception of the two infantry divisions of the Sixth Corps, under Count Lobau, on the Charleroi road, well supported by artillery. In reserve, the Imperial Guard drew up infantry, cavalry, and artillery right and left of the road. These dispositions of Napoleon were as judicious as circumstances would admit of, and he was free to move his columns of attack against any part of the English which might seem the weakest, while his own position was such as to render a direct attack by a force not superior to his own dangerous in the extreme.

About ten o'clock on the morning of Sunday, the 18th, a great stir was observed along the French line; and presently a furious attack was made upon the château of Hougomont, occupied by a detachment of the brigade of guards under Colonel Hepburn and Lord Saltoun, who maintained the post throughout the day despite the repeated and desperate assaults by large bodies of the enemy. While the enclosures of Hougomont thus continued to be furiously assailed, the artillery on both sides thundered along the whole extent of each line. Under cover of the cannonade, Ney formed his columns of attack against the left and centre of the British position. This dense mass, consisting of at least sixteen thousand men, supported by seventy pieces of cannon, ranged along the brow of the height, led by D'Erlon, at about two o'clock moved forward to attack the left centre of the British under a murderous fire from the allied artillery.

The divisions of Alix and Marcognet, pressing onward, had opened fire on the Dutch-Belgian line, when the latter lost all order and fled. Picton's division, consisting of the brigades of

Kemp and Pack, numbering altogether little more than three thousand men, deployed into line to receive not fewer than thirteen thousand infantry, besides cavalry; but Picton, nothing daunted, as soon as the enemy halted and began to take ground to the right, shouted, "A volley, and then charge!" The order was so rigidly obeyed that the enemy, taken in the act of deploying, were borne back in the utmost confusion. The success was however dearly purchased—Picton was mortally wounded by a musket-ball in the temple; but Kemp gallantly supplied his place, and the line moved on, driving before it all resistance. A body of cuirassiers bearing hard upon the Hanoverian infantry, the Household Brigade, led by Lord Edward Somerset, came thundering forward, and the *élite* horsemen of the rival nations met in close and desperate strife.

The British prowess at length prevailed, and the enemy, overpowered, fled in wild confusion; but as the French far outnumbered the allies in cavalry, their reserve coming up in excellent order once more turned the tide of battle. Our dispersed horsemen fell back, experiencing considerable loss. Covered by the horse artillery and supported by Vivian's hussars, they however succeeded in reaching the crest of the position, where they re-formed under protection of the infantry. But the ground was covered with the dead and dying; and among the former was Major-General Ponsonby. While great efforts continued to be made by the French to gain possession of Hougomont, and the right of the line was threatened by a body of lancers, Donzelat's division pushed upon La Haye Sainte. The interval between became filled by such a display of horsemen as had never been looked upon by the most experienced soldier in the allied army.

Forty squadrons, of which twenty-one consisted entirely of cuirassiers, descending from the French heights in three lines began to mount to the English position; and despite the murderous discharge of the allied artillery, these resolute horsemen continued to advance at a steady trot, their cannon thundering over them. Arriving within forty yards of the English guns, with a loud shout they put their strong horses to their speed, and in a moment all the advanced batteries were in their possession. At this period all the allied regiments were in squares along the crest of the glacis, with their front ranks kneeling. Nevertheless the cuirassiers would not shrink from the trial. Once again the cry arose, "*Vive l'Empereur!*" and, with the noise of thunder, they rushed on. But their pace slackened as they approached; and they no sooner received a fire than they broke off from the centre by troops and squadrons.

Thus passed the whole line of cuirassiers, while the second and third lines—the former consisting of lancers, the latter of chasseurs—plunged headlong into the same course, and the British infantry became enveloped by the enemy. But they were not left long to maintain the combat single-handed. Lord Uxbridge, gathering as many squadrons as were available, launched them against the assailants, and drove them back over the declivity in confusion. They however soon rallied under their own guns, and, driving back the English beyond their squares, the game of the previous half-hour was played over and over again. Round and round these impenetrable masses the French horsemen rode, individuals here and there closing upon the bayonets and cutting at the men, but not a square was broken. The repulse of Ney's cavalry, and the failure of the attempts upon Hougomont and La Haye, determined Napoleon to make another effort upon the main position of the allies. Kellermann was ordered to move forward with his corps, while Ney adding the cavalry of the guard, no less than thirty-seven squadrons formed in rear of the broken force which had begun to rally; and in a short time the whole extent of the field between Charleroi road and Hougomont was covered with these splendid corps of horsemen. Again were the squares assailed without success, and again did Lord Uxbridge come to the rescue.

Having failed to make an impression on the first line, composed entirely of British and German troops, a large body of French cavalry passed over the ridge, and threatened the Dutch-Belgians in the second line. Great was the commotion in that part of the field from which whole masses of men began to move off without firing a shot. Lord Uxbridge again led the remains of his cavalry forward, and the enemy were driven back, pursued by Somerset's brigade; but the Dutch-Belgian carbineers disregarded the exhortation of Lord Uxbridge to follow him in the same course. Instead of advancing to the attack they went to the right about, and, galloping through the Third Hussars of the German Legion, fairly fled the field.

Never did a battlefield present such an anomalous spectacle. To all appearance the French were masters of the position of the allies. Their cavalry rode round the English infantry, and their strength of numbers overawed the allied horse. Scarcely an English gun gave fire, and most of those in front were actually in the possession of the enemy, the gunners having sought shelter within the squares. Yet the guns were safe, for the artillerymen had left neither harness nor limber, and thus the cavalry were deprived of the means of carrying them off. Meanwhile, the right of the English line had been sharply assailed, but Adams's brigade, consisting of the Fifty-second, Seventy-first, and Second battalions of the Ninety-fifth Regiment, under the immediate direction of Wellington, drove the enemy back over the hill.

Napoleon, finding that all his attempts upon Hougomont had failed, in order to make a lodgment in front of the main position, pushed forward Donzelat's division against La Haye Sainte, which, after a sharp opposition by Major Baring, was carried.

It was now about half past four o'clock, when the British regiments, although reduced to skeletons, still held their ground; and the Duke rode along the line, encouraging his diminished battalions, when the welcome sound of Blucher's approach was heard, as the Fifteenth and Sixteenth Prussian brigades debouched from the Wood of Paris, moving upon the right flank of the French army. Lobau, with the Sixth Corps, had been detached to resist this movement; but the Prussians continued to receive reënforcements, and at six o'clock they had brought thirty battalions, twenty-seven squadrons, and sixty-four guns into action. In vain Lobau, with half that force, sought to maintain his ground; and abandoning Planchenoit, he drew off toward the Charleroi road.

At this critical moment Napoleon, observing the masses of Prussians pouring into the field, determined to attack the right centre of the English position with a column of the Imperial Guard; while a second, in support, moved nearer toward Hougomont. The cavalry were at the same time to advance *en masse;*

and this movement was to be made under cover of the whole of their powerful artillery. The interval between these masses was to be filled up with cavalry, and Donzelat's division, now gathered round La Haye Sainte, was to dash forward. These preparations were met by Wellington filling up the gaps already made in his line; and these arrangements were still in progress when forth from the enclosures of La Haye Sainte Donzelat's corps came pouring.

They advanced in dense skirmishing order, and brought several pieces of artillery to bear within a hundred yards of the allied line—doing such dreadful execution on the German legion that Kreuse's Brunswickers wavered until sustained by Du Plat's Brunswickers and the Nassau regiments, gallantly led by the Prince of Orange, on which occasion he was severely wounded. The Duke's presence restored order, and the battle was renewed. The Imperial Guard, led by Ney, Friant, and Michel, after filing past the Emperor, now passed down the descent from La Belle Alliance. There was a cessation in the firing of the French artillery, and simultaneously with this advance the corps of D'Erlon, *en échelon* of columns, moved partly upon Lambert's brigade, while their right was engaged with the Prussians; and Reille, with some of his battalions penetrating the Wood of Hougomont, advanced boldly with another portion upon the centre of the English line.

It was now seven o'clock—the third corps of Prussians had arrived; and their whole force, close at hand, was little less than fifty thousand men, with one hundred pieces of cannon. The French batteries, which had remained silent until the rear of the advancing column had cleared their muzzles, opened with rapidity and precision, doing fearful execution upon the regiments that came within their range. As the leading column of the guard approached, the English batteries played upon them: yet they never paused a moment, but continued boldly to advance, despite the havoc occasioned by the murderous fire. Michel nobly fell, Friant was severely wounded, and Ney, who rode at the head of these veterans, had his horse shot under him; but, nothing dismayed, he led them on foot, and driving in the light troops, they reached the summit. Then Wellington directed the brigade of guards, under Major-General Maitland, to attack this imposing force. Pouring in a destructive volley, they moved upon the enemy with the bayonet, and spite of every effort of the officers to rally, this *elite* of the French army ran down the slope, closely pursued by the British guards.

Napoleon, seeing his guards falling back in confusion, his broken squadrons fleeing, his guns abandoned, and having no reserve to fall back upon, shortly after eight o'clock galloped from the field. A cheer was now heard on the right, which flew swiftly along the entire position of the allies, and the whole line rushed forward. Darkness soon set in, and such confusion prevailed that the advanced cavalry got so completely intermingled among the crowds of fugitives that they could with difficulty extricate themselves, and more than one awkward rencounter took place. Guns, tumbrels, the whole *matériel*, in short, of the routed army, remained in the possession of the British. Then as the Prussians came furiously advancing upon the routed enemy, the Duke, feeling that the day was won, caused the order for a general halt to be passed; and the weary but victorious English lay down upon the position they had so gloriously gained.

Almost every individual of Wellington's personal staff was either killed or wounded. The Duke, after following the flying army far beyond La Belle Alliance, was on his way back when he met Blucher. Many congratulations passed between the two generals; and the latter readily undertook to follow up the pursuit. Thus was fought, and thus ended, one of the greatest battles in modern times; and if its results be taken into account, perhaps the most important recorded in history.

VICTOR HUGO

Those who wish to form a distinct idea of the battle of Waterloo need only imagine a capital A laid on the ground. The left leg of the A is the Nivelles road, the right one the Genappe road, while the string of the A is the broken way running from Ohaine to Braine l'Alleud. The top of the A is Mont St. Jean, where Wellington is; at the left lower point Reille is with Jerome Bonaparte; the right lower point is La Belle Alliance, where Napoleon is. A little below the point where the string of the A meets and cuts the right leg, is La Haye Sainte; where the left cuts it, is Hougomont; and in the centre of this string is the exact spot where the battle was concluded. Here the lion is placed, the involuntary symbol of the heroism of the Old Guard.

The triangle comprised at the top of the A between the two legs and the string is the plateau of Mont St. Jean; the dispute for this plateau was the whole battle. The wings of the two armies extend to the right and left of the Genappe and Nivelles roads, D'Erlon facing Picton, Reille facing Hill. Behind the point of the A, behind the plateau of St. Jean, is the forest of Soigne.

As for the plan itself, imagine a vast undulating ground; each ascent is commanded by the next ascent, and all the undulations ascend to Mont St. Jean, where they form the forest.

The two generals had attentively studied the plain of Mont St. Jean, which is called at the present day the Field of Waterloo. In the previous year, Wellington, with prescient sagacity, had examined it as suitable for a great battle. On this ground and for this duel of June 18th, Wellington had the good side, and Napoleon the bad; for the English army was above, the French army below.

All the world knows the first phase of this battle; a troubled, uncertain, hesitating opening, dangerous for both armies, but more so for the English than for the French.

It had rained all night; the ground was saturated; the rain had collected in hollows of the plain as in tubs; at certain points the ammunition-wagons had sunk in up to the axletrees and the girths of the horses; if the wheat and barley laid low by this mass of moving vehicles had not filled the ruts, and made a litter under the wheels, any movement, especially in the valleys, in the direction of Papelotte, would have been impossible.

The action was begun furiously, more furiously perhaps than the Emperor desired, by the French left wing on Hougomont. At the same time Napoleon attacked the centre by hurling Quiot's brigade on La Haye Sainte, and Ney pushed the French right wing against the English left, which was leaning upon Papelotte.

The attack on Hougomont was, to a certain extent, a feint, for the plan was to attract Wellington there and make him strengthen his left. This plan would have succeeded had not the four companies of guards and Perponcher's Belgian division firmly held the position, and Wellington, instead of massing his troops, found it only necessary to send as a reënforcement four more companies of guards and a battalion of Brunswickers. The attack on the French right on Papelotte was serious; to destroy the English left, cut the Brussels road, bar the passage for any possible Prussians, force Mont St. Jean, drive back Wellington on Hougomont, then on Braine l'Alleud, and then on Halle—nothing was more distinct. Had not a few incidents supervened, this attack would have succeeded, for Papelotte was taken and La Haye Sainte carried.

There is a detail to be noticed here. In the English infantry, especially in Kemp's brigade, there were many recruits, and these young soldiers valiantly withstood our formidable foot, and they behaved excellently as sharpshooters. The soldier when thrown out *en tirailleur*, being left to some extent to his own resources, becomes as it were his own general: and these recruits displayed something of the French invention and fury. These novices displayed an impulse, and it displeased Wellington.

After the taking of La Haye Sainte, the battle vacillated.

There is an obscure interval in this day, between twelve and four; the middle of this battle is almost indistinct, and participates in the gloom of the *mêlée*. A twilight sets in, and we perceive vast fluctuations in this mist, a dizzying mirage, the panoply of war at that day, unknown in our times; flaming colbacks, flying sabre-taches; cross-belts; grenadier bearskins; hussar dolmans; red boots with a thousand wrinkles; heavy shakos enwreathed with gold twist; the nearly black Brunswick infantry mingled with the scarlet infantry of England; the English soldiers wearing clumsy round white cushions for epaulettes; the Hanoverian light-horse with their leathern helmets, brass bands, and red horsetails; the Highlanders with their bare knees and checkered plaids, and the long white gaiters of our grenadiers—pictures, but not strategic lines; what a Salvator Rosa, but not a Gribeauval, would have revelled in.

A certain amount of tempest is always mingled with a battle, *quid obscurum, quid divinum*. Every historian traces to some extent the lineament that pleases him in the hurly-burly. Whatever the combination of the generals may be, the collision of armed masses has incalculable ebbs and flows; in action the two plans of the leaders enter into each other and destroy their shape. The line of battle floats and winds like a thread, the streams of blood flow illogically, the fronts of armies undulate, the regiments in advancing or retiring form capes or gulfs, and all these rocks are continually shifting their position: where infantry was, artillery arrives; where artillery was, cavalry dash in; the battalions are smoke. There was something there, but when you look for it it has disappeared; the gloomy masses advance and retreat; a species of breath from the tomb impels, drives back, swells, and disperses these tragic multitudes. What is a battle? An oscillation. The immobility of a mathematical plan expresses a minute and not a day. To paint a battle, those powerful painters, who have chaos in their pencils, are needed. Rembrandt is worth more than Vandermeulin, for Vandermeulin, exact at midday, is incorrect at three o'clock. Geometry is deceived, and the hurricane alone is true, and it is this that gives Folard the right to contradict Polybius. Let us add that there is always a certain moment in which the battle degenerates into a combat, is particularized and broken up into countless detail facts which, to borrow the expression of Napoleon himself, "belong rather to the biography of regiments than to the history of the army." The historian, in such a case, has the evident right to sum up; he can only catch the principal outlines of the struggle, and it is not given to any narrator, however conscientious he may be, to absolutely fix the form of that horrible cloud which is called a battle. This, which is true of all great armed collisions, is peculiarly applicable to Waterloo; still, at a certain moment in the afternoon, the battle began to assume a settled shape.

Everybody is aware that the undulations of the plains on which the encounter between Napoleon and Wellington took place are no longer as they were on June 18, 1815. On taking from this mournful plain the material to make a monument, it was deprived of its real relics, and history, disconcerted, no longer recognizes itself; in order to glorify, they disfigure. Wellington, on seeing Waterloo two years afterward, exclaimed, "My battlefield has been altered." Where the huge pyramid of earth surmounted by a lion now stands, there was a crest which on the side of the Nivelles road had a practicable ascent, but which on the side of the Genappe road was almost an escarpment. The elevation of this escarpment may still be imagined by the height of the two great tombs which skirt the road from Genappe to Brussels: the English tomb on the left, the German tomb on the right. There is no French tomb—for France the whole plain is a sepulchre.

Through the thousands of cartloads of earth employed in erecting the mound, which is one hundred fifty feet high and half a mile in circumference, the plateau of Mont St. Jean is now accessible by a gentle incline, but on the day of the battle, and especially on the side of La Haye Sainte, it was steep and abrupt. The incline was so sharp that the English gunners could not see beneath them the farm situated in the bottom of the valley, which was the centre of the fight. On June 18, 1815, the rain had rendered the steep road more difficult, and the troops not only had to climb up but slipped in the mud. Along the centre of the crest of the plateau ran a ditch, the existence of which it was impossible for a distant observer to guess. On the day of the battle this hollow way, a trench on the top of the escarpment, a rut hidden in the earth, was invisible, that is to say, terrible.

Napoleon was accustomed to look steadily at war; he never reckoned up the poignant details; he cared little for figures, provided that they gave the total—victory. If the beginning went wrong, he did not alarm himself, as he believed himself master and owner of the end.

At the moment when Wellington retrograded, Napoleon quivered. He suddenly saw the plateau of Mont St. Jean deserted, and the front of the English army disappear. The Emperor half raised himself in his stirrups, and the flash of victory passed into his eyes. If Wellington were driven back into the forest of Soigne and destroyed, it would be the definitive overthrow of England by France; it would be Crécy, Poitiers, Malplaquet, and Ramillies avenged; the man of Marengo would erase Agincourt.

The Emperor, while meditating on this tremendous result,

turned his telescope to all parts of the battlefield. His guards, standing at ease behind him, gazed at him with a sort of religious awe. He was reflecting, he examined the slopes, noted the inclines, scrutinized the clumps of trees, the patches of barley, and the paths; he seemed to be counting every tuft of gorse. He looked with some fixity at the English barricades, two large masses of felled trees; the one on the Genappe road defended by two guns, the only ones of all the English artillery which commanded the battlefield; at the one of the Nivelles road, behind which flashed the Dutch bayonets of Chassé's brigade. The Emperor drew himself up and reflected; Wellington was retiring, and all that was needed now was to complete this retreat by an overthrow. Napoleon hurriedly turned and sent off a messenger at full speed to Paris to announce that the battle was gained. Napoleon was one of those geniuses from whom thunder issues, and he had just found his thunder-stroke; he gave Milhaud's cuirassiers orders to carry the plateau of Mont St. Jean.

They were three thousand five hundred in number, and formed a front a quarter of a league in length; they were gigantic men mounted on colossal horses. They formed twenty-six squadrons, and had behind them, as a support, Lefebvre Desnouette's division, composed of one hundred sixty gendarmes; the chasseurs of the guard, eleven hundred ninety-seven sabres; and the lancers of the guard, eight hundred eighty lances. They wore a helmet without a plume, and a cuirass of wrought steel, and were armed with pistols and a straight sabre. In the morning the whole army had admired them when they came up at nine o'clock, with bugles sounding, while all the bands played *Veillons au salut de l'Empire*, in close column with one battery on their flank, the others in their centre, and deployed in two ranks, and took their place in that powerful second line, so skilfully formed by Napoleon, which, having at its extreme left Kellermann's cuirassiers, and on its extreme right Milhaud's cuirassiers, seemed to be endowed with two wings of steel. The aide-de-camp Bernard carried to them the Emperor's order: Ney drew his sabre and placed himself at their head, and the mighty squadrons started.

Then a formidable spectacle was seen: the whole of this

cavalry, with raised sabres, with standards flying, and formed in columns of division, descended, with one movement, and as one man, with the precision of a bronze battering-ram opening a breach, the hill of La Belle Alliance. They entered the formidable valley in which so many men had already fallen, disappeared in the smoke, and then, emerging from the gloom, reappeared on the other side of the valley, still in a close compact column, mounting at a trot, under a tremendous canister fire, the frightful muddy incline of the plateau of Mont St. Jean. They ascended it, stern, threatening, and imperturbable; between the breaks in the artillery and musketry fire the colossal tramp could be heard. As they formed two divisions, they were in two columns; Wathier's division was on the right, Delord's on the left. At a distance it appeared as if two immense steel lizards were crawling toward the crest of the plateau; they traversed the battlefield like a flash.

Nothing like it had been seen since the capture of the great redoubt of the Moskova by the heavy cavalry: Murat was missing, but Ney was there. It seemed as if this mass had become a monster and had but one soul; each squadron undulated and swelled like the rings of a polyp. This could be seen through a vast smoke which was rent asunder at intervals; it was a pell-mell of helmets, shouts, and sabres, a stormy bounding of horses among cannon, and a disciplined and terrible array; while above it all flashed the cuirasses like the scales of the dragon.

It was a curious numerical coincidence that twenty-six battalions were preparing to receive the charge of these twenty-six squadrons. Behind the crest of the plateau, in the shadow of the masked battery, thirteen English squares, each of two battalions and formed two deep, with seven men in the first lines and six in the second, were waiting, calm, dumb, and motionless, with their muskets, for what was coming. They did not see the cuirassiers, and the cuirassiers did not see them: they merely heard this tide of men ascending. They heard the swelling sound of three thousand horses, the alternating and symmetrical sound of the hoof, the clang of the cuirasses, the clash of the sabres, and a species of great and formidable breathing. There was a long and terrible silence, and then a long file of raised arms, brandishing sabres and helmets and bugles and standards, and three thousand heads with great mustaches, shouting "Long live the Emperor!" appeared above the crest. The whole of this cavalry debouched on the plateau, and it was like the beginning of an earthquake.

All at once, terrible to relate, the head of the column of cuirassiers facing the English left reared with a fearful clamor. On reaching the culminating point of the crest, furious and eager to make their exterminating dash on the English squares and guns, the cuirassiers noticed between them and the English a trench, a grave. It was the sunken road of Ohain.

It was a frightful moment: the ravine was there, unexpected, yawning almost precipitous, beneath the horses' feet, and with a depth of twelve feet between its two sides. The second rank thrust the first into the abyss; the horses reared, fell back, slipped with all four feet in the air, crushing and throwing their riders. There was no means of escaping; the entire column was one huge projectile. The force acquired to crush the English crushed the French, and the inexorable ravine would not yield till it was filled up. Men and horses rolled into it pell-mell, crushing each other, and making one large charnel-house of the gulf, and when this grave was full of living men the rest passed over them. Nearly one third of Dubois's brigade rolled into this abyss.

A local tradition, which evidently exaggerates, says that two thousand horses and fifteen hundred men were buried in the sunken road of Ohain. These figures probably comprise the other corpses cast into the ravine on the day after the battle.

Napoleon, before ordering this charge, had surveyed the ground, but had been unable to see this hollow way, which did not form even a ripple on the crest of the plateau. Warned, however, by the little white chapel that marks its juncture with the Nivelles road, he had asked Lacoste a question, probably as to whether there was any obstacle. The guide answered, "No"; and we might almost say that Napoleon's catastrophe was brought about by a peasant's shake of the head.

Other fatalities were yet to arise. Was it possible for Napoleon to win the battle? We answer in the negative. Why? On account of Wellington, on account of Blucher? No; on account of God. Bonaparte, victor at Waterloo, did not har-

monize with the law of the nineteenth century. Another series
of facts was preparing, in which Napoleon had no longer a place:
the ill-will of events had been displayed long previously.

It was time for this vast man to fall; his excessive weight in
human destiny disturbed the balance. This individual alone
was of more account than the universal group: such plethoras of
human vitality concentrated in a single head—the world, mounting to one man's brain—would be mortal to civilization if they
endured. The moment had arrived for the incorruptible supreme equity to reflect. Streaming blood, overcrowded grave-
yards, mothers in tears, are formidable pleaders. Napoleon had
been denounced in infinitude, and his fall was decided. Waterloo is not a battle, but a transformation of the universe.

The battery was unmasked simultaneously with the ravine
—sixty guns and thirteen squares thundered at the cuirassiers
at point-blank range. The intrepid General Delord gave a military salute to the English battery. The whole of the English
field artillery had entered the squares at a gallop; the cuirassier
has not even a moment for reflection. The disaster of the hollow way had decimated but not discouraged them, they were of
that nature of men whose hearts grow large when their number
is diminished. Wathier's column alone suffered in the disaster,
but Delord's column, which he had ordered to wheel to the left
as if he suspected the trap, arrived entire. The cuirassiers
rushed at the English squares at full gallop, with hanging bri-
dles, sabres in their mouths, and pistols in their hands.

There are moments in a battle when the soul hardens a man,
so that it changes the soldier into a statue, and all flesh becomes
granite. The English battalions, though fiercely assailed, did
not move. Then there was a frightful scene; all the faces of the
English squares were attacked simultaneously, and a frenzied
whirl surrounded them. But the cold infantry remained impas-
sive; the front rank kneeling received the cuirassiers on their
bayonets, while the second fired at them; behind the second
rank the artillerymen loaded their guns, the front of the square
opened to let an eruption of canister pass, and then closed again.
The cuirassiers responded by attempts to crush their foe; their
great horses reared, leaped over the bayonets, and landed in the
centre of the four living walls. The cannon-balls made gaps in

the cuirassiers, and the cuirassiers made breaches in the squares. Files of men disappeared, trampled down by the horses, and bayonets were buried in the entrails of these centaurs. Hence arose horrible wounds, such as were probably never seen elsewhere. The squares, where broken by the impetuous cavalry, contracted without yielding an inch of ground; inexhaustible in canister, they produced an explosion in the midst of the assailants. The aspect of this combat was monstrous: these squares were no longer battalions, but craters; these cuirassiers were no longer cavalry, but a tempest: each square was a volcano attacked by a storm; the lava combated the lightning.

The extreme right square, the most exposed of all, as it was in the air, was nearly annihilated in the first attack. It was formed of the Seventy-fifth Highlanders; the piper in the centre, while his comrades were being exterminated around him, was seated on a drum, with his pipes under his arm, and playing mountain airs. These Scotchmen died thinking of Ben Lothian, as the Greeks did remembering Argos. A cuirassier's sabre, by cutting through the bagpipe and the arm that held it, stopped the tune by killing the player.

The cuirassiers, relatively few, and reduced by the catastrophe of the ravine, had against them nearly the whole English army; but they multiplied themselves, and each man was worth ten. Some Hanoverian battalions, however, gave way; Wellington saw it, and thought of his cavalry. Had Napoleon at this moment thought of his infantry, the battle would have been won, and this forgetfulness was his great and fatal fault.

All at once the assailers found themselves assailed; the English cavalry were on their backs, before them the squares, behind them Somerset with the one thousand four hundred dragoon guards. Somerset had on his right Dornberg with the German *chevaux-légers*, and on his left Trip with the Belgian carbineers; the cuirassiers, attacked on the flank and in front, before and behind by infantry and cavalry, were compelled to make a front on all sides. But what did they care? they were a whirlwind, their bravery became indescribable. In addition, they had behind them the still thundering battery, and it was only in such a way that these men could be wounded in the back. For such Frenchmen, nothing less than such English-men was required.

It was no longer a *mêlée*, it was a headlong fury, a hurricane of flashing swords. In an instant the one thousand four hun-dred dragoons were only eight hundred; and Fuller, their lieu-tenant-colonel, was dead. Ney dashed up with Lefebvre Des-nouette's lancers and chasseurs; the plateau of Mont St. Jean was taken and retaken, and taken again. The cuirassiers left the cavalry to attack the infantry, or, to speak more correctly, all these men collared each other and did not lose their hold. The squares still held out after twelve assaults. Ney had four horses killed under him, and one-half of the cuirassiers remained on the plateau. This struggle lasted two hours.

The English army was profoundly shaken; and there is no doubt that, had not the cuirassiers been weakened in their at-tack by the disaster of the hollow way, they would have broken through the centre and decided the victory. This extraordinary cavalry petrified Clinton, who had seen Talavera and Bada-joz. Wellington, three parts vanquished, admired heroically; he said in a low voice, "Splendid!" The cuirassiers annihilated seven squares out of thirteen, captured or spiked sixty guns, and took six English regimental flags, which three cuirassiers and three chasseurs of the guard carried to the Emperor before the farm of La Belle Alliance.

How far did the cuirassiers get? No one could say; but it is certain that on the day after the battle a cuirassier and his horse were found dead on the weighing-machine of Mont St. Jean, at the very spot where the Nivelles, Genappe, La Hulpe, and Brussels roads intersect one another. This horseman had pierced the English lines. The cuirassiers had not succeeded, in the sense that the English centre had not been broken. Every-body held the plateau, and nobody held it; but in the end the greater portion remained in the hands of the English. Welling-ton had the village and the plain; Ney, only the crest and the slope. Both sides seemed to have taken root in this mournful soil.

But the weakness of the English seemed irremediable, for the hemorrhage of this army was horrible. Kemp on the left wing asked for reënforcements. "There are none," Wellington replied. Almost at the same moment, by a strange coincidence which depicts the exhaustion of both armies, Ney asked Napoleon for infantry, and Napoleon answered: "Infantry! where does he expect me to get them? Does he think I can make them?"

Still the English army was the worse of the two; the furious attacks of these great squadrons with their iron cuirasses and steel chests had crushed their infantry. A few men round the colors marked the place of a regiment, and some battalions were only commanded by a captain or a lieutenant. Alten's division, already so maltreated at La Haye Sainte, was nearly destroyed; the intrepid Belgians of Van Kluze's brigade lay among the wheat along the Nivelles road; hardly any were left of those Dutch grenadiers who in 1811 fought Wellington in Spain on the French side, and who in 1815 joined the English and fought Napoleon. The loss in officers was considerable: Lord Uxbridge, who had his leg interred the next day, had a fractured knee. If on the side of the French in this contest of the cuirassiers Delord, L'Heretier, Colbert, Duof, Travers, and Blancard were *hors de combat*, on the side of the English, Alten was wounded, Barnes was wounded, Delancey killed, Van Meeren killed, Ompteda killed, Wellington's staff decimated—and England had the heaviest scale in this balance of blood.

The Second Regiment of foot-guards had lost five lieutenant-colonels, four captains, and three ensigns; the first battalion of the Thirtieth had lost twenty-four officers and one hundred twelve men; the Seventy-ninth Highlanders had twenty-four officers wounded, and eighteen officers and four hundred fifty men killed. Cumberland's Hanoverian Hussars, an entire regiment, having Colonel Hacke at its head (who at a later date was tried and cashiered), turned bridle during the flight and fled into the forest of Soigne, spreading the rout as far as Brussels. The wagons, ammunition-trains, baggage-trains, and ambulance carts full of wounded, on seeing the French, gave ground, and approaching the forest, rushed into it; the Dutch, sabred by the French cavalry, broke in confusion.

From Vert Coucou to Groenendael, a distance of two leagues on the Brussels roads, there was, according to the testimony of living witnesses, a dense crowd of fugitives, and the panic was so great that it assailed the Prince de Condé at Mechlin and Louis XVIII at Ghent. With the exception of the weak reserve échelonned behind the field-hospital established at the farm of Mont St. Jean, and Vivian's and Vandeleur's brigades, which flanked the left wing, Wellington had no cavalry left, and many of the guns lay dismounted. At five o'clock Wellington looked at his watch, and could be heard muttering, "Blucher or night!" At this moment a distant line of bayonets glistened on the heights on the side of Frischemont. This was the climax of the gigantic drama.

Everybody knows Napoleon's awful mistake: Grouchy expected, Blucher coming up; death instead of life. If the little shepherd who served as guide to Buelow, Blucher's lieutenant, had advised him to debouche from the forest above Frischemont, instead of below Planchenoit, the form of the nineteenth century would have been different, for Napoleon would have won the Battle of Waterloo. By any other road than that below Planchenoit the Prussian army would have come upon a ravine impassable by artillery, and Buelow would not have arrived.

It was high time for Buelow to arrive. He had bivouacked at Dieu-le-Mont and marched at daybreak, but the roads were impracticable, and his division stuck in the mud. The ruts came up to the axletrees of the guns; moreover, he was compelled to cross the Dyle by the narrow bridge of Wavre; the street leading to the bridge had been burned by the French, and the artillery train and limbers, which could not pass between the two rows of blazing houses, were compelled to wait till the fire was extinguished. By midday Buelow's vanguard had scarce reached Chapelle St. Lambert.

Had the action begun two hours sooner, it would have been over at four o'clock, and Blucher would have fallen upon the battle gained by Napoleon. Buelow was obliged to wait for the main body of the army, and had orders to concentrate his troops before forming line; but at five o'clock, Blucher, seeing Wellington's danger, ordered Buelow to attack, and employed the remarkable phrase, "We must let the English army breathe."

A short time after this, Losthin's, Hiller's, Hacke's, and Ryssel's brigades deployed in front of Lobau's corps, the cavalry of Prince William of Prussia debouched from the Bois de Paris,

Planchenoit was in flames, and the Prussian cannon-balls began pouring even upon the ranks of the guard held in reserve behind Napoleon.

The rest is known—the irruption of a third army; the battle dislocated; eighty-six cannon thundering simultaneously; Pirch the First coming up with Buelow; Zieten's cavalry led by Blucher in person; the French driven back; Marcognet swept from the plateau of Ohain; Durutte dislodged from Papelotte; Donzelat and Quiot falling back; Lobau attacked on the flank; a new battle rushing at nightfall on the weakened French regiments; the whole English line resuming the offensive and pushed forward; the gigantic gap made in the French army by the combined English and Prussian batteries; the extermination, the disaster in front, the disaster on the flank, and the guard forming line amid this fearful convulsion. As they felt they were going to death, they shouted, "Long live the Emperor!" History has nothing more striking than this death-rattle breaking out into acclamations.

Each battalion of the guard, for this denouement, was commanded by a general: Friant, Michel, Roguet, Harlot, Mallet, and Pont de Morvan were there. When the tall bearskins of the Grenadiers of the Guard with the large eagle device appeared, symmetrical in line and calm, in the twilight of this fight, the enemy felt a respect for France; they fancied they saw twenty victories entering the battlefield with outstretched wings, and the men who were victors, esteeming themselves vanquished, fell back; but Wellington shouted, "Up, guards, and take steady aim!" The red regiment of English guards, which had been lying down behind the hedges, rose; a storm of canister rent the tricolor flag waving above the heads of the French; all rushed forward, and the supreme carnage began. The Imperial Guard felt in the darkness the army giving way around them, and the vast staggering of the rout: they heard the cry of "*Sauve qui peut!*" substituted for the "*Vive l'Empereur!*" and with flight behind them they continued to advance, hundreds falling at every step they took. None hesitated or evinced timidity; the privates were as heroic as the generals, and not one attempted to escape suicide.

Ney, wild, and grand in the consciousness of accepted death, offered himself to every blow in this combat. He had his fifth horse killed under him here. Bathed in perspiration, with a flame in his eye and foam on his lips, his uniform unbuttoned, one of his epaulettes half cut through by the sabre of a horse-guard, and his decoration of the great eagle dinted by a bullet —bleeding, muddy, magnificent, and holding a broken sword in his hand, he shouted, "Come and see how a marshal of France dies on the battlefield!" But it was in vain, he did not die. He was haggard and indignant, and hurled at Dronet d'Erlon the question, "Are you not going to get yourself killed?" He yelled amid the roar of all this artillery, crushing a handful of men, "Oh, there is nothing for me! I should like all these English cannon-balls to enter my chest!" You were reserved for French bullets, unfortunate man.

The rout in the rear of the guard was mournful; the army suddenly gave way on all sides simultaneously, at Hougomont, La Haye Sainte, Papelotte, and at Planchenoit. The cry of "Treachery!" was followed by that of "Sauve qui peut!" An army that disbands is like a thaw—all gives way, cracks, floats, rolls, falls, comes into collision, and dashes forward. Ney borrows a horse, leaps on it, and without hat, stock, or sword, dashes across the Brussels road, stopping at once English and French. He tries to hold back the army, he recalls it, he insults it, he clings wildly to the rout to hold it back. The soldiers fly from him, shouting, "Long live Marshal Ney!" Two regiments of Durotte's move backward and forward in terror, and as it were tossed between the sabres of the hussars and the musketry fire of Kemp's, Best's, and Pack's brigades. A rout is the highest of all confusions, for friends kill one another in order to escape, and squadrons and battalions dash against and destroy each other. Lobau at one extremity and Reille at the other are carried away by the torrent.

In vain does Napoleon build a wall of what is left of the guard; in vain does he expend his own social squadrons in a final effort. Quiot retires before Vivian, Kellermann before Vandeleur, Lobau before Buelow, Moraud before Pirch, and Domor and Subervie before Prince William of Prussia. Guyot, who led the Emperor's squadrons to the charge, falls beneath the horses of English dragoons. Napoleon gallops along the line of fugitives, harangues, urges, threatens, and implores them; all the mouths that shouted "Long live the Emperor!" in the morning, remained wide open; they hardly knew him. The Prussian cavalry, who had come up fresh, dash forward, cut down, kill, and exterminate. The artillery horses dash forward with the guns; the train soldiers unharness the horses from the caissons and escape on them; wagons overthrown and with their four wheels in the air, block up the road and supply opportunities for massacre. Men crush one another and trample over the dead and over the living. A multitude wild with terror fill the roads, the paths, the bridges, the plains, the hills, the valleys, and the woods, which are thronged by this flight of forty thousand men. Cries, desperation; knapsacks and muskets cast into the wheat; passages cut with the edge of the sabres; no comrades, no officers, no generals recognized—an indescribable terror. Zieten sabring France at his ease. The lions become kids. Such was this fight.

At Genappe an effort was made to turn and rally; Lobau collected three hundred men; the entrance of the village was barricaded, but at the first round of Prussian canister all began flying again, and Lobau was made prisoner. The Prussians dashed into Genappe, doubtless furious at being such small victors, and the pursuit was monstrous, for Blucher commanded extermination. Roguet had given the mournful example of threatening with death any French grenadier who brought in a Prussian prisoner, and Blucher surpassed Roguet. Duchesne, general of the Young Guard, who was pursued into the doorway of an inn in Genappe, surrendered his sword to a hussar of death, who took the sword and killed the prisoner. The victory was completed by the assassination of the vanquished. Let us punish as we are writing history—old Blucher dishonored himself. This ferocity set the seal on the disaster; the desperate rout passed through Genappe, passed through Quatre-Bras, passed through Sombreffe, passed through Frasnes, passed through Thuin, passed through Charleroi, and only stopped at the frontier. Alas! and who was it flying in this way? The grand army.

Did this vertigo, this terror, this overthrow of the greatest bravery that ever astonished history, take place without a cause? No. The shadow of a mighty right hand is cast over Waterloo; it is the day of destiny, and the force which is above man produced that day. Hence the terror, hence all those great souls laying down their swords. Those who had conquered Europe, fell crushed, having nothing more to say or do, and feeling a terrible presence in the shadow.

At nightfall, Bernard and Bertrand seized by the skirt of his coat, in a field near Genappe, a haggard, thoughtful, gloomy man, who, carried so far by the current of the rout, had just dismounted, passed the bridle over his arm, and was now, with wandering eye, returning alone to Waterloo. It was Napoleon, the immense somnambulist of the shattered dream, still striving to advance.

CHRONOLOGY OF UNIVERSAL HISTORY

EMBRACING THE PERIOD COVERED IN THIS VOLUME

A.D. 1800–1815

JOHN RUDD, LL.D.

CHRONOLOGY OF UNIVERSAL HISTORY

EMBRACING THE PERIOD COVERED IN THIS VOLUME

A.D. 1800–1815

JOHN RUDD, LL.D.

Events treated at length are here indicated in large type; the numerals following give volume and page.

Separate chronologies of the various nations, and of the careers of famous persons, will be found in the INDEX VOLUME, with references showing where the several events are fully treated.

A.D.

1800. Washington becomes the seat of the United States Government. Jefferson and Burr receive the largest number of electoral votes; last election at which electors did not specify vote for President and Vice-President. Convention between France and the United States; from this arose the French Spoliation Claims.

Legislative " UNION OF IRELAND WITH GREAT BRITAIN." See xv, 1.

Beginning of Robert Owen's social experiments at New Lanark; they fail.

Submission of the Chouans. Battles of Messkirch and Biberach; victories of Moreau. Napoleon crosses the Alps; defeats the Austrians at Marengo. Kléber assassinated in Egypt.

Genoa, after two months' desperate defence, capitulates to the Austrians.

England rejects the French overtures for peace. Capture by the English of a Danish frigate and convoy. Capture of Malta by the British. Dispute respecting the close of the century; Lalande decides that December 31st is last day of the eighteenth century. Earl Stanhope introduces his improved printing-press.

Manifesto of Paul, Emperor of Russia, against the British seizure of neutral ships; he seizes all British property in Russia.

393

1801. "RISE OF THE DEMOCRATIC PARTY." See xv, 18. John Marshall first Chief Justice of the United States. Beginning of war with the pirates of Tripoli.

Czar Paul withdraws Russia from the European coalition; his alliance with Napoleon. Peace of Lunéville; France gains Germany west of the Rhine.

Battle of Alexandria; defeat of the French by the English. Denmark enters into the northern league of armed neutrality; Nelson bombards Copenhagen and defeats the Danish fleet. Duckworth captures the Danish and Swedish West Indies. First attempt to navigate a steamboat on the Thames. Passage of the first Factory Act. George III renounces the title of "King of France"; removal of the quartering of the lilies from the royal arms.

1802. Founding of the Military Academy at West Point.

Peace of Amiens between France, Spain, and Batavia and Great Britain.

Napoleon declared Consul for life. Piedmont united to France. Rebellion in Switzerland; restoration of order by the French. Haiti subjected by the French; treacherous capture of Louverture, who is taken to France. Institution of the Legion of Honor.

Vote of £10,000 to Doctor Jenner. English newspapers prohibited in France.

1803. Ohio admitted into the Union. Lewis and Clark appointed to explore the western portion of the United States. Congress receives the report on the British impressment of seamen from American ships. "PURCHASE OF LOUISIANA;" see xv, 39.

Act of Mediation; Napoleon reorganizes the Swiss Confederacy; the cantonal system reintroduced. Press censorship in France. Occupation of Hanover by the French.

Wellesley (later Duke of Wellington) achieves brilliant successes against the Mahrattas. England declares war against France. Peltier convicted of libel on Napoleon. Rebellion of Emmet in Ireland; he is executed. Threatened invasion by Napoleon causes immense preparation for defence.

In Haiti the negroes expel the French.

Sheep farming begun in Australia.

The British and Foreign Bible Society founded.

Craniology promulgated by Doctor Gall.

The Lyceum, London, lighted with coal-gas.

1804. "THE LEWIS AND CLARK EXPEDITION." See xv, 84.

Death of Hamilton after a duel with Burr. Jefferson reëlected President. "THE TRIPOLITAN WAR;" see xv, 58.

Abduction and execution by Napoleon of the Duc d'Enghien; Fouché said: "It was worse than a crime—it was a blunder." Publication of the *Code Civil des Français* (*Code Napoléon*). Napoleon declared emperor of the French; his coronation and that of Josephine, in Paris. See "CORONATION OF NAPOLEON," xv, 76.

Wilberforce's Slave-trade Bill read a third time in the Commons; thrown out by the Lords. Savings-banks originated by Priscilla Wakefield's "Frugality Bank."

Dessalines (first governor) assumes the title of Jean Jacques I, Emperor of Haiti.

1805. Impeachment and trial of Judge Samuel Chase. Treaty of Peace with Tripoli; end of the payment of tribute.

Napoleon acquires the crown of Italy; formation of the third coalition against Napoleon. Bavaria invaded by the Austrians. "BATTLE OF AUSTERLITZ;" see xv, 115. Treaty of Presburg, between France and Austria. Bavaria and Wurtemberg created kingdoms.

Battle of Trafalgar; destruction of the French and Spanish fleets; death of Nelson. See "BATTLE OF TRAFALGAR," xv, 105. Strachan captures four of the escaping ships after Trafalgar.

Jerome Bonaparte, brother of Napoleon, having married an American, Miss Patterson of Baltimore, is refused permission by Napoleon to enter France.

1806. Attempted filibustering scheme of Aaron Burr in Texas.

Napoleon issues his Berlin decree declaring Britain under blockade and forbidding intercourse with her. Prussia humiliated and oppressed by Napoleon; war ensues and the Prussians are subjugated at Jena. See "PRUSSIA CRUSHED BY NAPOLEON," xv, 140.

Francis II, on the dissolution of the Holy Roman Empire, assumes thenceforth the title of Emperor of Austria.

Holland a kingdom; Louis Bonaparte on the throne.

A French squadron is captured by Admiral Duckworth. The new administration of "All the Talents" formed in England. "THE BRITISH ACQUISITION OF CAPE COLONY;" see xv, 127.

1807. Arrest and trial of Aaron Burr. The British war-ship Leopard attacks the U. S. frigate Chesapeake. An embargo laid by Congress on shipping destined for foreign ports. Abolition of the slave-trade in the United States. "THE FIRST PRACTICAL STEAMBOAT;" see xv, 159.

Battle of Eylau. Napoleon defeats the Russians at Friedland. Conference between Napoleon and Alexander I.

Duckworth forces the Dardanelles. Abolition of the slave-trade throughout the British Empire. Treaty of commerce with the United States. Siege of Copenhagen by the British; it falls and the Danish fleet is captured. Heligoland taken from the Danes.

Deposition of Sultan Selim III by the Turkish Janizaries; Mustapha on the throne.

Westphalia made a kingdom for Jerome Bonaparte.

1808. Election of James Madison as President of the United States.

Knavish acquisition of the throne of Spain by Napoleon for his brother Joseph; a national revolt follows; crushed with merciless severity. See "WELLINGTON'S PENINSULAR CAMPAIGN," xv, 170.

Convention of Cintra; Junot compelled by Wellington to evacuate Portugal.

Murder of the deposed Selim III ; recurring revolutions in Constantinople.

1809. Beginning of Madison's first administration. Substitution of Nonintercourse for the Embargo.

Renewal of the struggle by Austria against Napoleon; invasion of Bavaria and the duchy of Warsaw. Defeat of the Austrians at Abensberg, Landshut, and Eckmuehl. Napoleon enters Vienna. Archduke Charles defeats Napoleon; Austrians defeated at Raab. Battle of Wagram; defeat of the Austrians. Peace of Schoenbrunn between France and Austria. The Illyrian provinces created by Napoleon. Annexation to France of the Papal States by Napoleon; he is excommunicated by Pius VII. The Pope arrested and removed to France. Napoleon divorces Josephine.

Russia declares war against Austria.

Battle of Corunna; death of Sir John Moore. Gambier and Cochran, English admirals, destroy a French fleet. Collingwood takes the Ionian Islands. Wellesley gains the Battle of Talavera de la Reina. Disastrous Walcheren Expedition of the English.

Finland ceded by Sweden to Russia.

1810. Third census of the United States; population 7,215,791.

"REVOLUTION IN MEXICO." See xv, 189.

Buenos Aires and Chile revolt against Spain; they achieve complete separation. See "UPRISING IN SOUTH AMERICA," xv, 205.

Louis Napoleon abdicates the throne of Holland; it, with the Hanse towns and the Swiss Valais, is annexed to France. Napoleon marries Maria Louisa of Austria. Bernadotte made crown prince of Sweden.

Battle of Busaco ; Wellesley (Wellington) defeats Masséna. Guadaloupe taken by the English. O'Connell, at a meeting in Dublin, moves for a repeal of the Anglo-Irish Union.

1811. Battle of Tippecanoe; defeat of the "Prophet," brother of Tecumseh, by General Harrison.

Masséna retreats from Portugal. Beresford defeats Soult at Albuera.

Revolutionary uprising in Paraguay. Venezuela and New Granada declare themselves independent of Spain. The revolution in Mexico continues; Hidalgo is captured by the Spaniards and executed.

Financial bankruptcy of Austria.

"MASSACRE OF THE MAMELUKES." See xv, 223.

Java comes under the dominion of the English. Institution of the regency in Great Britain of the Prince of Wales. Luddite riots in Nottinghamshire and adjacent counties to destroy machinery.

1812. Beginning of war between the United States and England ; see "WAR ON THE CANADIAN BORDER," xv, 241. The Federalists oppose the war. Louisiana admitted to the Union. Reëlection of President Madison.

Napoleon declares war against Russia; the Grand Army advances into Russia; French victories at Smolensk and Borodino; Napoleon enters Moscow; the city is fired by the Russians; disastrous retreat of the French; passage of the Beresina. See "NAPOLEON'S RUSSIAN CAMPAIGN," xv, 231.

Peace of Bukharest between Turkey and Russia.

Assassination of Prime Minister Perceval, England. Wellington takes Badajoz by storm; he defeats Marmont at Salamanca; the British enter Madrid.

1813. Battle of Frenchtown; defeat of the Americans by the British. York (Toronto) captured and burned by the Americans; an expedition sent against Montreal; the British surprise Fort Niagara and burn Buffalo; capture of the Chesapeake by the Shannon. "PERRY'S VICTORY ON LAKE ERIE," xv, 268. Outbreak of the Creek Indians.

An alliance concluded between Russia and Prussia. Bernadotte heads a Swedish army against France. Battle of Luetzen; victory of Napoleon over the Prussians. "BATTLE OF THE NATIONS AT LEIPSIC;" see xv, 281.

Bolivar successfully advances through Venezuela and New Granada; he receives the title of "Liberator" at Caracas.

Peace of Gulistan; Russia compels the cession of large Persian territories.

Wellington defeats the French in the Battle of Vitoria; defeats Soult in the Pyrenees; pursues Soult into France. England and Austria make a renewed coalition; Russia also joins it.

Abolishment of the Inquisition by the Spanish Cortes.

Holland recovers independence; William, Prince of Orange, proclaimed ruler.

Publication of Thomas Moore's *Irish Melodies.*

1814. Battles of Chippewa and Lundy's Lane; siege of Fort Erie. "BURNING OF WASHINGTON BY THE BRITISH;" see xv, 295. Naval war on Lake Champlain. The Federalists oppose the war at the Hartford Convention; see "HARTFORD CONVENTION," xv, 326. Negotiation of the treaty of peace at Ghent.

Murat deserts Napoleon; France invaded by the allies; unsuccessful campaign of defence by Napoleon; Paris surrenders; abdication of the Emperor; he is retired to Elba; return of the Bourbons, Louis XVIII King.

"CONGRESS OF VIENNA." See xv, 310.

Return to Rome of Pope Pius VII; restoration of the Jesuits.

Union of Holland and Belgium forming the Kingdom of the Netherlands.

Dictatorship in Paraguay of Doctor Francis.

Ferdinand abrogates the Spanish Constitution of 1812; the Cortes abolished; reëstablishment of the Inquisition.

Building in England of the first steam locomotive by George Stephenson. The American frigate Essex captured by the British. Wellington created a duke.

Treaty of Kiel; Denmark cedes Norway to Sweden.

1815. "BATTLE OF NEW ORLEANS;" see xv, 343. War of the

United States with the Dey of Algiers; Decatur imposes terms upon him; he also demands and obtains reparation from Tripoli and Tunis.

Escape of Napoleon from Elba; he lands in France; Ney with his army passes over to him; flight of Louis XVIII from Paris; beginning of the Hundred Days; the alliance against France renewed; Napoleon defeats Blucher at Ligny; Ney repulsed at Quatre-Bras. "BATTLE OF WATERLOO;" see xv, 363. Second abdication of Napoleon; the allies enter Paris; Louis XVIII reënters Paris; he is restored to the throne; Napoleon surrenders himself to Captain Maitland of the British war-ship Bellerophon; he is taken to St. Helena.

Formation of the Germanic Confederation.

Protectorate of Great Britain over the Ionian Islands. The Corn Laws passed in England, to maintain the price of breadstuffs.

Murat attempts to recover his kingdom of Naples; he is shot by order of court-martial.

Ney is executed.

New Granada overrun by the Spaniards under Morillo.

END OF VOLUME XV